"A fine genre-bender mixing sf, fantasy, thriller, horror, and New Age elements into a heady brew."

— *Locus*

THE CHRONICLES OF GALEN SWORD
BOOK ONE

Sword heard a sound behind him and froze. It had been too loud, too massive to be another person. He heard heavy breathing. Felt a soft wall of heat reach out to him. Smelled an odor far worse than anything he had smelled from 'Bub or Martin.

"Hello, Galen," a deep, hollow voice said to him. An inhuman voice.

Sword turned. Sword looked up. Seven feet to Seth's smile and all the glistening, needle fangs that bristled in his mouth.

"Welcome back," the werewolf said.

" ... an intellectual feast ... *Shifter* is a real page turner ... the suspense is heartstopping ... memorable and overpowering ... "
— *Science Fiction Research Association Newsletter*

"[*Shifter* is] one of the best fantasy novels of 1990."
— *Science Fiction Chronicle*

SHIFTER

THE CHRONICLES OF GALEN SWORD BOOK ONE

SHIFTER

THE CHRONICLES OF GALEN SWORD BOOK ONE

JUDITH & GARFIELD
REEVES-STEVENS

BABBAGE PRESS • 2003

THE CHRONICLES OF GALEN SWORD #1: SHIFTER

ISBN: 1-930235-18-6
October, 2003

Babbage Press
8740 Penfield Avenue
Northridge, California 91324

www.babbagepress.com

Printed in the United States of America

For Campbell Kingsburgh, Galen's first fan

THE RETURN OF GALEN SWORD:
INTRODUCTION TO THE BABBAGE PRESS EDITIONS
OF THE FIRST THREE CHRONICLES

Over the years, we got used to it. The phone messages that would turn up on our answering service, left by people we'd never met, from British Columbia, or California, or Alaska, once even from Italy. The e-mails that came to us through addresses for other projects and books. The earnest inquiries made at conventions and signings, even at the United States Naval Academy. Always the same thing.

When's #3 coming out?

Over the years, our answer was always the same thing, too.

No idea.

We weren't stumped. No writers' block for us. We knew the very last line of the very last Galen book (#9) before we wrote the first line of the first Galen book, *Shifter*.

In fact, we had written the complete manuscript for the third Galen book, *Dark Hunter*, before the second, *Nightfeeder*, hit the stands. We got editorial notes for the third book, made a few tweaks and polishes, turned in a revised manuscript, and got paid in full by our publisher.

Then, just like every other Galen fan out there, we waited for *Dark*

Hunter's publication.

And we waited. And ...

Well, twelve years later, here we are.

What happened?

Life.

Sometime after Galen #2 was published, the science-fiction/fantasy market was deemed to go "soft." Our original publisher cut its list in half. And despite Galen #1 having sold reasonably well, and Galen #2 having sold better than #1, and foreign rights being sold to the U.K. and Italy, Galen #3, was on the wrong side of that 50/50 dividing line.

But we'd been paid for our *Dark Hunter* manuscript, so the publisher retained the right to publish it at some unspecified time in the future. Until then, it was theirs, not ours. They held the reprint rights to *Shifter* and *Nightfeeder*, too. End of story. Or, at least, of that particular chapter.

We moved on to other publishing projects, wrote many books and scripts, but never forgot Galen. About as frequently as we were asked by readers about when Galen #3 was coming out, we asked our literary agent when we could recover the rights to our series.

As it turned out, we were only two of many other writers whose rights to unpublished manuscripts had been similarly affected by the publisher's downsizing of its list. Our agent's answer to our question was a friendly, if world-weary, "Get in line."

So we did, and as the seasons passed and the universe unfolded, eventually we made it to the front of that line and many years after we had written *Dark Hunter*, its publication rights finally reverted to us, along with the reprint rights to the first two Galen books.

Which meant we were free to take all three books to another publisher.

Which meant, of course, that it was time for another complication to arise, one of our own making.

By this time, we were with a new publisher with whom we'd published *Star Trek* fiction and nonfiction, and we had written a new novel for them: *Icefire*. The book was different from anything we had written before — a military-themed technothriller — and it became a *Los Angeles Times* bestseller. Stephen King, whom we do not know personally but to whom we do light candles of thanks on a regular basis, called it, "The best suspense novel of its kind since *The Hunt for Red October.*" A year later, we wrote another novel in the same vein: *Quicksilver.* It was a *New York Times* bestseller. *Publishers Weekly* said the book "ensured our entry into the technothriller elite."

All that was the good news.

The bad news was that because of the success of our technothrillers, our new publisher no longer considered us science-fiction writers.

We said, Tell that to William Shatner and a couple of hundred thousand *Star Trek* fans.

Our new publisher said, Doesn't matter, your future is "mainstream" now; science fiction is in your past. However, we would like you to write these three *Deep Space Nine* novels for us ... We still haven't figured that one out.

The last delay in Galen's resurfacing arose in our other world — script writing — specifically on a television series we joined in its second season and continued with in its third: *Sir Arthur Conan Doyle's The Lost World,* an Indiana-Jones like adventure set in the 1920s on a lost plateau in South America. (Note: There's a special prize for whoever is first to find the Galen reference we planted in one of the *Lost World* episodes we scripted.) But finally, by Spring 2003, we had turned in all three Galen manuscripts to Galen's knight in shining armor: Babbage Press.

Which brings us to the new editions of the first two Chronicles of Galen Sword — *Shifter* and *Nightfeeder* — and the long-awaited first edition of the third — *Dark Hunter.*

Is *Dark Hunter* exactly the book we wrote twelve years ago? Mostly yes, a little bit no. The story is exactly the same. Same number of chapters. Virtually identical last chapter — and please don't read it until the end. But we do admit to cleaning up the language a bit, tweaking the action scenes, adding some details that could prove useful for the future Chronicles. (Future Chronicles?! See the Afterword in *Dark Hunter.*)

We undertook the same type of minor editing for the new editions of *Shifter* and *Nightfeeder* as well, but there are no major changes, and very few minor ones. For those who know the original editions by heart, we updated a few cultural references for new readers. Example:

Ja'Nette now watches *South Park* instead of *Arsenio*. Rest assured, though, that Martin still remains a fan of Hulk Hogan because, after all, some things are timeless.

Oh, and we also corrected one tiny continuity error in the out-of-print version of *Nightfeeder* that no one but us seems to have noticed. (Happy hunting!)

So that's it.

No more delays.

The wait is over.

For everyone who's never heard of us or Galen, we hope this is the first of many times our paths will cross.

For everyone who's read our other work, and who's trying out Galen for the first time, we think you'll recognize our favorite themes, despite the presence of werewolves and vampires in the place of Navy pilots and Klingons.

And for those of you who shared Galen's first two adventures and have been anticipating his third for many years, welcome back.

We've missed Galen as much as you have.

And this time, we think, he's here to stay.

J&G
Toronto – Los Angeles
1988 – 2003

ONE

Galen Sword had lost.

He kept his dark eyes fixed on the steady pinpoint lights of the dashboard video map display. Each dot on the glowing grid represented a motion sensor hidden at chokepoints in the web of alleys nearby. Each light was green. The werewolf had eluded him again.

Melody Ko's voice crackled in Sword's ear. He touched a finger to the tiny Mitsubishi transceiver there, to better hear her over the steady drumming of the night rain. The woman's words were crisp and to the point, as always.

"Four AM, Sword. No previous sightings past three before." It was Ko's way of saying it was time to go back to the Loft. To quit. Sword sighed and stretched his arms against the leather-wrapped steering wheel. Maybe it was time to quit everything.

Another voice broke in, but it said nothing. It was only a long yawn triggering a VOX circuit in one of the transceivers each of the team wore on a job.

Sword recognized the yawn. "Still with us, Ja'Nette?" he asked, keeping his eyes locked on the unchanging display.

"Bore-*ing*," the child answered sleepily. "How come you let me do this stuff but you won't let me stay up to watch *South Park?*"

Sword didn't answer, didn't even smile. There was no humor in him this night. Three tedious months spent narrowing down the operating range of a werewolf in Manhattan, three long years spent trying to find some way back into the hidden world, and all that time, all that money, had come to this, another failure.

He looked out through the rain-rippled windshield of his Porsche. This far north in the city, there were few streetlights still working. Only a handful of them were smeared into orange streaks through the windshield, dimly illuminating the deserted streets. Yet Sword was certain there was something beyond their light, in the darkness. It was only a question of knowing where to look, and when. He knew the answers were there. He knew he had been close enough to touch them in the past three years. He knew he had once been part of them himself, so long ago.

Sword leaned back and closed his eyes. He saw another rain-swept night, the werewolf in Greece, trapped in the ruins, close to speaking, felled by the swift whisper of a silenced silver bullet. Sword saw the woman again, atop the crumbling wall, her cloak billowing in the wild wind, rifle held ready as her quarry bled out its immortal life on marble twice a thousand years old and shifted painfully back into its human form, taking its secrets into darkness.

Sword and the woman had faced each other in that night until the dying creature had raised a claw to the blackness from which the rain swirled, turned its now human eyes to Sword, and called out with its dying breath, "*Galen!*"

Lost in a country not his own, confronted by a creature others thought only a legend, Galen Sword had been *recognized* by his prey. He had seen that same flash of instant knowledge widen the eyes of the woman who had killed the beast, just before she had turned back to the night and leapt from the wall and disappeared into shadow. Even now, safe in the dry, technological cocoon of his car, Sword felt the hairs on his arms bristle with the memory of that night and what it might have meant.

There *were* secrets in the darkness.

And other hunters.

He opened his eyes. He touched the transceiver in his ear. It was time to quit, but only for the night.

Then a green light on the display changed to red and began to flash. And in his earphone, he heard the familiar mechanical sound of a shell pumped into place as Ko cocked her weapon.

The hunt began again.

To the creature's eyes, the alleys were a jungle, the city a continent of secret lairs, hidden prey, sudden death. But tonight he had no need to hide, no need to fear. Tonight he ran with the force and the fury of the storm. Tonight he flew with the wildness of the cold autumn rain. Tonight, for just this little while, this tiny escape, he was free as no human could ever be.

His name was Martin and he was what he was. The false term "werewolf" meant nothing to him. And this night he had a destination. His favorite place.

Martin's heavy feet slapped over the filthy asphalt and paving bricks of the back alleys. His large hands, cold rain streaming from their sparse fur, smacked against the glistening walls and alley paths, propelling him forward with perfect balance and elegant gait. Freedom fueled him. He knew his clanmates were too busy with their preparations to realize his absence for hours.

Martin rounded a corner, transferring his momentum and motion so perfectly he didn't slip or slide. With a leap that seemed to require no effort, he was at the lip of a bent and buckled dumpster. But before the metal could even creak with the pressure of his landing, he had flipped up against the rain-slicked wall, pushed off with his feet, rolled twice through the air over an eight-foot-tall rotting wooden fence, and hit the ground on the other side with no greater sound than that of an ordinary footstep, and no break in the rhythm of his running. Yet the cloak of his silent progress was broken by his howl of delight because, for this night at least, he believed he ran without pursuit. He did not scent or see the motion sensors as he triggered them.

In the final alley, Martin came to a sudden stop, so still in the shadows that he became almost invisible. His nostrils flared as he scented the approach to his destination. Even through the rain and the

3

city's perpetual stink of garbage, cars, and buses, Martin could tell that humans had passed by recently. The rotting stench of the fruit and vegetables that oozed through their pores, clung to the night air, unavoidable to his refined olfactory sense. At least by now he was used to the foul odor enough that he no longer felt like gagging as he had as a child.

But the human spoor in the final alley was strong enough to keep him from moving again. His instincts were more than a match for his goal that night, no matter how rare and hard-won his freedom. If there were even a chance that humans were in the alley, he would not continue. Above all, Martin knew he must survive.

His nostrils flared again as he tasted the air with a sensitivity greater than two parts per billion. Then he smiled, his dark face split by perfect teeth which by human standards were marred only by incisors remarkably too long and too sharp. Martin recognized alcohol. Lots of it. Whatever human might be hidden in the alley would be unconscious, or too drunk to notice Martin's presence.

Martin pursed his lips and mouthed a silent howl of victory, then moved into the open alley on the last leg of his journey.

The old back door, battered wood splotched with flaking remnants of dirty green paint, was protected by a hinged black iron grill held in place by a thick chain and heavy padlock. Martin didn't pause. He reached out and took the padlock in both hands. His eyes rolled back in his head. A faint, electric blue glow sputtered between his fingers and palms and the lock clicked open. His clanmates called it a blue power, but to Martin it was just a legacy from his father, a way to get into places he wanted to get into. What it was or how it worked, he didn't know or care.

Carefully, he unthreaded the chain from the grill, swung it open, and touched the doorknob. It wouldn't turn until a second blue flash glimmered beneath his palm. He pushed the door open. He had arrived. The crudely-painted delivery instructions on the door were topped by a sign that said, NOAH'S PET SHOP EMPORIUM, but Martin couldn't read them. His nose had told him what waited for him inside. Soft animals, small animals, young animals.

His favorite.

⌒

A moment after the back door to the pet store swung shut, Melody Ko stepped forward from the narrow inset in the alley wall opposite. The young Japanese woman's face was tense with concentration, not fear. Her eyes were narrowed not in apprehension, but for protection from the rain that ran without slowing through the short razor-cut bristle of her hair.

"It's in the pet shop," she said softly, then brushed at her nose to clear it of the smell of the whiskey Forsyte had instructed her to pour at her feet, to camouflage her scent.

She heard the rasp of Sword's breath in her earphone as he ran for his position. "I'll cover the front," he said, voice resonating with the impact of his running.

Ko frowned. Sword always stated the obvious. Of course he would cover the front. That had been Forsyte's plan. And Forsyte had never been wrong. Except that once.

"What have we got, anyway?" Sword asked, breathing harshly with his exertion. He never kept to the exercise program she had devised for him.

Ko scanned the dark alley. She heard Ja'Nette's footfalls approaching. "Humanoid. No pronounced snout. Sparse fur. Maybe five-four, five-six standing up." She guessed the creature was young. Some of Sword's sources had put the height of mature werewolves at over seven feet. But there were always so many contradictions among the observers who had survived, making it extremely difficult to formulate theories.

A small dark shape appeared at the corner of the alley: Ja'Nette. Ko held up a hand to silently stop the child, twelve years old but looking ten, no evidence of womanhood about her.

Ja'Nette instantly froze in position, and not necessarily because of Sword's incessant training. She treated whatever Ko told her to do as a command from heaven, or from the parents who haunted her dreams.

"Sword?" Ko said. Coming from her, it was a complex question.

His reply came through the transceiver. "In position ... *now*." She could hear that he had stopped running. Then he added, "Adrian, are you on line?"

There was a long pause, then a flat mechanical voice answered, "YES." Ko felt her stomach tighten as it always did when she heard Forsyte's voder, knowing the real voice that lay behind it, forever stilled.

"Is Ja'Nette in position?" Sword asked.

"We are proceeding," Ko replied. It was answer enough.

Keeping her modified assault rifle aimed at the back door of the pet shop, Ko turned to Ja'Nette twenty feet away and nodded her head, then pointed silently back to the door.

Ja'Nette pulled off the hood of her red nylon windbreaker to reveal her richly black features tense with expectation. Ko saw the girl cross her wrists and lift her clenched fists to her shoulders, then begin slowly rocking. Her soft humming came over the transceiver. An old Michael Jackson tune, greatly slowed down.

The falling rain quickened for a moment, sending a curtain of spray through the alley. Ko ignored it, turning back to the door, finger on the trigger, poised on the brink of sudden action.

The chain moved like a snake on the ground.

"Focus," Ko said softly.

Ja'Nette's humming rose. From the corner of her eye, Ko saw the child's rocking increase.

"Focus," Ko repeated like a mantra.

The chain became motionless. The doorknob moved. The door swung silently open.

There was nothing on the other side.

"Open and safe," Ko announced. She hefted the gun, knowing what would come next.

"PROCEED," Forsyte's voder said.

"In position," Sword confirmed.

Even without the transceiver, Ko could hear the sound of Ja'Nette vomiting at the end of the alley. When would the girl learn not to eat before one of their excursions? But Ko did not turn to the child, nor speak to her. There was no time for that. Instead she held her rifle ready and moved toward the open door. It was time to make Galen Sword's day. It was time to catch a werewolf.

Pudgy fat puppies yipped with bellies round and swollen like berries about to burst. Puffs of kittens mewed as they tumbled over each other in a furry avalanche. Martin peered into the cages full of life and slowly licked his lips. His favorite place.

Without turning his head, Martin reached out and grabbed a package from a shelf, then crept back through the dark pet store until he came to the door that opened onto the room at the back of the cages. He needed no blue power to open it. It was unlocked, unprotected. He went inside and closed the door behind him. He didn't want a single one of them to get away.

The puppies were first. They always were. *Excitable,* Martin thought. That was the word his clanmates used for him as they laughed, as they hunted.

Martin opened the cage door. Eight-week-old beagles erupted in rush of high-pitched squeals. Martin's huge hand reached into the cage, found the first puppy, engulfed it, and Martin grinned in anticipation. Next would come the kittens.

Best for last, Martin thought. *Best for last.*

Ko moved through the back storeroom until she stood in the doorway to the main part of the shop. She could hear the muffled barking of puppies and mewing of kittens, but saw nothing moving in the shop except for the lazy passage of tropical fish in five softly-lit aquariums along one wall. But the rippling light from the tanks was weak and there was no way of knowing what was hidden in the shadows.

Carefully, precisely, Ko slipped a Starbrite Viewer from a loop on her black canvas equipment vest, and flicked the device once, scattering beads of rain from its slick casing. Then she flipped the switch on its side as she held the viewer to her eyes like binoculars, squinting at the bright multicolored image it produced.

A five-second scan revealed nothing hiding in the shadows, but she suddenly heard the puppies in the cages at the side of the store begin to howl. Quickly Ko slipped the viewer back onto her vest. There was a small room running the length of the wall of cages at the side of the shop. The door to it was closed. Ko didn't want to do it, but Forsyte had worked out the procedure as the safest, so she pressed the call button on her locator band three times.

She heard Ja'Nette answer, very tired now, "Comin'."

Twenty seconds later, Ko heard Ja'Nette behind her. Ko pointed to the cage room door, then moved into position five feet in front of it. Now, the cries of kittens filled the shop, high-pitched and plaintive. She tried not to think of what might be going on in there.

Ja'Nette hummed softly. Michael Jackson again.

The handle on the cage-room door began to move by itself.

The cage-room door slammed open.

Ko lunged forward and screamed in attack, bringing the gunsight to her eye and ...

... there was nothing there.

Ko halted in the open doorway. She moved her head cautiously so she could see past the gunsight. The creature had been at least five-four. It *had* to be close to her eye level.

"What's going on in there?" Sword asked in her ear. But Ko shut him out. He always talked too much.

A kitten tottered into view on the floor. Ko looked down, gun barrel reflexively following the new motion. The kitten stopped, looked up at Ko and her rifle, and mewed. A gigantic dark hand with black nails and tufts of rain-soaked fur snaked out, scooped up the kitten and drew it back behind a row of cabinets.

"Melody?" Sword asked. "Ja'Nette?"

Ko could hear Ja'Nette retching behind her in the storeroom.

"Proceeding," Ko announced firmly and stepped into the cage room.

She heard a deep growl as she entered, a warning in any language, human or otherwise.

"Show yourself," Ko said. Her voice was steady and calm. What little emotion was in it was excitement. Sword had hopelessly screwed up the photographs he had taken of the werewolf in Greece — that incident had been before she and Forsyte had joined up with him — and Ko was eager to see what such a creature looked like. Electrophoresis of its DNA promised to be a blast, too.

The creature growled again. She heard one puppy yip, another bark.

A standoff, Ko decided, except she was the one with the rifle. She stepped further into the cage room, brushing against an open cage door and swinging it shut with a metallic clink. She heard another warning growl. Ko took a breath and prepared to —

"Hold your position," Sword said. "I'm coming in."

Ko heard a tremendous crash as the storefront window exploded inward. The creature hidden behind the counter howled deafeningly. "You asshole!" Ko shouted at Sword, but she leapt forward anyway, raising her gun barrel.

The creature, dark and squat, naked and muscular, was crouched on the floor behind the counter. Its eyes were wide and its thick arms and powerful hands encompassed a writhing armload of small animals.

"*Nooo!*" the creature shrieked at Ko.

But it made no move to stand up. No move to protect itself.

Ko stopped in surprise. The creature was more human in appearance than she had anticipated, and was definitely a *he.* And he wasn't attacking. Almost as if ... as if he were worried about ... She saw an open box of dog biscuits on the floor. Two of the puppies beside the creature were happily digging into it.

"Please," the creature said. "Don't hurt ... don't hurt ... "

Ko hated the unexpected, but she never denied it. "You mean ... the puppies?" she asked.

"Kittens, too," the creature said, and dipped his eyes in supplication. "Don't hurt."

Ko lowered her rifle. Then Galen Sword was beside her, rivers of rain still dripping from the black leather jacket covering his equipment vest, gas pistol held ready at his side.

"You're not going to believe this, Sword," Ko said, "but — "

Sword fired.

The creature screamed and jerked back against the wall, sending his kittens and puppies flying.

He writhed and gurgled and in seconds was still, only the slow movement of the red tag of the tranquilizing dart giving evidence that he was still alive.

Ko clenched her jaw in anger. "Why the bloody hell did you do that?"

Sword glanced at her. "You okay?" Without waiting for an answer, he knelt down beside the creature and lifted its limp arm. "Look at that musculature," he said, shaking his head. He absently pushed a puppy out of the way as it tried to lick the creature's face.

"I said, why did you do that?" This time, Ko's voice wavered with rage. Sword was perhaps the only person who could affect her that way. "I had everything under control. He was just sitting there! He came to *play* with the animals. Look at the dog biscuits!"

"Good, good," Sword said, ignoring her as he forced open one of the creature's eyes and shone a penlight beam into it.

"For God's sake, Sword," Ko said.

Sword stood up beside her, studied her for a long moment. "Bring the van around and we'll load it in."

Ko cleared the tranquilizing charge from her rifle and snapped the gun's strap over her shoulder. "Ja'Nette was sick back there. I'm looking after her."

"Ja'Nette knows better than to eat before translocating," Sword said. He was almost six feet tall and he towered over Ko, but she refused to be intimidated.

"She's just a child, remember?"

"She's on the payroll," Sword said. He kept glancing down at the unconscious creature and Ko sensed an elation in him that she had never known before. "Just get the van, Ko. Adrian doesn't know how long the drug will last."

"Oh, go to hell," Ko muttered as she stormed from the cage room.

Behind her, almost softly enough that she didn't hear, Galen Sword said, "What makes you think I'm not already there?"

Fuming and grumbling all the way, Ko brought the van to the store before seeing to Ja'Nette. After all, this was Sword's big night. After three years of ineffectual effort, he had finally caught himself a were-wolf. Now, as far as Ko was concerned, it was time to see which of the two was the bigger monster.

TWO

At his brilliantly lit workbench in his private study on the Loft's third level, Dr. Adrian Forsyte blinked his eyes twice in urgent desperation. His on-chair computer detected the interruption in the narrow beam of light emitted from the fiber-optic strands that were embedded in the frames of his glasses and positioned to reflect from the white of his eye. The small computer then sent a short-range FM signal to the Loft's mainframe, a Cray-Hitachi Model II safely enshrined in the renovated warehouse's second basement. The mainframe promptly relayed a command through the Loft's smart wiring harness to the bookstand in Forsyte's study. With that, approximately half a second after Forsyte's double blink, the small metal tube at the top of the bookstand flipped down to the corner of the page in front of Forsyte, sucked the paper against it, and began to swing out to turn the page.

Forsyte moaned and closed his eyes, holding them shut to abort the command. He heard the bookstand's suction pump cut out and saw the half-turned page fall back into place so he would be able to resume his study of the equations describing eleventh-dimensional gravitational distortions through superspace. It was the best framework he had found so far that might provide a testable theory for Ja'Nette's abilities.

But that work for Sword could come later. For now, exhausted from his evening's efforts, the scientist slumped against the crossed, double chest-belts that chafed against him, holding him upright in his chair. His left index finger moved slowly to the sensitive miniature joystick and control pad on the chair's left arm. He toyed with it for a moment, thinking the old thoughts, the dangerous thoughts. Thinking how easy it would be to push the stick all the way forward, rolling the chair along the workshop balcony, through the railing, then plunge three stories down to the equipment bay. The chair's motors and treads could exert enough force to break through the railings. He had seen to that when he had designed the chair and Ko had built it.

But Forsyte opened his eyes again and saw the green ready light on the narrow display screen attached to the chair's right arm come on. *All systems ready for action*, he thought. *Except me.*

He wanted to cry then, one of the few things he could still do on his own. But he refused to give in. Because, more than crying, more than killing himself, more than finding the people who had done this to him, right now what the most brilliant physicist in the world wanted more than anything else was to scratch his damned nose.

He took another breath and began again. This time, he remembered to push down on the center keypad button in front of the joystick before blinking twice, and the on-chair computer at last recognized the proper sequence that shifted command priorities from the study's equipment to the chair. The ready light flashed and Forsyte blinked twice again. This time, it worked. An intricate antenna-like structure of plastic rods swung out from the chair's high back and in front of his face. He pushed against it, rubbing his nose back and forth against the various textures.

These days, it was as close to ecstasy as he was likely to get. Until he found *them.*

After savoring his small victory, Forsyte leaned back against the headrest, rewarding himself with a vision of what he would do to the people, the creatures, whatever they were, who had done this to him. His vision was vicious, violent, and if he had ever articulated it to the psychiatrist Sword insisted he visit, Forsyte knew he would probably be committed. But what he wanted to do to those who had taken his body from him was no less than they deserved. And it made him feel so good to imagine the moment of his revenge: moving his hands and arms and legs again, shoving, striking ... moving.

Someday, he thought. Someday he would end the spell or the curse or whatever it was they had done to him. But until that day came, at least he could still dream, at least he could still use his mind. At least he could still imagine his revenge. First against his enemies, and then against the man responsible: Galen Sword.

The vision ended. He opened his eyes as a soft mechanical vibration passed through the open ironwork of ramps and levels that filled the cavernous Loft. Three stories down, the equipment-bay barricade door ground up, opening onto the cold rainswept night of the SoHo streets, and Forsyte heard Melody Ko's voice in his ear. "We're home." He heard the familiar rumble of the van and the powerful hum of Sword's Porsche.

Forsyte smiled, the expression lopsided but recognizable, and his finger pressed the new code sequence he had developed for his voice synthesizer. The mechanical voice said, "WEREWOLF ... WEREWOLF ... WEREWOLF." Forsyte nodded slightly, approving the intonation he had programmed into the voder, as he brought his chair to life. Its central stalk rose as the motorized treads rotated in opposite directions to turn the chair to take him to the open elevator and down to the equipment bay. The safe way.

Whatever else Forsyte thought about Galen Sword, at least working for the obsessed fool was interesting.

The examination chair in the main lab on the second level had been built just before Sword had gone to Greece two years earlier. It was proportioned for the werewolf he had hunted then. The creature who was strapped to it now, by his arms, legs, chest, and waist, barely took up two-thirds of the chair's length. He still breathed slowly and regularly, and Ko had thrown a thick wool blanket over him to cover his nakedness and, she said, to keep him warm.

"HE DOESN'T LOOK LIKE A WEREWOLF," Forsyte played on his voder. Most words and phrases could be generated by a preprogrammed letter and number code. Other words could be built, painstakingly, phoneme by phoneme.

Sword paced around the reinforced metal chair, hands in the back pockets of his black jeans. His hair and face were still damp from the rain and his angular features glinted beneath the multicolored lights of the banks of equipment that lined the walls.

"That's what I told him," Ko said. She was standing by a metal locker, methodically removing from her equipment vest the devices she hadn't used that night, stowing them back in their proper positions, connecting them to battery rechargers or removing their detonators as was appropriate. "I said, if that thing was a real werewolf he'd be drinking our blood by now."

Ko hung up her empty vest and Forsyte saw her glance with annoyance at Sword's vest, piled carelessly in a heap on a swivel chair by the main computer workstation. The scientist saw his number one student, his only student these days, grimace as she clanged shut the locker door. But her resolve didn't matter, Forsyte knew. Sometime in the next hour she would no longer be able to stand the absence of order in the lab. She would swear, she would proclaim that she hadn't signed on to be Sword's keeper, but she would pick up his vest, stow its equipment, and hang it neatly in the locker anyway. The truth of it was that she *was* Sword's keeper. Someone had to be.

"Maybe it's a young one," Sword said finally, brushing his wet black hair from his forehead. "No matter how long they live, they've still got to be born. Somehow." He bent down to look into the creature's unconscious face. Forsyte saw Sword wrinkle his nose and pull away sharply.

"BAD BREATH?" Forsyte's machine asked.

"Worse than 'Bub's," Sword said, then he stepped back as Ja'Nette approached with a tangle of wires and EEG pickups.

"Thought you could only get turned into a woofer if they chomped you or somethin'," Ja'Nette said, concentrating on the wires. Forsyte watched enviously as she sorted them by hand, not by translocation, an indication of the exhaustion she felt.

"There's no full moon out there tonight," Sword said, distracted. "We can't count on the old legends being reliable. Remember that vampire we heard about, the one that escaped in daylight?"

"Least this one didn't escape," Ja'Nette said. "*Fii*-nally."

Slipping into their rehearsed routine, Ko joined Ja'Nette by the chair and helped her apply the pickups to the creature's head, smearing on the conducting gel and aligning the sensitive leads in what would be normal positions for a human. When each of the adhesive disks was in place, Ko handed the interface plug to Ja'Nette.

"Which one does it go into?" the child asked.

Ko pointed over to the main workstation as she checked each pickup's placement. "Any one of the three plugs under the disk slot. Then select MEDICAL from the library menu, select NEUROLOGY, select MONITOR, input the number of the plug you used, and run EEG, normal mode, filtering out muscle echoes and deep-wave enhancement."

Ja'Nette didn't move. "Say what?"

"Just do what we did this afternoon, Ja'Nette."

"I know," Ja'Nette said and went over to the workstation, trailing the input wire behind her.

"Any coffee?" Sword asked.

"Same old place," Ko answered, watching over Ja'Nette's shoulder as the child brought the medical subroutines on line.

Sword shrugged. He went to stand by Forsyte. "This going to work?" he asked.

The two fingers Forsyte could still control moved over his keypad. "IF IT DOESN'T YOU CAN FIRE ME," the voder said.

"If that thing breaks those straps, I might not have to. Ever seen musculature like that before?"

Forsyte had, but he knew the details would have to wait until he could write up his notes. For now, he just had the voder say, "GREAT APES."

Sword nodded impatiently. "I'll be waiting for your notes."

Across the lab, Ja'Nette called out, "Online."

Ko sighed, then leaned past the girl and typed an additional command into the keyboard. The large workstation screen flickered and seven horizontal graphs appeared. Slow golden lines zig-zagged from left to right across them.

"Oh, right," Ja'Nette said. "Okay, *now* we're online."

"On the big screen, please," Sword said.

Ja'Nette pressed a switch at the side of the keyboard and the image on the workstation monitor appeared on a projection video-screen eight feet up the wall. Sword had had it and others like it installed throughout the Loft so Forsyte could keep track of the computers' work without the necessity of rolling over to a screen each time his attention was required.

Sword watched the slow crawl of the EEG traces with his arms folded across his chest. "So what does it tell us?"

Forsyte's voder said one word. "WAKING."

Ja'Nette swung around in her swivel chair and started to stand up. Ko pushed her firmly back into place and crossed over to Sword and Forsyte, circling the examination chair well out of arm's reach. And the creature had long arms.

"Are you certain?" she asked. "I hadn't expected to get a one-to-one match on the wave frequencies so quickly and it could easily — "

"NOW AWAKE," Forsyte's machine said.

"Extremely fast metabolism," Sword said appreciatively.

"Ja'Nette," Ko commanded softly. She pointed to the equipment locker. "Gas pistol. Red flagged dart."

Ja'Nette ran over to the locker and opened it excitedly. The metal door squealed and Forsyte saw the tracing in the third graph suddenly peak.

"SEE GRAPH THREE."

"He obviously heard that," Ko said, taking the pistol Ja'Nette handed to her. Forsyte saw her check it quickly and frown. "You took the safety off," she said to the child.

"The woofer's awake," Ja'Nette protested.

"What have I told you about guns?" Ko asked.

Ja'Nette frowned. "Yeah, yeah. But I figure be ready. That woofer jumps, we're not talking junior firearm safety while he chomps you, y'know."

Ko touched Ja'Nette's shoulder. "Upstairs. Now."

The child's eyes widened as she looked at Ko in disbelief. She turned to Sword. "Just when it's getting interesting?"

Sword glanced at Ko and Forsyte could feel the tension between them. The logical part of him admired the little girl for how quickly she had learned to play Sword and Ko against each other. Ko had figured out what was going on even if Sword would probably be forever blind to it. He didn't appear concerned about Ja'Nette remaining in the lab with the werewolf.

"Go up to your room and watch everything on the monitors," Ko said conspiratorially, ignoring Sword. "Pay attention because we might need you in reserve if this guy acts up. Deal?"

"Yeah, okay." Ja'Nette gave Ko a quick hug. "G'night, Adrian." She kissed Forsyte's cheek and put her hand on his for a moment. She turned to Sword. "G'night, Sword." She was gone before he could turn to her.

"If we plan on keeping this guy here," Ko said, after waiting until she heard Ja'Nette's rapid footsteps on the metal stairs to her sleeping quarters on the fourth level, "we might think about moving Ja'Nette out of the Loft. Could get hairy. The situation, I mean."

"She'll be fine," Sword said. "She likes to be in the center of things." He moved closer to the creature in the chair. "A were*ape?*" he asked uncertainly. Then he held his hands as if to clap them by the creature's ear.

"Don't," Ko said sharply. "He doesn't need that now."

"It's awake, isn't it? So let's get it acting that way." Sword stared down at the beast. "I want to know if it can talk. It *has* to be able to talk."

"Bloody hell, Sword, *it* is a *he.* And whether he can talk or not, let's show him some respect."

Reluctantly, Sword lowered his hands. "*He's* a werewolf, Melody. I've hunted his kind for three years. I have to know if — "

"Then you can damn well give him three more minutes."

Forsyte's voder interrupted. "PATIENCE, BOTH OF YOU."

Sword exhaled noisily and walked away from the chair. He chewed at a thumbnail. "So what do you want to do with him?" he finally asked. "Serve him dinner?"

Ko cocked her head in thought. "Why not? His calorie requirements must be enormous. But he went to that pet store to *play* with the puppies and kittens, not eat them."

"Great," Sword said. "Maybe we should have brought them back with us instead of wasting so much time crawling around to find them all and put them back into their cages. Maybe that would give him something to wake up about."

"Good idea," Ko said. She turned to smile at Forsyte, then pursed her lips and made a series of kissing sounds.

"Oh, no," Sword said. "Not her."

Ko placed the gas pistol in one of the side carriers on Forsyte's chair, beside the equipment ports that carried the chair's taser guns. Sword believed in everyone being overprepared. Then Ko crouched down and held her hand out. "Here, 'Bub. Thatsa good girl. Good girl."

Forsyte turned his head in the direction Ko faced. Two electric copper eyes blazed out from the darkness beneath a worktable.

"Good girl, 'Bub," Ko said, her voice low and reassuring.

The eyes moved out of the table's shadow, revealing themselves as belonging to an opulent white Persian cat. Forsyte corrected himself: what *appeared* to be an opulent white Persian cat.

"Is her collar on?" Sword asked.

"She's here, isn't she?" Ko answered as the cat slowly approached her, obviously suspicious.

"Is it on tight?" Sword clarified.

Ko scooped the cat up and chucked her under the chin. Six feet away, Forsyte could hear its strange, almost sing-song purr. "Of course it's on tight," Ko said, nuzzling the soft, white mass. "We know what happened last time, don't we, 'Bub?" The cat closed her eyes and flexed her front paws, kneading empty air.

"Check it," Sword persisted.

Ko slipped her finger under the scarred surface of the old green leather collar 'Bub wore. The two-inch-long clear crystal pendant that hung from it was firmly in place. "Satisfied?" she said.

Sword smiled sarcastically. "Maybe our friend will eat her. Then I'll be satisfied."

"Don't you listen to him," Ko crooned to the cat, then walked over to stand in front of the strapped-in werewolf.

Forsyte maneuvered his chair to a better observation point. Surprisingly, after the cat opened her eyes once to look at the creature in the examination chair, and had sniffed the air briefly with her mouth partially opened, she settled back in Ko's arms, purring loudly, not at all disturbed by the creature's presence.

Forsyte glanced at the EEG traces on the big screen. "LOOK," he had his voder say. "GRAPH THREE, FIVE, SIX."

"You like cats, don't you?" Ko said to the creature.

"LOOK AT HIS EYES," the voder said. Forsyte could see the heavy lids tremble.

Ko leaned closer to the creature. "Go ahead," she said kindly. "Take a look at our cat. Her name's 'Bub. See? She's big, and soft, and white. Do you like cats?"

The creature opened his eyes.

Forsyte heard Sword's intake of breath.

"I like cats," Ko said. "I think you like cats, too."

The creature spoke. "Catss." Coarse, gravelly, but intelligible.

"This cat's name is 'Bub."

"'Bub."

"Do you have a name?"

The creature nodded.

"Can you tell me?"

The creature shook his head.

Ko frowned. "Why not? My name's Melody. I'd like to know your name. Can't you tell me?" She knelt down beside the creature, holding the cat up so he could see it easily.

"They will hunt me," the creature said. "They will catch me." He looked nervously around the room for a moment, then his eyes, large and brown, returned to the cat. "They will eat me."

"Who will?" Ko asked.

"The keepers."

Sword stepped forward, his eyes as wide as the creature's. "You have keepers?" he asked excitedly, too loudly. "People who look after you? You're organized? You're — "

The creature moaned and squeezed his eyes shut and pulled his massive head in closer to his barrel chest.

Ko turned to Sword and hissed at him. "Will you calm down. You're ruining everything." She turned back to the creature. "It's all right," she said softly. "Would you like me to put the cat in your lap?"

The creature's eyes fluttered.

"Would you like to pet her? She's so soft. And she loves to be petted. Can you hear her purr?"

"Yess," the creature said. He opened his eyes again, glancing furtively at Sword.

"Here you go," Ko said and deposited 'Bub on the blanket covering the creature's broad lap. The cat lay on her side and stared up at the large dark face above her. The creature smiled and Forsyte was amazed by the teeth he saw inside, trying unsuccessfully to place them within the family of the known great apes.

Ko stood up and moved to the side of the chair.

"Think it through," Sword advised, seeing what she was planning.

Ko ignored Sword and undid the strap holding the creature's right arm. Hesitantly, eyes flicking from Sword to Ko to 'Bub and back, the creature brought his hand down to the cat and touched, then scratched her ears. 'Bub melted into a thick white puddle and her purring increased.

"You do like cats, don't you?" Ko asked, going back to kneel before the creature.

"Yes, yes," he said, smiling, "Martin likes cats. Martin likes — " He looked up suddenly, frowning.

Ko smiled. "Is that your name? Martin?"

The creature said nothing.

"We can keep it a secret. We won't tell the keepers that we know."

The creature nodded sheepishly. An odd expression for such a bestial face, Forsyte thought.

Sword approached the creature again, this time speaking slowly and deliberately. "Martin, look at me. Do you know *my* name, Martin?"

Forsyte looked from Martin to Sword. He remembered how shocked Sword had been when he returned from Greece and said that the werewolf he had hunted there had recognized him, and had known his name. Would Martin know Sword's name as well?

But the creature shook his head. "You just dark hunter," he said and turned his concentration back to 'Bub.

"What's a dark hunter, Martin? You can tell me," Ko coaxed. She brought her hand up to scratch at 'Bub's ears, too. Forsyte could see she was gaining the creature's trust. Martin no longer started when she moved.

"Dark hunters evil. Dark hunters kill clanmates."

Sword took a deep slow breath. "Who are the clanmates, Martin?"

"My clanmates," the creature said, apparently puzzled by the question. "Clan Arkady."

"Do you belong to a clan, Martin? Is that what you call it?" Sword loomed over the creature.

Martin flinched. "Everyone belongs to clan," he said.

"Do we belong to a clan, Martin?" Ko asked, keeping a soothing rhythm going as she and Martin stroked the cat. "The Clan ... Pendragon. Have you heard of it?"

Martin's eyes flickered, but he frowned and turned away. "No," he said like a child told a piece of nonsense. "You have no clan. You are human." He made a sound like a chuckle.

Sword brought his hand down to 'Bub. The cat immediately stopped purring and opened her eyes to stare at the man. Martin tensed. Sword took his hand away and 'Bub closed her eyes again. "If we're human, Martin, then what are you?"

Martin jerked his chin upright and proudly said, "I am adept."

"Adept at what?" Sword asked, puzzled.

The creature frowned. "I am adept. You are human. This is cat. Everything is what it is."

"This is *fantastic*," Sword said, startling Ko and Forsyte with his sudden excitement. "There *is* an organization. Keepers. Another clan in addition to Pendragon." He turned to Forsyte. "Remember, I told you. I told you they'd have to organize to stay hidden. I knew it." He beamed at the creature. "So, you all call yourselves adepts. Is that it?"

"Call myself Martin."

Sword rolled his eyes. "But you are an adept?"

Martin nodded and stared at 'Bub.

"Would you call yourself a werewolf, Martin?" Ko asked.

Martin shook his head ponderously. "Martin not werewolf. Werewolves big. Werewolves keepers."

Sword was elated. Forsyte had never seen him this way. Sword was rarely so unguarded, so easily read. Whatever his true feelings were, he usually kept them hidden, along with the other secrets of his life. Forsyte, for one, was just as happy they stayed that way.

"You've *seen* werewolves? You *know* werewolves?"

"Martin Clan Arkady," Martin said, confused again. "All clanmates shifters. Wolves, bears, lions, other ... things."

Sword hooted and Martin jumped against his bonds. 'Bub instinctively tried to scramble away but Ko deftly caught her.

"Shifters! This is *it!*" Sword cried out, clenching his fists at the ceiling. "*Yes!*"

Martin cowered as Sword's voice echoed through the Loft.

"It's all right," Ko said to Martin as she shot a murderous glance at Sword. "He won't hurt you. He's just happy. He's been looking for someone like you for a long, long time."

"Why?" Martin asked, watching Sword suspiciously.

"He wants to find werewolves."

Martin's eyes narrowed in thought. "Humans do not find werewolves," he said slowly. "Werewolves find humans. That's why werewolves keepers. To keep all clans safe."

"All clans?" Sword said. "You mean, more than just Arkady and Pendragon?" He mock-punched Ko on her shoulder and she stumbled against Martin's knees. "Are there more than two clans? Is that what you mean?"

Martin turned his head from Sword to Ko. "Keepers say I should not talk. You humans. You do not know about First World. I should not tell." He sucked his lips in like a child about to hold his breath.

"First World ... ?" Sword whispered in delight. "A whole organization — no, a world — based on clans. A name for it all ... " Forsyte could feel his intensity.

"You're wrong, Martin," Ko said suddenly before this newly awakened Sword could confuse the creature again. "We're not like most humans. We do know about the First World." Forsyte could hear the bluff in her voice but felt quite sure no one else could. Ko stared into the creature's doubting eyes. "Here," she said. "I'll show you." She placed 'Bub on Martin's lap. "Go for a walk, 'Bub?"

'Bub instantly sprang to all fours, staring expectantly at Ko.

"Forget it, Melody!" Sword warned. "Not in the damned lab!"

"Hold the cat tightly," Ko said urgently to Martin. "Don't let go."

Martin's giant hand swept around the cat, holding her close to his chest. Ko's hands worked at the fittings on 'Bub's collar. The hanging crystal chimed against her nails as if it were made of thin, light metal.

"Melody!" Sword warned. "I said no!"

"There!" Ko pulled the old collar and crystal away.

And Martin gasped as the cat he held melted away into absolute transparency. "Light Clan!" he whispered. "With humans!"

"What did he call it?" Sword demanded. "He called it a what clan?"

"Don't let go," Ko cautioned Martin. "Let me put the collar back on."

She moved her hands to the empty space contained behind Martin's powerful right arm. Then Forsyte saw she remembered it was easier if she kept her eyes shut. The collar closed over empty air. 'Bub cried out like something four times her size, then sparkled into sight again.

Sword was back beside Martin's chair. "What did you call that cat?" he asked. "What kind of clan?"

"Light Clan," Martin said as if it was the most obvious thing in the world. "Not cat."

"Then what is it?"

"'Chanted." He spat out the word as if it were a curse. "Poor Light."

"Incredible," Sword said.

Martin stroked 'Bub. "Poor 'chanted Light," he said sadly. "Who put collar on you?"

"I did," Sword said. "But that's not important. What I want to — "

"Did this to Light?" Martin asked, turning his head slowly to face Sword. Forsyte did not like the challenge that was suddenly in the creature's eyes.

"Yeah," Sword said, missing the obvious. "I had to when the guy sold her to me. Anyway — "

"Put *collar* on *Light?*" Martin's deep voice had become a growl.

"Ah, Sword ... " Ko said cautiously, easing back from the creature. "Maybe you'd — "

"I put the collar on the damned Light," Sword said flatly. "Now listen — "

"Then you *bad!*" Martin roared as his massive fist shot out at a speed Forsyte could not follow and Sword flew back and crumpled to the floor, limp and bloodied.

As Ko scrambled for the medikit, Forsyte couldn't help himself. He smiled. Sword had finally gotten the werewolf he wanted, and the werewolf had given Sword exactly what he deserved.

THREE

Galen Sword.

He hears someone say his name.

Jesus Christ, it's Galen Sword.

The lights hurt his eyes. White on, red off. White on, red off. No red lights in the Loft, he thinks.

Jesus, what was it? A Lamborghini?

Ah, the accident, he thinks. This is before the Loft. Before Forsyte. Before Greece. Before Askwith. Before everything.

A Ferrari maybe? Not much left.

White, red, white, red. Spinning slowly, spiralling down, heading down the long lonely tunnel into ... into ... is it before the werewolf? Three years before. Three years before everything. This is the accident, he thinks. This is the beginning.

How much one o' those things cost anyhow?

Not much wrapped around the post like that.

They laugh. He hears them laughing down the tunnel. But he can't laugh with them. His laughing seems to be over. Oh, well, he thinks. Not much to laugh about anyway. He feels a pain in his side as the numbness fades. Champagne must be wearing off. What had he told the girls? You can't buy a good Chateau LaFitte '64 anymore. You can only rent it. He wonders what happened to them.

Jesus, is there someone still in there?
Two of them.
Two of them? Christ, isn't she ... from the magazine ... ?
Yeah, that's her.
Some guys.
Yeah, some guys have all the bucks.

Yeah, he thinks. They want them, he gets them. Not much challenge but no time alone. That's a good thing. No time alone. Might think too much. Might remember too much. It's bad to remember. The light is really starting to bother him now. Maybe it's time to go all the way down that tunnel. Looks nice and dark and safe down there. Did the werewolf do this to me? No, it's the accident. Again.

Who's the other one?
Let me see, let me ... oh, Jesus. Oh, Jesus, Mary, and Joseph.
Who?
Can't tell. Don't know.
No face.

No faces needed down that long, dark tunnel, Sword thinks.

Goddamned bastard should die.
Look at him. Poor bastard's gonna die.

He feels himself lifted up but stops a few miles short of heaven. Just being slipped onto a stretcher, into the ambulance, through the streets and over the hills to grandmother's house ... Don't have a grandmother, he thinks. Don't have a grandfather or a father or a mother or a sister or anyone. All I have is their money. Much too much of their money.

The light again. White that stays on. Bumping and bouncing, not down a tunnel. Down ... a corridor. Into ... an emergency room.

Who's this one?
Got a wallet?
Got a big wallet. Christ a'mighty ... who is this guy? Looka the cash.
But no license.
That got suspended last year.
How do you know?
Don't you recognize this creep? It's Galen Sword.
Oh, yeah. That guy in the Post. *Got a place at the Trump Tower, the*
bastard.

Never stays in it. Always off —
Think there's anyone we should call there?
Card here says notify Askwith and Marjoribanks. Lawyers?
Lawyers. Don't you remember anything? This guy's got no family.
This guy's got nothing.

Not even hope, he thinks. Not even hope.

Slow night, gentlemen. Let's see what we can do.
You got it, doc.

He feels a cold circle of plastic against his mouth. A cool dryness floods past the clots of blood and torn flesh in his throat and reflexively he gasps, drawing the oxygen deeper inside. The ragged ends of his ribs grate deep within him.

Hundred and fifty cc's, stat.

All that pain and he can still feel the needle slip into him. More, he thinks, want more and more to slip and slide and go away and forget it all.

Funny, he thinks. At times like these aren't you supposed to see your whole boring life pass before your eyes? Why do I just want to forget mine? Forget everything.

We're going to have to open him up.

Here? With those injuries? God, look at his ribs. They're all over the place.

Get an O.R. set up. Pump him and purge him and pray he lasts the five minutes it's going to take to —

Police shootings! Officers coming in now! It's bad. It's bad.

But ...

C'mon, doc, this guy's had his chance. No one's going to miss him. Work here long enough and you'll understand.

They don't even say goodbye. He hears only the quiet rattle of the curtain drawn around him. He hears only the soft bubble of the oxygen. He's had his chance. No one is going to miss him. He misses no one. Except those people he never had. Mother. Father.

Galen Sword is alone. The tunnel waits.

Open your eyes.

And he does.

For the first time since the lamp post flew in front of his Testa Rossa at eighty miles an hour in downtown Manhattan, Galen Sword opens his eyes and he can see. The emergency-room cubicle mists around him. The sounds of the wounded police officers being treated and saved seem far away and muffled. He looks up, angry to be pulled away from the soft darkness. He looks up and sees ... himself?

No, no, he thinks. My hair is black, his is blond. My nose is straighter, thinner, his is rounder. But his eyes ... I've seen his eyes before ... his mother's eyes?

How could you?

So much sadness in those eyes, those words, those ... his lips hadn't moved. Sword tries to speak, to tell the man he's wrong to talk that way, it's bad to talk that way, but his throat will not work.

You have a destiny.

I have pain, Sword thinks. I have emptiness. I have sorrow and pity and wish to surrender as I have surrendered all my life. I have no destiny.

You must fight.

I cannot fight.

No one else can fight for you.

I will not fight.

No one else can fight for us.

I ... must not fight.

I know. But that will change.

No.

The man's hand floats down to Sword. For an instant, it seems to fade into the darkness of the shadows and the tunnel as it covers Sword's eyes. And then Sword realizes that he can still see it, lit with a gentle blue light. A blue light that grows from the hand itself.

No, Sword thinks. He recognizes the color of that light. He knows he must not recognize the color of that light.

Yes.

I can not.

Remember.

I must not.

Remember.

I.
Remember.

⌒

His mother's laughter. Was there ever a sound that more thrilled him? More comforted him?

His mother's laughter and a day of play in the enclave's garden.

The sun was bright. It danced in his mother's hair like sparkles in water like gold. His mother laughed and he giggled and he fell on the yielding grass and giggled even more. He was not afraid of falling here. He had seen the enclave's gardeners at their work, with their crystals and their spells. There was nothing in the garden that could possibly hurt him. Never had been. Never would be. Because his father ... his father ...

Sweeping down with laughter, his mother scooped him into her arms and spun him through the warm summer air. She kissed him on his round baby's cheek. He kissed her back. "The ball!" he cried. "The ball! The ball!" And his stumpy little legs thumped across the grass of perfect hue and length and he grabbed at the brilliant yellow ball that waited for him.

He stooped over it, awkwardly bending at his waist and wrapping his arms around the ball and heard his mother's footsteps rushing up behind him.

He couldn't help it. He shrieked with the helpless anticipation of her fingers brushing his tiny sides from behind. He collapsed in giggles before his mother even touched him.

He rolled over, saw her kneeling over him, laughing as he laughed. As beautiful as anything he had seen in all his five long years of life.

Her beauty caught him for that moment and he stopped his laughter. He felt the bond between them as her face imprinted itself upon his mind. The gold of her hair in the sunlight. The sparkle of the day in her eyes. The magical swelling of her stomach where she said a special surprise grew for him and his father. A new playmate. A sister. Or a brother.

Life was a never-ending adventure of magic and ... something even more important. Something that gave purpose to that magic, and to all the days of play in the enclave's garden.

His mother's arms wrapped around him.

"I love you, little Galen."

She smelled like sunlight and summer grass and soft breezes on warm days and he nuzzled into her shoulder and knew his life would be forever perfect.

She smelled like antiseptic and her scalpel cut deep into his chest ...

Holy shit. His eyes are open.

Light.

I don't believe it. They're dilating.

Are you sure? Look in here. He's got bone fragments spearing his heart. His lungs should be useless. Blood pressure ... nonexistent.

His goddamned eyes are dilating.

We're getting brain activity over here.

Whatta we do?

Get some practice, I guess. Boost the gases and let's go in.

How long do you give him?

Ten minutes ago, pal. Ten minutes ago.

The pressure in the plastic circle over his mouth and nose increases. The circle of lights above him spin around and around, changing from blue to yellow, changing from a circle to a sphere. Becoming ...

His big yellow ball flew through the air and he jumped for it, seconds too soon. It landed on his head and bounced to the grass and he chased it, tiny legs pumping until the ball rolled into a small, laden apple tree and stopped.

He picked it up, one small hand on either side, and ran back, almost waddling, to toss it to his mother. Four feet from her, he stopped, concentrated, took a mighty breath, and pushed the ball away. His mother reached quickly to the side, caught the ball with one hand and bounced it up to where she could catch it easily.

"Good boy, Little Galen. Good boy." His mother hugged the ball as she had held him.

"Again!" Galen called, clapping his pudgy hands together. "Again! Again!"

"No."

Galen recognized the voice. He hadn't ever known Tomas Roth to be at home when his father wasn't. The boy dropped his hands to his side and lowered his head, afraid to look up. Playtime was over.

"That's not good, Little Galen," Tomas said. The tall, dark man stalked across the grass to Galen's mother. He took the ball from her. "That's bad, Little Galen. Bad. Do you understand?"

Galen felt his bottom lip quiver. He kept his head down and studied the way his feet pushed into the grass. He heard the man coming closer to him. He looked up.

Tomas knelt in the grass four feet away from Galen. The sun didn't dance in his hair because he was bald, with only a dark, trimmed fringe around his temples and the back of his head. And his face and features were hard and square, precise and cold as if he had been made like the gargoyles that protected the old school. He cast a shadow in the sun, on the grass, that fell at Galen's turned-inward feet.

"Like this, boy. Throw the ball like this."

Tomas held the yellow ball upon his open palms. The ball jiggled once, twitched up into the air, hung for a moment, then floated across to Galen and settled gently into the boy's reluctant open arms.

"See," Tomas said. His smile clicked on like a working crystal's sudden flare. The child could see it was false. "That's how you throw a ball, Little Galen. That's the good way to throw a ball. Now you do it that way, too."

Galen held the ball in his outstretched palms but the ball was too big and it rolled off and hit the ground.

The dark man's smile flickered. "Again, boy. Try again."

Galen grappled with the ball, held it once more as he had been taught in the old school. But he didn't know what to do next. He looked at his mother but didn't understand the expression in her eyes, such beautiful eyes. He looked back at Tomas. Eyes like empty pits.

The boy trembled. The boy threw the ball to the side and ran for his mother, little hands reaching up to her, small tears trickling down flushed cheeks.

He was lifted by her, consoled by her, but even her whispers could not blank out the man's words between the boy's sobs.

" ... keep telling you? ... not like us ... something wrong ... congenital ... a freak ... can no longer stay ... stay ... "

... stay with us, stay with us ... that's it.

This is too much. Are you sure the EEG's connected properly?

He's breathing, isn't he?

Yeah, good job on that lung. I thought it would have to —

I didn't touch his blasted lung! It just ... it just ...

There go his eyes again.

Can't you control the blasted anesthetic!

Everything's textbook perfect. It's just that he's not metabolizing it the way the textbook says he should.

That's ridiculous.

Like his lung, right?

Okay, okay, as long as he's not moving around. Let's stitch up those rips in the ventricle wall.

Uh, what rips, doctor?

The ones in ... oh, shit. The bone fragments ... they're ...

This isn't happening, right? I mean, this is impossible, isn't it? Isn't it?

"It's impossible," Tomas said.

Galen looked up from his secret fort under the dining-room table, nested deep among the strong, dark, wooden legs of a dozen chairs, which were intricately carved with overlapping leaves. Quietly, he closed the cover of the book he had with him. It was large, and heavy, with a rich smell of the library, all leather, and secrets, and dust. He watched two pairs of legs enter the room, until he recognized the slow, shuffling steps of his uncle, Alexander, and the crisp march of Tomas Roth. He turned back to his book. He didn't care for adult business. He didn't understand it.

"I'm afraid he's become a liability," Tomas said. "Politically as well as practically."

Galen ran his hand over the heavily-textured design and type engraved on the thick leather cover of the book. He could not read the language it was written in yet, but he had heard the title of the book a hundred times. It was his favorite source of bedtime stories, all about the 'good old days' his father called them, smiling as he said the words. The title of the book was *History of the Greater Clan Pendragon,* and the design was the sword and dragon that his father and mother wore on their rings. Someday, Galen had been told, he would wear the design, too.

"But how?" Alexander asked. The old one sounded tired. "How many generations have we bred true?"

Carefully, Galen opened the book again. The pages were so thin he guessed they had working crystal somewhere in their making. They fell open so gently they made no sound. It was a good book to be reading in a secret fort.

"Perhaps ... " Tomas replied, "perhaps the fault is not with the weight of ... generations?"

Galen looked up as Alexander coughed. "You dare suggest a ... a halfling?"

Galen put his fingers to his lips. He had never heard old Uncle Alexander swear. It sounded funny coming from him. He looked back at the book, searching through it for pictures.

"He is as powerless as a human," Tomas said.

"I will not let my sister be insulted," Alexander said sternly. "He's just slow. He just needs time."

Galen wondered who his Uncle Alexander's sister was. He had never known his uncle had any little brothers or sisters. He thought they might be nice to play with. Galen was only five years old.

"You know what the conditions are like, old one." Tomas sounded angry. "There is no more time. How can any of us face the Gathering knowing the heir is without substance?"

Galen found a picture he enjoyed, an intricate etching of a battle in the Great War. In the picture's center, a noble warrior was heroically clad in ornate armor which Galen's father said was in a museum somewhere Galen couldn't remember. The warrior swung his sword through a heaving mass of hunched-over monkeylike things, all fangs and claws. The boy knew the words that were written on that page, too: *The Battle of Florence during the Great War with the Lesser Clans.*

Galen traced the path of the sword with his finger, caught up in imagining what life would be like in those days so long ago. He touched the warrior's face, studying the handsome points on his ears, the radiant fighting light shown emerging from his eyes, so much of the working crystal about him, so much inner substance as well.

"There is no other choice," Tomas said loudly, startling the boy. "Little Galen *must* be sent away!"

Galen dropped the book from his lap and it hit the floor with an audible thud. Had they been talking about him the whole time? Sent away?

Tomas bent down and peered in at the boy through the forest of chair legs. For an instant, the man's expression was like those on the faces of the monkeylike things, feral and hungry and crazed. "See what I mean?" Tomas complained. "He's so powerless he hasn't even got an aura. He's been here all along."

Moving carefully, Alexander bent down as well. His face was softer, kinder, and he smiled as he saw the boy and what he was doing. "Ah, Little Galen, going through the family album again, are you?"

The old one moved a chair out of the way and reached in to lift up the book from where it had fallen open. He saw the picture Galen had been looking at, and smiled, ignoring Tomas.

"Ah, Lysander at the Battle of Florence. A great day for the greater clans." He held out his hand to Galen, inviting the boy out from his fort. His smile emphasized the deep lines in his face and comically pushed the points of his own ears up against his balding temples. "Lysander Sword was a great hero to the clans, little one." He glanced for a moment at Tomas and Galen saw a flash of fighting light, barely held back, grow in his uncle's eyes. "He is my ancestor, you know, and no matter what some might say, he is *your* ancestor as well."

Galen felt his uncle's hand fold around his own. The old one's skin was warm and dry and comforting.

"Don't ever forget that, little one. Don't ever forget that."

Galen stared into his uncle's eyes, so much like his mother's, and heard Tomas's angry footsteps leaving the room.

"I won't," the boy said uncertainly, without any idea of why his uncle's glowing eyes had tears.

⤴

There're his eyes again.

Sword? Can you hear me? Do you know where you are?

No response here.

But they're dilating.

Blood pressure's coming back up, too.

Impossible. We haven't given him enough.

I don't think we had to give him much, doctor. A lot of his bleeding seems to have come from his scalp and when you wash the blood away, he's not really in all that bad shape.

Uh, there aren't any scalp wounds.

What?

There were other people in the car, maybe their blood ...

Is he stable, now, for Christ's sake? Then get him into X-ray. I don't like this. I don't like this one bit.

Come on, Sword. Do you know where you are? Look at me.

⤴

"Look at me, young master."

Galen didn't like the way his mother had brushed his hair. It was still wet and his scalp tingled from the harsh strokes she had used to slick it back. And he didn't like the sweet smell of flowers that came from the breath of the small creature in front of him.

"Little Galen," his mother said from across the room. "Look at Herr Slausen when he speaks to you."

Galen peeked over at his mother. No sunlight danced in her hair this time. The curtains were shut against the night in the family library and the glowing facets hovering in the air by the ceiling were turned down low. She stood by an old man he had never seen, a tired old man leaning on a cane as if he had no substance. Galen wondered where his father was.

"Young master?" Herr Slausen said gently.

Galen turned his eyes to the creature, about his own height but more wrinkled even than Uncle Alexander. His eyes were colored solid with the blue power, matching the perfectly tailored little suit he wore. In one small wrinkled hand, he held a yellow orb of waiting crystal.

"Yes sir," Galen said. Why was everyone so sad? Was it because of what Tomas had said last week? That Little Galen must go away?

"Look into the orb, young master. See what drifts within."

Galen focused his eyes on the center of the waiting crystal. He knew from his lessons that he should be able to fill it with ... something. But he didn't know what, didn't know how.

"Mother ... " the boy said.

The creature cut him off with a wave. Galen heard his mother sob and from the corner of his eye saw her sag against the old man with the cane. Her stomach looked so full. A brother. A sister.

"Look, young master." This time, Herr Slausen's lips had not moved. "The crystal waits for you. What do you see? What do you give it?"

Tears, only tears from his eyes.

The creature sighed and the scent of roses flooded the boy's nostrils. Herr Slausen slowly lowered the orb and turned to Galen's mother, shaking his small head.

"*Tut mir leid, meine Dame*," the creature said softly. "There is no change ... nothing ... I am sorry."

Galen's mother pressed her eyes against the shoulder of the old man, her hand covering her mouth. Galen saw her back tremble and, for the first time, he felt afraid.

Then Tomas entered the library. Also for the first time in a long time, Galen saw that the dark man looked pleased. He placed a hand on Galen's mother's back.

"It's all right, my lady. All the arrangements have been made," Tomas said. He turned to Herr Slausen and nodded.

Galen wanted to yell at Tomas, to tell him to take his hand from his mother, to demand to know why he remained in the house while Galen's father was gone. But the scent of the flowers held him. Somehow, he could not turn away from the creature before him, the creature who now held up a crystal vial, frothing with blue.

"Drink this, young master," Herr Slausen said. The scent of flowers was overwhelming as the creature spoke.

Galen had no choice. The vial was at his lips, beyond his control. His mother was weeping. Tomas was smiling. Galen's father was gone.

"Drink this, young master, and forget."

Forget his father. Forget his mother, the growing swell of his brother or sister. Forget his house, his enclave, his books, his games.

"Forget everything," the creature said, frothing with blue, with flowers overwhelming.

Forget the old school and the gargoyles. Forget the book, Lysander, Alexander. Forget everything.

The blue coursed through him.

"Forget everything."

Everything.

Forget.

You have a destiny.

I remember.

" ... do you remember?" the voice asked. "Do you remember what happened?"

Galen Sword opened his eyes and the light was blinding. The long dark tunnel was gone.

It was a nurse who spoke, leaning over him, holding his wrist, patting his face. "Do you know your name?"

"Galen Sword." He tried to sit up, saw he was in a bed. The roughened sheets were harsh against him.

"Do you know where you are?"

He had to think. An ambulance. Something about doctors? "The hospital?" he guessed.

"Do you remember what happened?"

The first thing that came into his mind was an accident. The girls laughing. Going too fast. The road suddenly shifting away and going straight into ... but it was more than an accident. Someone had come to him in the emergency room. Someone had come to him as he was poised above empty blackness and that someone had told him ... told him ...

Galen Sword's hand clasped solidly around the wrist of the nurse.

"Mr. Sword," she said, a tinge of fear in her voice. "Do you remember what happened?"

"Yes," Sword said. "I remember ... everything."

And for the first time in almost twenty years, he did.

FOUR

Marcus Askwith looked up from the police reports carefully arranged on his immense, leather-covered desk. A pair of thin half-glasses rested precariously on the tip of his nose and his brilliant pink scalp shone through a few wispy strands of white hair brushed up and over from his temples. But the mind within the ancient trappings was as sharp and fast as any youngster's he might face in court.

He cleared his throat, announcing his intention to speak. "They tell me you're quite a lucky man, Galen." His voice had a hint of age's waver in it, but was still strong, tempered by the precise modulation learned during almost fifty years before the bar.

Galen Sword stood by the floor-to-ceiling windows overlooking Central Park, thirty stories below. He glanced down at the small plaster cast on his left wrist.

"Police estimate you were doing close to eighty miles an hour when you hit the lamp standard," Askwith said, glancing down at the reports in his thin hands. "One woman dead, another ... well ... another probably wishes she were, and you walk away with a minor fracture."

"My chest was crushed," Sword said without emotion, repeating what wasn't in the reports, but what the charge nurse had told him. "Five ribs splintered. Collapsed lung. My heart pierced by bone fragments. Skull shattered."

"I don't doubt it felt that way," the lawyer conceded, offering a comradely and calculated laugh. "To tell the truth, when I got the call, I thought you had been drinking again and I thought — "

"I had been." Sword's voice was low and flat in the dark panelled opulence of the old law office.

Askwith shrugged as he flipped through the sheets of paper he held. "Hospital report shows no trace of alcohol in your blood at the time of the — "

"I was doing more than just alcohol, too."

"No trace of *anything* in your blood, Galen."

Sword turned around to face the man. "I should have died, Marcus."

The lawyer studied his young client for a moment, then slipped his reading glasses off, folded them carefully, and placed them to the side of his desk blotter, by a sterling silver tray holding an antique desk set. "I understand," he said, folding his hands together on his desk. "You feel guilty about the women."

"Damn right I do. And your firm will make the necessary adjustments to my trust fund to see that everything is taken care of for them and — "

"Doing anything for them, or their estates, at this time could be construed as an admission of guilt in a court — "

"For God's sake, Marcus! I *am* guilty." Sword's hand slashed the air for emphasis. "I was drunk. I was high. I was speeding."

Askwith slapped his hands on his desktop. "*No*, young man, you were not *any* of those things. I have the hospital reports right here — your blood was clean. I have the police reports — three reliable witnesses have come forward to say you swerved to avoid the cab that tried to cut you off. At worst, at *worst*, you face misdemeanor fines for having three people in a two-seater vehicle and driving while under suspension. And that, young man, is *it*."

Sword dismissed the lawyer's outburst, cynically. "That's crap and you know it."

"I know no such thing." Askwith tugged down on his vest and huffed.

Sword turned away to stare out of the windows again. "Tell me about my parents," he said.

"I never knew them," Askwith replied.

"You answered too quickly," Sword said. "You always answer too quickly when it comes to answering questions about my past." He breathed on the glass before him and watched it fog, then clear, revealing the park anew. "How did you come to be administrator of my trust fund, then, Marcus? If you didn't know my parents?"

Askwith cleared his throat again. "Your father dealt exclusively with Miss Marjoribanks — "

"Retired these many years."

"Quite correct. Your father arranged the trust through this firm, with Miss Marjoribanks as administrator, until her untimely ... accident, at which time I took over respon — "

"Tell me how my parents died." Sword faced Askwith again, and saw an uncustomary nervousness appear in the old man's eyes. Odd how he had never noticed that before.

"Plane crash. New Zealand. You were two years old. You — "

"I was five years old, Marcus."

Askwith looked down and rubbed his forehead. "No, no. You were five years old when Miss Marjoribanks retired and you were placed in — "

Sword struck. "I was five years old when my parents *sent me away* because I had no powers. Like the rest of my clan. Name 'Pendragon' mean anything to you, Marcus?"

It was as if Askwith had been hit by lightning.

"You're losing it, Marcus. You give a reaction like that in court and the jury will bury you."

Askwith tried to speak, couldn't, tried again, coughing. "I ... I don't know what you're talking about, Galen. A dream perhaps. A nightmare brought on by the anesthetic. No one wants to be an orphan, after all. You just dreamed that — "

"I am not an orphan, Marcus. I've got a mother, and a father. I've got an uncle named Alexander. I've got an ancestor named Lysander. My God, my mother was pregnant when I was sent away. I've got a brother or a sister out there someplace. I've got — " Then lightning struck Sword. He remembered the eyes of the man in the emergency room.

"My God, Marcus. I *do* have a brother."

Askwith's face was white. "No, Galen. You don't understand. You can't have a brother."

Sword leaned over the old man's desk. "Oh, no. You're the one who doesn't understand. I should have died in that crash last week. I *was* dying. But a man came into the emergency room. He spoke to me, Marcus. He spoke to me without moving his lips. And he looked at me. He looked at me and his eyes were just like mine. Just like my mother's. Our mother's."

"No," the old man said. Pleaded. Prayed.

"Yes," Sword threw back at him. "He spoke to me and he told me to remember and I did remember. 'You have a destiny,' he told me."

"He *told* you that?"

"'You must fight,' he told me."

Askwith moaned. "And that? Brin told you *that?*"

Sword stopped instantly. "'Brin'? Is that his name? You know him?"

"No," Askwith said. "I don't know him. I can't know him. You can't either. You musn't."

"How do I find him, Marcus? How do I find *them?* My family?"

Askwith held a large white linen handkerchief to his face. He blew into it, folded it, used it to wipe at his brow as he caught his breath. When he spoke again, a semblance of control had returned. But it was fragile, Sword sensed. Like a spider's web.

"Galen, do you have any idea how much your trust fund is worth?"

Sword sat on the edge of Askwith's desk and folded his arms. "What the hell does that have to do with anything?"

"Do you?"

Sword gestured aimlessly at the ceiling. "Forty ... fifty million. Somewhere around there."

Askwith raised his eyebrows and shook his head. "One hundred and ten."

"About my family, Marcus — "

"I could have it doubled for you." Askwith's eyes were crystal clear and steady. "I could have it tripled."

Sword had never heard the lawyer more serious. More than anything else he could have asked for at that moment, Askwith's offer was the proof he needed that what he had experienced wasn't a dream. "Thank you, Marcus," he said.

"All that you'd have to do is promise that you wouldn't go looking for ... well, looking into any of this."

"My delusion. The anesthetic."

Askwith sighed with relief. "Exactly, my boy. Exactly."

Sword stood up and paced across the thick Persian carpet in front of Askwith's desk. "You know, Marcus, you've been the only constant in my life. I had a new guardian every year, but I've been coming to your office four times a year ... forever, it seems. You've had me to your townhouse for holidays. To the Hamptons in the summer. Taught me about life as you wrote out the checks."

"I've tried to," Askwith said hesitantly.

"And buying my way out of a problem is certainly one of those things you've taught me well."

"It's a method which works for those who have the means."

"And I have those means, don't I, Marcus?"

"Very much so."

"And you're offering me something like three hundred million dollars to buy *your* way out of the problem *I've* presented."

"Put bluntly, yes."

Sword stopped pacing and stood in front of the man who had been the closest thing to family he had had for almost twenty years. "Well, I'm offering whoever will take it one hundred and ten million to buy my way out of *my* problem. I think that kind of money can find out a lot of things, don't you, Marcus? Track down a lot of missing people?"

Askwith's mouth dropped open. "You can't, Galen. You'd be ... "

"What?" Sword asked. "In danger? I don't think so. I was going to die last week and my brother" — he smiled tightly at the old man — "Brin, saw to it that I was ... healed." Sword picked up the antique silver letter opener from the tray on Askwith's desk. It was shaped like a dagger. "Brin placed his hand on me, it glowed with the 'blue power' — see how much I remember, Marcus? — and my body put itself back together." He held the dagger to his stomach. "I think that if someone wanted me killed, they would have killed me when I was five years old. I think that I could go looking for my family and I wouldn't be in danger." He lightly bounced the point of the dagger against himself. "I think that if anything does happen to me then that blue power will — " he raised the dagger to thrust.

"*Noo!*" Askwith jumped from his chair and grabbed for the letter opener. "No," he said, and there was no control left in his voice at all, only age. "It ... the blue power, it ... doesn't last. You aren't protected anymore. It doesn't work like that."

Sword released the dagger into Askwith's waiting, trembling hand. "Then how *does* it work?"

The lawyer slumped back in his chair. Sword felt he had just taken the first step on a long journey.

"I can't say." Askwith's voice was a whisper. "Because I ... don't know." He looked up at the young man whose life he had tried to order. "I'm not part of their world, Galen. You must believe me."

Sword nodded. There was no more denial in Askwith's eyes. The guardian had conceded. "What can you tell me?" He made his voice sound as gentle as he could.

Askwith shook his head slowly and, for a long moment, Sword wondered if the man even remembered his client was there. "I'll have to ask permission," the lawyer finally said. "It's the only way."

"Who gives permission like that?"

Askwith sighed. "I have a number I can call."

Sword concentrated on keeping his voice level and unthreatening. He didn't want to lose any of the advantage he had gained. "Will ... whoever it is give permission?"

Askwith raised his empty hands. "I don't know. If I had asked last week, the answer would have been no. But with Brin back ... I can't say."

Very calmly, Sword asked, "*Is* he my brother?"

Askwith looked past Sword, out through the windows to the park. "Please, Galen, they'll know what I've said, all that I've told you. They have ways of ... ask me again tomorrow."

"What if 'they' don't give permission for you to tell me anything?"

Askwith fixed his eyes on Sword, as if trying to pass on some hidden message he couldn't commit to spoken words. "Then we'll deal with it tomorrow, Galen." He held out a hand to his client, as Alexander had so long ago, encouraging the boy forward, telling him not to forget his heritage. "Trust me on this one, Galen. You've waited this long. Give it one more day."

Sword held the old man's gaze but could extract no meaning from it. Finally, he reached across the desk and shook the lawyer's hand. "All right," he said. "One more day."

Their hands separated with hesitation, as if Sword were afraid to relinquish anything that might lead him toward his goal.

"You should leave now," Askwith said.

"So you can make the call?"

The lawyer shook his head. "I can't make it now." He saw the question unspoken in Sword's eyes. "The number is only answered after ... after the sun has set."

Sword raised his eyebrows. "They only answer the phone after sunset?" He laughed nervously. "What kind of people are we dealing with here, Marcus?"

The lawyer looked away, too many secrets in his eyes. "They're not people at all, Galen. They're not people at all."

FIVE

The accident had only been a week ago, yet still Galen Sword felt as if he were a ghost in his own home: somehow insubstantial and not belonging, out of phase with the reality of his past. Despite what his brother Brin had done to him in the emergency ward to bring him back from death, Sword knew that his old life really had ended on that night of the accident. But he still had no idea what had begun in its place.

It was early morning and he walked through the marble-floored hallway of his Trump Tower apartment. If he had slept last night, he couldn't remember. It was still a novelty to pass through an evening undulled by alcohol or other distractions. He watched the dawn from thirty stories above Fifth Avenue — golden shafts of light lancing through the canyons of the city — and realized he had not seen a day begin through unaltered eyes since he had been ... had been a boy. The city seemed new.

Sword stretched in the morning sunshine and cautiously moved his wrist within its short cast, wondering why he had been healed of everything except this one small fracture. But he had more important questions to think about now. Askwith had had his day — his night, rather — to talk to those who might give him permission to tell his client the truth, and after almost twenty years of being kept from that truth, Sword could not be patient any longer. He went to his study. It was time to make a call of his own.

The study was tastefully furnished — so his exorbitant designer had assured him — with antique oak panelling resurrected from some grand old mansion from the days when Manhattan had farms north of Houston Street; a magnificent inset saltwater aquarium teeming with creatures whose names he could not pronounce, carefully tended to by a biweekly service; and on all the walls and all the shelves, mementoes of his dabbling at digs around the world: burial masks from Mycenae; crude clay Lares and Penates from the Romans' Gaul; even a bizarre out-of-place artifact, suspiciously Phoenician, from the Starkey excavation just out of sight from Uluru — formerly Ayer's Rock — in Australia.

He paused for a moment in the doorway of the study, staring at the objects so elegantly and so meaninglessly arranged within it. The terms of the trust fund had been clear: ridiculous wealth in exchange for the pursuit of a university education and a career of his choice in a field which would expand humanity's knowledge of itself. Perhaps, he now realized, he had been searching for his own past in his journeys, and not the past of humanity.

But whatever had fuelled that one avocation of his past life — maintained, he knew, by the money he was able to donate to various field excursions and not by his scholarly abilities — the use and worth he had given his study of archaeology could be clearly seen in the backlit glass cabinet that ran behind the long leather couch by the study's fireplace. The case was filled with a completely unprofessional assortment of ornate phalluses, erotic sculptures, and fertility fetishes spanning three thousand years and fifteen cultures. The collection had worked its magic for Sword on that couch, before that fireplace, more times and with more women than he could remember. He looked away from the case. That morning, when the city felt new, he found his entire study filled him with sadness, with emptiness. There would be changes in his life now, he thought. It was time for everything to become new.

He went to his desk, another meaningless antique purchased without joy, only with a check. He reached to the phone to turn the ringer control back on, pushing aside a mass of unopened mail and magazines to reveal the message light on his answering machine. It was flashing. Someone had called, unheard, in the night as he had stared into the darkness, waiting for sleep.

Eeeeeeep. "Galen, it's Marcus. Are you there? If you're there, pick up the phone, Galen. Damn you, pick up the phone." The lawyer had paused long enough that the VOX circuit sensed the silence and disconnected the line.

There was a second message. Sword heard in Askwith's voice something he had never heard in it before. The old man had been drinking. Sword knew the effects well. "It's Marcus again. Calling about ... what, midnight? One? I'm not sure ... I'm not ... look, Galen. I made the call. I asked. I said I would ask and I asked and ... they said no."

"I'm not surprised. You shouldn't be, either." The old man laughed bitterly. "They kept it from you for almost two decades, after all. You can't expect them to give that up, to stop hoping that they might keep it up just a little while longer. That's all they think it's going to take. Just a little while longer." Askwith paused. Sword heard his sigh, long and tired. A drunk old man late at night. He had paused too long. The machine cut out again.

There was a third message. "Marcus here. I ... I suppose what I want to do is apologize to you, Galen. I tried to make it up to you, you know. Tried to give you what I could of a ... human life." The hair on Sword's arms stood on end. "That's what I am. That's what ... They have to use a lot of us, you know. In the past, when things were simpler, not the way they are today with computers and satellites and these damned machines, well, they could take care of themselves. Mostly, that is. I suppose that's when the legends all started. When they made their mistakes.

"Then things got more ... complicated. Little mistakes could become big mistakes. So they need a lot of us to keep things ... hidden. Keep things organized." He laughed again and coughed. Sword heard him sip something, heard the clink of ice. "I mean, I've *seen* some of them in my day. The real ones. It's not as if they could just ... walk into a bank and sign their own withdrawal slips." Another sigh. "I'm sorry, Galen. I'm rambling. An old man. So much to tell you. So much to apologize for." Another pause. The machine clicked off.

Sword swore in the silence of his study.

There was a fourth message.

Askwith's voice was dry and tremulous. "You don't belong to this world, Galen. But you're not an outcast. No. That's not the term they use for you. But you should find the outcasts. Oh, they say there aren't any. They say they were an aberration of the past. But they're there, in the shadows. That's where you've got to look. Halfway between. In the shadows."

"For what?" Sword shouted to the machine. "What am I looking for?"

"So hot in here," the message continued. "So late and so tired. I'm sorry Galen. Did I tell you that? I'm sorry for what they did to your parents. But ... but that was after. You wouldn't know. Not even Brin ... " Askwith sighed again, a deep breath as if he were trying to clear his mind. "Look, I'd better start at the beginning because ... because they're not going to let me see you again. They can't risk it. You'll understand when I've told you why you were sent away. Why they ... " The lawyer hummed for a moment. A short single note, less than a second in duration. Or had it been a sound from elsewhere near his phone? He continued speaking. "Your name is truly Galen Sword. They're bound by so many oaths that they couldn't take that from you. It was one of the conditions. I don't know what all of them were, but that was definitely one of them." A second brief hum. "Listen, you were born first in your line, heir to the Victor of the Greater Clan Pendragon. Brin was right, Galen. You *do* have a destiny. You *must* fight. First for your Clan, and then for the re — "

Without scream or cough or pause for an intake of breath, Askwith stopped talking. Sword heard a faint electric crackle from the speaker, the clunk of a phone handset hitting a hard surface, and then a moment of silence before the machine cut off again.

There was no fifth message.

That early in the morning, cabs were easy to get and without traffic Sword expected that the ride to Askwith's townhouse on East 64th would take only minutes. But the firetruck, ambulance, and police cars on Askwith's block had congested all routes in the area. Sword ran the last two blocks without once thinking that the emergency vehicles were for anything or anyone other than Marcus Askwith.

What was left of the lawyer's body had already been bagged and taken away by the police so it was not difficult for Sword to gain entrance, claiming that he was an old family friend and that Askwith had failed to make a breakfast appointment that day. He said nothing about the messages on his machine.

A plainclothes detective who introduced himself as Trank, bleary-eyed, bored, fat in rumpled clothes, brought Sword into Askwith's kitchen.

"Anything missin'?" the detective asked.

Sword made a show of looking carefully around the room. The counters and cabinets were immaculately white. The copper pots and utensils hanging in place on a stainless-steel grid attached to the wall were precisely arranged. It was a working chef's kitchen, as fully and expertly equipped as any fine restaurant's. Only a handful of details spoiled the illusion that Marcus Askwith might step in at any moment to prepare one of his legendary Sunday brunch menus.

An open bottle of Tanqueray Sterling vodka stood on a counter beside the refrigerator. Its silver label was charred and flaking from the glass. A crystal tumbler was beside the bottle, blackened on one side and cracked.

In the center of the ceiling, an oily black smudge soiled the smooth white enamel paint. Beneath the smudge, a white phone with a dozen extra buttons in addition to the standard number pad hung over the edge of another part of the counter. Its handset cord trailed down toward the floor but ended abruptly, cleanly cut off. On the floor beneath the phone was the most chilling detail of all. Forensics technicians had used thick white tape to trace what could only be the outline of Askwith's body: the outline took the shape of a near perfect circle less than three feet in diameter. The floor within the circle was charred black and the vinyl floor tiles had melted and lifted from the scorched wood beneath.

"What happened?" Sword asked, seeing without comprehending.

Trank rubbed at his face. "Aaah, punks broke in. Doused 'im with gas. Torched the guy. Nothing but ashes."

There had been no sound of break-in on the machine but Sword couldn't bring himself to mention it. Too many other things had been recorded. "Why?" he asked. "In God's name, why?"

"Aaah, crackheads. Happens alla time." The detective grabbed a handful of paper towels from an under-the-cabinet roll and blew his nose, then examined the contents of the towels carefully.

"But," Sword said cautiously, "if it was gasoline, why isn't anything else burned up?" There was the smudge on the ceiling, the charred spot on the floor, and nothing else except the heat-scarred label on the vodka bottle five feet away. The white phone, except for its missing handset, was undamaged and unmarked.

"One of those mysteries of life, kid," the detective said without conviction. "So, like, y'know what this kitchen's s'posed to look like mosta the time, right?"

"Yes," Sword said.

"So, like I said, anything missin'? Address book? Filin' cabinet? Rare cookin' doohickeys?"

"Just the telephone handset," Sword said.

"Aaah yeah, we know about that. Had to cut it off 'cuz the guy was still holding onta it, y'know."

Sword looked at the perfect circle of the technicians' tape. "I thought you said there was nothing left of him but ashes."

The detective balled up the paper towels and stuffed them into his wrinkled jacket pocket. "Well, yeah, mostly there was only ashes. But, like, his hand, y'know, his hand didn't get burned up hardly at all. It was just sorta layin' there in the middle of the ashes, still holdin' onta the phone. Guess he was tryin' to call for help."

Trying to call to *offer* help, Sword thought as Trank took him by the arm and led him away from the kitchen to let a video camera crew from channel five come in for *News at Noon* footage.

"I don't understand," Sword said to the detective. "How can ... how can someone burn up entirely, *except* for his hand, without anything else being damaged?"

The detective stood in the doorway to the kitchen, watching the camera operator's light cut across the counter and the floor like a searchlight in fog. "Whaddaya mean, nothin' else damaged? Looka the ceiling."

"Look at the countertop," Sword said. "The laminate should have bubbled. The phone's got a plastic case, for God's sake. Shouldn't it have melted?" No crackheads had broken in and torched Askwith, Sword realized suddenly. The lawyer had been stopped from revealing what he had known. He had asked permission, it had been denied, and then, suspecting Askwith would tell Sword anyway, whoever had denied that permission had arranged Askwith's permanent silence. But how?

He heard Askwith's voice replay in his mind, as if in answer: *They're not people at all, Galen. They're not people at all.* And Askwith had said that Sword himself didn't belong to the human world.

"Dear God," Sword said softly to himself. "What am I?"

The detective misheard. "Aaah, forget it, kid. It happens, y'know. Whole city's goin' to hellinahanbaskit. The guy was old, he did okay. Just think of it like it was his time, y'know?"

Sword turned to the detective, about to swear, but the microphone abruptly thrust in front of his face stopped him.

"Kendall Marsh, LiveEye News!" The arresting voice belonged to a tall, broad-shouldered black woman with a brilliant smile and carefully lacquered hair. "Did you know the victim, sir?"

Sword covered his eyes from the glare of the camera light and turned away.

Marsh didn't interrupt the rhythm of her delivery and moved the microphone over to the detective like an industrial robot reaching for a new part. "Detective Trank, any theories as to why Marcus Aurelius Askwith, noted lawyer, friend to the Mayor, fell victim to such a horrifying death?"

Sword watched as Trank leered at the camera. "No comment until afta the autopsy."

Marsh moved in closer, waving the microphone like a weapon. "But Detective, our sources have informed us that there is virtually no body remaining to conduct an autopsy upon. Would you comment, please, sir?"

"Aaah, we got summa the body."

"Detective Trank, sir," Marsh said sincerely, "We understand what you have is a hand."

Trank straightened his jacket without noticeable effect, and looked up at Marsh. "A hand is good. They can do the tissue stuff with a hand. Y'know, bloodwork an' all that."

"Are you aware, sir, that the circumstances of Mr. Askwith's death fit in precisely with other known cases of spontaneous human combustion?"

Trank opened his mouth in a grating laugh. "Oh yeah, sure. Right afta the UFOs got 'im. Gimme a break, darlin'."

Marsh's eyes brightened and she spun back to the camera. "There you have it," she said dramatically, lowering her voice to a confidential tone. "A police official confirms there might be a UFO link to the tragic SHC death of noted attorney Marcus Aurelius Askwith, found dead this morning at the age of seventy-four in his ... "

Sword walked out of the townhouse, leaving the detective and the reporter to their games. He sat on the stone balustrade by the open front door and stared out at the street without seeing it. The firetruck and ambulance were gone. A fire department supervisor's car and two police cars remained pulled up on the sidewalk, but not far enough to let the garbage truck that was stopped behind them pass. The truck's crew stood around drinking coffee from paper cups, being paid by the hour and in no mood to rush fellow employees of the city.

Sword had finally found a path into his past only to have it shut down completely and forever. He had no idea what to do next, where to take his search. Not even Askwith had known where his partner, Miss Marjoribanks, had gone after her accident. Perhaps that was the lead to follow. Marjoribanks had known his parents. Perhaps she was still alive someplace. Perhaps even his parents were —

"Coming through," growled a voice from inside the townhouse. It was Kendall Marsh's camera operator, Betacam balanced on his shoulder like a bazooka. He lowered the camera gently to the stone porch, then pulled out a pack of cigarettes and lit one. "Pretty atomic weird in there, huh?"

Sword waved away the offer of a cigarette, surprised to realize that he hadn't had one in more than a week. Since the accident. "Ever seen anything like it before?" he asked.

"Spontaneous human combustion?" the operator said with a laugh, then a cough. "Naa, not for real."

"It's not real or you've never seen it for real?"

The man took a long pull on his cigarette and narrowed his eyes. "I've never seen it for real. You a detective or something?"

Sword shook his head. "But you've heard about it? This ... combustion?"

"Yeah, sure," the operator answered. "I mean, Kennie's always trying to do specials on that kind of crap. Great for ratings during the sweeps. Astrologers, psychics, UFOs. All sorts of stuff like that. People love it."

"So where does spontaneous human combustion fit in?"

"SHC," the operator said. "Easier that way. But who the hell knows where it fits in? I mean, it's been around for a couple of hundred years, I guess. There was some big case in the fifties in Florida that the FBI was called in on. Same sort of thing. Person sitting in an armchair, watching the tube. All of a sudden, poof, they're toast, the chair's incinerated, nothing else in the apartment's touched except for ... what was it ... oh yeah, the plastic frame around the television screen across the room is all warped like from heat. And that's it. No other damage. This guy's feet are even still sticking out of the ashes, still wearing slippers. Not a mark on them. Police took lots of photos."

"You're serious, aren't you?" Sword said. He had never heard of anything like it or, he thought tentatively, if he had, it was as if he had driven the subject from his mind, forced himself to forget.

The operator shrugged. "So the story goes, pal. I'm just saying what was on a TV special, that's all."

Maybe there was a connection among the SHC cases, Sword thought. Maybe that was the way to find a new path. Linking Askwith's death to others. Searching for a pattern. Like sifting through an archaeological field excursion.

"You have any of the research that was done for that show at your station?" Sword asked.

The operator dropped his cigarette to the porch and stamped it out. "We're not set up for that, pal. A lot of the researchers are freelance, or Kennie just goes out and buys a pile of books. Say, that's what you should do. We did interviews with a bunch of bookstore owners. You know, the occult-type shops down in Greenwich. Why not head into one of them? Floating eye in the pyramid, that sort of thing. They got all sorts of weird shit there. Books on everything. Maybe you can find what you're looking for there, okay?" He hefted his Betacam to his shoulder again. "Look, I got to go. Nice talking with you." He headed back inside the townhouse.

The bookstores, Sword thought. Of course they're there. How many times had he walked by them, ignoring them? How many times at parties had he heard people discussing psychic phenomena, ghosts, channeling, all types of subjects from the paranormal, and turned away or changed the subject? Almost as if a block had been in place. Almost as if he had somehow been instructed not to think about such things. Not to learn about such things.

Not to remember such things.

In the shadows, Askwith had told him. *That's where you've got to look. Halfway between.*

It was that day, in that new morning, when Galen Sword's new path opened. He had no concept of where it might end, but he at last knew where it must begin.

In the shadows.

SIX

He awoke in shadows, seeing city streets flash by, a large pole suddenly in front of him, rushing at him, through the windshield. A pole with fur and a hand with claws. The fist of a werewolf called Martin.

Sword opened his eyes. Ko stopped patting at his face. "You okay in there?" she asked without real concern.

He tried to rise up from the floor and felt fire shoot down his neck into his shoulder. He relaxed again, gasping. There was something soft beneath his head; his folded jacket.

"You want to say something to let me know what I should do next?" Ko asked. "Ambulance, hearse, what have you?"

Sword looked past her and saw the reassuring lights of the main lab's computers and equipment. "What's the time?" he asked, trying not to move his jaw. How long had he been lost in the memories of how his search had all begun?

Ko studied him for a few seconds, then stood up, deciding he wasn't severely injured. "You've been out about ten minutes."

Sword cautiously touched his face where Martin had connected. The skin was hot and felt tightly drawn over the swollen flesh beneath it. He could work his jaw though each movement brought fresh pain to his neck and shoulder. "Didn't even see it coming," he said. Then he saw that the examination table was empty and sat up with an explosive groan. "Where is it?" he asked in alarm.

Martin, unbound, clothed only in the blanket Ko had given him, crouched in a corner of the lab. Ja'Nette knelt on the floor beside him, caught up in her game, and childishly unconcerned about Sword's condition. A small chain of brightly-colored paper links floated in the air between the two. Forsyte was a few feet away, observing.

"He's cool," Ko said. She held out a hand to Sword. "Want to try to get up?"

It took two attempts but Sword made it to his feet. He stood with his head tilted to the right, rubbing at his neck. "You feel that's safe? Ja'Nette and that thing?"

"I explained about 'Bub," Ko said. "Once Martin was convinced that you hadn't ''chanted the light,' he calmed down. I'm guessing he meant 'enchanted.'"

"How did you explain 'Bub?" Sword watched as Martin made playful grabs at the floating paper chain, laughing softly as Ja'Nette made it dance out of reach. He found it disconcerting to see the child using her ability just for a game. Translocation took a lot out of her, he knew. She should be saving it for training. But first Sword decided he had to know more about the creature called Martin, especially how he might react if his game were abruptly called off.

"I explained 'Bub by telling the truth about her," Ko said, glancing sideways at Sword. "Radical concept I know. But it worked. I just told Martin that she came that way, crystal, collar, and all, when you bought her from that guy in New Orleans."

"And that was enough to make him decide that I wasn't 'bad' anymore?"

"I let him check out 'Bub's collar. Couldn't have been made by a human, Martin said. Definitely First World." Ko smiled at Sword, waiting for his obvious question.

But Sword didn't stop with one. "Did he tell you what the First World was? Where it was? How to find —"

"It's a lot simpler than that," Ko said, raising her hand to stop him. "Essentially, the term 'First World' appears to be the same thing we always called the hidden world. It's what the adepts call it, at least.

They're the ... people, I guess, who live in it, at least, according to Martin," she added, indicating that she hadn't completely accepted these new details.

"So ... it's not an actual place?" Sword couldn't keep the disappointment from his voice.

"It's their organization, their clans, keepers ... a blanket term."

He nodded, thoughtful. "If I go up to him, is he going to attack me again?"

Ko shrugged as if she didn't know or care and Sword couldn't tell if she meant it or if she was simply baiting him again. He knew she did that to him more times than she thought he was aware of and he still couldn't think how he could convince her that he wasn't the cold and uncaring fanatic she thought he was. But someday soon, he knew, he would have to make her understand. He needed her as much as Forsyte did, though the search too often took precedence.

"Cover me," Sword said to Ko, then walked stiffly to the corner where Ja'Nette and Martin played.

"Don't I always?" Ko muttered to his back.

Ja'Nette glanced up as Sword approached and the paper chain fluttered to the floor.

"Yo, Sword," the child said. "You okay?"

"Fine." Sword looked at Martin. The creature glanced up for a moment, then stared down at the floor and poked idly at the motionless paper chain with a black-nailed finger. "I want to ask you some questions ... Martin."

Martin cocked his head but didn't look up. "Melody say Martin go any time. Free to go. Don't have do anything."

Sword looked up at the ceiling. "Well, let me tell you what I say," he began.

But Ko came up from behind Sword, interrupting him before he could continue. "A moment, Sword. While you were napping on the floor, I explained to Martin how we wanted him to be our friend. Isn't that what you've always said? A real First World friend for 'Bub and Ja'Nette. And friends can come and go as they please. Whenever they want."

"And friends don't have do anything don't want to," Martin said quietly to the paper chain.

Sword turned to Ko. He could feel the uninjured side of his face flush with anger. "I wasted three years tracking down a werewolf that — "

"But that doesn't mean you've got one now!" Ko snapped. She turned to the creature. "Martin, tell Sword here, are you a werewolf?"

"Already say not." He still didn't look up.

"Martin," Ko continued, "do you think Sword *could* catch a werewolf?"

This time, the creature did look up at Sword. He shook his head. "Not Arkady werewolf. Eat human heart before human even know Arkaday werewolf hunt."

"I've seen a werewolf *die*," Sword said indignantly.

"Not Arkady werewolf," Martin said, still shaking his head.

"I saw a human woman shoot and *kill* a werewolf in Greece."

Martin stopped shaking his head. His eyes grew round. "Silver bullet," he whispered in awe.

Sword smiled triumphantly at Ko, and looked back at Martin. "You know anything about that, do you?"

"Not Arkady werewolf."

Sword slapped his side, then gasped and grabbed at his neck as the pain from the sudden movement shot through him. "Then are there other clans of werewolves? Of shifters?" he asked through clenched teeth.

"Lots," Martin said simply.

Sword blinked. "How many?"

Martin shrugged.

"How about a guess?" Sword asked.

"Lots."

Sword began to swear.

"FIVE-YEAR-OLD," Forsyte's voder said behind him.

Ko turned to the scientist in his wheelchair. "That would seem to be about right," she said.

"What's right?" Sword asked.

"Martin's developmental age," Ko explained. "How old are you, Martin?"

"Two and a half," he answered proudly.

"Years?" Sword asked, almost feeling shocked at the ramifications. How could cells grow and intelligence develop so quickly?

"Changes," Martin said. "Two and a half Changes."

"How long is a Change?" Ko asked. "How many years?"

"Lots," Martin said.

"Oh, God." It was too much for Sword. He moaned and turned away in frustration.

Ko spun around to Sword. "Will you lighten up? Don't you see the opportunity you've got here? Are you trying to screw this up on purpose or what?"

Sword lowered his voice. "Don't you even joke about that, Melody. You don't understand what they did to me. What they took from me. I know what I'm doing."

Martin shifted into a crouch beside Ko. He stared up at Sword, opened his mouth slightly, and began to softly growl.

"Well, what the hell *are* you're doing?" Ko demanded.

"I'm trying to get some damned answers!"

"You've *got* them, damn *you*. Look at him. Look at Martin." Ko reached down and rubbed her hand over Martin's head. His growling stopped as he leaned into her caress. "He's First World, Sword. He's part of it. What you've always wanted. He's got your answers."

"You can hear him as well as I can," Sword said despairingly. "The problem is, he doesn't know how to tell us those answers." He put his hand to his temple and massaged it carefully.

Ko shook her head. "The problem, Sword, is that you don't know how to ask the right *questions*." She waved her hand at him. "Oh, just go make coffee or something. Let me handle it, all right? You're only going to upset him."

Sword pressed the heels of his hands to the sides of his head. "Fine, fine. I've got to get out of here, anyway." He headed for the staircase, then paused on the first step. "And be careful, will you? Don't trust him too easily."

Behind him, Martin's growl became louder.

The sun was coming up when Ko came to Sword's quarters, but no morning light entered through the thick layers of curtains he had pulled over the windows. He sat in darkness, elbows on the arms of his blanket-covered chair, steepled fingers held lightly against his chin. Except for a simple ebony chest of Japanese design, and an open futon bed, the chair was his bedroom's only furniture.

"Come," Sword said in answer to Ko's knock.

Ko entered with a digital videocassette. "A lot of good stuff on this. You're going to like it."

"Is it anything like I thought it might be?" His voice was slow and hesitant.

Ko shook her head.

"So, three years wasted," he said bitterly. Martin's capture was to have been the pay-off. His entry back into the hidden world, the First World. His way back to his family and his destiny, whatever it was meant to be. Instead, Martin had become the biggest anti-climax of his life.

Ko took her time replying. She looked around. The austere room was barely lit by the light spilling in from the hallway. The walls were bare. It was a monk's cell.

"Not wasted, Sword," she said at last and he was surprised that the usual biting edge to her words seemed to be missing. She spoke to him as if she were speaking to Forsyte. "Misdirected, maybe. But necessary."

"Necessary for what?" He waited for her usual sharp reply.

Instead, he only heard her sigh. "What have you had to go on, Sword? Really, what brought you this far?"

He said nothing.

"Damn little, that's what," she continued. "You got your lawyer's last messages from your answering machine. A ... jumble of memories from when you were a kid. Most of them make no sense. You got Detective Trank feeding you inside leads on any weird crimes that happen in this city. You got a couple of reporters doing the same. And you've got Greece. Four pitiful days in Greece when you might have been as close to the First World as you are now, but that chance was taken away."

"Don't forget that vampire we heard about," Sword murmured. "Or Ja'Nette."

"Or what happened to Adrian." Ko couldn't keep the bitterness from her voice. "We've all had our run-ins with them, Sword. We just don't know who *they* are. But you're the one who's the closest to understanding how to get to them. You're the one who brought us this far." She held up the tape again.

"Martin really is part of it? Of them?"

Ko nodded. "He's too young, or too ... simple to lie to us. I think it's just that he's too young."

"But he's not a werewolf?"

"If you believe him, it's bigger than werewolves. According to what Martin says, the whole First World is a lot more complicated than you thought. Werewolves are just a small part of his clan."

"Then what is he?"

She shrugged in the halflight. "Won't say. Having 'Bub and Ja'Nette around really calmed him down so I don't think he's afraid of his ... keepers. I think he won't tell us what he is because ... well, he's embarrassed or something."

"Maybe he doesn't know." Sword could understand that, not knowing.

"Maybe he doesn't." There was much understanding in Ko's voice, very unlike her, as if she knew what he were thinking. "Maybe he's what your lawyer told you to look for. An outcast of some sort. Someone caught halfway between the First World and ours."

"But he knows who his clan is. Where it is. Doesn't he?"

"He's gone back to them," Ko said quietly.

Sword closed his eyes as those words dug into him. Just like Greece. The opportunity had slipped away again. Had Ko been right? Was he doing this to himself on purpose?

"But," she added. "He did say he was coming back."

"Why?" The word came out choked and dry. It was starting again and he knew he wouldn't be able to talk much longer.

"To help 'Bub," Ko said. "He asked if we wanted to help 'Bub not be 'chanted anymore and I said yes so he said he'd come back and help, too."

"When?"

"Tonight. He had to leave before sunrise. He was very serious about that. But he said he'd be back tonight."

"To help 'Bub."

"Yes."

Sword frowned. "We still don't even know what the hell 'Bub's supposed to be, either."

"It's a start," Ko said. "At least it's a start."

There was a long silence before Sword spoke again. "I, uh, want to apologize for the way I sounded ... when you said ... asked, if I were doing this ... on purpose."

"You sound that way every day, Sword," Ko said coolly.

"I'm sorry." It was almost a whisper.

"Not important."

"But," he continued, not hearing her anymore, "I don't know if I am doing it on purpose. They made me forget, Melody. They made me forget so much. And then they ... conditioned me not to think about so many different things. To even think about werewolves, about the crystals, about anything from their world, at all ... " He sighed again, closed his eyes. "It's ... very hard for me to concentrate on it all, Melody. Very hard."

She walked to his chair and stood close to him. "I know, Sword. It's hard for all of us."

He kept his eyes closed. "Just so you know."

After a long moment, she reached down to place the small cassette on the arm of his chair. She didn't touch him.

"Want me to open the curtains?" she asked. "Get you some coffee?" From Ko, it was the ultimate offer of reconciliation.

"Keep them closed," Sword said hoarsely.

"The headache again?"

He nodded slightly, eyes squeezed tight.

"Do you want anything?"

"Just to be left alone."

Ko walked back to stand in the doorway, hand resting on the door handle.

"I'm sorry, too, Sword," she said. "Buzz down when you want something."

"I want it to be night," Sword said to her from the darkness. "I want him to come back."

"So do I," Ko said, and silently closed the door.

Sword spoke to the blackness. "I want him to come back and help me." And then the headache took him in all its fury.

SEVEN

Kenny had just been eaten by rats again when Ja'Nette heard the faint scratching noise at her window. She slowly twisted her head to the left and the volume-control bar on the screen of her television set moved the same way, dropping the sound of Stan's shocked protest. Then she looked out her window.

Four stories straight up, with no balcony, fire escape, or ledge, Martin stared in at her. His large mouth split in half and his fangs glistened. He was smiling.

"All riiight!" Ja'Nette said excitedly and bounded from her bed, heading for the window. But before she got there, Martin had raised one immense hand and there was an almost unnoticeable flash of blue light behind the window latch. Then the window swung open on its own, letting in a cool breeze from the darkening twilight beyond.

Martin slid through the open window as smoothly as water, landing silently on his bare feet.

"Wow," Ja'Nette said, "I didn't know you could translocate, too. You never told me."

Martin blinked at her. "Ja'Nette not know Martin do what?" he asked.

Ja'Nette smiled. "No, no, Martin. If you don't know what I said, you're s'posed to say, 'Say what?' Okay? Say it."

Martin's thick brows knit over his eyes. "Say what?" he asked, very uncertainly.

"Yeah, you got it," Ja'Nette said happily. "Now, what I meant was that last night, or this morning, I guess, when I was dancing the paper chain around, you never told me you could make things move by themselves on your own, the way I can."

Martin shook his head at all the words running together.

"How'd you open the window, Martin?" Ja'Nette finally asked.

"Blue power," Martin said. He looked around room, then laughed when he saw a faded color poster above Ja'Nette's cluttered desk.

"What's a blue power? What's so funny?"

Martin loped over to the desk to look more closely at the vintage poster. In it, a man with a golden mane of hair and a symmetrically-cleft upper lip, reminiscent of a large cat's, stood with his arms wrapped protectively around a woman in a flowing gown. "Blue powers do different things. Martin blue power opens closed things." He pointed to the man on the poster. "Silly silly. Not Arkady werewolf. Not Arkady shifter." He laughed again and patted the poster with his hand.

"He's just a pretend woofer from an old show," Ja'Nette said as she went to stand beside him. "Like, is that why I thought I saw a blue flash or something when the window opened? Did you make the light?"

Martin turned, crouched down, his oversize brown eyes even with hers. "Blue power makes own light. Blue power opens things for Martin."

"I don't make a blue light come on when I translocate things," Ja'Nette said.

"Ja'Nette not have blue power," Martin said. His eyes flashed around the room, then widened. "TV," he said appreciatively and crossed over to it. On the screen, an animated herd of black and white cows was staring, mute, at a large bovine-faced clock.

"What's the difference between your blue power and what I can do? Both make things move without having to touch them, right?"

"Cows 'chanted," Martin said to the television screen. He pushed a few buttons on the set experimentally but nothing happened. He turned to Ja'Nette. "Ja'Nette make things move. Martin blue power opens things. Big big difference." He looked back at the set. "Time for wrestling? Stone Cold Steve Austin? Triple H?"

Ja'Nette looked around for a television guide. "I don't think so. But how come I don't make a blue light come on or anything?"

Martin followed behind Ja'Nette until she was on her knees, digging through a pile of books and magazines and comics by her bed.

"Ja'Nette live with dark hunter?" Martin asked.

"Say what?" Ja'Nette stopped digging, thought for a moment. "You mean Sword?"

"Yes," Martin said with a nod. "Bad man Galen Sword."

Ja'Nette sat down crosslegged on the floor. "Sword's not really a bad man, Martin. He's just ... I don't know. He gets busy with all sorts of other things so sometimes he seems rude, you know?"

"Ja'Nette parents Melody Galen Sword?" Martin asked.

"No way!" Ja'Nette said, feeling that she wanted to laugh but also feeling the ache she always felt about her mother and father. "Melody and Sword, they just ... look after me, that's all."

Martin nodded and looked down at the pile of magazines between them. "Ja'Nette. know where parents?" He didn't look at her as he spoke. It was the same way he had talked with Sword early that morning, when it had been obvious that Martin was uncomfortable with the subject they discussed.

Ja'Nette shared Martin's discomfort. "No. I don't."

"Oh," Martin said, still not looking up.

"Why do you want to know?"

He reached out to move the magazines around. "What Ja'Nette know about parents? Melody Galen Sword tell Ja'Nette things?"

"No," Ja'Nette said uncertainly, not wanting to call up the past. "Not a lot, at least. Why?"

"Then Melody Galen Sword good. Not tell Ja'Nette ... bad things."

Ja'Nette leaned forward, annoyed by what Martin had said. "What d'ya mean, bad things? There's nothing bad about my mamma. What are you talking about?"

Martin squirmed and turned back to the television.

"C'mon, Martin. What did you mean about bad things?" Martin didn't respond so Ja'Nette scrunched her face up and translocated all the bushy black hair on Martin's head so it stood straight on end. "I'm talking to you!" she said.

Martin slapped both hands to his head and yowled as he rolled away backward from the bed. He landed on his knees with a thud and smoothed down his hair. Then he snorted. "Felt funny," he said. "Ja'Nette surprise Martin."

"Yeah, well, I can surprise you again if you don't tell me what you meant by calling my mamma bad," Ja'Nette said, trying to sound angry as she also tried to stop from laughing because of the way Martin was sitting. "And, like, you should probably put on some clothes or something, you know?"

Martin stood up, naked as he had been when they had cornered him in the pet store. "Why?" he asked.

Ja'Nette turned away, giggling. "'Cause you're not wearing any, dummy." He was furry enough that she hadn't really noticed until he had flipped away from the bed. "Here, take this." She pulled the duvet off her bed and held it up for him, without looking, until she felt him take it from her hand.

"Better?" Martin asked.

Ja'Nette tried looking again. Martin's head emerged from a mountain of rainbow-colored fabric. "Much better," she said seriously, still trying not to laugh. "Now are you going to tell me about my parents or ... ?" She made a face of concentration.

"No, no," Martin said, patting his head. "Martin tell."

"Do you know my mamma and poppa?" Ja'Nette asked. Not even Sword and Melody said they did. Or would admit it. Ja'Nette always felt that they knew something they weren't telling her. As if there could be anything more she would ever want to know about her poppa.

"Martin not know Ja'Nette mamma poppa," Martin said sadly. "But Martin can tell Ja'Nette about mamma poppa." He cocked his head at the door that led from Ja'Nette's room to the corridor outside. His large nostrils flared. "Melody outside door." He sniffed again. "Has gun for making sleep."

Ja'Nette frowned. "Melody!" she called out. "You there?"

Ko's voice, calm and measured, came back through the door. "Are you all right, Ja'Nette?"

"I'm fine."

"Is Martin with you?"

"Yes," Ja'Nette said. "And you don't need your gun, neither."

"May I come in?"

Ja'Nette hesitated. There was nothing she wouldn't do for Ko. But she had to know what Martin was going to tell her and she suspected that Martin wouldn't speak if Ko joined them. She looked at the creature wrapped up in her duvet, then made her decision.

"Can you wait just a minute?" Ja'Nette asked. "He'll come right out." She looked at Martin. "You will come out, right?"

Martin nodded.

"You're sure you're okay?" Ko asked from behind the closed door. "That was a pretty loud thump."

"No problem," Ja'Nette said. "Five minutes, okay?"

"I'll be down the hall," Ko said.

Martin watched the door and sniffed the air. After a few moments, he said, "Melody go away. Take gun."

"She's just being careful," Ja'Nette explained. "With that noise you made, she mighta thought a woofer was in here."

Martin glanced at the open window. The night sky outside was black now. "Martin *not* werewolf," he said softly. "Martin parents like Ja'Nette parents." Martin looked at her. Hiss eyes were full and soft and sad. "Martin like Ja'Nette."

"What do you mean, Martin?"

Martin rolled to his knees beneath the duvet and moved over to be beside Ja'Nette. His voice was a whisper. He was looking away from her again.

"Martin father Arkady shifter. Big shifter. Strong shifter. Many Changes. Humanform shifterform. Many times back forth. Good hunter. Good keeper." He rocked back and forth as he spoke, as if reassuring himself with his words.

"What was his name?" Ja'Nette asked.

"Astar," Martin said proudly, still keeping his voice low. "Powerful Arkady shifter."

"How about your mamma?"

Martin held a hand to his mouth, covering his lips. "Ja'Nette mamma adept," he said.

"Say what?"

"Ja'Nette mother powerful adept. Elemental Martin think. Greater clan."

"Like Clan Arkady?" Ja'Nette asked, trying to weave together all the strands of what Martin was revealing to her.

"No, no," Martin answered, looking down. "Clan Arkady shifter clan. Elementals other clans. Clan Hiroyoshi, Clan Pendragon, Clan Marratin. Ja'Nette mamma one of those clans Martin think."

"Why?" Ja'Nette asked. She moved closer to him, feeling the heat his body generated even through the duvet, smelling the sweat of him. "Why do you think that?"

Martin sucked in his bottom lip and chewed on it. He spoke as if he were concentrating hard on each word. "Blue power ... father. Mother power not blue. Different. Like Ja'Nette. Not blue."

Ja'Nette nodded, at last hearing something that made sense to her. "I get it. Your power came to you from your poppa, so it's a blue power. My power came down to me from my mamma, so it's a ... what? An invisible power?"

Martin rocked his head back and forth. "Not invisible. Hard to say. Hard for Martin remember all right words."

"How about your mamma?" Ja'Nette asked. "What did you get from her?"

Martin flinched and pulled into himself. "Same as Ja'Nette poppa." He moved as though to glance at her but his eyes never made contact. "Nothing."

Ja'Nette was confused again. "I don't get it. Why nothing?"

"Ja'Nette poppa Martin mamma ... " Martin reached out a hand to squeeze Ja'Nette's. Her small fingers were lost in his. "Both no power both ... human."

At first, it was as if Ja'Nette hadn't heard what Martin had said. She waited in silence for him to go on, but he didn't. Then it hit her. "Hold on ... " she said, pulling her hand away from his. "Are you saying I'm only *half* a human being?" Martin's eyes finally came up to look at hers. He nodded. "Get outta town!" Ja'Nette said.

"Bad word," Martin said apologetically. "Martin know. Very bad bad word."

"What is?"

"Word for Ja'Nette," Martin said. "Word for ... Martin." He reached for her hand again. He dropped his voice to a whisper. "We ... halflings." He shook his head with embarrassment. "Bad bad word."

"Halflings?"

Martin flinched at the sound of it. "Not human not adept. Half each," Martin explained.

"Halfling? Half-human, half-adept? That's what we are?"

Martin nodded again. " Bad bad word. Martin sorry tell this. Melody Galen Sword good not tell this."

Ja'Nette slumped back against the side of her bed, pulled up her knees and wrapped her arms around them. Somewhere deep inside her, some connection was being made. Martin had just made more sense to her than Ko and Forsyte had made to her in the past year. As for Sword, he rarely talked to her about such things. But when he did, it seemed to make him sad.

"You know, Martin," Ja'Nette said after a few moments of silence, "I wish they *had* told me this. It sort of makes sense, you know? I mean, I always felt different. A little different, at least. And not just 'cause I could move things around on their own, neither. I mean, I learned to keep that pretty much to myself early on, you know. After my poppa got ... well, left me. But I can sort of remember my mamma. Real hazy-like, a long time ago. I musta been a baby, I guess. And she was, well, different, too, I guess, but not different to me." Ja'Nette squeezed her arms around her legs, reaching for that memory of her mother's own arms.

"How different?" Martin asked.

"Her eyes were black," Ja'Nette said, closing her own eyes to see her memory more clearly. "Completely black, no whites, no irises, no nothing. Sort of scary-like, you know. But I was never frightened of 'em. Like I knew that was the way they were s'posed to be."

"Black eyes," Martin repeated. "Clan Marratin. Ja'Nette mamma Clan Marratin."

Ja'Nette's eyes flew open. She turned excitedly to Martin. "Yeah? Really? You know where my mamma mighta been from?"

"Not where," Martin said. "Martin not know where Clan Marratin enclaves. But black eyes Clan Marratin. Powerful elementals. Greater clan."

"Wowww," Ja'Nette said. "I'm part of a greater clan. Neat."

"Oh, no," Martin interrupted. "Ja'Nette not clan. Ja'Nette cursed. Ja'Nette worthless. Ja'Nette halfling."

Ja'Nette was so angry she couldn't speak. She jumped up to her feet and sputtered. "Now you just hold on right there. I am Ja'Nette Conroy. I am not cursed. I am not worthless."

"Ja'Nette halfling," Martin repeated sadly. "Like Martin."

"And you aren't cursed and worthless neither!"

Martin sighed. "Ja'Nette halfling. Martin halfling. We ... cursed worthless."

Ja'Nette held out her hand to the creature. "Martin," she said, "you and me are gonna have to have a talk about attitude."

Ko was motionless on the edge of the metal stairway that led down from the sleeping quarters to the Loft's working areas. She held the tranquilizing rifle ready in her hands and kept her eyes fixed on the door to Ja'Nette's room. Ko didn't like it but she had to give Ja'Nette the benefit of the doubt this time. The girl and Martin had shared some unspoken affinity when they had played with the paper chain that morning and Ko suspected that some deeper connection existed between them. If she were to hear anything at all from Martin like the jarring sound that had first alerted her to his presence, she wouldn't hesitate rushing through the door. But as long as things remained quiet, Ko trusted Ja'Nette to handle herself and the situation in the way she had been trained.

At last, ten minutes after Ko had spoken to Ja'Nette through the closed door, she saw the door handle start to move. Ja'Nette and Martin emerged from the room holding hands. Martin used his other hand to hold together a makeshift robe that Ko recognized as Ja'Nette's duvet.

"Hello, Martin," Ko said, making her words sound ordinary, not letting the relief she felt color them in any way.

The creature began to smile at her, then his eyes moved to the rifle in her hands and the smile disappeared.

Ko didn't pause for even a moment. She broke the gun, popped out the tranquilizing cartridges, checked to see that the underbarrel was clear, then held the gun out. "It's all right, Martin," she said. "It can't hurt anyone. You take it."

Martin's eyes met hers and held them, and in that moment Ko understood that she was right not to underestimate him. She must never confuse his lack of ability in spoken language with lack of intelligence or emotional depth. Martin knew what her offer of the weapon meant and returned the trust that was given with it.

"Martin thank Melody," he said carefully, then shook his head. He did not need to see her weaponless. Ko's offer and Martin's polite rejection of it had forged a small bond of trust between them. Ko held the weapon to her side and smiled. This time, the smile was returned in full.

"Martin said we're halflings!" Ja'Nette blurted.

Ko was puzzled to see Martin shudder at Ja'Nette's words.

The girl turned to him. "What did I tell you? It's not a bad word. It's a good word. It means we're something special." Ja'Nette looked back to Ko. "Doesn't it, Melody?"

"You're very special," Ko said. She went to Ja'Nette and gave the child a hug. Then she felt Martin's eyes on her.

"Martin special?" he asked.

Why not? Ko thought, and she hugged Martin, too. His muscles were like smooth iron, completely immovable beneath her arms and hands.

"But you just have to tell me one thing," Ko said as she stepped back from the two friends. "What's a halfling?"

Martin sighed and Ja'Nette frowned at him. "He thinks it's a bad word," Ja'Nette said. "But what it means is that my mamma was an adept and my poppa was a human being. I'm part of the Clan Marratin," she added proudly.

"Is that right?" Ko asked. Someday, she decided, she would have to tell the child what she knew of her mother, despite what Sword had said.

"And Martin's poppa was an Arkady shifter," Ja'Nette continued, "and it was his mamma who was human."

"Ahh," Ko said. "That would explain a great deal." She started down the stairs and Ja'Nette and Martin followed.

Ja'nette burbled happily on. "And Martin has a blue power that can open all sorts of things and it came from his poppa and my power isn't a blue power 'cause it came from my mamma and Martin doesn't know what it should be called but we're both just the same." She stopped to laugh. "Well, sort of."

"Sounds like you two had quite a talk," Ko said. They were on the Loft's third level now and she glanced off through the large doors to Forsyte's quarters and private study. He wasn't there. She went over to the stairway that led down to the main lab on the second level.

"Yeah," Ja'Nette said, stopping to pick up part of Martin's impromptu robe so he wouldn't trip, though Ko doubted he could ever do anything so clumsy. "We're friends."

"Good," Ko said. It was nice to know that someone could still afford friends these days.

Forsyte was in the main lab, working at a computer station that Ko saw was displaying band patterns from the electrophoresis of Martin's DNA. She went to stand beside Forsyte before she spoke so he wouldn't be startled. "Half human," she said, "on the mother's side."

The fingers on Forsyte's left hand tapped on their keypad. "EXACTLY," his voder said. "HOW DID YOU KNOW?"

"Martin told us." Ko gestured back to the center of the lab and Forsyte's chair turned in place. The counter-rotating rubber treads of it squeaked against the raised circular dots of the black Pirelli floor covering.

"HELLO, MARTIN," the scientist's voder said as he saw Ja'Nette with her new friend.

Martin nodded in greeting but said nothing. He angled his head back to watch the false color computer display of his DNA that was projected on the large screen above the computer station.

"Is Sword up yet?" Ko asked.

The voder said, "BEHIND YOU."

Ko turned in time to see Galen Sword emerge from the stairway opening that connected the main lab with the tool shop on the main floor. His eyes were shadowed and his skin pale. He was still recovering from the morning's migraine. They always struck when the pressure was off, as if he could only survive under tension.

"So," he said as he approached Martin. "You did come back. Any idea how he got in, Melody?"

"Came in through my window," Ja'Nette said.

Sword nodded. "Probably safer if we barricade it. I had thought four stories would be protection enough." He stood by Martin and looked down at him. "And we'll teach you how to use a door. Now, you're going to help us help 'Bub, right?"

Martin nodded. "'Bub 'chanted."

"And how do we get her un-'chanted?"

Martin looked away from the display. "Say what?"

Sword blinked and Ja'Nette laughed. "All riiight, Martin," she said and slapped her hand against his.

"How do we help 'Bub?" Sword tried again.

Martin rose from his crouch. "Maybe Martin take Galen Sword ... to place where maybe 'Bub get help."

Sword took in a sudden breath. "Where, Martin?"

Martin hesitated, as if he were about to speak a secret. "Somewhere ... " He changed his mind. "First Galen Sword must make promise."

Ko watched as Sword slipped his hands into the back pockets of his black jeans. His hands still trembled. "Sure," he said. "What kind of promise?"

"Galen Sword must promise be good," Martin said solemnly.

"Why?" Sword asked.

Ko shook her head. When would Sword just learn to just go along with it all?

"If Galen Sword not be good in place where Martin take Galen Sword then Galen Sword be dead."

At that, Ko smiled. Perhaps tonight would be the night that Sword finally learned a lesson.

EIGHT

Galen Sword tapped his fingers against the dashboard of the van as Ko screeched in beside a fire hydrant. Behind the front seats, Martin bounced and nodded excitedly. "Here, here," he said. His huge hands made both seats shake and his moving mass made the van rock.

"Keep it down, Martin." Ja'Nette reached over from her own bench to touch his shoulder. "Chill out, okay?"

Martin patted Ja'Nette's hand. "Martin not be cold," he said. He picked at the empty black canvas equipment vest Ko had given him, and the baggy grey track pants that Forsyte had donated. Martin had brought up the matter of clothing by himself. It was necessary for Soft-wind, he had told them. But he wouldn't explain what Softwind was. Ko had told Sword that Martin probably wasn't trying to withhold infor-mation. It was just that no one had asked him the exact type of question he could understand.

"Where, exactly, is this Softwind supposed to be?" Sword asked, leaning forward to peer through the windshield. They were parked on a downtown sidestreet. All Sword could see was an unending row of metal-shuttered buildings and, at the corner of an alley, a small bar, still open, with a sign saying Art Engoron was being held over. The place was packed. "Do you mean the bar over there?"

Martin snorted. "Bar human. Softwind not. Martin Galen Sword go from here." He began fiddling with anything he could grab on the van's side door, trying to open it.

"I'll get it. I'll get it." Ja'Nette squeezed past him.

Forsyte's voder spoke from the back of the van where the scientist and his chair were locked in position. "REMEMBER TRANCEIVERS AND LOCATORS."

Sword held his right hand up to check that his own locator band was operational. It appeared to be a flat black metal bracelet, two inches wide and a quarter-inch thick. On the outer wrist surface, four different colored LEDs glowed and a clear plastic panel protected four small flush-mounted buttons from being accidentally triggered. Pressing the proper combinations of those buttons could send an audible or vibration signal to any of the other locator bands, or activate a proximity beacon the other bands could home in on. Forsyte had designed the bands as a backup to the radio transceivers each of the team wore and Ko had taken his original plans — which had described something the size of a toaster — and made the design fit neatly and efficiently into the slim bracelet casing. From the corner of his eye, Sword saw Ko and Ja'Nette checking their own bands.

"We'll give you a level on the radios when we get outside," Sword told Forsyte. Then he opened his door and started to slide out, just as Ko did.

"No no," Martin said urgently, calling them back.

Sword and Ko leaned into the van.

"Not all go Softwind. Martin can't take all."

"Why not?" Ko asked.

Martin shrugged. "Galen Sword buy 'Bub. Galen Sword go Softwind for help. That all."

Sword looked over to Ko. Ko asked, "Martin, is it dangerous in Softwind?"

Martin thought about that. "Not for Martin," he decided.

Ko shook her head. "I don't like it, Sword. Without knowing what it is, we — "

"Softwind place for help," Martin interrupted.

"Is it part of the First World?" Sword asked.

Martin shook his head.

"But it's not part of the Second World, either?" Ko used the term Martin had said was used by the adepts to describe the ordinary world of humans.

"Softwind Shadow World." Martin spoke quietly. "Half First half Second." He looked at Ja'Nette and tried to smile. "Special. Like Martin."

"So, will there be other humans in Softwind?" Sword asked.

"Sometimes."

Sword gestured to Ko. "Sounds safe to me."

But Ko wasn't convinced. "Will there be werewolves in Softwind? Powerful shifters?"

"Sometimes," Martin repeated. "Many humans. Many adepts. All things meet in Softwind."

"I'm going to go," Sword said. "No argument. You wait here." He shut the passenger door and slid open the side door. "Come on, Martin, let's go visit the Shadow World."

Martin hopped from the van and began to scamper along the sidewalk toward the bar. With every third or fourth step, the backs of his hands grazed the ground. He stopped at the mouth of the alley by the bar and waved to Sword to join him.

Sword paused by the open window of the van. "Aren't you going to tell me not to do anything stupid?"

"Waste of breath."

"Then, why don't you pull forward so you can see where we go in?"

"Gee, what a good idea, Sword. Why didn't I think of that?" Ko put the van in gear and pulled out.

Sword joined Martin by the alley. "Down here?" he asked the creature.

"Softwind," Martin said, and took off between the buildings.

Sword glanced quickly over his shoulder at the van, then sprinted after Martin, thinking the beast had virtually flown away. He reached a bend in the alley, charged around it into near darkness, then felt Martin's powerful hands slam into him, stopping him and holding him up at the same time.

"Very slow. Very noisy," Martin said.

Sword touched the transceiver in his ear, gasping to recapture the breath that had been knocked from his lungs. "We're just around the first corner. Do you copy?"

Forsyte's mechanical voice whispered, "YES," in Sword's ear.

Martin watched Sword suspiciously. "Hear Galen Sword in van?"

Sword nodded and tapped his earphone. "Radio," he said.

Martin grinned. "Top forty," he said, then turned to the alley wall. In the gloom, Sword's eyes could just make out a door, where it seemed no door should be. Triple padlocked and nailed shut in a thick wooden frame, inset into a field of dark bricks. Martin walked up to the door and whispered something Sword couldn't hear. The door creaked without appearing to move. Martin reached out and a sudden flare of blue fire sparked from his hand and ran along the edges of the door, leaving a spidery yellow afterimage in Sword's eyes.

Then the door swung open, frame and all, and Sword realized it had been disguised. Martin stepped up into the open doorway and it flickered oddly. Behind the creature, Sword could see a small partition wall and, past it, from a high ceiling, dim shafts of light in thick smoke. He could hear music and the din of many voices talking over one another. The space beyond seemed cavernous.

"How long has this been here?" Sword asked as Martin waved him forward.

Martin shrugged. "Moves around. Have to ask. Different places different times. Softwind." He added the last, as if it were explanation enough. "Hurry hurry Galen Sword. Door must close."

Sword stepped up to the doorsill, half-expecting to have some feeling of being teleported someplace. But the door was only a door and the space it led into was an ordinary part of an ordinary building. Only the music seemed out of place — an eerie instrumental that reminded him of Peruvian pipes played to the rhythm of the sea.

Once Sword was inside, the door swung shut behind him and the noise of the place became almost as overwhelming as the smell. There was the scent of tobacco mostly, but harsh and pungent, as if it had been cured in heavy wines. Beneath the smoke were undercurrents of wood fire, cinnamon, and other spices he couldn't identify. There was also sweat, cutting and acrid, and — inescapable he supposed — the stench of old beer.

Sword bent down so Martin could hear him. "Whatever else this place is, it's still a bar, isn't it?"

"Softwind," Martin said and walked ahead, around the partition wall that screened the doorway from the rest of the enormous room.

Sword followed and suddenly heard Ko's voice in his ear. "We're getting a huge commotion over the link, Sword. Not getting many words. If you're receiving this and okay, give us a band signal."

Sword brought his arm up, slid the plastic cover on his locator band to the side, and pressed the two buttons that would send a confirming signal to Ko's band.

"Okay," Ko relayed. "We got that. Use the band if you need anything. There're four people heading down the alley your way. Big guys. Must be a busy place."

Sword sent another confirming signal back, then looked up as he realized that Martin had halted in front of him. And then Galen Sword saw Softwind for the first time.

Obviously, the space had begun as an old warehouse. It was at least three hundred feet on a side and the ceiling was twenty feet above them, studded with wide metal light fixtures from which cones of smoke-filled light shone down. Everything, walls and ceiling and support pillars, was made of huge wooden timbers bound by metal bands. The floor was smoothly polished wood as well. Sword smiled. It was covered with sawdust.

Martin took Sword's arm and began to walk into the center of the room, weaving a path through more than a hundred closely packed tables of all different sizes, all occupied. There were glasses and bottles on each table and Sword's first impression was that Martin had brought him to a well-established 'blind pig' serving liquor without benefit of a license and without regard for legal business hours. But then he started paying more attention to the people sitting at the tables. At least, he corrected himself, most of them appeared to be people.

Sword felt his pulse race, his heart thunder in his chest. Maybe half the customers here could have been ordinary patrons of any late night, downtown bar. But the other half ... There was a man with pointed ears and glowing eyes. A table full of creatures built like Martin, but covered in luxuriant red fur. Another table of small, roundly obese females who seemed to be having a heated argument with an ornate copper box — East Indian, Sword's trained eye saw — that sat in the middle of their table and twitched from side to side.

The confusion of the sounds of Softwind rumbled in Sword's ears. For three years he had searched for just one member of the First World and in this one night, in this one moment, he knew he must be in the company of hundreds of them. He opened his mouth to take a deep breath and clear his head, but the smoke and the clamor were too powerful for him. He stumbled, pulling back against Martin's guiding hand.

"No, no, Galen Sword," Martin said rapidly. "Must keep moving. Must keep moving."

Sword bumped against a table and saw violet eyes glare at him. He saw dwarves scuttling with trays of beer bottles. A black horse — a *horse* — was tethered to the end of a large, metal-covered bar at the far end of the room, a design like a silver bolt of lightning gleaming on its flank. Sword couldn't make sense of all he heard; he couldn't keep what he saw in order. The impressions bombarding all his senses were too overpowering, too alien. He lost all sense of movement and of place until he felt Martin's hands pushing him into a wooden chair.

The room seemed to steady. Martin sat across from him at a tiny round table. He reached out and took Sword's hands in his. Sword focussed on Martin's more-or-less familiar face and found something he could center on.

"This is incredible," Sword said. "This is ... "

"Softwind," Martin said.

A small person with an elaborate white moustache and a face intricately lined with fine wrinkles appeared at the side of the table, wearing a powder-blue apron. When he spoke, Sword smelled a wave of roses roll from him and for an instant he thought he was back facing Herr Slausen in his family's library on the night he had been sent away.

"*Guten Abend, Herr Arkady*," the small creature said to Martin. "First time?" he asked, indicating Sword.

Martin nodded. "Water for friend," he said and Sword realized that the tiny person was their waiter. "Water for Arkady."

Sword laughed as the waiter walked away. A First World *waiter*! He leaned over the table to Martin. "What was that? What clan?"

Martin shook his head. "No questions here Galen Sword. All supposed to know. Many ears. No questions."

"But later? Later you can tell me?"

"If still want to know," Martin said enigmatically.

Sword decided not to press the issue. He glanced around the room. Sitting down, the overall strangeness of the place was not quite as disconcerting. Martin had taken them to a section of the room where most of their neighbors were ordinary humans. Sword saw two men whom he recognized — musicians he recalled seeing play on a late-night television talk show. He looked away before his staring became apparent.

Someone else had joined their table while Sword had looked away, a thin nervous woman with a totally bald head and a dingy white suit. Her thick black eyebrows gave her face a stretched-out, animalistic cast that reminded Sword of a ferret. The woman sat down, pulling in close to the table, leaning over, eyes darting. She held out a closed fist to Martin. "Arkady," she said in greeting.

Martin swept his hand across the table, brushing his knuckles against the woman's. "Tantoo," Martin said.

Tantoo jerked her head around to Sword and slid her fist toward him.

"Human," Martin said before Sword could give his name.

Tantoo nodded as if she could accept that limitation on Sword's part, then she opened her fist and lightly brushed Sword's knuckles as quickly as Martin had brushed hers. Sword began to see a structure of status and hierarchy at work.

Tantoo folded her hands together. She bobbed her head in counterpoint to the reedy music still playing. "So, you the guy with the 'chanted Light who wanted to see me?" she asked looking at Sword.

"Yes," Martin said.

Tantoo's eyes danced back and forth. "Who'm I dealing with here, Arkady?"

"Deal with Arkady," Martin said.

"But, it's his Light?"

Martin nodded.

"I don't like it, Arkady. Could be a set-up. I'm feeling very uncomfortable." She turned to Sword. "What's your name, pal?"

"Pal Arkady friend." Martin held up a hand to instruct Sword to be silent.

Tantoo smiled and sat back, narrowing her eyes. "What's the deal here, Arkady?"

"Deal simple." Martin kept his lips drawn tightly over his fangs. "Arkady friend buy Light. Good Light. 'Chanted Light. 'Chanting soft. Hard to know. Arkady friend *not* know. Arkady help friend Arkady help Light. Tantoo help Arkady."

Tantoo rubbed her nose in silence. She squinted in Sword's direction. "Where'd you buy this Light?"

Sword glanced at Martin, saw him nod, then answered, "New Orleans," all the while wishing to God he knew what was going on.

Tantoo nodded as if it had been a proper answer, as if there were nowhere else one could buy an invisible cat. "Get it from a woman named — "

Martin tapped the table with his heavy knuckles. "Softwind," he said in warning.

Tantoo shifted in her chair and straightened her collar. She leaned in toward Martin again. "Look, my talkative friend. In my line of work you don't go around lifting 'chants without knowing what you're dealing with. If I break a punishment 'chant, I'm growing gills. Know what I mean?"

"Not punishment," Martin said. "Clear crystal bond."

Tantoo thrust out her lower lip and tugged at it. "Okay, that sounds like it's on the up and up." She slid over to Sword. "So, what's this Light look like when it's 'chanted?" She slid back to Martin. "If I'm permitted to know that much, that is. But if I'm not, I walk right now."

"Tell," Martin said to Sword.

"It's a cat."

"We talking lion, tiger, sabre-toothed — "

"Persian. A white, Persian cat. Twenty pounds, tops."

"A housecat?" Tantoo frowned. "Why would anyone bother?" She shook her head. "So, okay, what's the clear crystal bond? A leash? A collar?"

"A collar," Sword said. He couldn't get over it. Tantoo was acting as if this were an everyday occurrence. In her line of work, maybe it was.

"Green leather? Sort of beat-up?"

"That's it," Sword said.

"Well, that's not *it*, pal. Stuff like that's pretty common." She winked at Martin. "That don't make it any less expensive, though, Arkady." Back to Sword. "So, can you take the collar off?"

"Yes."

"And ... ?" Tantoo prompted. "Turns into a reptile, right? A snake or something?"

Sword shook his head. "Turns ... invisible."

Tantoo's eyes widened and she spread her hands out across the table as if holding on for support. "But you say it's just a white Persian housecat?"

"Appears to be," Sword corrected.

Tantoo waved her hand. "Yeah, yeah, *appears* to be. You're probably a lawyer in the Second World, huh, pal?" She leaned back in Martin's direction. "Look, Arkady, I hope your friend here didn't pay too much glitter for this Light. You know what I'm saying? I mean, invisibility wasted on a twenty-pound housecat? Like, this has got to be a grudge 'chant or else ... " She shook her head again. "Naa, no way. But anyhow, assuming that there really is a Light under the fur and the clear crystal bond, we're talking *beaucoup* the crystal to lift, you know what I mean? I mean, that's one soft 'chant." She leaned back to Sword. "Say pal, like, who told you the beast was a Light, anyway? Sure you're not being slipped a flaw?"

Sword looked at Martin and felt the first intimation that something might go wrong. It had been Martin who had identified 'Bub as a member of a Light Clan, whatever that was. What if Martin had been wrong? He fought the urge to grab Tantoo by her jacket and drag the scrawny woman back to the Loft for questioning. How many secrets did Tantoo possess that she just took for granted?

"If too hard for Tantoo to lift," Martin said, ignoring Tantoo's question, "Arkady find counter who can."

Tantoo did a take on that as if Martin had insulted her. "Hey, Arkady. You're not going to find a counter better than me through the whole North Shore, know what I'm saying? I can lift the 'chant" — she shot a glance at Sword — "*if* you're sure that's what you want to do, pal" — she glanced back to Martin. "What I'm not sure of is whether or not you can afford a lift that big. Know what I mean?"

At last they were in an area Sword felt he had some knowledge of. If humans in the Shadow World could be bought as easily as humans in the Second World, Sword knew he had enough money to buy all the answers he could ever need. "What's it going to cost?" he asked.

Tantoo squinted at Sword as she sucked on her teeth. "Fifty," she said finally. "It'll cost you fifty."

Sword knew the woman couldn't mean fifty dollars. There was only one other meaning. "You mean thousand?" he asked, just to be sure. He felt a sudden rush of relief. If it were going to be this easy, he'd pull out a few million in cash and be in the middle of the First World by tomorrow night.

But Tantoo shook her head in disgust. "What fifty *thousand*, pal? I mean fifty *million*. Hell, I mean fifty *billion*." She pushed her chair back from the table and grimaced at Martin. "Don't be wasting my time, Arkady. You'd think management would know better than to let shirleys in here. Coldblasted know nothings." She started to get up.

"Tantoo mean fifty *whole*," Martin explained to Sword. "Tantoo can't lift 'chant so Tantoo ask stupid price. Tantoo have no power. Waste Arkady time."

Tantoo stood by the table and looked around trying to find the other Tantoo that Martin must have been talking about. She stared down at the creature in disbelief. "Hey, Arkady. This is Tantoo up here. You can't be saying that about me."

"Fifty whole to lift clear crystal bond?" Martin asked skeptically.

Tantoo thought for a few seconds, looked around, looked up to the ceiling, then back at Martin. "Okay, Arkady. What would *you* say was fair?"

Martin pursed his lips. "Arkady say ... ten whole."

Tantoo's eyes bulged. "You're insulting me!" She turned to the people at the table beside her. "The best counter on the North Shore and he's insulting me!" She sat back down at Sword's table and pulled her chair closer to Martin. "What did I ever do to you, Arkady? Why would you want to treat me this way?"

Sword leaned back and tried not to smile. He didn't know what kind of currency they were talking about, but he had no doubt that Martin was negotiating a realistic bargain because Tantoo was sitting at the table again and was getting ready to make a counter offer. Maybe Ko was right. Maybe Martin wasn't simple, just smart in ways that Sword hadn't yet discovered.

The bargaining went on for five more minutes. Tantoo waved her hands, looked to the ceiling for help, hit her forehead on the tabletop in despair, but didn't stand up again. She paused in her histrionics only long enough to let the waiter deposit two plain glasses of what seemed to be ordinary water. As soon as the waiter had left, the bargaining commenced again and Sword listened intently, his admiration for Martin increasing with each downward adjustment in Tantoo's demand. Finally, the negotiations hit the last phase. Tantoo was holding firm at twenty whole — whatever that meant — while Martin was offering thirty in four — whatever that meant.

"Look, Arkady," Tantoo said, leaning forward, patting her hands to her chest. "I got expenses. It's going to take ten whole just to do the lift. I got to eat, you know?"

Martin looked away. "Take six in ten to lift."

Tantoo leaned against her open hand and sighed. Sword could feel a deal about to close. "Look, Arkady, we seem to have a legitimate difference of opinion on what it's going to take to lift the Light's 'chant. Am I right or am I right?"

Martin stared at her and said nothing.

"Okay, so here's what I propose. You give me a fifteen whole and a five whole." She held up her hand to stop Martin's objections. "That's twenty in two. And then, you provide whatever it takes to lift the 'chant. If it's six in ten — that's all you pay. But if it takes ten whole, well, you got to pay that, too."

Martin thought about the offer. "Arkady only pay what lift take?"

"Plus fifteen whole and five whole."

"No fifteen," Martin objected. "Straight twenty in two."

Tantoo frowned. She hesitated.

Martin held out his fist, knuckles first. "Worst Tantoo do two ten wholes ... "

"Ahh, what the hell," Tantoo said and brushed her knuckles against Martin's fist. She turned to Sword. "Your furry pal here sure talks a tough deal, don't he?" Tantoo straightened her collar and winked at Sword. "Guess I should have started the bidding with the Crystal of the Change Arkady and taken it from there, right, pal?"

Sword smiled awkwardly. "Yeah, sure," he said. But he had hesitated and that seemed to bother the woman in the white suit.

"The Crystal of the Change Arkady?" Tantoo asked him. "You've heard of that, haven't you?"

Sword glanced at Martin, uncertain how he should respond.

"Don't be looking at him," Tantoo said. She grabbed Sword's chin and jerked his head away from Martin's gaze. "You look at me, shirley! You tell me what the Crystal of the Change Arkady is!"

Sword grabbed the woman's wrist and pushed it down to the tabletop. "I don't know."

"Then you're no friend to Arkady, are you?" Tantoo said angrily. She twisted to Martin. "And you! With a shirley who doesn't even know about the Change. I mean, that's why you're all in town these days? Isn't it?" Tantoo's eyes narrowed again as she stared intently at Martin. "Hold on ... " she muttered, then reached out to grab Martin's face as she had held Sword's.

Martin snarled, baring his teeth. Tantoo laughed and snapped her hand back.

"I tell you, my little two-fanged friend," Tantoo spat out as she rose from the table again, "you're not getting Tantoo mixed up in no clan war. You either got fixed halfway through your last Change ... or you're nothing but a coldblasted Seyshen halfling!"

Martin roared and leapt at the woman. The table splintered beneath his fists. Sword pushed away from the table and jumped to his feet. He saw Tantoo fly back with Martin wrapped around her torso. He heard screams. He started to go for Martin, to pull him back from the woman. And then he felt two iron clamps dig into his shoulders.

Sword gasped in agony. He felt his whole body twitch in the sudden, electric shock of something sharp impaling both trapezius muscles. He couldn't even lift his arms to push whatever it was away. He heard something in both shoulders crunch — the muscle being ripped and torn. Then one shoulder was released and he felt himself being slowly turned around. The disturbance of Softwind passed before his pain-blurred vision, then was replaced by an expanse of soft blue fabric and an ornate, silver crucifix, twisted and flowing as if it had originally grown in wood.

Sword shook his head to clear it and realized he was looking at someone's chest, someone very tall: the person who had stopped him, who still held him. He looked up. A death's head looked back.

It was not a person who had prevented him from helping Martin. It was a living skeleton, with dead-white translucent skin stretched hideously over a skull swollen grotesquely at the cranium, and rippled and dented as if no flesh and blood lay upon it. What lips the creature had were stretched taut like thin cords, forming a mindless grimace over long, gumless teeth, blotched and stained with thin rust-red cracks. But it was the eyes that held Sword and made his heart shudder and the hair on his neck bristle. The eyes of the creature, only inches from his own, were solid orbs of translucent blue, filled with swirling, sparkling silver flecks, but without any recognizable inner structure.

The monster looked down on Sword. The cords of its lips drew up in a quivering grin. A monstrously deformed hand appeared by Sword's head. It was all flexing tendons beneath tight white skin, with long fingers ending in two-inch pearl white claws. Sword cringed as he felt one of those claws scrape against his scalp. He felt a stunning burst of red-hot pain on his head and watched as the creature's hand withdrew, trailing a small hunk of his hair, one end joined by a rag of bloody skin.

"*Bad,*" the creature said and its voice was hollow and stank of damp soil and death.

Sword gagged and suddenly he was falling, the pressure on his shoulder gone.

He hit the floor and lay there, pressed into the sawdust. His arms felt useless. Somewhere behind him, he heard Martin bellowing and Tantoo screaming. Dimly, he was aware of Ko calling his name in his ear. He forced himself to his hands and knees. He heard Martin's sudden squeal of pain and fright. He put one foot beneath him, the other, then he stood.

The creature loomed over Martin. All around the other patrons of Softwind had pulled back.

"Martin!" Sword shouted in warning.

But the skeletal creature, clothed in loose-fitting, pale blue trousers and top, wrapped its bony fingers around Martin's neck and wrenched him into the air as if he weighed only a handful of pounds.

Tantoo scrambled to her feet, panic on her face. She held one hand out toward Martin as if holding a gun. But in her hand, instead of cold metal, a single red gemstone blazed with an inner light.

"'Chanted halfling!" Tantoo shrieked.

The creature dug a hand into Martin's side and turned him around, still keeping him suspended in the air. Martin's face collapsed in terror when he saw what held him. He screamed mindlessly. The creature moved a claw to Martin's scalp and began twisting a lock of his stiff black hair.

Sword had seen enough. He ran at the creature, locking both fists together and smashing his full weight against its back in a desperate, two-armed blow. It was like hitting sculpted marble, without give. But the shock of the blow made the creature drop Martin and whirl around to face its attacker.

The hideous mouth stretched into a gaping smile that grew half-way around the creature's face. Its open hand shot out and slapped Sword like a fly, bashing him to the floor. Then it held up its other fist, opened its fingers like a spider unfurling its legs, and showed what it held in its palm.

Sword blinked to force his vision to come back into focus. The creature held the bloody strands of hair it had pulled from Sword's scalp. It slapped its other hand on top, cupping both around the hair. Sword was aware of a hundred voices gasping in surprise. He heard chairs and tables overturn, the shattering of glasses and bottles as feet and hooves scraped away across the sawdust-covered floor.

And then he heard a hum, pure and clear above the other noise. A hum he recognized even as he felt a burning vibration enfold him. A hum he still had on his answering machine. A final message.

Blue fire flared through the creature's fingers. Blue light blazed from its translucent eyes.

Martin's shriek echoed through the chaos.

The creature jerked forward with Martin's feet planted on its back. The silver cross and heavy silver chain bounced up from around the creature's neck. Its hands flew out to break its fall and Sword saw the strands of his hair burst into flames as they floated through the air.

Then Martin's hand closed on Sword's arm and he was dragged through the now empty tables. He couldn't decipher a word of what Martin was bellowing, but he understood the urgency of his tone.

Sword glanced back as he stumbled after the halfling. Behind them, the skeletal creature was on its hands and knees on the floor, moving around blindly, searching for its crucifix. Its eyes were dark, black, unseeing.

Sword bumped against the small partition wall as Martin dragged him to the entrance. Martin rammed the door with his solid shoulder and the door slammed open into darkness and they both tumbled through it, into the sludge and the damp of a forgotten alley.

Sword lay on his back, feeling the cold of the wet ground seep into him, bringing back full awareness. He was surprised to find that the city air smelled sweet and clean to him after the smoke of the room. His shoulders blazed with pain, his forearms still vibrated from the useless blow against the creature's rock-solid back, but he felt himself calming. Then he heard Martin whimpering and saw him huddled against a wall, folded over, hugging himself.

"Are you hurt?" Sword asked. He struggled to his feet, his ears ringing in the absence of noise. He went to Martin and knelt beside him. "Are you all right, Martin? Should we keep running?"

Martin shook his head. "Softwind gone," he blubbered and could say no more. Sword put his arm around Martin's shoulders and sat beside him, deciding that if Martin felt safe here, then there was no need to keep moving. As his eyes became adapted to the night, he saw that they weren't in the same alley from which they had entered Soft-wind. Must have been a second door, Sword thought. But he was sure they had run out the same door that they had entered.

He raised his finger to his ear and felt that his transceiver was gone, lost in the fight, so he activated the proximity signal on his locator band to let Ko know it was time to come and get them. The red LED on the band pulsed silently in time to the signal. Sword squeezed his arm around Martin, still feeling the adrenalin coursing through them both.

"It's going to be okay, Martin," Sword said, and in some strange way, despite all that had happened, he actually found that he believed his own words. He had taken his first steps into the First World.

But Martin wouldn't stop crying, wouldn't stop quaking. "Not okay," he sniffled, holding his hands over his face. "Never okay again."

"Why, Martin? Why do you say that?"

"Dmitri try to kill Galen Sword."

So the skeletal creature had a name, Sword thought. "But he didn't," Sword said. "Dmitri failed."

But Martin shook his head and sniffed again. "Dmitri never fail. Dmitri try again and again." He turned to look at Sword, eyes streaming with tears. "Galen Sword already dead."

NINE

Forsyte closed his eyes and felt the main lab spin around him — each ghost limb sensing the rush of air flowing past. The scientist still had no understanding of how his body reacted to what had been done to him. There was no physical damage to his nervous system. That much had been confirmed more than two years ago by the best medical specialists the Sword Foundation's money could buy. And judging from the way Forsyte felt himself responding to the excitement that grew in him as he listened to Sword's account of what had happened in the place called Softwind, his endocrine system was also unaffected. But why should he respond to such stimulation by feeling his entire body in such exquisite, yet false, detail? Why was it that when his eyes were open, the only physical sensations he was aware of came through his head and neck and the two fingers of his left hand? Why the sensory illusions when he closed his eyes? Why had they done this to him? Why had Sword allowed it? His whole world spun. Why?

"Adrian, are you all right?"

Forsyte opened his eyes and the sensation of spinning evaporated. Sword was in front of him, bending down to check him. The scientist tapped his finger against the pad on the arm of his chair. His voder said, "FINE."

"We could take a break if you'd like," Sword offered. His face was still drenched in sweat and his bare chest was streaked with blood. But Forsyte could see in Sword's dark eyes the same rush that he himself felt. Damn, but they were close on this one. How could Sword think of stopping even for a moment?

"NO, NO, NO," the voder chanted.

"All right." Sword held his hands up. Forsyte could see they still trembled with what he had been through. "Just checking."

"Back here, Sword," Ko said. She stood by the examination chair where Sword had been sitting before he had checked on Forsyte. Ko wore surgical gloves and held a folded pad of cotton bandage dipped in disinfectant. "Or would you like to bleed to death?"

"Another time," Sword said and settled back into the chair.

"CONTINUE," the voder prompted.

"Watch it!" Sword jerked away from Ko's hands as she tried to clean out the wounds the thing called Dmitri had inflicted on his shoulders.

"You want to do it?" Ko tossed a bloodstained bandage into the plastic pail beside her.

Forsyte pressed the repeat button on the keypad and the voder prompted Sword again. He marvelled at how well Sword could put up with Ko's damned irascibility, no matter how highly he valued her services. If Ko hadn't insisted on living away from the Loft most of the time, Forsyte was certain the two of them would have had a major blow-up by now. As things were, though, the inevitable was only being delayed, not prevented.

"Okay, okay." Sword flinched as Ko swabbed out the three puncture marks on his left shoulder. "I was telling you about the negotiations with Tantoo. Uh, that could be either her name or her clan. Everyone called Martin 'Arkady' the whole time we were in there."

"YOUR NAME?" Forsyte's voder asked.

Sword paused, looking up. "Martin wouldn't let me use my name. He just told Tantoo I was a human, and ... Tantoo called me a shirley a couple of times. Derisively," he added.

"Other one." Ko pushed Sword to the side so she could work on his other shoulder.

"So, anyway," Sword continued, "Martin said that all the figures they were spouting back and forth when they were bargaining were measurements for crystals. When Tantoo said she wanted fifty whole in payment for lifting the enchantment from 'Bub, she meant she wanted a single gemstone with a mass of fifty carats. The price they agreed on — twenty in two — meant that Martin would pay her with two crystals with a combined mass of twenty carats. That could mean a fifteen whole and a five whole, or two ten wholes."

"TYPE OF CRYSTAL?" Forsyte punched out on his keypad.

"Some type of red crystal. Martin didn't know what humans called it."

"Rubies?" Ko asked, breaking open a new package of cotton swabs.

"Now, why didn't I think of that?" Sword glanced at Ko over his shoulder. "Martin said that even he knows the difference between rubies and crystals with *real* worth."

Ko squeezed the disinfectant liquid all over the four puncture wounds on Sword's other shoulder and smiled as he shivered. "Oh, sorry," she said cheerfully.

Sword turned back to Forsyte. "Anyway, Martin did a great job of negotiating with this woman and they agreed on a price. Apparently, in the First World instead of shaking hands, you brush knuckles with the other guy. The one with the least status makes the tightest fist."

Forsyte punched out a single word on his pad, phoneme by phoneme. "COMBATIVE."

Sword nodded. "Ritualized combat, sure. Could have originated from that. Humans shake hands in the Second World to show their hands are empty of weapons; adepts in the First World exchange blows to prove they're equal. Good as any explanation I can think of."

Forsyte punched again. "WARLIKE CULTURE."

"As in: could be dangerous?" Sword asked.

"We already know that." Ko dabbed at Sword's shoulders to help dry the disinfectant.

"NEXT?" the voder asked.

"Well, the deal broke down. Tantoo said something to me about the ... Crystal of the Change Arkady, and she was very disturbed that I didn't understand what she meant by it. She was nervous the whole time. One of the first things she said was that she was suspicious that the meeting was a set-up."

"For what?" Ko asked. She tore strips of adhesive tape from a roll.

Sword shrugged and grimaced as he moved his shoulders experimentally. "I don't know. She and Martin both called what had happened to 'Bub a 'soft enchantment.' Tantoo seemed skeptical that someone would go to all that trouble to make something as small as a housecat invisible."

"What else are you going to do to a housecat?" Ko asked lightly.

"Tantoo expected 'Bub to turn into a reptile or a snake." Sword's answer was serious.

"Oh."

"So, when I admitted I didn't know what the Crystal of the Change was, that's when Tantoo got mad."

"And called you a shirley?" Ko arranged fresh cotton bandages over the wounds as she talked.

"Actually," Sword said, "she called me a ... know nothing, cold-blasted, shirley. She also identified Martin as a halfling. Said he wasn't Arkady. Said he was, uh, Seyshen. That's when Martin jumped her and ... Dmitri came along."

"THE BOUNCER," Forsyte's voder said.

Sword smiled. "That's it, Adrian. The Softwind bouncer. Absolutely nonhuman. Martin said he was Clan Ronin."

"*Clan* Ronin or just Ronin?" Ko asked.

"Just Ronin," Sword said after a moment. "Oh, you mean, as in a Japanese samurai for hire. No allegiance. Could be." He nodded his head in thought as Ko taped the bandages in place. Then he said quietly, "Dmitri is the one who killed Marcus Askwith."

"REPEAT," the voder said.

"Try that one again?" Ko asked.

Sword watched the floor as he spoke. "He did something with the hair he yanked out of me ... cupped it in his hands." He looked up at Forsyte. "He has a blue power. He focused it on my hair. I ... felt it."

"Felt what?" Ko walked around to be in front of him.

"The heat," Sword said. "The heat he was putting into that piece of hair was coming out in me."

"SHC?" Ko asked. "You're not suggesting that this Dmitri is able to ... induce it in others?"

"I'm not *suggesting* anything." Sword pushed himself from the chair abruptly. "I felt it. I heard it."

"Heard it?" Ko repeated.

"That same damn tone that's in Marcus's last message. That hum. You remember that hum? Happens twice. The technician I hired from the FBI sound lab could only say it wasn't produced by the phone system or by my answering machine. It's something linked to the combustion process. It has to be."

Forsyte flicked his chair's joystick and rolled forward, pivoting to be by Sword. "YOU SAW OTHERS LIKE MARTIN. WHY COULD THERE NOT BE OTHERS LIKE DMITRI? WHY DO YOU SAY HE DID IT?" Forsyte asked, laboriously typing in the words that weren't already preprogrammed.

Sword squatted by Forsyte's chair and put his hand on the scientist's. "Because I felt it, Adrian. I saw it in his ... eyes. If they were eyes. It was Dmitri."

Ko closed up the medikit. "What's going on here, Sword? You catch a case of ESP or something from those First World types?"

"I know it's hard to believe." Sword stood up again. "But I was there. It happened."

Ko snapped off her surgical gloves and tossed them into the plastic pail. "I believe what I see, Sword. You track down Martin because Trank feeds you a few weird peeping Tom reports, and I believe that Martin exists. You say your lawyer got spontaneously combusted? I see the police photos and I believe he's dead and a lot of heat was involved. But just because *I* can't bloody well say what killed Askwith is absolutely no reason for you to say, 'Then it *must* be SHC,' or some crap like that. I go along with what I can see, and hear, and taste, and smell on my own. If it's in front of me, I'll believe it. But all these stupid explanations ... clans, and crystals, and — "

"We came out in a different alley, Melody! Five blocks from where we went in. Something ... moved us."

Ko shook her head. "You were dazed, Sword. You couldn't know how far Martin dragged you."

"Then, how about 'Bub's crystal?" Sword interrupted. "You admit that works, don't you?"

"*Something* works, Sword. Some *thing*. It might be the crystal. It might be the collar. It might be some combination of the two with something we know nothing about. Or even a whim of 'Bub's that she only makes herself transparent to photons when the useless collar is off. The phenomenon is real — no question — but using all this other crap as an explanation for it ... no way."

Forsyte spun his chair around to face Ko. She was being uncharacteristically emotional. There must be something else bothering her but he was too far removed from her personal life to know what it was. And, as usual, Sword was too obsessed to even notice.

"Martin believes it," Sword said, folding his arms.

"Martin has a developmental age of five," Ko retorted. "Who knows what he's been told by whoever raised him? Most five-year-olds believe in Santa Claus and the Tooth Fairy, too."

"Well, maybe they should. Maybe they're based on First World legends. That's what Askwith said. The clans got into trouble, made mistakes, and that's when the legends started."

"Oh, give it a bloody rest!" Ko yanked open an equipment locker and threw the medikit back inside without bothering to see where it landed.

But Sword was on a roll. "Adrian, this could be it! This could make sense! A whole network of ... of supernatural beings ... a different species from us ... you know, like Cro-Magnon, Neanderthal, and ... adepts, let's say. Their special powers, special attributes, let them advance more rapidly. They reproduced within their clan lines, stayed hidden. When the world's population was small, it was easy. But as ordinary humans spread out, it became more difficult. Humans started running into the adepts, not knowing a lot about them but seeing enough to start the legends. *All* the legends. Werewolves, vampires, witches, warlocks, demons ... " Forsyte saw Sword's eyes blaze with the ferocity of the vision he pursued.

"Let's not forget little green men and the Loch Ness monster," Ko added sarcastically. She slammed the equipment locker shut.

"Well why the hell not?"

Ko turned to face Sword, her hands on her hips. "C'mon, Sword, don't screw around like this!"

"I am not screwing around! I've been there! I've seen them in Softwind" Sword dropped his voice to an intense whisper, as if willing Ko to understand him. "They're what I remember, Melody. They're what was taken from me. I belong with them."

Ko erupted. She took a step toward Sword. "No, you *don't*! That's insane! You're *not* like Martin. You're *not* like Ja'Nette. You're just an ordinary man. A *human* man. This search is bullshit. And it's getting crazier by the minute. Tantoo, Softwind, Ronin ... you can't be serious. You just can't!" Ko's pale face flushed as she struggled for control of her emotions.

Doesn't Sword see it? Forsyte thought. *Can't he tell that it's something else that's upsetting her?*

"But I am serious about it, Melody," Sword said. "Deadly serious."

Ko wiped at her eyes with a quick angry gesture. "Deadly. That's my point, Sword. Do you know how close those punctures on your shoulders came to ripping up your arteries?" She shook her head at him. Forsyte could see she fought back tears. "Goddamnit, Galen, you almost died tonight."

Sword held out his hand, confusion in his voice. "Melody ... ?"

"This isn't a rich boy's game anymore. This is real life. And real death." She turned away from him and ran to the stairway leading down to the street level.

Sword turned to Forsyte, confusion still in his eyes. "Adrian? What should I ... ?"

"STAY," Forsyte punched into his voder, cursing his silence.

Sword read the conflict in his eyes, saw how much was inside him, straining to get out. "Stay, and ... wait for your notes?" he asked quietly.

"NO," the voder said. "WAIT FOR MARTIN TO RETURN."

Sword shook his head. "He was badly frightened, Adrian. I don't think he will come back."

"HE MUST," the voder said. "HE IS WITH JA'NETTE."

"But they're both halflings," Sword said. "They don't belong in our world."

Forsyte punched out the phonemes on his pad. "NEITHER DO YOU."

TEN

Martin took the final bite of his fourth Big Mac and swallowed without chewing. Then he dropped the cardboard container to the streaked surface of the roof he sat on, leaning against its small circling wall.

"Mar-*tiiin?*" Ja'Nette said, halfway through her second burger. "What did I tell you?"

Martin sighed and flopped his arm down to snatch the burger container from the roof. Then he shoved it into the brown McDonalds' bag with the rest of the trash from their meal, though he didn't understand why. It was night, it was only a roof, and there were thousands of other roofs they could go to when this one became too cluttered with trash.

"Better," Ja'Nette said, and bit into her burger again.

But Martin couldn't resist. As soon as Ja'Nette looked away, he tossed the bag into the air, arcing it over the roof to fall to the street twenty stories below. There were more streets than roofs in this city anyway. There was room for lots of trash.

But the bag stopped in mid-air. Martin blinked in surprise. The bag rotated twice, then sped back as if it had been launched from a giant elastic band and beaned Martin between the eyes.

Ja'Nette laughed at her friend's reaction, then began to gag as the effort of her translocation rebounded through her digestive system.

"Serves Ja'Nette right," Martin said, rolling the bag into a tight ball and hiding it from Ja'Nette by placing it behind his back.

"Worth it," Ja'Nette said weakly, then drew a mouthful of chocolate milkshake through her straw until she made a satisfying slurping sound.

Martin laughed, grabbed his own shake, and sucked on the straw to make his own slurping noise. But he sucked too hard and the empty cup crumpled inward because of the sudden vacuum.

"Stupid cup," Martin muttered and started to toss it over his shoulder, stopping only when he caught Ja'Nette's glare. He sighed again and put the cup behind him with the bag. "Ja'Nette have too many rules."

"Don't you have rules where you live?" the girl asked.

"Not stupid rules."

Ja'Nette stuck her tongue out at him, then looked serious for a moment. "Where do you live, Martin?"

"Martin Clan Arkady," he said, thumping at his chest. "Not Seyshen. Never Seyshen. Stupid Tantoo," he grumbled.

"Say what?" Ja'Nette asked.

"Martin Clan Arkady," Martin repeated. "That all."

Ja'Nette shrugged as if she still didn't understand him. "But that's your family, right? What I mean is, where do you and your family live? Like in a house somewhere? Or on roofs or something?"

"Oh," Martin said. "Martin sleep eat Arkady enclave."

"Earth to Martin," Ja'Nette said, shaking her head. "So where's this enclave? And what is it?"

"In city." Martin shook his own head back at her. Humans could ask so many pointless questions.

Ja'Nette put her burger down in its container and wiped her hands on her jeans and red nylon jacket. "Okay," she tried again, "let's do this the way Melody would do it. Let's start right at the beginning and go one step at a time." She took a deep breath. "One: when you go to sleep, are you out in the open or are you under a roof?"

That made sense. "Roof," Martin said.

"Is there a floor and walls?"

"Lots," Martin answered. He leaned forward. These were good questions.

"Sooo, if there's a roof and a floor and walls, then you sleep in a room, right?"

Martin nodded. "Martin room."

"And if there're lots of walls, then there're probably lots of other rooms next to your room, too. Right?"

Martin nodded happily. "Arkady enclave."

"Now, are all these rooms in a big building like this one? Or a medium building like the Loft? Or a teeny tiny building like, um, one of those houses on television?"

Ja'Nette had gone too fast for him again, or was she trying to play a joke? "Arkady enclave bigger than TV," Martin said knowingly. She wasn't going to fool him.

"You're bigger than a TV, Martin. But how big is the enclave?"

Martin considered the question for a moment, then tapped the roof. "This big."

Ja'Nette whistled. "And it's full of woofers?" Martin narrowed his eyes and the girl elaborated. "You know, werewolves? Shifters? A whole building full of them?"

Martin nodded. Once again it was back to being a stupid question. "Arkady enclave ... Arkady shifters. What else?"

"How many Arkady shifters are — no, never mind. I know the answer to that one: lots, right?" Martin nodded. "So how come nobody knows about you? Like, how come everybody isn't seeing you guys all over town or something?"

Martin smiled proudly. "Good rules. Shifterform never go out in daytime. Never never never. Shifterform never more than three go out together. Shifterform hunt only tagged prey. Shifterform never eat prey in open."

Ja'Nette pursed her lips. "Martin, what's 'tagged prey' mean?"

Martin looked away uncomfortably. He didn't want to explain it to the child. She was too human. She might not understand. "Hunter stuff," he said. "Martin not know everything."

"Are tagged prey humans?" Martin squirmed at the girl's question. "Martin? Are they?"

"Sometimes," he admitted.

"And shifters hunt humans, and ... *eat* them?"

"Sometimes."

"Ewww, gross," Ja'Nette said. Then her eyes widened. "Holy cow, Martin, you haven't ... I mean ... have you ... you know?"

Martin cringed but said nothing. She was just a child. She wouldn't understand.

"Yuk." Ja'Nette clutched her arms around herself. Then she grabbed her tray of food and held it out to him intently. "You want the rest of my burger? How about my fries? Whatever you want."

"Martin not hungry." He reached out to Ja'Nette and brushed the back of his hand against her leg. "Ja'Nette Martin friend. Ja'Nette not worry. Okay?"

"Okay," Ja'Nette said skeptically, then put her tray down. "So what's shifterform, anyway?"

"Not humanform."

"Oh, I get it. Like sometimes you look like a human and then you change — you shift — into something else. Like a wolf or something."

"Not Martin," Martin said glumly. "Martin halfling. Martin always this way."

"Yeah, but the other shifters, they change from humans to animals, right? Like during the full moon, right?" Ja'Nette glanced for a moment up at the night sky.

"Full moon stupid. Shifters change during Change."

"Oh, so pardon me, okay?" Ja'Nette stood up and stretched her legs. "So, like, when is this Change? Every month? Every year?"

"Every Ceremony of the Change." Martin stood up, also.

Ja'Nette sighed. "And when is the Ceremony of the Change?"

Martin worked it out on his fingers. "Four more sleeps."

"Wow, four more days?"

"Nights, too."

"I know that, Martin. I just meant that's soon. And all the shifters are going to change into animals then?"

"Most change to shifterform. Some back to humanform."

"How come?"

"Humanform no rules. Go out in day. Do things. Help keep enclave."

"Oh yeah, you were talking about the keepers. Humanform shifters, huh?"

Martin nodded, then turned and put his hands on the edge of the low barrier wall. "Morning soon. Must go now."

Ja'Nette patted him on the back. "Back to the enclave?"

He shook his head. "Not go back there."

"How come?"

"Fight in Softwind. Keepers hear. Know Martin with human. Bad bad. Never never. Martin break rules."

"What will they do, Martin?"

"Tag Martin. Hunt Martin. Eat Martin."

"Ewww." Ja'Nette grabbed Martin by the shoulders and tried to turn him around to face her, but she wasn't strong enough to make him move even an inch. "Then you gotta come back to the Loft with me."

"No. Cannot."

"Why not? You can be safe there. Melody's got all sorts of neat stuff. And Adrian's real smart. And Sword can buy anything we need to protect you."

Martin gently took hold of Ja'Nette's hand and moved it from his shoulder. "Dmitri never fail. Galen Sword dead."

"I keep telling you, no he's not. You rode back to the Loft with us. He told us you saved him, remember?"

"Dmitri kill Galen Sword. Dmitri Ronin. Dmitri kill anything for crystal."

"Sword will *kill* stupid Dmitri!"

"Galen Sword not real Sword. Galen Sword human. Human cannot kill adept."

Ja'Nette shook her hand free of Martin's. "What do you mean, Sword's not a 'real' Sword?"

Martin hopped up to the wall ledge and squatted, rocking over the edge and back again, sniffing the night air. "Some names same in First World Second World. Galen Sword Second World human. But Sword name First World strong."

"Say what?"

"Martin Second World name. Martin First World name, too. Same for Sword. Human name. Adept name. Strong name. Used to be."

"What do you mean, used to be?"

Martin wiggled his toes forward until they hung over the side of the wall. There was little wind. He pictured himself pushing off, hitting the support beam of the fire-escape walk on the opposite building fifteen feet away, swinging around once, then flipping down the outside of the building, window ledge to window ledge. It was the safest way down. He turned to Ja'Nette. He would miss her.

"Bad war," Martin said, lightly touching her face with the back of his hand. "All with Sword name die or 'chanted. Sword not name in First World anymore. Used to be. Bad to say now."

"Like, there was a Clan Sword?"

Martin shook his head. It wasn't Ja'Nette's fault she knew so little. She had been raised by humans. "Sword not clan name. Sword family name. Sword clan Pendragon." He checked the wind again. "Must go now Ja — "

"That's Sword's clan!" Ja'Nette shouted excitedly. She grabbed hold of Martin's arm and he almost lost his balance.

Martin pulled away from the girl. "Galen Sword not have clan. Galen Sword human."

"No, no, he's not!" Ja'Nette jumped up and down, clapping her hands. "Listen, Martin. Sword's always talking about when he was a little boy. He says he grew up in a clan. But he didn't have any powers or anything. So they made him go away. They made him forget everything. That's why he's doing this. He's trying to find his way back to his family."

Martin stared at the child for a moment. "Ja'Nette make joke again?"

"No way! This is straight. He says he's ... he's ... oh, poop, what was it ... ? Oh, yeah, 'heir to the Victor of the Clan Pendragon.' That's it."

Martin slapped his hands to his ears and shook his head. "Bad to joke," he warned Ja'Nette.

"I'm not joking, swear to God."

"Galen Sword say Heir to Victor?"

"All the time. He's like nuts about it, you know? He's got this recording he keeps playing with some guy telling him he was born heir to the Victor. You know what that means?"

"But Clan Pendragon elementals. Greater clan. Galen Sword human." The child must be insane. Or worse, Galen Sword was for telling such lies. The Shadow World was piled high with the bodies of humans who had tried to pass between the First and Second Worlds without invitation. Martin had heard the legends. No Swords remained within the First World. No Swords *could* remain.

But Ja'Nette kept up her tirade. "Of course he's like human. That's why they sent him away! Like he was a freak or something! They didn't think he was special, Martin. He was just ordinary to them. They didn't want him."

"Not possible," Martin said after a long silence. "Galen Sword human. That all."

"But what if he's like a shifter? What if he's in ... humanform or something? How could you tell if he was only a human or a humanform adept?"

"Shifter tell by smell." Martin scratched at his face. "But if smell 'chanted ... shifter not know. Wizard could tell. Maybe elemental. Maybe others."

"Come on, Martin! Come back with me and tell all this to Sword. He's dying to know this kinda junk."

"Galen Sword dead now," Martin said sadly. No, he was sure of it, there could be nothing to what Ja'Nette was saying, and there was nothing he could do for the human. He had to go now. Had to hide.

"But what if he's right, Martin? What if he *is* an adept? Then he could fight back against Dmitri, couldn't he? He'd have a chance!" Ja'Nette clutched at Martin's arm. "Give him a chance, Martin. Please. Sword's been nice to me. At least he's tried the best he can."

Martin felt the child's small hands grip him as if she were suddenly afraid he might leave her. He felt the safety of the night call him.

"Please don't go, Martin. Please don't."

Martin stood poised on the wall ledge, thinking thoughts more complex than he had ever tried before. What if there were a Sword of the First World still free? Could it make any difference after all this time?

He moaned in inner conflict. To stay was to enter the Second World — the world of sunlight and danger. To run was to embrace the safety of darkness — the security of the Shadow World.

"Don't leave me," Ja'Nette cried against him, and Martin, despite the risks he knew the decision would bring, realized that he could not.

He cradled her head, feeling her warm tears on his arm. "Little halfling sister. Martin not leave Ja'Nette."

"Really?" Ja'Nette asked, her dark face glistening.

"Really," Martin promised. He held her tight. "Ja'Nette come with Martin," he whispered to her.

And then he leapt from the roof, taking her with him into the night.

ELEVEN

Ko heard the tapping on her window and the first thought to come to her mind was, *Martin*. She had a second thought, too, and that made her reach for the taser shock prod she kept on her bedside table. Her apartment was on the third floor of a renovated Greenwich apartment building and none of the countermeasures she had installed could make her windows inaccessible to someone with a long enough rope or a tall enough ladder. But, once they had reached her windows, Ko felt confident any ordinary criminals would be unable to progress past that point. Unfortunately, since coming to work for Galen Sword, she had run into an inordinate number of criminals who were anything but ordinary.

The tapping came again. She heard someone whisper her name from outside the window. It was Ja'Nette. Ko replaced the shock prod and rolled out of her bed. The water mattress undulated behind her but the massive black Danish bed made no sound. Ko pulled a sheet off the bed, wrapped it around herself, then went to the window and peered between two of the vertical slats on the blind. Ja'Nette was pressed against the window. Behind her, apparently holding her up only by exerting outward force on the edges of the window, Martin bared his fangs, smiling.

But Ko made no move to unlock the window. "Are you all right, Ja'Nette?"

"As long as I don't look down. Are you going to let us in, or what?"

Satisfied that Martin wasn't using the child as a hostage, Ko unlatched the window and slid it up. Ja'Nette tumbled in with a whump of expelled breath and Martin followed gracefully. The old wooden floor didn't even creak under his broad bare feet.

"Couldn't you have opened the window?" Ko asked. "With your blue power."

"Need hand free for blue power," Martin explained, looking around Ko's bedroom, sniffing the air. "Why you not stay Loft?"

"Sword lives at the Loft." Ko scanned Ja'Nette, checking for any sign of injury. "I live here."

Martin nodded. It was the sort of answer he could accept.

"Have you been out with him all this time?" Ko asked Ja'Nette.

"Yes'm. We went to McDonalds for food and then Martin hoisted me up to a roof" — Ja'Nette looked at Martin with admiration — "he's real strong, isn't he? And we just kept talking after that."

"You were supposed to go back to the Loft."

"You're not there."

"That's different."

"I don't see how. Why do I always — "

"Ja'Nette tell Martin Galen Sword not human," Martin interrupted impatiently. "Ja'Nette tell Martin Galen Sword adept."

Ko looked from the girl to Martin. "Sword *thinks* his original family might have had some connection to ... an adept clan."

"Clan Pendragon," Martin said.

Ko nodded. "Is this important?"

"I'll say," Ja'Nette answered.

"Martin not know," Martin said. "Melody tell Martin now what Galen Sword say about family." He held a finger to his lips to silence Ja'Nette. "Ja'Nette say nothing now."

Ko looked at Martin with new respect. He was smart enough to compare sources without letting them influence each other. She did as he had asked. "Sword believes he has memories of being born into a family of adepts involved in the Clan Pendragon."

"How involved?" Martin asked.

Ko wiped her eyes free of sleep. "According to what his lawyer told him, Sword was born heir to the Victor of the Clan Pendragon. Is that what you mean?"

Martin turned to Ja'Nette. "Not make joke."

"Told you."

Ko pulled the sheet tighter around her. "Is this somehow important, Martin?"

Martin nodded slowly, his brown eyes wide, his mouth set in a tight line. "Most important thing Martin know. Most important thing in Worlds."

"Not now," Sword moaned.

"Look, this is important," Ko said. Her words were clipped and tense. "I'll even apologize for what I said last night." She peered into the darkness of Sword's room. He was sprawled on his futon cover, naked except for the bandages on his shoulders. His face was in shadow.

"I can't." Sword's voice was dry and rough. "And will you shut the door? The light ..."

Ko stepped farther into the room and pushed the door shut behind her. "Martin is frightened, Sword. I don't know if I can keep him here until tonight. Especially if he doesn't think you can help him."

"Help him," Sword rasped miserably. "Look at me. I can't move my damn arms. I can't see. My head is — "

"Oh, stow it! You've got a migraine. You always get migraines. But you're managing to talk to me so let me bring Martin up here so you can talk to him."

"I ... can't ... think straight," Sword said through clenched teeth.

"So what else is new," Ko complained under her breath. Then, more loudly, she added, "He knows about your family, Sword. He knows you're all supposed to be dead or ... bloody enchanted. There, I said the damn word 'enchanted,' okay? So you were right. You've always been right, okay? Now will you at least talk to him?" She heard Sword shift on the futon.

"Just ... don't ... yell ... anymore."

"Do I bring him up?"

"Bring ... him up," Sword whispered. Ko said nothing. "Something else?" he asked.

"Yeah." Ko opened the door wide enough to send light from the hall across Sword, making him twist his head into his pillow. "Put something on so you don't frighten Ja'Nette."

An hour later, Sword's room was silent except for the tapping of Ko's foot. Sword lay on his futon — under the covers this time — with a wet cloth over his eyes. Martin crouched on the tatami-covered floor, and Ko and Ja'Nette sat on chairs they had carried in from Sword's attached study. Forsyte was participating in the meeting through the intercom system. Every level of the Loft was accessible to his chair except for the split-off fourth level that separated Sword's quarters from Ja'Nette's bedroom and four other unused rooms.

"Shhh, Melody," Sword said quietly.

Ko flattened her foot against the floor, silencing it.

"Adrian," Sword said then, "based on everything Martin has told us, I can only see one way to move on this. How about you?"

Forsyte's voder came over the intercom. "ONE WAY. YES."

Ko could only see one way as well, but she refrained from saying it out loud. If Sword had thought Softwind was dangerous, how could he even consider this new option?

"I'm going to attend the Ceremony of the Change Arkady," Sword said with the voice of someone who had made an unalterable decision.

Martin popped up like a jack-in-the-box. "No no no," he chanted and patted his hands against his ears.

Sword grimaced at Martin's loud voice. "Calm down, Martin. It's the only way in."

"Gathering of the Clan for Arkady only. No humans."

"But I'm an adept, Martin. You admit that now yourself, don't you?"

"Galen Sword not have power. Galen Sword 'chanted. Soft soft 'chant good as human. Go to Ceremony good as dead."

"But you told Ja'Nette that shifters can't tell the difference between a humanform adept and a human. So, if I do go to the Ceremony, how will they know I'm not one of them?"

"Galen Sword not have Clan ring. Galen Sword not change."

"I'm going to leave before the change part, Martin. But I've got to talk to someone there. I've got to find out how to get in touch with Clan Pendragon."

Martin sat back on the floor, hugged his knees, and rocked. "No good no good no good," he said.

Sword sat up in his bed and the wet cloth fell from his eyes. They were red-tinged and ringed with dark circles. His skin was pale and cheeks sunken. But the full force of his voice was coming back.

"Stop that and listen to me," Sword said. "You told us there was a war among the clans. You said the Swords were defeated, that Clan Pendragon lost its supremacy and now none of the greater clans can stand against the lesser clans. You say there will be another war soon. A First World war that will spill out into the Second World. That war has to be stopped, doesn't it? Doesn't it?"

"Should be," Martin sighed, still rocking. "Can't be."

"My brother told me I had a destiny, that I had to fight and — "

"Bad destiny to fight," Martin said. "Not right destiny. Brother wrong."

Sword carefully edged back in his bed, trying not to use his arms. When he had moved far enough, he rested his head against the wall. "What is it going to take to convince you to tell me where the Ceremony of the Change Arkady is going to be held?"

Martin looked over at the man on the bed. "Say what?"

"Keep the sentences short, Sword," Ko advised.

Sword sighed. "You know where the Ceremony is going to be held, correct?"

"Yes," Martin said.

"I want you to tell me where."

"Martin won't."

"I know that, Martin. What I'm asking is what can I do that will make you tell me?"

Martin stopped rocking and slowly eased into a readiness crouch. "Galen Sword beat Martin?"

"No, I'm not going to beat you. I want you to *want* to tell me where the Ceremony is. I want you to *want* to help me. Do you understand, Martin?"

"No. Galen Sword go to Ceremony. Galen Sword die."

Ko couldn't stand the impasse any longer. She stood up and went to Martin. "Martin, you thought Dmitri was going to kill Sword, didn't you? But Dmitri didn't. He tried, but he couldn't."

"Still time," Martin said. "Dmitri Ronin."

"Martin," Sword said forthrightly, "why will I die if I go to the Ceremony?"

"Human always dies at Ceremony," Martin said, then immediately looked down at the floor.

"What human?" Ko asked, peering down at Martin's hunched shape.

"Oh, oh," Ja'Nette said. She got up from her chair and joined Ko. She patted Martin on his back. "Is there like, a tagged human at the Ceremony, Martin?"

Martin nodded his head.

Ja'Nette looked at Sword's and Ko's expectant faces. "He told me that the Arkady shifters hunt and ... eat humans. Humans that've been tagged as prey."

"Is that right, Martin?" Sword asked. "Is killing and eating a human part of the Ceremony?"

Martin nodded his head again.

"Bloody hell." Ko turned back to her chair and sat down to think. The situation was even worse than she'd imagined. Sword wouldn't just be in the presence of hundreds of werecreatures, they'd be werecreatures primed for human flesh. "Well, I guess that's that," she said with finality.

"What do you mean?" Sword asked.

"You can't go into that kind of a situation, Sword. Even you aren't that crazy."

But Sword just swung his long legs around and sat at the side of the futon frame without protest. Ko swore to herself. His headache was leaving. That meant there was tension coming back into his life. That meant he had an idea. Bloody hell again.

There was no hesitancy in Sword's tone now. "Martin, do elementals ever kill or eat humans?"

Martin stared at Sword and stuck out his tongue.

"He means no," Ja'Nette translated.

"So, it must be risky for shifters to kill humans, right? Big chance of being caught. Letting the Second World know that shifter adepts are around." Sword watched Martin nod again. "So I'm guessing that the elemental clans don't like it when Arkady has these ceremonies because humans die. Am I right?"

"Always bad," Martin agreed. "Council meetings. Many fights. Sometimes wars. But shifters must change. Have to."

"I understand that, Martin." Sword raised a hand to gesture in agreement, but let it fall again as Ko saw his shoulder go into a spasm. "But what I also understand is that the elemental clans, like Clan Pendragon, might be happy if the Ceremony were stopped. Somehow."

"Oh, no, Sword." Ko rose to her feet in alarm.

"Say what?" Martin asked.

Sword stood up. His covers fell from him. Ja'Nette giggled. Sword reached down for the covers, forgetting about his torn muscles, swore, then flopped back onto his futon, finally covering himself again.

"Good move, Sword," Ko said. "That's really convincing me you're up to this."

"All of us," Sword said faintly. Then he summoned enough strength to call out, "Are you with me on this, Adrian? We find out where the Ceremony is being held, we go to it, disrupt it, get them to put it off, let the Clans know that a Sword is back! What do you say?"

Ko put her head in her hands as Forsyte's voder answered, "MAKE THEM COME TO US. YES."

Ko moaned. "Sword, that's insane. You don't understand enough about how these people are organized. You don't understand what the repercussions might be. You don't — "

"Galen Sword not kill Arkady shifters?" Martin asked suddenly.

"I'll stop the Ceremony, rescue the sacrificial human, but I'm not out to kill anyone." Sword looked at Ko and added, "Or anything."

"Galen Sword do this to get Pendragon help?"

"It's my clan, Martin. I have to get back in touch with them."

Martin looked thoughtful. "Bad to stop Ceremony. Sometimes shifters stop halfway. Not change whole way." He shivered at whatever image he pictured.

Then Ja'Nette was beside him again, scratching the back of his neck behind his ears. "When you were getting ready to leave me this morning, you weren't going back to your enclave, were you?"

"No," Martin agreed.

"Because if you went back there, you said the keepers would tag you, right? Tag you, hunt you, and *eat* you, right?"

"Fight at Softwind. Bad to be with human."

"Bad for a shifter, maybe," Ja'Nette said. "But you're like me, remember, Martin? We're both half human, too. It's not bad for *you* to be with humans. And humans won't kill you." She rocked her head back and forth, considering what she said. "Well, these humans won't, at least. So it's okay to help us. It's okay to help Sword find his clan." She reached for his massive hands and squeezed them reassuringly. Her fingers could barely stretch around two of his. "It's all going to be okay." She looked up at him affectionately. "Hey, trust me, big bro. This is your little sister talking, remember?"

Martin stared into Ja'Nette's eyes and chewed on his lip. "Little halfling sister," he said. "Little halfling sister right."

Ko felt her stomach twist. This wasn't right at all. They still knew too little.

But Sword wouldn't be stopped. "So where is the Ceremony going to be held, Martin?"

Martin turned to Sword and took a deep breath. "American Museum of Natural History." He pronounced each word with such precision that he seemed to be speaking a foreign language.

"No way," Ja'Nette said.

"Yes way," Martin countered.

"But I go there on school trips! It's a regular place."

"Keepers say go there for Ceremony. That all Martin know."

"And the Ceremony's there in three days?" Sword asked.

"Three nights too," Martin added.

Ko didn't like the expression on Sword's face. "What are you getting at?"

"Nothing," Sword said. Ko hated it when he smiled that way. "I was just thinking it was too bad I threw out all my fancy clothes when I bought this place."

"You and your bloody tangents."

Sword got to his feet again, carefully, and this time remembered to hold onto his covers. "I'm not going off on a tangent, Melody. First of all, Martin's going to tell us how I can get a Clan ring for the evening, and then I'm going off to rent a tuxedo."

Ko could actually see the color coming back into Sword's face, masking the shadows, bringing life to his complexion. He grinned, with no sign of the migraine that had flattened him just over an hour ago. "It seems, my friends, that the one thing Martin hasn't told us is that the Ceremony of the Change Arkady is a black-tie affair. I read that in the newspaper." He laughed at the dismayed expressions he saw.

But Ko didn't find it all funny. Martin had the mind of a child, and she was certain there were many other things he hadn't told them. Things that were important.

And deadly.

TWELVE

The night called out to him and he embraced her, running free beneath the stars as he was born to do.

The cool night air raced past Martin's ears as he sped across the rooftops of the brownstones, effortlessly switching from pushing feet to swinging arms and back again, without sound or disturbance to any who lived beneath the roofs that were his path. His breath came in easy, regular lungfuls. He could count the number of cars and buses that passed below him simply by the smell of their exhaust. He knew which houses were occupied, which were empty, and which were the domain of Clan Arkady, his clan no longer.

It was still strange for Martin to find himself thinking in that way, but the truth of the thought was inarguable. He was a halfling and he could just as easily abandon Arkady for his other side. His human side. He reached a gap between a brownstone and an old apartment building and without pause deftly somersaulted twice in twenty feet to land like a spider on what seemed to be a smooth brick wall. But Martin knew that brick walls were never smooth, never without purchase, as long as one had the strength and the skill he had.

He scaled the featureless wall as expertly as an athlete climbing a rope, and when he had reached the roof, high over the city, the thrill of the hunt became overwhelming and he howled into the night-wind. Martin of no clan, that's how he travelled through this night, and the lack of affiliation did not frighten him. Because tonight he ran the shadows for Galen Sword, heir to the Victor of the Greater Clan Pendragon.

Martin called to the night and the night embraced him.

"Hey, Martin," Ko's voice crackled in his ear. "If that was you, you'd better keep it down. We heard it all the way to station two."

Martin shook his head at the sound of the radio transceiver Ko had given him. It was too small to fit snugly in his ear canal and he refused to wear it there anyway. At night, it was necessary to be able to hear everything that was around him. How else could he grab at posts and beams in utter darkness if he could not hear the wind blow around them? So Ko had taped the transceiver behind his ear and turned up the volume. It was annoying, but when Galen Sword's 'chant was lifted, Martin hoped Sword's power would enable him to talk mind-to-mind. That was much better than stupid radios that couldn't play top forty.

"Martin stay quiet." Martin felt foolish for speaking to himself.

"Just until we get him," Ja'Nette added. "Then you can howl all you want, right, Sword?"

"No unnecessary traffic," Sword answered.

"How come you just don't tell me to be quiet like you usually do?"

"Be quiet, Ja'Nette."

The girl's laughter over the radio made Martin's ear itch.

"You in position, Martin?" Sword asked.

"Soon," Martin answered, then leapt to the edge of the roof and raced along, inches from a fifteen-floor plunge.

When he reached the other side of the apartment building, he stopped to pick out the best way down, finally deciding to climb down ten floors along the building's corner, then flip backward into a tree which grew in a small patch of a garden behind one of the brownstones in the same row as the one they were all heading for. It would be fast and easy, except for the other thing Ko had done to him that night — made him wear clothes.

He thought about the clothes he had on for a few moments: another pair of Adrian's sweat pants and a black canvas equipment vest to which Ko had added an extra panel so he could fasten it over his chest. This time, he even had special equipment in it, just like the others. But he knew he couldn't climb down the building with all these cumbersome extra layers and bulges. That made the answer to his problem very easy. He would take everything off.

Martin rolled onto his back and wriggled out of the pants in a second. He fumbled with the zipper on the vest for a few moments, couldn't work it, so took a deep breath to expand his chest to its limit and used his fingers to rip the strained zipper out of its seams. The vest was off him in two seconds and he felt much better, except that the wire from his transceiver now was pulled tight between the back of his ear and the transmitter and battery unit in his vest pocket. Melody had said it was very important that everyone stay in touch with each other, so Martin found he had to stop and think again. It was a disruptive and delaying thing to have to do on a hunt, but he realized he had no choice. At least when he did think, he knew he did it well. It must be his human side, he decided. Perhaps it was good for something.

Within two minutes, Martin had removed the transmitter from the vest and taped it against his chest with long wide strips of the thick gray tape which Ko had said was good for keeping glass quiet when a window had to be broken open. With his blue power, Martin didn't understand why they might think he would ever have to break a window to get through it, but since everyone else carried the tape, he had agreed to take it, too.

"How's it going, Martin?" Sword asked.

"How what go where?" Martin asked. Sword was clever, Martin knew, but he couldn't talk as sensibly as the keepers could.

"Are you in position, Martin?" Ko asked.

"Soon soon," Martin said testily, then naked at last, he slipped headfirst over the edge of the building and began to climb straight down, thankful that the time for thought had passed.

Ko watched the brownstone that Martin had identified as their target. The lights were still out. Maybe they had missed him. Ko hoped so. Beside her in the van, Ja'Nette yawned.

"Look," Ko said without turning to the child, "when this guy comes — *if* this guy comes — why don't you just stay in the van?"

"No way." Ja'Nette was indignant at the suggestion.

"It's not safe. And this isn't a game anymore."

Ja'Nette sat up straight in the passenger seat. "The guy's going to be in humanform, Melody. The four of us can handle him." She took Ko's hand from the steering wheel and held it. "Besides, I'm not afraid."

"That's my point," Ko said, squeezing Ja'Nette's hand in return. "We've been running around like this for more than a year and nothing's happened. So now, when something finally is happening, we're not treating it any differently. Maybe someone should be afraid."

Ja'Nette smiled and her expression was so pure and her face so young, that Ko had to fight an incredibly strong impulse to just hug the child and drive away from Sword and the city as fast as the van could travel. But, unfortunately, she knew that wouldn't solve anything.

"Melody, you're real smart, Martin's real strong, Sword can get everything we need, and I can punch out anybody's lights from fifty feet away. We're a great team. What's there to be afraid of?"

Ko looked into Ja'Nette's eyes, sorry to say what she knew must be said. "Adrian."

Ja'Nette's smile faded. "Oh, yeah. They made him that way, didn't they?"

"And he's probably one of the smartest people in the world."

The silence in the van was finally broken by Sword's voice over the radio link. "Target approaching from station one. Are you in position, Martin?"

Ko peered down the street and saw a lone figure walking along the sidewalk on the opposite side, passing steadily from one streetlamp's pool of light to another.

"Martin in position," Martin broadcast.

"I'll be careful, Melody," Ja'Nette said, also catching sight of the target and crossing her arms over her chest, preparing to send out her power. "But I'm part of the team, too. And maybe what we find out can help Adrian."

Without taking her eyes from the figure coming closer, Ko released the restraining tab on the rifle between the seats and reached for the door handle. "That's the only reason I'm here," she said.

It was time to go to work.

Galen Sword felt wondrously alive. The cool of the night air was electric to him. Even his shoulders didn't ache as they had just an hour ago. He was close, he knew. He would not lose again.

The man who had turned the corner, heading for the brownstone where Martin said he lived, was Saul Calder, and he was exactly as Martin had laboriously described: five-and-half-feet tall, barrel-chested, thick dark beard and long bushy hair, with a bow-legged gait which was almost a waddle. His shifterform, Martin had said, was a bear. Or something close to a bear. Forsyte was busy back at the Loft, still analyzing Martin's blood samples and trying to formulate a new theory of DNA which might explain how the whole shifter phenomenon could be real. But Sword didn't think about the science. He didn't think about Ko's caution or Ja'Nette's age. Tonight, he thought only about winning.

He felt the familiar vibration from his locator band as Ko sent a silent signal. She and Ja'Nette were ready. Sword took a breath and climbed out of his Porsche. He pulled the transceiver from his ear and slipped it into a pocket so it wouldn't alarm Calder. Then he tugged down on the equipment vest he wore beneath his long black leather coat and began walking quickly after the man. *The adept*, he corrected himself. His ticket to the Ceremony of the Change Arkady.

The adept slowed his pace as Sword's footsteps clicked loudly on the deserted street. He turned to see who had joined him in the night. For a moment, Sword thought he saw the adept's eyes glow, though he knew it could only be a sudden reflection from the overhead streetlight.

"Hey!" Sword shouted, his voice echoing down the street. "Hey, Arkady!"

Calder stopped in midstride and slowly turned. He had been carrying a white plastic shopping bag in both arms but now lowered it to his left side, freeing his right hand.

Sword caught up to the adept, whose eyes were completely hidden in the dark shadow cast by his thick, furrowed brow. "We have to talk," Sword said.

"I don't know you," Calder replied. His voice was surprisingly high-pitched. His accent, midwestern neutral.

"It's a big clan," Sword said, extending his hand.

Almost in reflex, the adept began to lift his hand to take Sword's. But he hesitated, and Sword could see him tensing, preparing for action.

Then Sword made a fist and Calder relaxed. He continued bringing his hand up to brush knuckles with Sword and a brief smile flickered on his face as he saw how small and tight a fist Sword made, acknowledging who had more status. "Adrian Ko," Sword introduced himself. "I'm new in town and the keepers said I should talk to you about a few things."

"Which keepers?" The adept wasn't as tense as before, but there was still suspicion in him.

"John and Brenda." Sword used the names Martin had given him.

"And what things are we to talk about?"

"The halfling, Martin, has gone rogue."

Calder laughed. "Halflings are rogue by birth."

"But you heard about the fight in Softwind? Martin was there with a ... human. Talking about the Ceremony, Dmitri reported."

The adept passed his shopping bag from one hand to another and glanced over Sword's shoulder. At last Sword saw the glimmer of gold he had been looking for on Calder's left hand — his clan ring.

"What does that have to do with me? Or with you?" the adept asked.

"Martin is to be tagged."

With that, Calder relaxed completely. "I've been telling John and Brenda that for the past two Changes." He checked out the street again, then nodded at Sword. "Come in with me, Adrian. We shouldn't be talking on the street."

"Of course," Sword said, and fell into step behind Calder as he walked up the stone steps leading to the adept's front porch. Sword was surprised to see that Calder had not locked his door. "Is that wise?" he asked, trying to determine if there might be protective enchantments at work which Martin hadn't known about. "I mean, in this neighborhood?"

Calder turned to Sword and tilted his head as if trying to understand the question. "It's quite all right, Adrian," Calder said with a smile. "My mate is home. And she's in shifterform." He pushed the door open and gestured for Sword to step through.

"I'm back, dear," he called out. "And we have company."

Ignoring the sudden pounding of his heart, Sword had no choice but to step into the shifter's home.

"Oh, shit," Ko swore as she watched Sword go through Calder's front door and the lights in the brownstone come on. She held her hand to her transceiver and spoke quickly. "Martin! Did you hear that? You didn't tell us Calder had a mate!"

Martin's voice was broken up as he answered over the link. "Galen Sword not supposed go inside. Galen Sword take ring outside. That plan."

"It's not the bloody plan now." Ko swore again, wishing that Adrian were in the loop this evening. But he was intent on completing the DNA-match comparisons on Martin's blood and had said that he would only be as far away as the radio link.

Ja'Nette tugged on Ko's arm. "What do we do, Melody?"

"A moment, Ja'Nette, give me a moment." Ko's hands were like ice on her weapon; even in the cold night air she preferred to go sleeveless for easy movement and handling of her rifle. Her mind raced with the possibilities. Of course Sword couldn't have gone through with the plan to attack Calder on his front porch, stunning him long enough to drag him back to the van to slip off his clan ring. Not even Sword would risk that kind of action knowing a changed shifter waited on the other side of an unlocked door.

"Martin," Ko said into her transceiver, "do you know what his mate's shifterform is?"

"*Tagonii*," Martin answered. "No human word. Small like Martin. But lots fangs."

"Will the silver work?"

"Silver always work on Arkady," Martin answered. "Keep away from Martin."

"I know, I know."

Ja'Nette hopped from foot to foot. "We gotta do something, Melody."

Ko nodded. There was no time to find a perfect plan. She would have to go with the first thing that had come to mind. "Martin, I'm going to go ring the doorbell. I'm expecting Calder to come to the door and I'll take him out with the spray. When I do that, I'll shout and you go in the back, get Sword, and drag him out." Ko looked down at Ja'Nette. "I'll stay by the front door to split their attention. You're watching my back from the sidewalk. No closer, understand?"

"Yes'm," Ja'Nette promised.

"On your mark, Martin. I'm crossing over."

Ko slung the rifle over her shoulder, barrel down, hoping to keep it unobtrusive, then jogged across the empty street, checking to be sure that Ja'Nette was maintaining a safe distance behind. As she climbed the stone steps to Calder's front door, she slipped a slim metal aerosol can of silver halide spray-on photo emulsion from her vest. *So much for the ozone layer,* she thought. Then she grabbed the thick metal knocker in her hand and pounded against the door.

There was an intercom box by the door frame and she cursed silently as it suddenly clicked on. This wasn't going to be easy. "Who is it?" It was Calder's voice.

"Melody Ko," she blurted, making it up as she went along. "I've got to see my brother. The halfling's gone to the ... the New York *Times*. They're sending a photographer to the museum on Friday night. Let me in!"

Whatever unknown language Calder spoke in next, Ko could recognize oaths when she heard them. She heard what sounded like rapid footsteps from behind the door. Then the lock clicked and the door swung inward.

"Hurry, hurry," a low voice urged, but Ko saw no one standing in front of her. Then she saw a hand with improbably long fingers on it grasping the door handle and the lanky arm attached to the hand trailed *up,* toward the ceiling. Ko followed the arm, watching as it changed over the four feet of its length from being covered with dark skin to being covered with long black fur. Then she saw what the arm was attached to. *Tagonii.*

Like an orangutan, the creature's body was small and round and compact, and branched into four long limbs, each indistinguishable from the other. The *tagonii*'s arms and legs were all four feet long, and ended in grotesquely-stretched grasping appendages. An identical hand and foot clutched at a rope web strung against the ceiling and the other two limbs dangled down, one resting on the door. Ko fearlessly stared into the creature's eyes — its most human feature — spaced far apart in a flattened head ringed with an outward spray of stiff black fur. The creature blinked at her and opened its mouth. Ko didn't know which surprised her more — the fact that the creature wore bright red lipstick or that every tooth in her mouth was a wickedly sharp, inch-long fang.

"Is something wrong, my dear?" the *tagonii* asked.

"Not at all," Ko said evenly, then brought up the aerosol can and sprayed a mist of silver into the creature's face.

The *tagonii*'s shriek of pain drowned out Ko's shouted signal to Martin. The small fur-covered body snapped up against the ceiling as its limbs contracted, trying to escape, but Ko charged forward into the front hall, spraying madly over her head.

Suddenly, a high-pitched voice bleated beside her and Ko wheeled to see Calder standing in a doorway, staring in shock at the attack on his mate. Sword appeared behind the adept and brought both hands down on his neck, then up against his ears. Calder dropped stunned to his knees.

Sword glanced up at Ko. "Good work, I was getting — *look out!*"

But it was too late. The *tagonii* had unfolded her limbs and snapped down from the ceiling web directly on top of Ko. Ko crashed to the floor, feeling the solid weight of the creature as she crawled over Ko, angling her head to align with Ko's. Then the creature's face appeared above her. Half of it was swollen with pulsating red blisters where the silver spray had made contact, with more lesions bubbling up as Ko watched. The *tagonii* howled in pain and rage. Her fangs clicked open and shut, sounding like knife blades sharpening, as thick ropes of saliva dripped down on Ko's face.

Ko tried to shake the creature from her, but the *tagonii* was even heavier than Martin. There would be no escape by mere physical force.

"*Die!*" the *tagonii* screeched as her wet and flashing fangs descended for Ko's throat. But Ko would not give up. Even as she shrank back from the *tagonii*'s open mouth, she concentrated on removing a concussion grenade from her vest to detonate it behind the creature's back, coolly estimating the odds of the *tagonii's* thick body protecting her from the blast. If only she could last through the grenade's five-second delay.

And then the spray of fur that ringed the *tagonii's* ruined face suddenly folded in on itself like a flower closing, covering the creature's mad eyes like a mask. The *tagonii's* ears snapped out from the side of her head, stretched painfully from her skull by a pair of translocated hands. The *tagonii* screeched again, even louder than before.

"More, Ja'Nette! More!" Ko shouted as she pulled the concussion grenade from her vest.

The *tagonii's* head began to shake from side to side as the swollen lesions were suddenly pummeled by child-sized invisible fists. The creature could take no more. She abruptly launched herself straight into the air by flexing her limbs, hit the floor, and rolled backward in a ball, howling in agony from both the spray and Ja'Nette's attack.

Like a gymnast, Ko sprang straight from her back to her feet, grenade held ready in her hand, just in time to see Calder reaching out to his mate from the floor. "My darling," he called to her. "My darling ... " Then Sword's foot connected with Calder's rib cage and the adept went down again, curling up like a baby.

For a moment, there was silence in the front hall, and then came the sound of Ja'Nette slumping to her knees on the porch and vomiting everything she had eaten in the last four hours.

In the corner of the hall, the *tagonii* wheezed harshly, and unfurled one long arm across the floor to brush her fingers against the limp hand of her mate. She wheezed again, trying to talk, but nothing more came out. Her body settled without a sound. Ko returned the grenade to her vest.

"Dead?" Sword asked, standing behind Calder's unconscious body.

Ko unslung her gun and used the barrel to poke at the dark fur of the balled-up creature. There was no resistance. The tagonii's face was a mass of harsh red blisters. "Dead," Ko said. "Anaphylactic shock. Adrian was right."

Calder moaned and rolled his head on the floor, trying to get up. "Simone," he whispered. "Simone ... " He collapsed and lay silent.

Sword bent down to take the adept's gold ring.

Ko frowned. "Sword, before you start looting the dead, you want to tell me how we're going to handle this now? It's a lot more complicated than we planned."

Sword held the gold ring up to examine it. It appeared to be a plain gold band, a half-inch wide. "Engraving on the inside," Sword said, peering at the ring as he stood up. "And how's it more complicated?" He slipped it into his coat pocket.

"Holy cow," Ja'Nette gasped from where she knelt on the porch.

Ko and Sword turned to the girl but she pointed a trembling finger inside the house. "Not m-me ... look at *her*."

In a darkened corner of the front hall of a Manhattan brownstone, the *tagonii* underwent her final Change.

Ko immediately slipped a half-frame Olympus from her vest, snapped out its flash unit, and told Sword to do the same. Then she held the camera to her eye and started the motordrive, clicking off an entire roll of film. But Sword stood motionless, watching wordlessly. "Come on, Sword," Ko urged. "Adrian's going to need this. Ja'Nette, get Sword's camera."

A few seconds later, lit by the double strobelike flashes from the two whirring cameras, the *tagonii* seemed to jump from stage to stage in its transformation back to humanform. First, the arms and legs twitched in closer to the body, shrinking in length as the torso and the head stretched out. Ko could hear liquid crunching sounds as she saw bones rearrange their shapes beneath the body's black skin, now gleaming and exposed as the dark fur slipped back into the epidermal layers.

The blank, staring eyes of the creature moved slowly closer together as the skull reshaped itself. The red lipstick grew more vivid as the lips it was painted on shrank back to smaller, more human size. Breasts grew from the narrow ribcage. Claws shrank back into ordinary fingernails.

"Just like Greece," Sword said softly.

At last the transformation ended. The body of a naked black woman lay in the corner of the hallway. A thin gold chain hung around her neck, and from it dangled the gold band of her clan ring. Ko took the last picture on the roll. Unlike the legends, there was no last smile of relief or release on the woman's still face. Only a dying grimace of agonizing pain.

"Shouldn't we cover her up or something?" Ja'Nette said, voice shaking.

"Wait outside," Sword told her.

"Not in this neighborhood," Ko protested. She held out her hand to the child and hugged her as Ja'Nette wrapped her small arms around Ko's waist. "Shut the front door, Sword."

"Why don't we just go?" Sword asked. "We have the ring."

Ko held Ja'Nette tightly to her. "In case you haven't noticed, what we don't have is Martin."

All of the ceilings in the brownstone were covered in heavy rope netting, but other than that, each room was normal. Except for the kitchen.

Sword went into the unlit room first, silver halide spray can held ready. Ko followed and had Ja'Nette walk in front of her so the child would be protected by an adult, front and back. Ja'Nette walked stiffly and Ko knew that the attack the girl had unleashed on the *tagonii* was probably the most violent use of her power she had ever attempted. Forsyte had warned that Ja'Nette was close to forming ulcers as it was. Who knew what other damage she might be inflicting on herself?

"There's a red light above the back door," Sword said over his shoulder as he peered through the kitchen door. From the layout of the brownstone, Ko had determined that the kitchen should have a door that would open out onto a small garden or patio deck. It would have been the best way in for Martin, if he had made it that far.

"Any other lights?" Ko asked. "Any sign of broken glass?"

"Or children?" Ja'Nette added.

Ko tensed. She hadn't thought of that.

"*Nada,*" Sword said. "I'm going to try to find the light switch ... got it." Light flooded through the door as the ceiling-light fixtures blazed on through the rope web. "It's empty," Sword announced, and stepped into the room.

Ko entered behind Ja'Nette and found Sword staring at the red light shimmering above the door leading outside. It didn't appear to be an ordinary light fixture. It seemed to be a circular brass shelf, only a few inches across, nailed above the transom and holding a ...

"That's a crystal!" Sword said. "That's one of those red crystals like the one Tantoo had in her hand at Softwind." He walked over to the door and reached up to the small shelf over it.

"Is it safe to touch?" Ko asked. She kept one hand on her rifle, the other held Ja'Nette's hand.

Sword waved his hand close to the red glow. "Doesn't seem to be any heat coming from it." He tapped a finger to the crystal and its light momentarily wavered. "No shock or anything." Then he snatched it from the shelf and its light faded out completely in his hand.

Before Sword could say anything more, there was a loud thud from outside the door, then a flash of blue light from both the doorknob and deadbolt lock. The door swung open and Martin bounced in.

"Martin, what happened?" Sword asked.

"Martin, what happened to your clothes?" Ja'Nette snickered.

Martin looked around self-consciously, then hopped up to crouch on a countertop. "Door 'chanted." He looked down at his hands. "Try blue power on door but 'chant coldblast Martin."

Sword held out the red crystal, now dark and dull. It was small, about the size of a pea and cut in an irregular pattern of facets. "Could this have caused the enchantment?" Sword asked Martin. "It was glowing up on that shelf there." He pointed to the brass circle above the door.

Martin took the crystal from Sword's hand and studied it closely, even sniffed it. "Good five whole," he said. "Martin lucky glitter run out or Martin be coldblasted till Saul Calder lift 'chant." He shook his head. "Loud 'chant too. Not even soft. Martin stupid." He handed the crystal back to Sword. "Where Saul Calder?"

"Tied up in the living room," Sword said. "Simone's dead."

Martin looked grim. "Simone Calder change to humanform?"

"Yes," Sword said.

"Then Simone Calder dead." Martin nodded gravely. "Now Galen Sword must kill Saul Calder."

THIRTEEN

Forsyte stared in rapt attention as the digitized images of Simone Calder's post mortem shapeshift appeared on the large screen in the Loft's main lab. Only the knowledge that Ko herself claimed these photographs represented exactly what she had seen occur, and Forsyte's own familiarity with the bizarre world of quantum physics where matter and energy could be created out of nothingness without regard for cause and effect, enabled his rigid, scientific mind to accept what he saw as real. He blinked again and the signal created by the interruption of the tiny laser beams reflecting from his eyes instructed the Cray-Hitachi II in the basement to display the next picture.

"I wish I had had a video camera," Ko said as she stood beside Forsyte, watching the pictures with him.

Forsyte's two fingers pecked madly at his keypad as he spelled out his own wish list. "MICROSCOPE. BLOOD SAMPLES. TISSUE CULTURES. BONE FRAGMENTS," his voder recited. "DISAPPEARING MASS. WHERE DID THE EXTRA MOLECULES GO? WHERE DO THEY COME FROM WHEN THE CHANGE GOES THE OTHER WAY?"

Ko patted Forsyte's hand. "Next time, Adrian."

Forsyte glanced up and caught her eye. He made a crooked smile for her. "SO MUCH FOR DNA," his voder said. Ko laughed and went back to the workbench where Sword and Martin studied Calder's ring.

Forsyte cycled through the rest of the images, then instructed the computer to construct in-between frames estimating the rate of body-tissue change between pictures, assuming that the motordrives of both cameras had been operating at a constant speed. With so much mass and energy being absorbed by the body in so short a time, Forsyte was convinced that the excess heat that must have been generated couldn't have instantly evaporated into nothingness. It would have to have been stored somewhere for gradual release. But before he could even begin to flesh out the equations for describing such a heatsink, he would have to have a much more precise idea of the rate at which mass had been disappearing from Simone Calder's body as it changed from *tagonii* to human.

The Cray-Hitachi flashed a dialog box on the main screen that effectively said it would get back to Forsyte when it had finished, without offering any estimate of how long the calculations would take. Forsyte sighed, blinked an acknowledgement, then directed his chair to take him to the workbench.

"PROPER RING?" Forsyte had his voder ask as he rolled into position beside Ko.

"Plain on outside," Martin said. "So no one notice."

"All the inscriptions are on the inside," Sword added. He turned away from the large, self-lit magnifying glass and the jeweler's clamp that held the ring to show his sketchpad to the scientist. Forsyte was impressed by Sword's efforts. It was apparent that even if Sword had never given anything except money to the study of archaeology, it was clear that archaeology had taught him the value of meticulous detail when it came to drawing representations of unusual artifacts.

"RECOGNIZE THE SCRIPT?" Forsyte's voder asked as the scientist studied the curlicues and flowing lines of what was obviously a written language, but unlike any he had ever seen.

"If I close my eyes and squint," Sword said, "I'd guess some early form of Arabic script. But none of the letterforms conform to anything I know. It's not even like the letters I remember seeing on that family album I used to read when I was a child."

"CAN MARTIN READ IT?" the voder asked.

"Martin only know Arkady marks," Martin said.

JUDITH & GARFIELD REEVES-STEVENS

Sword held his pencil under a section of the reproduced script which he had darkened with shading. "From here to here," he indicated. "That's what Martin reads as 'Arkady.' He thinks the rest of the script would show Calder's family names, Clan descent, and words to describe his shifterform."

"Martin think," Martin added. "Martin not have ring. Martin not know."

Forsyte would have frowned if he could. "TOO BAD," he punched out.

Forsyte felt a surge of frustration as Sword looked at him without understanding what his comment had meant. But Ko leaned forward before the scientist began to type in a long explanation. She was in tune with him and understood his sometimes cryptic shorthand. "Adrian's worried that you won't be able to wear the ring on Friday," she said. "It might not have the right words to describe you, or someone might recognize it as not belonging to you." She looked into Forsyte's eyes. "Is that right?"

Forsyte blinked once for yes. Sometimes, when Ko's insight brought even a few seconds of relief to the struggle he faced trying to communicate his thoughts, Forsyte could feel tears of gratitude fill his eyes. He still wanted an end to this struggle but now that the team this close to the shifter phenomenon, suicide no longer seemed a necessary alternative. Who knew what unsuspected knowledge might lie waiting for them in the next few days?

"Martin says I can only get away with wearing the ring until the Ceremony actually begins," Sword said. "Then there's some sort of formal roll call and I wouldn't be able to respond correctly."

"So you'll have to disrupt the Ceremony before it actually begins," Ko concluded.

"That's the plan. Apparently there will be representatives of other aligned clans present — "

"Including Pendragon?" Ko asked.

Martin tapped his fists together, knuckles to knuckles, then quickly pulled them apart. "Arkady Pendragon apart in Council."

"Not friendly with each other," Sword translated. "But word will get out through the other representatives. Martin says they all get together from time to time." He turned to Martin to check his explanation. "A Gathering is one clan meeting with all its families. A Grand Gathering is more than one clan meeting together. And the Council is like a ... United Nations or something. Representatives of all the clans meet together to try and resolve any differences, but never really accomplish much. Correct?"

Martin nodded.

"If they never accomplish anything," Ko said, "then they really are like the United Nations. So where do they hold this Council?"

Martin shrugged. "Martin never go. North Shore? South Shore? Martin not know."

"Where we are is what the adepts call the North Shore," Sword explained before Ko could ask. "It includes all of New York City and Martin doesn't know how much more."

"Have you showed him maps?" Ko asked.

Sword nodded, then said to Martin, "Tell Melody what you told me about the maps I showed you."

Martin bit his lip as he tried to remember. "Martin know maps. Martin see many maps. Martin good with maps. Galen Sword show Martin bad maps. Martin not know."

"I don't get it," Ko said.

"Martin knows how the city is laid out. He had no trouble guiding us through the streets to Softwind, remember? But when I show him a standard map of New York City, and show him where we are, where your place is, where Calder's brownstone is, even where he took us to Softwind, Martin says it's all wrong. It doesn't make any sense. Doesn't look like any map he's ever seen."

"Martin, can you draw a map of the city the way you know it?" Ko asked.

Martin looked away and Ko recognized the action as a sign that Martin felt embarrassed. "Martin not know read write."

"I've already talked to him about it," Sword said. "Writing and map drawing seem to be the same skill where he comes from. He doesn't have either."

"Oh," Ko said.

Forsyte couldn't take the frustration any longer. He liked Martin, in addition to being professionally fascinated by him, but Martin was no longer their only entry into the First World. He tapped his fingers against his keypad and everyone turned expectantly to him, waiting for the voder to speak. "WHAT ABOUT SAUL CALDER?"

"He didn't tell us anything in the van coming back here," Ko said. "All he did was growl at Sword and curse him to a thousand deaths. Stuff like that."

"Saul Calder not elemental," Martin said with relief. "Good thing."

"MATE DEAD" Forsyte punched out. "UNDERSTAND."

"I know you do." The understanding was rich within Ko's eyes again.

"But there's no way Calder can get out of the holding cell."

Forsyte fought against the memories coming back. He needed distraction. "SEE THE BODY NOW?" his voder asked.

Ko frowned and crossed her arms. "Did you call your lawyer, Sword?"

Sword shook his head. "What am I going to say, Melody? We've already been through this."

"There's a dead woman in the van, Sword. How about you start with that?"

Sword stood up from the workbench and Forsyte felt a sudden pang of envy at the quick movement. "That's not the body of a woman. It's the body of a dead shifter in humanform. I don't think we're going to find any federal or state statutes concerning the deaths of were-wolves. We've got nothing to gain by — "

"But we have everything to lose!" Ko slapped her hand on the workbench and the jeweler's clamp and a mug full of pencils jumped in response. "You're not thinking through the full implications of what we did tonight. Saul Calder was passing as *human*, get it? He either rented or owned that brownstone. He paid taxes on it. He went shopping in the neighborhood. Remember the shopping bag he had? And he probably gets mail there. Maybe even has a job."

"What's the point, Melody?"

"The point is that all of a sudden, Calder's vanished. Poof! Gone like magic. He's — "

"Not like magic," Martin interrupted. "Magic make — "

"Not now, Martin," Ko said curtly. "The point is that as far as New York is concerned, a human being is missing. In a couple of days, the police are going to come calling at his place, break down the door, and find evidence of a struggle."

"So?"

"So our van with 'Sword Foundation' plastered all over it was parked there for two hours tonight. Your bloody Porsche was sticking out like a sore thumb up the street, and we made enough noise fighting with Calder's mate that even if no one called the police they're sure as hell going to remember it when the police poll the neighbors."

"That's back there," Sword said and Forsyte readily detected the irritation in his voice. "We're here. Miles away."

"And what if the police track down a black van and a black Porsche 928S4 or whatever the hell it is to this address? There's a kidnap victim drugged into unconsciousness downstairs and there's a body leaking all sorts of forensics evidence wrapped up in the van. The police won't care what she *was*, Sword. They'll only care what she is — a bloody dead human being."

"All right, all right. I'll get rid of the body, Melody. And I'll buy a new van."

Ko rolled her eyes. "Oh, good thinking, Sword, that won't make the police suspicious at all."

"What do you want me to *do*?" Now Sword had given up any semblance of trying to remain in control of himself. "Call up Trank and turn myself in?"

"No! I'm trying to get you to prevent that! Use your bloody head and your bloody money and call a lawyer and get ready for when Trank calls *you!*" Ko turned her back on Sword. "God, no wonder they kicked you out of the clan, Sword. You're a moron!"

One of the benefits of his present condition, Forsyte suddenly realized, was that he didn't have to worry about trying to hide his laughter. It couldn't come out in any event, no matter how much he felt like laughing. And he felt like it now. He was sorry to see those two dark splotches appear on Ko's cheeks, but he enjoyed watching Sword's face redden with exasperation, especially in reaction to someone he couldn't fire without risking losing Forsyte's own services.

Sword slammed his sketchpad down on the table, knocking over the pencil mug. "Well, excuse me, Ms. Ko, but I've never fought a *tagonii* before so maybe I'm not up on the proper etiquette."

"Well, I've never killed anyone before!" Forsyte heard Ko choke as she turned and headed for the street-level stairway, leaving the rest of them in silence.

After the sound of Ko's feet on the metal staircase died out, Forsyte heard the sound of the van's back doors clanging open in the parking area. Martin kept his head down and idly reached over to gather up the spilled pencils and place them back in the mug.

Sword stood quiet for a moment, then looked at Forsyte. "Do you suppose that's why she's ... you know?" He looked stricken.

Forsyte knew it for a fact. "LET ME," he punched out on his voder, then instructed his chair to take him to the lift and the woman who shared his thoughts.

Ko stood at the open back door of the van and stared at the shapeless mound of black plastic sheeting that lay there, across the metal tracks designed for holding Forsyte's chair. In that gleaming darkness lay the body they had wrapped within it. And no matter what else it had been, it was now, in death, Simone Calder, mate to Saul, whom Saul had called his darling.

And Ko had killed her. She fought the tears she felt, trying to ignore what was in front of her, trying to shut out all the sounds of the hateful Loft, anything at all that reminded her of Sword. She wanted to leave, to run away, to have nothing more to do with him and his obsession. But she couldn't leave Forsyte. And she couldn't abandon Ja'Nette. Not to Galen Sword.

"SHE TRIED TO KILL YOU," Forsyte's voder announced behind her.

Ko hadn't been aware of the hum of his chair or the soft ripping noise of its treads coming up behind her from the lift, but she wasn't startled by his presence. She needed a friend now. She had wanted someone to come to her. Even Forsyte.

"I know," Ko said without turning, and without any sense of accepting it as the truth.

Forsyte rolled to a stop beside her, also staring into the back of the van. In the shadows of the Loft's garage, broken only by the shafts of light that shone through the grids of the crisscrossing metal stairs and open catwalks, the lasers within Forsyte's wide glasses turned his eyes into glowing red dots.

"WOULD YOU HAVE KILLED A BEAR IF IT HAD ATTACKED YOU?" the voder asked.

"I would have tried to frighten it away first."

"BUT WOULD YOU HAVE KILLED IT? IF YOU HAD TO?" The mechanical voice echoed eerily in the garage.

"If I had to. I didn't have to kill Simone, though."

There was no silence between their words to each other. The pauses were filled by the quick clicking of keys as Forsyte typed in his next response.

"DID YOU KNOW YOU WOULD KILL HER?"

"Martin told us silver could kill any shifter."

"SILVER BULLETS," the voder said. "SILVER BLADES. I DID NOT THINK HALIDE SPRAY WOULD BE AS TRAUMATIC."

Ko sighed. "The point is, it was."

"THEN WHY NOT BLAME ME?"

Ko knew the answer to that, but how could she tell him what the truth of it was? How she felt about him? If it was possible to torture him even more than he was being tortured now, she didn't want to know.

"THEN WHY NOT BLAME ME?" the voder repeated.

"Because I was there and you weren't. Because I did it and you didn't." She felt angry tears stream down her face. She had taken a life.

"I WOULD HAVE DONE IT," the voder said.

Ko turned to him and took his hand. "Oh, no," she said, "not you Adrian. Never you, my — "

"Why Melody cry?" Martin asked from above.

Ko looked up, startled by Martin's presence as she hadn't been by Forsyte's. The halfling hung ten feet above the van like a trapeze artist, upside down from an iron support beam that spanned the parking area.

"I killed Simone Calder," Ko stated, as if saying it to herself as well as to Martin.

Martin swung back and forth a few times, then dropped from the beam, flipped over once, and landed with only a gentle sound of impact beside Forsyte's chair. He peeked inside the van and sniffed the air.

"Simone Calder *tagonii*." Martin said. "Simone Calder Arkady shifter. Arkady shifter kill humans. Human kill Arkady shifter. First time."

"It's wrong to kill, Martin. That's what I believe."

Martin watched the lights flicker on the small computer display screen on the left arm of Forsyte's chair. He pushed out his lips. "Melody want to kill Simone Calder?"

"No," Ko said truthfully.

"Martin believe wrong *want* to kill. Sometimes *have* to. Difference."

"This wasn't an accident, Martin. Killing a person is killing a person. That's all there is to it."

Martin stretched his arm over Forsyte's chair and brushed the back of his hand against Ko's arm. "No no. Melody wrong." He hopped into the van and its suspension creaked beneath his mass. "Simone Calder Arkady shifter." He reached out for an edge of the black plastic sheet. "Simone Calder *tagonii* shifterform." He looked back at Ko, both hands gripping the sheet, and made his eyes big and round. "Powerful Arkady shifter." He began to pull the bundle forward, unrolling it open.

"Please don't, Martin. I ... I can't, please."

"Powerful *old* Arkady shifter," Martin said gravely as he snapped the plastic sheeting into the air, and it rose as if there were nothing hidden within it.

Ko stepped back in surprise as the sheet billowed out to her like a black wave. She tensed as she expected to see the limp arms and legs and staring eyes of the woman she had killed flop out at her, accusing her, marking her.

But there were no arms or legs or staring eyes. No body at all. Only a gentle white dust that puffed out like pale smoke, dissipating even as it fell from the air.

"Old old old Arkady shifter." Martin let the empty plastic fall from his hands.

Ko turned to Forsyte to seek confirmation of what she had seen. Galen Sword stood silently behind him.

She looked up to Sword, seeking understanding. But all she saw was his hand reach out to grasp at the indistinct white cloud that was all that remained of the dead *tagonii*. And all she was aware of was the fascinated smile on Sword's face.

Martin had given Ko back her innocence.

Galen Sword gave her back her hate.

FOURTEEN

Ja'Nette heard the familiar scraping on her bedroom door and told Martin to come in. He entered quietly, closing the door behind him, then loped over to her, hands brushing the room's thick white shag carpet.

Ja'Nette had been sitting on the side of her bed, staring out her window at the small patch of blue sky she could see between two large buildings to the south. Whenever Sword got her actively involved with his search, she realized she rarely had a chance to see the daytime sky. He preferred the night. She patted the bed beside her and Martin hopped up to it and sat down, staring out the window with her.

After a few moments, he tilted his head and asked, "What Ja'Nette Martin do?"

"Woolgathering," Ja'Nette said.

"Say what?"

"That's what my poppa called it. Just sort of sitting around and doing nothing."

"Ja'Nette feel better inside?" Martin asked, still peering out the window.

"I don't think I'll be eating burgers for a while, but I'll be okay."

Martin suddenly raised his hand and pointed out the window with a long, black-nailed finger. "Airplane!"

Ja'Nette smiled as she saw the silver speck move slowly between the buildings. Twilight was coming on. "Ever been on one?"

Martin shook his head. "But want to."

"Sword'll probably take you on one. He's taken me to London, and to San Francisco. And he let Melody take me to Disney World."

Martin tilted his head again. "Disney World like First World? Second World? Shadow World? Martin not know."

Ja'Nette laughed. "It's like a big playground." She patted his hand. "You'd like it. Fit right in."

"Melody take Martin?"

"Sure. She likes it, too. And sometimes Sword is just as happy to get us out of his hair for a while." Ja'Nette stretched out her legs to the floor. "Want to watch TV? We don't have to go for an hour or so."

"Wrestling?" Martin asked hopefully.

"Not till tomorrow night," Ja'Nette said.

Martin shrugged. "Watch then." He looked thoughtful. "Galen Sword should buy videos. Then wrestling always on." He stretched out his legs like Ja'Nette's. "Wrestling at Disney World?"

"I guess so," Ja'Nette said. "Is that what you did where you lived before? At the enclave? Watch videos and stuff?"

"Sometimes. Keepers not let Martin out most times so Martin do things inside."

"Keepers are sort of like parents, huh?"

Martin looked down at the bed cover and poked at it. "Ja'Nette remember parents?"

"Well, my mamma with her black eyes. Clan Marratin, you said. But I really don't know all that much about her."

"Human poppa?"

Ja'Nette closed her eyes and saw her father's face — skin as rich and black as the night, the trim moustache, the special smile he had made her think was just for her. "He went away when I was six, I guess."

"Where poppa go?"

Ja'Nette opened her eyes to stare out the window again, but still saw herself a child of four, sitting cross-legged in the RV her father drove, playing with her dollies, making them move and dance and fight without touching them. She saw her father's face when he watched her do that. She saw his special smile. Felt again the love she had thought had filled her then, before she had known better. Remembered the games they had played together, when he would put her dollies to the side and have her play with his toys instead: the dice. By the age of five, Ja'Nette could make them act as if they were rolling normally and still have them come up seven more than half the time. She was poppa's little angel, he had told her.

"Ja'Nette know where poppa go?" Martin asked from what seemed far away.

Vegas, first they had gone to Vegas. Her father with a thick stack of money, more than Ja'Nette had ever seen him with before. And her poppa had told his angel that together they would make the stack even bigger, so big that they might even be able to find mamma again. To six-year-old Ja'Nette, the first drive down the strip, all afire with the the casinos' twinkling lights, had been more exciting than Christmas Eve.

But she hadn't been allowed into the casinos. Not the parts where her poppa wanted her to go, at least. The casino people had misunderstood her poppa's insistence and had offered free babysitting and cartoons and ice cream — which had sounded all right to Ja'Nette. But her poppa explained it to her when they were alone in the RV that she had to come with him so she could watch him play with the dice and so she could make seven come up more than half the time.

They had finally found a small place in Reno with the right set-up. Ja'Nette could sit at a table in an elevated restaurant section and look between some wooden posts and an old wagon wheel and see her poppa ten feet away at a big green table where grown ups could play with the dice.

It was difficult being that far, not being able to see the dice all the time. Once she had made a die bounce after it had stopped and the grown ups got angry with each other. But, mostly, she could make the dice do what her poppa wanted, and every once in a while he would look up at her through the posts and the spokes of the wheel and give her that special smile.

Sitting on her bed in the Loft, feeling the heat radiating from Martin's heavy body only a few feet away, Ja'Nette knew that the innocence with which she remembered her poppa existed only because of the age she had been at the time. She knew now that the smile had not been for her. It had been for her mother's gift of translocation. She knew now that she had never been poppa's little angel. She had been an easy way out of trouble, poppa's little free ride.

Ja'Nette squeezed her eyes shut and saw the woman in the dress that barely covered her, holding on to her poppa's arm and laughing and laughing as he'd roll the dice and Ja'Nette would make them do what poppa wanted. And she saw the special other smile that her poppa gave that woman and she suddenly knew that he would never, not ever, go looking for her mamma.

That night, in the RV, Ja'Nette had lain awake in her cot all by herself, clutching her blanket up tight to her face, jumping in fear each time another RV or a car would grind by in the gravel outside, sending quick stabs of headlights through the windows. She cried for her poppa who had left her alone. She cried for her mamma, lost in the night.

Her father had come back to her as the sky outside had turned pink with the dawn. His hair was mussed and he walked unsteadily and spoke thickly the way he did when he went out to play with other grown ups. And when he bent down to give his angel a kiss, he had smelled like perfume. That woman's perfume.

Ja'Nette had pushed her blanket aside and wrapped her arms around her poppa's neck and then felt herself yanked into the air as the Big Men pulled her poppa back.

The Big Men had come into the RV behind her poppa. There were two of them and they were taller than her poppa and broad and mean with angry bad faces which still haunted her dreams. The Big Men threw Ja'Nette back onto her cot and didn't care that she was crying. The Big Men hit her poppa and said bad words and reached inside his jacket and and tore it and took out all the money that he had.

Her poppa had dropped to his hands and knees in front of her on her cot. He had blood in his moustache. His eyes were wide and running with tears. He begged his little angel to show the Big Men what she had done. He begged his daughter to show them that it wasn't just her poppa's fault.

She was frantic, hysterical, but she made her dollies dance for the Big Men, in the air, without touching them. It was the first time she had thrown up as she had used her gift. And of all the words that were said that night, the only ones Ja'Nette could remember clearly, the only ones she could still hear when she closed her eyes and thought about that day, were the words that one of the Big Men had said right then.

"Conroy, we don't like her kind around here. Never have. Never will."

And then the Big Men had taken her poppa away.

"Ja'Nette okay?" Martin asked.

Ja'Nette opened her eyes. Another silver jet floated past in the patch of darkening blue. "I don't know where my poppa went," she said. But as she had grown older, she had come to know what must have happened. Since the Big Men had obviously seen others who could do what she had done, for many years she had been surprised that they hadn't come back to punish her as well.

"Galen Sword like Ja'Nette's poppa now?" Martin asked.

Ja'Nette thought about that and decided Martin was right. "Just like my poppa," she said, feeling sad. At the age of twelve, she knew what it was like to be used. But at least Sword was honest with her. Sword was distant, preoccupied, and she mostly felt ignored by him, though sometimes she caught him watching her when he thought she was busy with her drills. But he had never mistreated her, and most importantly of all, he had never lied to her, either. She doubted she would ever feel anything like love for him. But she knew she would always respect him. And be grateful to him for taking her from the foster home.

"Melody like Ja'Nette mother now?" Martin asked.

"I guess," Ja'Nette said. She brushed the back of her hand against Martin's hand, knowing it was a small gesture of affection and friendship to him. She liked to see him smile when she did it. "I think she'd like to be, you know? Like it's her job or something. But ... well, when it comes to trying to teach me stuff, like being good and doing my lessons and stuff like that, sometimes she doesn't act right. She'd sort of rather leave it up to me, I think."

"Melody like sister?"

"Yeah, that's probably better," Ja'Nette said, glad that Martin had defined the relationship she had with Ko. She turned to smile at Martin. "I mean, we sure do look alike, don't we?"

Martin widened his eyes. "No," he said seriously. "Ja'Nette black. Melody not. Ja'Nette long hair wrapped up. Melody ... no hair ... almost."

"Yeah, but other than that?" Ja'Nette said playfully.

"Ja'Nette make joke?"

Ja'Nette reached out a finger and gently tapped Martin between his eyes. "Nyuk, nyuk, nyuk," she said. Then she brought her hand back to fiddle with her tightly-wound braids, thinking that Martin had just given her a killer idea.

"Hey, Martin, let's see your hands."

Martin held his hands up for her and Ja'Nette placed her own against them. Fingers fully extended, she could almost cover his palm.

"What Martin Ja'Nette do now?" Martin said.

"These are pretty fat fingers. Can you use scissors?"

"Martin like biting better."

"Ewww." Ja'Nette jumped from the bed and went to her dresser. "This time we'll use these." She held up a pair of scissors as she came back to Martin.

Martin looked at the scissors dubiously. "Halfling sister still make joke?" he asked.

Ja'Nette twirled a long braid around her finger and smiled, the same way she always saw Ko smiling. "Not this time, halfling bro." And then she laughed again. Happy once more.

"I can't do this if you won't stay still," Ko said grimly.

Sword stepped to the side of her to examine himself in the large dressing mirror he had swung out from the wall in his study. If his shoulders still didn't ache so much from the wounds Dmitri had inflicted, he could tie his own damn tie instead of putting up with Ko's awkward attempts. But putting the studs in his dress shirt had been difficult enough. "It's lopsided," he complained.

Ko muttered under her breath and jerked Sword back in front of her. "Bend down so I can see." She enlarged one of the wings of the tie, then tightened the crossknot. "Can you still breathe?"

"Barely."

"Too bad." She threw her hands back from Sword's neck like a cowpunch jumping back from a roped calf.

"Better," Sword said grudgingly as he checked the tie in the mirror. Then he reached for his tuxedo jacket.

"Not so fast." Ko roughly pulled the jacket from his hands. "I've still got to wire you."

Sword stepped back from her and held out his hands in exasperation. "What *is* your problem?"

"Hey, Sword, I don't have a problem. You're the one going to the Charity Ball from Hell, remember?" Ko snapped out the jacket, folded it shoulder to shoulder, then draped it carefully over her forearm. "The equipment's in my workshop." She turned away sharply.

Sword grunted, annoyed. If he didn't do something about the way Ko was acting right now, she'd probably try to electrocute him as she set up his equipment. "I'm sorry. Okay? I'm sorry for the way I've been acting this whole week. Does that help at all?"

Ko paused in the doorway between Sword's study and bedroom. "No," she said after a moment, then continued on her way.

Sword followed behind her, out to the catwalk balcony and down the stairs to her workshop on the third level, wondering how he could have ever thought that someone like her could work with him. Ja'Nette he could understand. She was a kid. Sword told her what to do, and she either did it or complained. If she complained, Sword had Ko cut off her allowance or her movies, and *then* Ja'Nette did what she was told. It was a very easy and understandable relationship.

Even Martin was shaping up promisingly. His main problem was that he tended to approach everything at a near-instinctual level and it was maddeningly difficult to get him to explain himself. But Sword was just coming to realize that if he scratched Martin on the back of the head and gave him a few words of praise every once in a while, he'd be as loyal as a dog.

And Forsyte was a joy. True, he had screwed up their first joint investigation into the First World and was totally responsible for what had happened to him, but Sword didn't hold that one misstep against the man. The fact was that Forsyte was brilliant, enthusiastic, and — perhaps because of his difficulties — wasn't one to waste time or words.

Sword knew he enjoyed Adrian Forsyte's singleminded approach because it was so much like his own.

But Melody Ko had always been a mistake. Sword remembered back to the misgivings he had had when Forsyte first proposed that they include Ko in their ongoing extracurricular investigations. He had known that Forsyte considered her his ablest student. Solid experimental background. Good grounding in theoretical work as well. Any department at MIT was ready to put Ko on the fast track to a Ph.D. as soon as she made up her mind about which specialty she wanted to pursue. A Nobel-quality mind, Forsyte had insisted, so Sword had agreed to sign her on.

It had been disastrous from the beginning. Instead of an eager young mind ready to contribute to his search, Sword had encountered an opinionated, close-minded, arrogant, aloof brat who only cared for herself. He couldn't understand how Forsyte could tolerate anyone with that attitude, let alone say she'd fit into the team. But reluctantly, he had acquiesced to Forsyte's wishes. And now, if he tried to replace Ko as a Sword Foundation lab assistant, he would be forced to find another equally intelligent and perceptive attendant for the difficult physicist. The only good thing about the situation was that Ko was able to serve in both capacities at once.

"Wake up, Sword," Ko said, bringing him back to the here and now. "And put your arms out wider."

Sword stood with his arms half extended. "My shoulders still hurt," he protested.

"You should be bloody well pleased that I got to them before they could get infected." Ko reached around him, connecting a thin black strap at his back. "This'll be the antenna lead. After I hook up the contacts, you can slide it under the cummerbund."

"How about the batteries?" Sword watched impatiently as Ko methodically sorted through a tray of small plastic drawers mounted to the wall above her biggest workbench. Her entire workshop was in such perfect order that it never looked as if she ever did anything in it, other than organizing all her gadgets and equipment into more and smaller containers.

"I'll get to them," Ko said.

Sword didn't like her tone. "I don't believe this. Inside two hours I'm going to make contact with the clans of the First World, my whole search will finally come to an end, and you sound as if this is so routine you'd rather be ... asleep or something."

"I would rather be asleep, Sword. I was up all night wiring these bloody things for you. Right hand."

Sword held his right hand out. Ko slipped a thick gold Rolex over his wrist and fastened the metal band. Two fine, beige-toned wires extended from beneath the watch's body toward his hand. Sword looked at the face of the watch closely. The second indicator wasn't moving in its window. "It's not working."

"I had to take the movement out." Ko opened another drawer.

"You took the movement out of *my* Rolex?"

"Relax, relax. I'll put it back. Turn your wrist up." She grabbed his hand and turned his wrist up for him.

"Why did you have to take the damn movement out? We've got small radios. I could put one in my pocket. I — "

Ko held up a thin gold cigarette case. "This is your radio, Sword." She tossed it over to land on his jacket, folded neatly on the side of the workbench. "Just keep your wrist up." She opened a small bottle with a tiny brush attached to the lid and painted two clear stripes along Sword's wrist to his palm. Then she carefully flattened the two beige-toned wires against the stripes and blew on them. Sword felt the stripes as cool patches on his skin — adhesive to keep the wires in place. For the first time he noticed that the wires ended in round, bare-metal tabs at the base of his palm.

"What is this thing?" Typical that Ko would go ahead and spend valuable time on some gadget without checking with him.

"Adrian came up with the idea after he did some comparisons of medical results between Martin and Saul Calder. It's a modified galvanic skin-response device," Ko explained as she used small tabs of beige adhesive tape to anchor the watch into position, partially hidden by Sword's shirt cuffs. "Measures the electrical conductivity of the skin."

"What for? So you can tell if I'm lying to someone?"

"That's a standard, if imperfect use of GSR. Basically, what Adrian found out was that Saul's temperature was as elevated as Martin's, even though Saul was still in his humanform. Shifter metabolism runs hotter than an ordinary human's. To shed that excess heat, they also sweat more. The more sweat on the skin, the more conductive it is to a small electrical potential on those two leads, and the higher the reading generated between them when a current flows."

"And ... ?" Sword encouraged her as he brought the gutted Rolex and his wired wrist up for closer scrutiny.

"And ... Adrian believes that when you shake hands with the other guests tonight and the skin of their hands completes the circuit between those two wires, this device should let us identify who are humanform shifters."

Sword whistled silently. "Great. But what happens if I start sweating up a storm? Or if I shake hands with a human who's doing the same?"

"Filter circuits. The sensitivity's turned right down, too. Shifter sweat appears to be slightly different. More conductive. Probably has a faster evaporation rate so they have more efficient cooling." She stopped working on the series of small black wallet-sized cases she had laid out and looked meaningfully at Sword. "Like Martin explained to me, Sword. Shifters aren't human."

Sword nodded, but said nothing. He was part of what was to happen next and Ko wasn't. Perhaps he should remember that more often. Perhaps that might explain why she sometimes seemed to over-react. All of this was new for Ko, and he knew he must always remember that she wasn't what he was.

She was only human.

Ko vaulted down to the main lab, three steps at a time, swinging from the double handrails for the final five. The whole team was running late. The reception was starting in less than an hour and the Friday-night traffic uptown was going to be deadly.

She stepped quickly to her locker and slipped her vest on over her tank top, then began pulling out all her precisely-stored equipment and placing it in the vest's custom pockets and straps. She heard Forsyte roll up behind her.

"GOOD ON THE STAIRS," his mechanical voice said. "TAKING LESSONS FROM MARTIN?"

"Took longer than I thought hooking Sword up to all the new stuff. We should have left ten minutes ago." She slipped three spray cans of silver halide emulsion into a long pocket on the vest's side, then looked around the lab. "Have you seen Ja'Nette and Martin? I need them down here now."

"I WILL CALL THEM," the voder said, and Forsyte blinked in the code that would shift his commands from the on-board voder to the Loft's intercom system. He pressed a sequence of keys and a moment later, Ja'Nette's voice echoed from the living quarters. "Comiiiing!" she called out. Martin howled at the same time for good measure.

"I guess this is it," Ko said to Forsyte as she filled the last of her pockets and took her rifle out of its rack.

"NERVOUS?" Forsyte's voder asked.

"Curious is more like it. I guess I never really believed Sword before. Now, since two nights ago, seeing it for myself, it seems I have no choice but to accept it."

"DOES THAT MAKE YOU UNHAPPY?"

Ko arched a single eyebrow. "If it's the truth, Professor Forsyte, then it cannot make me happy or sad. It is simply the truth."

Forsyte's two fingers moved quickly over his pad. "BUT YOU STILL SEEM UPSET."

"What happens after tonight? That's what I don't know. Someone went to a lot of time and trouble, and spent a lot of money, to get Sword out of the First World in the first place. He's going to go out of his way to make a big commotion tonight, but I can't believe it's going to make whoever sent him away open the doors for him again." Ko broke her gun and checked to make sure both barrels were clear. "And I don't think Sword has figured that out for himself yet."

"HAVE YOU TOLD HIM?" the voder asked.

Ko shook her head as she efficiently snapped a clip of tranquilizing darts to the rifle stock. Each cartridge had three times the dosage of the dart that had dropped Martin. She didn't want to face hand-to-hand with a *tagonii* again. "I can't tell him anything, Adrian. You know that. I don't think anyone can."

She looked up as she heard footsteps clanging down the stairs. Sword appeared and Ko had to admit that if she didn't know him, she'd think he was quite elegant in his tuxedo. Even if it was rented.

"I just hope they don't have metal detectors at the entrance," Sword said. "I feel like I'm half robot."

"If you set anything off, they'll just frisk you for a gun or a knife," Ko said matter of factly. "And all they'll find is your hearing aid, your pocket memo recorder, your cigarette case, lighter, portable FM radio, and ... a broken Rolex."

Sword held up his left hand. "Don't forget my clan ring," he said, showing Saul Calder's gold band. "Calder still sedated?"

"HE IS NOT GOING ANYWHERE," Forsyte's voder said. The human-form shifter was still unconscious in his basement cell.

"Good," Sword said. He looked at Ko. "Are we all set?"

From above, more footsteps clanged: Ja'Nette's multiple thumps, which sounded like a small avalanche, and the more widely spaced thuds of Martin, taking each staircase in two jumps.

"Just about," Ko said. "All we have to do is convince Martin to keep his clothes on this — bloody hell." She stopped dead.

Ja'Nette appeared at the bottom of the stairway, followed closely by Martin. The girl was smiling broadly, set for the evening in jeans and sneakers and her favorite red jacket. She even had her Mitsubishi transceiver already in place in her ear. Ko could tell that very easily because nothing obscured Ja'Nette's ears. Her braids were gone. Her scalp was covered with a faint even bristle of hair, barely an eighth of an inch long. Just like Ko's.

"What have you done?" Ko asked, instantly feeling foolish because she *knew* exactly what Ja'Nette had done. And why.

A flicker of confusion played across Ja'Nette's face and her pleasure slipped away. "I thought you'd like it."

"I ... your braids were very pretty, Ja'Nette."

Ja'Nette's lips trembled. "Your hair's pretty, too."

Ko regretted saying anything. She went to Ja'Nette and hugged the child. "My hair's not supposed to be pretty, Ja'Nette. It's just supposed to stay out of the way when I'm soldering. And running around with you guys."

Ja'Nette stepped back and grinned at Ko. "Sooo ... let's all get running around."

Ko glanced at Sword and narrowed her eyes at him, warning him with her expression that now wasn't the time to say anything about how late they were running.

Sword hesitated, about to say something, then went over to give Ja'Nette an awkward clap on the back. "I like it," he said. "Looks good."

"Yeah?" Ja'Nette beamed.

"Martin cut," Martin added, now that he saw it was safe. "Use scissors. Not bite."

"Good job," Sword said to Martin, then turned to Ko and silently mouthed, "*Okay?*"

"Okay," Ko said. "Let's get this show on the road."

Ja'Nette cheered as Forsyte's chair rolled over to the lift. "The whole family's running around tonight!" Then she turned to Sword and Ko felt her heart ache at the girl's next question. "That's right, isn't it, Sword? We are a family, sort of, aren't we?"

Sword looked over at Ko and she could see what he was thinking. The five of them were in the middle of a multi-million dollar computer center: a brilliant scientist confined to a wheelchair by a First World curse; a half-human, half-werewolf creature who could scale sheer walls; a child who could move objects with her thoughts; a millionaire who thought he wasn't human; and Ko herself, who was thankfully ordinary as far as she could tell.

"What the hell, kid," Sword said, reaching over to Ja'Nette's upturned hand to give her five. "It's a brand-new century, and we can be a family if we want to be."

Ja'Nette cheered again and ran around the lab, slapping Martin's hand and Ko's before jumping into the open lift to tap Forsyte's left hand.

Ko followed Sword and Martin over to the streetlevel staircase. "Thanks for that, Sword." She meant it.

Sword stopped at the top step. "Let's just make it work tonight, all right?"

Ko held out her hand to shake his. "We will."

But when their hands touched, it wasn't in a handshake. Nor did they didn't pull away from each other as they wordlessly declared a truce, and perhaps, Ko thought, something more.

The moment was broken when Ja'Nette called out from below, "Can 'Bub come, too?"

Sword dropped Ko's hand. "Not a chance in hell," he said as he turned and hurried off down the stairs. "I want to get through tonight in one piece."

So do I, Ko thought as she followed him down to the garage.

All of us.

FIFTEEN

The night sky had clouded over with the onset of an autumn storm and the swiftly passing clouds formed a low dark ceiling to the city. They roiled within the stationary disks of light cast by the searchlights that ringed the museum's entrance like columns of ice in an underground cavern. Sword found the image fitting as he approached. He felt he was an explorer about to delve deep within a lost world.

Sword cut his Porsche through a line of cabs and limousines and pulled up to the broad sidewalk in front of the main entrance to the American Museum of Natural History. A tall man in a long gray coat and matching top hat came around to the driver's side and asked to see Sword's invitation. Sword flashed it but the man said, "If I may, sir," and reached inside and took the white card to examine it more closely. Sword let it go with misgivings. That little card had cost him ten grand. But the man only raised a finger and a youth in a short red jacket ran over to give Sword a parking tag.

The man in the top hat opened the car door for Sword, passed back the invitation, and told Sword where to reclaim his car at the end of the evening. Then he moved on to the next car in line, and Sword was among the throng heading up the shallow stone steps into the museum.

Sword paused for a moment in the wide plaza before going in. The storm winds were picking up and he could hear the frantic flapping of the long banners hanging on either side of the huge pillars of the main façade. In French and English, the large signs welcomed the 105th Annual Ball of the Society of St. Linus. With Forsyte's patient help, Sword had finally determined from Martin's recollections that there were approximately seven years between Ceremonies of the Change. That meant Martin was about eighteen years old, and that some of the people in gowns and tuxedos milling around Sword right now had been attending these 'balls' for more than seven centuries. Sword drew his jacket closer to his body for protection from the suddenly colder wind.

"Is something wrong?" Ko asked. Her voice was tinnier than it usually sounded. For tonight, Sword had had to forgo his usual transceiver and replace it with what appeared to be a standard, behind-the-ear hearing aid. The gold cigarette case in his tuxedo jacket pocket served as the receiver, and then broadcast an attenuated signal over a range of about eighteen inches which was picked up by the small antenna in the hearing aid. Unfortunately, there was no way for Sword to reply unless he wanted to be seen talking to himself, so he held his hand to the hearing aid, turning around to catch sight of the black van parked by a fire hydrant across the street, and shook his head, *No*.

"We're here when you need us," Ko said.

"Go get 'em, Sword," Ja'Nette added.

"Sword? Galen Sword?" a voice suddenly called out.

Sword turned back to the museum and saw an arm waving to him from a brilliantly-lit pocket of people ten feet away. It was an elegant brown arm, dripping with an elaborate diamond bracelet, and holding a small microphone. He instantly recognized the woman to whom the arm was attached.

"Kill the lights, boys," he heard her say, then watched, surprised, as she pushed her broad-shouldered way through the other guests to come to him, leaving behind a video camera crew.

Sword bent down to kiss her lightly on the cheek she offered. "Kennie, I wasn't expecting — "

"That's *my* line, Galen," the woman laughed. The television reporter hadn't changed much in appearance since the first time they had briefly met, in the townhouse of Marcus Askwith, the morning after his death. Nor had she changed from all their subsequent meetings. She still maintained the intriguing combination of striking features and intense expression that kept her viewers tuning in day after day. But tonight Kendall Marsh was dressed in a way that Sword had never seen her choose before. She was stunning. And the diamonds blazing on her wrist were more than matched by the ones at her throat.

"Are you a member of the Society of St. Linus?" Sword asked, suddenly afraid to hear her answer, especially because of the months they had had together.

"Are you kidding?" Marsh hooted. "I'm just trying to get out of true crime for a change. How about you? Are you going back to your old party ways?"

Sword shook his head. It seemed his legend still lived on in a certain set of society.

Then Marsh's eyes flashed excitedly and she leaned conspiratorially close to Sword. "Or are you here to exorcise a few museum ghosts?" She laughed again. Sword remembered that she was always laughing, always enjoying the challenges and the intrigues of her life. She had a lot of them. "You still involved in that, Galen?" Her smile turned rueful with that question. It remained still a sore point, Sword could see.

Sword dismissed the question lightly. "Only one of many interests." He felt disturbed by the effect that Marsh was having on him. He had thought he had gotten over her. It seemed so long ago.

"Heard you had some trouble over in Greece a while back. State Department had to pull a few strings to get you home." He recognized the professional tone creeping back into her voice. It was his turn to laugh.

"Now that sounds like a reporter looking for a story," he said.

"Always thought there should be a good one in you, Galen." Sword could see it in her eyes. She was feeling the same way; surprised and not entirely displeased that the old feelings still lived. "Such a wild boy. Such a bad accident. And then, such a sudden interest in things that go bump in the night. I still think you had one of those near-death experiences."

"Maybe I will have a story for you," Sword said impulsively. He liked the way her eyes flashed. He had missed her. "Lunch next week?" he asked.

"How about dinner?" Marsh said. Then raised her eyebrows innocently. "Or breakfast?"

"I'll call your office," Sword said. Accepting her invitation, no matter how tempting, would be pushing things. He expected that his life was going to get fairly disordered in the next few weeks. He didn't need the return of an old complication to add to it.

"Yeah," Marsh said with a touch of disappointment. "Maybe your people and my people can get together and they have a real good time."

"Fat chance," Ko hissed in Sword's ear. He had forgotten that everything he said and everything that was said around him was being transmitted back to the van.

"It's good to see you again, Kennie. I mean that." Sword looked around and saw that the guests were thinning out. Almost all had already gone in. "I've got to get inside." He only had until the time that the Ceremony was scheduled to begin. After that, it would be too late.

"Me, too," Marsh said. "I'm covering the whole thing."

That stopped Sword. How could the Clan Arkady let a reporter and a camera crew in to observe their Ceremony? "You — you *are* a member?"

"What member?" Marsh said with a frown. "I'm a reporter. They invited me. What are you looking so surprised for? Anyone with ten grand to donate to their hospital fund can come to this party, Galen." Her sly smile came back. "Unless, of course, you really are here to exorcise some ghosts. I talk to Trank from time to time, you know. He keeps me posted on some of the more bizarre things you get up to."

"Trank just likes to tell a good story," Sword said lamely. He could see that his evasiveness was only making Marsh more interested. "Got to run, Kennie. Talk to you next week." He turned to go.

"Shake her bloody hand, Sword," Ko hissed into his ear. "Or don't you want to know?"

Sword took a breath. Of course, Ko was right. What if his search had been infiltrated? What if Trank and Marsh and all the others who helped him from time to time were somehow connected with the clans? That could explain a great deal, a great many failures. He turned back to Marsh. He didn't want to know, but he *had* to know.

"Kennie," he said, then stopped, wondering how he could manage it.

"Yes?" she said expectantly.

What the hell, Sword thought. He stuck out both arms and grabbed the hand that didn't hold her microphone. Then he shook it like a schoolboy, making sure the twin leads on his palm made tight contact with her own. "Really good to have seen you again," he said, feeling like a fool.

"NO READING," Forsyte's voder rasped through the hearing aid.

Sword wondered what Marsh would make of the sudden look of relief that came over his face. Then he quickly left her to go inside, to join the Gathering of the Clan.

"If we keep doing this sort of thing," Ja'Nette complained, "we're going to have to get Sword to buy a bigger van. Move over Martin."

Ko sat behind the wheel, watching Sword take the last few steps before he disappeared into the museum. The Marsh woman and her camera crew followed a few seconds behind him. The reporter's presence bothered Ko and she looked back into the passenger compartment.

There was no doubt that the van was overcrowded. The darkness within it, broken only by the flickering lights of the various pieces of electronics built along the right-hand wall only made its interior seem more closed-in. Ja'Nette said it reminded her of an old-fashioned space capsule. It made Ko feel ancient to hear the girl call space capsules old-fashioned.

"Martin, why would the clan invite a television reporter to the Ceremony. *Is* she part of it?" Ko asked.

Martin looked away from the display lights Forsyte studied. The halfling shared his seat with Ja'Nette, even though it was intended for only a single, human occupant. At least with his new sweat pants, sweatshirt, and Velcro-fastened running shoes that barely closed over his feet, Martin could pass at night as a short though powerfully-built weightlifter. But if the public ever caught sight of him in daylight, the news crews would be on him as if the saucers had landed, and not just because he'd probably be naked if it were up to him.

"TV woman not Arkady," Martin said. Then he closed his eyes and moved his lips silently. Ko could see he was trying to give her more information. He had been making a real effort in the past day or two to try and talk in longer sentences with more details. "Not everyone at American Museum of Natural History go to Ceremony of the Change Arkady. Some humanform shifters. Some just humans." He closed his eyes again and Ko didn't interrupt him. "Keepers use big word. To keep things hiding."

"Camouflage?" Ja'Nette suggested.

"Yes," Martin said, sighing in relief. "Many humanform shifters hide among many humans. Keepers smart."

"How many?" Ko asked, then regretted it.

A look of pain came to Martin's eyes and he made a soft *ooo*-ing sound in his throat. He tried to smile at Ko but couldn't carry it off. "Martin want say lots but Martin not supposed to."

"That's all right, Martin." Ko kept her expression calm and accepting. "Did you watch all the people going up the steps to the museum?"

Martin nodded. The custom-built van had a small, one-way mirrored passenger window on each side, near the middle.

Ko laid out the question for him. "Some of those people were human and some were humanform shifters. Can you tell us if half the people on the stairs were humanform shifters? More than half? Less than half?"

Martin stared down at his hands and spread out his fingers. Then he moved his hands apart as if trying to see half of the number ten. Ko was impressed by his effort. Martin nodded tentatively. "Half." He peered out through the passenger window. "All Arkady shifters together, cover half stairs. Almost."

"Wow," Ja'Nette whispered. "That is a lot of woofers."

"About eight hundred people are at that party," Ko said, looking back outside at the museum. A line of fifty limousines waited across the street. Their drivers were clumped together in groups, smoking and talking.

"MAKE SENSE," Forsyte's voder said.

"Sure does," Ko agreed, then explained for Ja'Nette. "A lot of the Arkady shifters are coming in from other places. Might be difficult to arrange for four hundred humans to turn up at one place in this city and not come out again. Makes sense to hide them among another group of people. No one's going to notice if not everyone who goes in comes out, as long as all the limousines leave."

Ja'Nette nodded. "Camouflage. I get it." She looked out the window with Martin. "But where do the woofers go *after* the change?"

"Back to enclave," Martin said. "Not be on street in shifterform. Rules."

"How do they get back there?" Ko asked. "Does a truck come or — "

Martin motioned with his hand. "Down below. Other streets."

"You mean tunnels?"

Martin nodded. "Other streets. Other maps."

"Martin, is the Arkady enclave far from here?" In all the time they had had with Martin, Ko had never asked that question. Somehow she had assumed that wherever the Ceremony was to be held was where the Arkady shifters would also live. But Arkady shifters seemed to live around the globe. She was realizing the First World was more complex, and disturbingly more real, with each new revelation and discovery.

"Not far," Martin said. "On other streets."

"RECEIVING LINE," Forsyte's voder interrupted. "STARTING TO SHAKE HANDS NOW."

Ko saved her other questions for the moment and pressed the transmit button on the radio unit she used to reach Sword's hearing aid. "We're right behind you, Sword," she broadcast to him.

Martin narrowed his eyes dubiously at her, but had learned enough not to say anything about the human's misuse of the language.

Sword folded his hands together as he waited in the receiving line and surreptitiously pressed a single button on the locator band he wore, sending back a confirmation signal to the van. The band looked plain enough that he and Forsyte and Ko had decided if anyone noticed it, it would simply be seen as a piece of fashion-forward jewelry, and ignored.

"Confirmation received," Ko transmitted.

Sword moved a few feet closer to the beginning of the reception line. So far, nothing he had seen had been out of the ordinary, except perhaps, the inordinate number of fur coats being worn by the women present. Such coats were relics of an earlier, less aware time and even in the days when Sword had been a fixture on the society circuit, the wearing of them had been declining. But tonight, among the guests of the Society of St. Linus, the number of different furs was enough to make Sword feel he had stepped back into the fifties. Or into a group where the wearing of animal skins had a different meaning.

The Society of St. Linus itself, judging from the huge panels of color photography and advertising copy set up around the museum's foyer, was legitimate as far as Sword could tell. The photographs showed a dozen hospitals around the world, mostly in less-developed countries, and told of the Society's ongoing efforts to eradicate certain specific tropical diseases. According to the charts displayed, the Society was doing a good job. At both wiping out disease, and hiding the true nature of about half its members.

But which half of those members Sword should be interested in, he didn't know. More than three-quarters of the people he had checked out so far with quick glances to their hands, wore simple gold bands. They could be either all married or all humanform shifters. The clans had obviously developed the art of camouflage to a high degree. He supposed they would have had to, to last this long.

Sword heard gentle coughing behind him and realized he was next to move down the line. The first person he shook hands with was an older woman with bushy white hair and the tight shiny skin produced by one too many face lifts. "NO READING," Forsyte's voder said as Sword introduced himself.

The woman's husband was next, short and round in his tuxedo.

"NO READING."

Sword moved on.

As he shook hands with the third of the ball's organizers, Sword glanced down the rest of the line of about thirty people. The people toward the end wore small tufts of folded blue and white ribbons, the colors of the Society, on their gowns and tuxedos. Sword decided that's where the clan members would have to be, among the most senior organizers. He wondered where the actual Ceremony would take place. In some forgotten museum basement? The roof? And where was the human who would be the Ceremony's sacrifice? Sword felt tension coil within him.

"SHIFTER," the voder hissed.

Sword looked into the eyes of the woman whose hand he held in his. She was in her twenties, blonde, fresh-faced, in a slim, long blue gown with sprays of blue feathers coming off the shoulders. She smiled at Sword. Her teeth and pale complexion were flawless.

Sword introduced himself.

She answered with a soft southern drawl and introduced her husband beside her. On her left hand, beside the thickly-clustered diamonds of her engagement ring, she wore a simple gold band, out of place in its simplicity.

The shifter's husband took Sword's hand next.

"SHIFTER," the voder announced.

Sword smiled and said his name again. The man looked absolutely ordinary, just as Saul Calder did, and he, too, wore a simple gold band.

The husband caught Sword looking at his ring. He glanced down, too, and saw Sword's. He gave Sword's hand an extra squeeze. "Cousin," the husband said softly, then turned to greet the next in line.

Sword moved through five more no-readings until he came to two women in formal saris. The first woman spoke to him with a gentle British accent and when their hands touched, Forsyte's voder said, "SHIFTER." Ko added, "Reading almost went off the dial." The woman wore no gold band, but she did have a beautiful red stone set in her right nostril. She looked at Sword's hand. "Cousin," she said and smiled.

The second woman said nothing as she took Sword's hand. The stone in her nostril was also red. Ko broke in over the mechanical announcement of the woman's status. "These readings are right near the top of the band, Sword. We weren't expecting anything like this. Might have to recalibrate."

Sword moved on, coming closer to the final ten people who wore the blue and white ribbons. He was disappointed that he hadn't come across more shifters, but then, he supposed, some of the people he had met might have been other forms of adepts from other clans — Sword himself could not trigger Ko's GSR device. But once the line was finished, he wondered how many of those who had been in it would move off to rapidly confer with others, to announce that Galen Sword had arrived. Or had returned. And that he was wearing an Arkady ring.

Sword looked down the line again. The last two people were a man and woman. The woman was unusual, perhaps his own age, he guessed, with ash-blonde hair cascading over honey-colored skin which seemed incandescent above the electric shimmer of the low-cut, metallic-green gown she wore. He could see that beside the small ribbons of St. Linus that she wore, she also had on an elaborate brooch of gold and silver. But the stone in it was a dull-brown color, not red.

The man at the end of the line, beside the woman, looked up just then and caught Sword's eyes for the briefest of moments. Sword had a sudden flash that he had seen the man before — darkly-tanned skin, fringe of black hair — but the man looked away without recognition and Sword decided it was the tuxedo. Every man who wore one looked familiar because there was so little difference among them.

He shook hands next with an eighty-year-old man who sat with rounded back in a wheelchair, smiling gamely as he extended a trembling arm.

"SHIFTER," the voder said.

Is this what seven hundred years looks like? Sword wondered, and moved on again.

When he was three people away from the woman in the metallic-green gown, Sword saw her listening to something the man beside her said. She nodded and the man excused himself, leaving the line prematurely. Sword was glad that the woman hadn't gone. He shook hands with two more no-readings, and then he was before her.

She was beautiful, with brilliant green eyes that matched exactly the dress she wore, and Sword amused himself by creating an instant history for her. A model by age eighteen he decided. International assignments, top dollar, meeting all the right people, deliberately choosing the wealthy escort who had been by her side, her senior by about ten years, who could keep her in suitable style, then a graceful resignation from her profession to devote herself solely to good works.

Sword smiled to himself, said his name, and tensed, hearing the voder's rasp behind his ear. The woman introduced herself as Morgan Lafayette, and their hands met.

Sword held the woman's hand a moment longer than he normally would, but there was no signal from Forsyte or from Ko.

"I'm so sorry that my partner had to leave so suddenly, Mr. Sword," Morgan Lafayette said sweetly. "Perhaps you could join us for a drink when the others have passed through?"

Partner, Sword thought, *interesting.* He quickly checked her delicate hands for a ring. But there was nothing. The only jewelery she wore was her intriguing brooch, intertwined arms of silver and gold holding the exotic brown gemstone.

"I'd like that," he said sincerely. "Very much."

Lafayette nodded, released Sword's hand, and turned to the next in line. And only as Sword walked away from the line to the nearest bar, did he suddenly realize that he had received *no* signal from Forsyte and Ko. Not even a 'no-reading.'

Odd, Sword thought as he joined another line to get a drink, but he simply assumed that they were recalibrating the equipment for the higher readings, as Ko had warned they might. He tapped the hearing aid behind his ear and told the bartender what he wanted.

So far, he decided, the evening had been slow. He hoped things would pick up soon.

SIXTEEN

Ko cranked down the window beside her to let the smoke clear from the van. "It's all right, Martin!" she called out. The van rocked as Martin jumped back and forth. "Ja'Nette! Get him to sit still!"

Ko slipped out of her seat, crouched over, and duck-walked to the back of the van where Forsyte's chair was locked into its floor tracks in front of the equipment console.

"FINE, FINE," Forsyte's voder said before Ko could ask. "POWER SURGE."

Ko squinted at the main communications board. Thin wisps of smoke still trickled from a few of the control panels. "We're only on the supplemental batteries, Adrian. There's no way we've got enough amps to burn anything. And the breakers should have popped first, anyway."

Forsyte's fingers scrambled over the pad. "LAST SIGNAL OFF DIAL."

Ko felt the fine hairs on her neck bristle upright. "Broadcast power?"

"WHERE ELSE COULD IT HAVE COME FROM?" the voder asked. "ON BATTERIES. BREAKERS SHOULD HAVE POPPED."

"Oh, shit," Ko said. Then pulled her transceiver from her vest, placed it in her ear, and flicked on the transmitter unit. The vest equipment was all self-contained. It should remain unaffected. Now if only it were strong enough to reach Sword behind all that stonework.

"Sword? Do you copy? Give me a confirmation. Whoever you last got a reading from was right off the dial. Feedback signal got past our breakers and burned out the feed lines to the van's comm equipment. Can you give me a confirm on that?"

Ko and Ja'Nette both pressed their locator bands into their wrists to feel for the vibration signal from Sword. Long seconds passed with no response. "What if he can't hear us?" Ja'Nette asked.

"Then we've go to go in," Ko answered grimly. She began to fasten her vest. "No other choice."

"What's that supposed to be?" Kendall Marsh asked.

Sword spun around, nearly spilling his Perrier as he awkwardly tried to hold onto his glass and send out the confirmation signal to Ko on his locator band. He could almost hear her in his hearing aid, about every other word at least, punctuated by strings of static. He guessed that the storm was moving closer and that lightning was beginning to interfere with their transmissions.

"What do you think it is?" Sword asked, buying time.

Marsh stared at the flat black metal bracelet around Sword's left wrist. "A disguised copper bracelet for your arthritis? A clue that you've just escaped from a chain gang?"

"Wanted criminal," Sword nodded. "Hold this." He handed Marsh his glass, then turned half away from her as he slipped two fingers under the band to send Ko her signal.

" ... repeat ... last person ... the dial ... out ... coming in ... " It was Ko's voice but it still wasn't making sense. Sword tried tapping the hearing aid again.

Marsh watched Sword's movements and pursed her lips in thought. "You're wired for sound, aren't you?"

"I beg your pardon?" Sword said. He had just heard that Ko had received the confirm but then Marsh had spoken over the rest of the signal.

"That thing on your wrist is probably some kind of cellular phone," Marsh said, dropping her voice, "and that hearing aid has got to be the earphone. There's nothing wrong with your hearing."

"Tinitis," Sword said, using the lie he had rehearsed. "Skeet shooting."

"Out your ass, Galen." Marsh took him by the arm. "Come tell Aunt Kendall what you're up to."

"I'm trying to go to a party," Sword said. "Haven't been to one for a while. You know that."

Marsh guided Sword behind a large panel of hospital construction photos. The sound of a dance band began to echo in the high-ceilinged stone-walled foyer. "Off the record, Galen, swear to Nielsen. Are you in here working for someone?"

Sword shook his head, trying to concentrate on what Ko was saying.

"Is this something you're doing on your own, then?" Marsh continued. She dropped her voice to a whisper. "For God's sake, Galen, is this something to do with your ghostbusting?"

Sword rolled his eyes. "I am not a damned ghostbuster. I ... investigate strange phenomena, all right? It's my hobby. I'm allowed." He looked away from Marsh again to focus on Ko's words. It finally made sense. The last person with whom he had shaken hands had generated a shifter signal so powerful it had blown out the van's supplemental power system. But who had been the last person he had shaken hands with? The people by the bar? The green-eyed woman in the reception line? He looked at Marsh. Their hands had touched when he had given her his glass.

"Give me your hand, Kennie," Sword suddenly said. He took Marsh's hand with his and squeezed his right palm against hers.

"What *is* this?" Marsh giggled without pulling away. "A new form of safe sex?" She blew Sword a kiss. "Was it good for you, too, darlin'?"

Sword drew his hand away as Ko said no signals were coming through yet. Marsh stared at her palm for a second, then grabbed Sword's right hand.

"Where did these two little indentations come from, Galen?" she asked as she flipped his hand over. "Oh, ho," she said as she saw the leads glued to his palm. "What have we here?" She pulled up his sleeve and saw where the wires vanished beneath his Rolex.

"It ... it's like a lie detector," Sword quickly improvised. "I'm trying to get market leads. That sort of thing."

"Uh uh. You never could lie to me, Galen. You're decked out like a regular James Bond and I want to know why. I'll be completely off the record about it if you want, but I've got to know. You know I do."

Sword shook his head in dismay. He did know. Once Marsh got onto something that puzzled her, the entire world could collapse around her and she would still ignore it until she had found an answer which would satisfy her.

"It's a long story," Sword warned her.

"I'm a good listener. Start talking."

"This probably isn't the place." He looked around, past the panel. Most of the Society's guests were in the rotunda with the band. He had to get back and keep track of them. Find out where the ones he had identified as shifters ended up, and follow them.

"Are you in trouble, Galen?" The playfulness had gone from Marsh's eyes.

"Not yet," Sword answered truthfully. "But honestly, *you* might be if you keep hanging around me."

Her face was deadly serious. "Are you into drugs, Galen? Because — "

"Of course not! Nothing illegal, all right? But ... some things aren't illegal because nobody has ever thought of writing laws against them. Now, really, Kennie, you've got to leave me alone. Just for now."

Marsh thrust the glass back at Sword, spilling some of the water in it on his jacket. "Sometimes you can be such an asshole."

"I have to be ready for — "

"Ah, Mr. Sword," a familiar voice suddenly said. "I was wondering where you had escaped to." Morgan Lafayette, radiant and resplendent in shimmering green, stepped around the photo panel and held out her hand to him, smiling warmly. "My partner has come back and would dearly love to make your acquaintance now."

Sword took Lafayette's hand as Marsh looked on icily. "I see you have a lot to be ready for, *Mr.* Sword," she said.

"I don't think we've met, Ms ... ?" Lafayette said politely to Marsh.

"You're right, we haven't," Marsh replied, then turned and left.

"My, my," Lafayette said as Marsh departed, high heels clicking sharply across the marble floor. "An old girlfriend?" She said it lightly as if it were no more than a joke.

"Apparently she is now," Sword said, watching Marsh's rigid back disappearing into the crowd. And then it hit him. It had been Lafayette's hand he'd been holding when he received no signal from the van.

"Shall we?" Lafayette asked, holding her arm out for Sword to escort her. "I think you and my partner will have a great deal to discuss."

A shifter signal that went right off the dial, Sword thought. He took her arm in his. Things were finally beginning to get interesting.

Ko handed Martin a black knit cap and told him to pull it down over his ears. "They're too pointed," she said. "And when you walk around out there, keep your back straight and your hands in your pockets."

"Martin not have pockets," Martin said as he pulled the hat over his bristling scalp hair.

"Then just don't let them drag on the ground, all right? We don't want to attract any attention."

"Then why leave the van?" Ja'Nette asked.

"These small radios aren't working at this distance. The walls of the museum are too thick. We've got to get out there, walk around, find out what part of the museum that shifter is taking him to, and be ready to help him when he needs it."

Martin shook his head as if to clear his ears. "Shifter have Galen Sword?" he asked with concern.

"Yeah," Ko said. "Ja'Nette, try putting Martin's transceiver under his hat. See if he can hear it there. I don't want to put tape on him where anyone can see." She tapped her own transceiver for Martin's benefit. "I've been listening in, getting some of it. The woman who set off the big signal is taking him to meet her 'partner,' whoever that is."

"What woman?" Martin asked.

"Morgan Lafayette," Ko said.

Martin howled like a beast possessed.

Off the rotunda, there was a small door labelled MUSEUM STAFF ONLY. Lafayette took Sword through it and they were in a long corridor of wooden office doors inset with frosted glass.

"Have you been working with the Society of St. Linus for very long?" Sword asked, wondering how long he should keep up the pretense. Probably as long as Lafayette did, he decided.

"Since the beginning, Mr. Sword," the woman said in her seductive, lilting voice. "I was one of its founders." She glanced at him, favoring him with a smile. "Named for one of the early popes of the Catholic Church, did you know? A charming man," she said wistfully, almost as if she had known the man personally, and still missed him. "Ah, here we are. A small reception suite away from the crowd. I'm sure you understand how important that can be?"

"Certainly," Sword said, hiding his sudden unease. He hadn't expected to make contact this way, so cut off from the others. Ko's voice was little more than the buzzing of a fly in his ear. He doubted that anyone back at the van would be receiving anything from his mike pick-ups.

"After you, Mr. Sword," the woman said, gesturing gracefully.

Sword stepped into the small room. At first glance, he was surprised to see that it was set up as a private reception area. There was a portable bar to one side, fully stocked as far as Sword could tell. A ring of brown-leather club chairs surrounded a low table set with trays of *hors d'oeuvres*. It appeared to be the main organizers' hideaway. It appeared to be deserted. Until he heard the voice beside him, from the shadows.

"Little Galen." A man's voice. Smooth and cultured. Cold and threatening. Sword definitely knew that voice. He turned to face its owner.

The man stepped out of the shadows. He had been the man at the head of the reception line, beside Lafayette. Dark eyes and tanned skin, a neatly-trimmed fringe of black hair circling his bald scalp.

"Tomas!" Sword blurted before he even realized he recognized the man. "Tomas Roth."

A look of regret, or pain, almost crossed the man's face. "So the stories are true," Roth said. He shook his head. "I don't know whether to be frightened or impressed by your feat of memory, Little Galen." He made a gesture with the fingers of his right hand, of something slipping through them. The movement seemed familiar to Sword. Something he might have done himself once, a long time ago. "Ah, well," Roth said in resignation. "Lost glitter, fairy glamour, it all means the same in the end, doesn't it?"

"You're the one who sent me away, aren't you?" Sword said. He found he could scarcely breathe. The excitement, the fear he felt, all confounded with the sudden swirl of childhood memories. On Tomas Roth's knee. Reading at his side. The old school. The watching gargoyles.

Roth's black eyes sparkled. "So you don't remember everything," he said, intrigued. "Brin must have done the job himself."

"What do you know about my brother?" Sword demanded. This was it! He was where the answers were kept. He had found the man responsible.

"Your ... brother? Is that all you what to know about?" Roth asked. "Have you no other questions after all this time?"

And the questions flew out of Sword. He prayed that Ko and Forsyte were reading him. "My parents. What happened to them? Why was I sent away? Who — "

"I only asked if you *had* other questions, Little Galen. I didn't say I wanted to know what they were."

Sword put his hand to his head, dizzy from the exhilaration, and now sudden apprehension. "Someone has to answer, Tomas. Someone has to."

"So some would say." Roth walked forward, into the center of the room. "What is your Clan, Little Galen?" he asked sharply.

"Pendragon."

"Your father's name?"

"I ... I don't know."

"What clan hosts this ceremony tonight?"

"Arkady."

"What is the name of this ceremony."

"The Ceremony of the Change Arkady."

"What are the attributes of the adept of Clan Seyshen?"

"I don't know."

"What is your mother's name?"

"I don't know."

Roth looked away for a moment, toward his green-gowned partner who stood by the door, as if his rapid questions were at an end, then abruptly turned his burning eyes back to Sword. "Who killed Marcus Askwith?"

"The Ronin Dmitri!" Sword said in an angry burst.

Roth exhaled audibly. "So you *were* at Softwind the other night, with the witless halfling from the Arkady enclave. Now I am impressed."

"What *is* my father's name?" Sword demanded.

Roth's smile lacked all humor. "His name, Little Galen, is one of those many forgotten things you are destined never to know."

Before Sword could protest once more, Roth raised his hands and moved his fingers through an intricate pattern. Behind him, Sword heard the door to the corridor swing shut. He turned around, but there was no one near it now. The green-gowned woman, Lafayette, was sitting calmly in a club chair, legs crossed, slowly swinging one slim foot.

Sword prepared to meet whatever Roth might throw at him. "I'm not alone," he warned, slipping his fingers beneath his locator band and triggering the alarm signal.

Sword's defiant statement merely caused Roth to smile with real pleasure. "How wonderful for you. Because, neither are we." Roth gestured again, fingers as nimble as a magician's. "Tell me, Little Galen, in that vast store of knowledge that Brin has so helpfully unlocked within you, do you by any chance recall your friend from the old school: Little Seth?"

The name was familiar, but Sword couldn't place it. *The old school,* he thought, *the old school.* What had it been like there? Why did he remember the name and nothing else?

"Too bad," Roth said, interrupting Sword's attempts to recall. "But then, Seth certainly remembers you, don't you, Seth?"

Sword heard a sound behind him and froze. A sound too loud to be another person. He heard deep, heavy breathing. Felt a soft wall of heat reach out to him. Smelled an odor far worse than 'Bub or Martin.

"Hello, Galen," a deep, hollow voice said to him. An inhuman voice.

Sword turned. Looked up. Seven feet to Seth's smile and all the glistening, needle fangs that bristled in his mouth.

"Welcome back," the werewolf said.

SEVENTEEN

The night felt surprisingly cold on Ja'Nette's newly bared head. She wished she had brought a hat like Martin's. But she wouldn't complain. Not with the way Ko looked. Not with the way Martin had howled when he had heard the name of the woman Sword was with. It wasn't Morgan Lafayette, the way Ko said it was. Martin had said the woman's name was really Morgana LaVey. And that she was the Victor of the Clan Arkady. Which meant she was the most powerful shifter of them all — their ruler.

"Don't run, Ja'Nette," Ko commanded sharply. "We can't attract attention."

Ja'Nette slowed her pace and tugged on Martin's arm to slow his, and though he could easily pick her up and run through the streets faster than most cars could go in the city traffic, Martin held back. Like Ja'Nette, he was putting himself in Ko's hands.

Ja'Nette looked back at Ko, following a few feet behind as they made their way along the sidewalk that ran beside the museum's north side on 81st, heading for the long driveway to the staff parking lot where Ko thought a staff entrance would be. Ja'Nette wished Ko had been able to bring her rifle with the darts, but that would have attracted too much attention, too, Ko had said. Ja'Nette thought attention was pretty much what they could use a lot of right now. But she wouldn't complain. Not to Ko. Not now.

"Is Adrian going to be okay?" Ja'Nette asked as they came closer to the wide gate in the low black iron fence that surrounded the museum grounds. If anything bad happened to Ko, Ja'Nette knew that Forsyte couldn't drive the van. Sword and the scientist had talked about modifying a second van so Forsyte could drive it, but the scientist had told Sword to put it off until a faster set of chips came along. Ja'Nette usually wasn't sure what all their computer talk meant, but she knew it did mean that for now Forsyte was depending on them to make it back, just as Sword was depending on them to get in there and save him.

"He'll be fine," Ko said. "We'll go down that far path." She pointed to a narrow asphalt strip that ran beside the driveway. Ja'Nette followed it with her eyes to the small lot by a museum wing. Sure enough, she could see a small open door there, light streaming from it. But she also saw something else.

"There's a policeman there!" As big as one of the Big Men, she thought, imposing in his long tunic and with his black club held ready behind his back.

"That's okay," Ko said. "He'll know we see him so he won't think we're trying to break in. We'll go straight to him without attracting attention."

Again with the attention, Ja'Nette thought. Being careful took time. Maybe too much time. Who knew if Morgana was going to give Sword the same amount? "*Then* what do we do?" Ja'Nette persisted, heading down the path with Ko and Martin.

"Leave that part to me," Ko said. Her words were getting clipped again and Ja'Nette knew that meant she wasn't in a mood to be disturbed about anything.

"Yes'm," Ja'Nette said without argument. But she sure thought that things would be a lot better if she could just somehow attract a little attention.

Sword was bound and blindfolded, tied by cutting cords to one of the club chairs. His head throbbed from the blow the werewolf had given him. Dazed, he felt sharp claws rake against the side of his head as Seth ripped off his hearing aid. He heard his jacket being shredded as the rest of his equipment was torn from his pockets and the antenna strap broken. He felt the locator band bend, then snap in two as it was forced from his wrist. They had found it all. He was cut off and on his own.

For a few lucid moments, he was aware that Roth, and the woman, and the werewolf were still in the room with him, though they said nothing. It sounded as if the werewolf was pacing back and forth impatiently. Sword wondered what werewolves might have to be impatient about, then decided he'd rather not know the answer.

Seth, Sword thought. The name was familiar, striking some hidden chord. Had he known Seth before, in his earlier life? Had he actually *known* a werewolf? Then he heard a door open. It didn't have the rattle of glass so he knew it wasn't the door to the corridor. There must be a second door, he realized. The one that Seth had entered through. A hidden door for hidden things. He wondered if shifters sat on the museum's board of directors.

He heard heavy footsteps again, a second set.

"If it's true," Roth suddenly said, very clearly, "then Herr Slausen grows gills. Do I make myself understood?"

Sword heard a deepthroated growl in reply. Then he felt the presence of something large and inhuman bending over him. He felt a sudden rush of heat crash against him like a wave, and he smelled an explosion of flowers on a summer's day, strong enough to cut off his breath, to make him reel and remember.

Seth.

His mother had taken him to see Seth because Galen was worried that his friend was sick.

Seth was older than Galen, but only by a few years, and they played together in the old school, wrestling and tumbling and trying to trick the gargoyles. Until the day that Seth did not come back.

"He is different now, Little Galen," his mother told him. "His substance is other than yours. His way will be different."

But Seth had been Galen's friend and the child would not stop his questioning. So his mother told him she would take him to see his friend. He didn't know when or where he would be taken, except that his mother had to wait until Galen's father and Roth had left the grounds. And then Galen's mother had taken him through the gardens to one of the fardoors and then ... even as a child, Galen knew he could be anywhere.

The gardens around Seth's house were different from his own. There were no flowers, only green things. And once Galen stumbled on an uneven stone and tumbled and his mother only kept him upright by pulling on his arm. Galen's arm hurt and the boy was surprised. He remembered that clearly. He wondered why Seth's parents did not use gardeners whose crystals could take all pain and danger from a garden.

Seth's house was towering tall to Galen's child eyes. It was warm brown in color, soft and carved like the smooth twists and turns of tangled trees. Galen brushed his hand against the stone of Seth's house and wondered why so much crystal should be used in building the house and not in maintaining the garden.

"Seth is different," he heard his mother say.

They were met by a troll whose pretty eyes and lovely full mouth ducked down in respect to Galen's mother. Galen watched as the two women spoke in a softwind language which Galen had not yet learned. The women laughed and Galen knew that everyone was at ease around his mother. The troll motioned them to follow her through a long corridor and up a staircase which Galen knew was not the sort for guests. The troll's legs were scarcely longer than the boy's, but Galen had to work hard to keep up.

In an upstairs hallway, they stopped by a carved wooden door whose two sides arched up to meet in a point. An old man waited by the door. Galen thought he looked angry. The man had fighting eyes like Galen's Uncle Alexander and those eyes flashed as he spoke with Galen's mother, as if he could barely keep himself in control.

"I don't care what Roth has told anyone," Galen's mother said. "The boys are friends. That must be honored. A warrior, of all things, must know that to be true."

"He has no substance," the old warrior said. "He will not understand."

"He is my son," Galen's mother said proudly. "It is his right."

The warrior's eyes flared, then dimmed. He dropped his head with the same respect the troll had shown. "As you wish, my lady." And then they entered Seth's room.

Galen smelled the stench of that room as the door was opened, and he was worried that his friend was hurt or dead.

"Just different, now," his mother told him. "He has gone through his first Change. He is not as you remember him."

It was not a child's bedroom. Galen knew that right away. The glowing facets gliding close to the ceiling sent out light of rippled green, like sunlight through forest leaves. The floor was covered in layers of rough woven mats. The furniture was unfinished wood and seemed to be more like playground barricades for climbing instead of dressers for storage. And the smell was like the garbage digs behind Galen's house, like what the gardeners used for flowers.

Galen heard a rasping, breathing noise, like a big dog. He thought, perhaps, that Seth had been given a pet or a Light as a present for being sick. "Seth?" he called out. His voice sounded flat, as if he spoke in a large outdoor area and not in a closed-in room.

"Galen?" a voice answered back. And Galen realized that the breathing sound had stopped as his name was spoken.

Behind a barricade, his friend Seth lay sprawled on a torn-up mound made from folded pads of the rough floor coverings. Galen called to him again as his hand slipped from his mother's, and Seth rolled over to greet him.

It was Seth and it was not Seth. He had changed.

The new image of his friend seared into Galen's mind. He had not been told, had not been warned. The thing before him still had Seth's eyes, green and wide. But his skin was gone beneath a thick cover of silver fur. His features replaced by dark bands which ran as shading down arms and legs now grown so long they looked deformed. And his face had stretched as well. His mouth had thrust out to become a snout, topped by the glistening black pad of his nose, and filled with teeth that gleamed with drool. But it still had the voice of his friend. The voice of Seth.

"Hello, Galen," Seth said slowly, as if he struggled to catch his breath. He pushed himself up from the coverings that made a nest beneath him. What had been hands were now covered in fur and ended in long black claws. And something stained them, as dark and as wet as the stains around his nose and mouth.

"What happened to you?" Galen asked. He knew about shifters. He had seen shifters talking with his mother and father. But he had never *known* a shifter.

"I'm a big boy, now," Seth said proudly. "I'm ninety months old." He smiled at Galen, pulling himself into a crouch, baring all his dripping fangs. "I've changed."

Galen stepped forward on his short stubby legs. The floor was all ripped up and uneven. "Are you going to come back to the old school?" he asked.

"Later," Seth said. He lowered his head and licked at one of his hands. His tongue, much longer now than it had been, came away red.

"How much later?"

"When I'm finished." The tongue flicked among his fangs, searching and cleaning.

"Finished what?" Galen asked.

"This," Seth said. Then he thrust his head down to his side and came up with what had lain beside him.

The arm of a human child.

Galen slipped backward and fell against his mother. Seth growled and shook the arm until it fell away and left a dripping piece of flesh in his mouth. He angled his head up and opened his mouth with quick biting movements, until the flesh had fallen within his teeth. Then he swallowed.

Galen trembled. "It is their way, Little Galen. You must know," his mother whispered.

Seth nudged the arm where it lay in front of him, running his nose along its length. Then he looked back at Galen and his nose twitched again. Seth's eyes looked puzzled. They seemed to roll back in his head as if he had been overcome. He got to his feet. All four of them.

"You smell ... different," Seth said uncertainly.

"We must go, Galen," his mother said.

"Why, mother?"

Seth stepped forward, rearing back on his hind legs, bringing his front claws up. He was five feet tall now. Almost two feet taller than when Galen had last seen him.

"You smell ... ," he began.

"Now, Galen, now." His mother pulled him back.

"Human!" Seth growled. He coiled to leap, all awareness gone from his eyes.

Galen screamed. His mother pulled him up, spun him around, protecting him with her body.

But the impact of the werewolf never came.

In front of Galen and his mother, the old warrior stood, eyes blazing with the fighting light, a fist-sized crystal radiant as the setting sun in his upraised hand.

Galen looked over his mother's shoulder. Seth was still coiled for the leap, unmoving, bathed in the light of the working crystal.

"What more proof do you need that Roth is right?" the warrior said to Galen's mother. "Even a child like Seth can tell he does not belong."

The rest was confusion. Running from the room, the house, through the garden, to the fardoor. Galen remembered the troll's tearful farewell to his mother.

The only other thing he remembered from that meeting with Seth, after the Change, was when he had tugged on his mother's hand, safe within the confines of his own garden, and asked her in a small, frightened tone, "Will I change, Mother?"

There was no understanding the look that passed over his mother's face at that question, no hints, no clues as to whether it was pain she felt, or shame, or a hunger for vengeance. But the moment had passed quickly and she had knelt down to her son to hold his hands firmly in hers, and with tears in her eyes she had answered him.

"In time, I fear, you must."

The dizzying wave of flowers left him and Sword drew in a gasp of unscented air. He felt human fingers at his blindfold, and then he could see again. The green-gowned woman stood before him. Roth was beside her. Sword turned his head to locate Seth and saw him standing by the door to the corridor. Then he heard movement on his other side and turned in time to see a tall thin figure in loose blue clothing disappear through what seemed to be an open panel in the wall. Dmitri, he suspected with apprehension, but was too late to see the creature's face and know for sure. The panel flickered shut and the room was ordinary again. Dazed, Sword wondered what the creature had done to him and why he had smelled the flowers.

"You don't remember fardoors?" the green-gowned woman asked.

Sword turned back to her. He tugged at the cords that bound him to the arms of the chair. His hands were going numb. "They were always in the garden," he said suddenly, remembering as he spoke. "They led to other ... houses. Other enclaves."

"See?" the woman said dismissively, arching her eyebrow at Roth. "A child's memory. Someone has lifted Herr Slausen's work, but whoever it was hasn't told him anything more."

"Except for the halfling," Roth said, sounding unconvinced.

Seth stepped forward from his place by the door. The claws of his feet clattered on the hardwood floor. "We should have tagged Martin years ago," he growled. "I told John and Brenda ... "

"Takes after his father," the woman said sweetly. Then she smiled at Sword. "Do you remember *me*, Galen?" She read the look in his eyes. "Pity. Forget what I told you in the reception line. My First World name is Morgana. My family name, LaVey. My family and your clan go back many years." She laughed mockingly as Sword's expression changed. "Ah," she said, "so you at least remember the humans' legends. Too bad they're only that. The humans would have you believe I was a Light and you were born to rule with sword and stone."

"You're a shifter," Sword said. Forsyte's device had confirmed it.

Seth leaned forward. His breath was foul in Sword's face. "My mother is the Victor to the Clan Arkady. And I am her heir." He growled. "I should have ripped out your throat when I had the chance so long ago. A child's flesh tastes so sweet."

Sword looked past the werewolf, defiant. "And I am the heir to the Victor of the Clan Pendragon."

"Oh, my," Morgana said to Roth, "Brin *has* been busy."

"This isn't a joke," Roth cautioned her. Sword was glad to see the man was worried. If he were a man. He tried to remember what Roth had been like in his childhood memories, but nothing notable came to mind, except that Roth had always travelled with his father. Except that once, the day that he himself had been sent away.

"Things have changed since you left," Roth said. "The heir to the Victor Pendragon was without substance. What with the tragic accident, a mysterious disappearance, the line of the Victor came to an ... untimely end."

"Who rules Pendragon now?" Sword risked another question. Whoever ruled be the adept to go to for help.

"There is no Victor at this time," Roth said, with a glance at Morgana LaVey who was checking her thin gold watch with a restless sigh. "I, however, am its Regent if you'd care to petition me for aid. You don't? Then, on the other hand, by caveat of the Council — if such things make sense to you — Seth is the new heir to the Victor of Pendragon."

"But Seth is a shifter, not an elemental."

Roth's eyes flashed. "Very astute, little Galen. But clan lines shift over the years. Long before the Great War with the Lesser Clans, Arkady was once a guild of crystal cutters, yet look at them today."

"Why waste this time, Tomas?" Morgana asked impatiently. "We know what we have to do. And the dawn," — she tapped her watch — "is only six hours away."

"There is more than Brin at work here," Roth said. "And more than the halfling."

"Askwith then?" Morgana asked. "Remember at the meeting that night? He had time to make a phone call before Dmitri ... " Morgana looked over to Sword. "Did you talk to Marcus Askwith on the night he died, Galen?"

Sword shook his head. Morgana frowned at Roth. "Marjoribanks?" she asked.

Roth looked pained. "She's a *human*, Morgana. She knows nothing."

Sword tried to keep his face blank. Roth had used the present tense. That might mean that Miss Marjoribanks, Askwith's partner and the lawyer who had set up his trust fund with his parents, was still alive.

"Then we'll just have to go to Herr Slausen again," Morgana said.

"Do we even know where he is?" Roth asked.

"Dmitri will. The doors can be aligned in time."

"And when the Council finds out we've involved the wizard again? He only works with crystal."

"What else do you suggest we do, Tomas? Beat it out of that?" Morgana waved a hand in Sword's direction, her gesture one of disdain.

Seth raised a claw. "That would be permissible under the oaths," he growled.

Roth ran a hand over his gleaming scalp. He sat down in a club chair next to Sword's. "I know you have a thousand questions, Galen. But the truth of it is, you're a pawn. You don't belong in the First World. Never have. Some adepts wanted you killed" — Roth glared at Seth as the werewolf laughed coarsely — "but as your father's advisor, I developed the other, less ... radical means of coping with you."

"Banishment," Sword said bitterly. "Exile."

"Don't think of it as losing your family, boy, think of it as gaining your life." Roth steepled his fingers together. "The bottom line is that you don't belong here tonight. You're a pawn. You've been set up. Someone is using you against ... us."

"Why? Especially if I don't belong?"

Roth shrugged, smoothing down his formal jacket. "That's hard to say, Galen. The politics of the First World are very complex. Perhaps you can remember how busy your father and mother were when you were a child? Perhaps not. It's not important. But some of the ... players in our game ... have been involved with each other for centuries. The animosities involved are far beyond anything you might have experienced in the Second World."

"My parents are dead, aren't they?" Sword said. Assassinated from the way Roth was talking, he thought with sudden, unexpected grief.

Roth looked away for a moment before replying. When he looked back again, he was very sincere. "Trust me, Galen. In the First World, there are many things worse than death."

"You're wasting time, Tomas," Morgana warned Roth.

"Let me deal with him," Seth urged. "We can use him in the Ceremony."

But Roth waved his hand as if to silence the mother and her son. "You see what I mean?" he murmured to Sword. "This is what I have to deal with."

"Why do you then?" Sword challenged. "Why not let me return and I'll deal with it."

Roth started, then laughed, the sound deep and hearty and false. "If only I could, Galen. If only you could. But the time for that is long passed. Perhaps you were an option once, but history has passed you by. There is no place for you here in our World."

"But you won't tell me why."

"The old reasons aren't important anymore," Roth said, dismissing them with a snap of his fingers. "As for the new reasons, when Seth becomes the Victor of Pendragon, the clan lines of Arkady and Pendragon will merge." He interlaced his fingers. "The two clans have had ... certain disagreements in the past — "

"Apart in the Council," Sword said.

Roth shot another glance at Morgana. "See what I mean?" he said. He looked back to Sword. "As you say, Galen, the two clans have been apart in the Council for generations now. But Seth will bring them together and this will bring great peace to the First World."

"Funny," Sword said, not to prove his knowledge but to disturb the man, "I had heard there was going to be war."

Roth stood up abruptly, his face darkening. "Can you call *this* a coincidence, Morgana?"

Morgana went to the man and lightly caressed his cheek. "There's going to be a Ceremony, Tomas. The rumors of war always fly at these times. But then, when the World sees that the Change from humanform to shifterform balances out the Change from shifter to human, it all calms down again. You know what the softwind is like."

"Except this time the Changes won't balance," Roth said angrily and pushed Morgana's hand from his face. "And he knows. He *knows.*" Roth wheeled around to confront Sword. His cheeks were flushed. His eyes sparkled dangerously. "The Seyshen dug you up, didn't they? That's who gave you all this information, isn't it?"

Seyshen, Seyshen, Sword repeated to himself, trying to take advantage of Roth's decreasing control of his emotions, trying to remember why the name 'Seyshen' was familiar. Of course, it was what Tantoo had called Martin, what had caused Martin to fly into his rage at Softwind.

Struggling to remember every strange First World word Martin had ever used, Sword regarded Roth with what he hoped was convincing scorn. "I wouldn't deal with those coldblasted, two-fanged halflings for all the glitter in the Worlds," he said contemptuously.

Roth snapped. "I *knew* it. I knew this was no accident." He lunged at Sword and grabbed him by his collar, lifting him and the club chair he was bound to and threw both back five feet to smash against the wall. Then before the chair could slide down the wall to the floor, Roth kicked aside the low table with its plate of *hors d'oeuvres* and came at Sword again.

Sword's chair landed upright. The sudden impact knocked the breath from Sword's lungs.

Sword was still gasping for air as the fingers of one of Roth's hands closed like talons around his neck. "Who sent you, you 'chanted bastard? *Who?*"

Roth's other hand dug into a pocket in his tuxedo jacket and brought out a dull red crystal, irregularly cut, about the size of human's fingertip. He held the crystal before Sword's face, small sparks of blue fire danced from Roth's open palm, into the crystal, and the crystal began to glow.

"Do you know what I can do to you with this?" the enraged man snarled in Sword's ear. "*Do you know what I can do to you?*"

Sword couldn't answer. The sound of blood thundered in his ears. His empty lungs strained to fill with air. He closed his eyes but the crystal's red glow was not diminished in his sight. It became blinding, overpowering, until —

"Nothing," Morgana said firmly. "You can do nothing to him."

Sword opened his eyes. He saw Morgana's hand slide into Roth's, cup the glowing crystal and take it away. Roth's hold on Sword's throat loosened.

"You know better than that," Morgana said.

Roth released his grip entirely, straightened up, and adjusted his formal evening suit. Morgana held out the glowing crystal to him. "Now turn this off."

Roth took the crystal, rolled it between his fingers, and the glow faded. He slipped the stone back into his jacket pocket as if he were holstering a gun.

"Much better," Morgana said and patted Roth's chest. Then she turned and gazed at Sword. "And now, Little Galen, we'll deal with you ... my way."

Seth howled.

EIGHTEEN

Can I help you?" the heavyset policeman in the museum's parking lot asked.

"No thanks," Ko said cheerfully. She didn't break stride as she walked up to him. "Just taking the kids to pick up my husband." Thankfully, Ko thought, it was dark enough in the small employee lot that the policeman couldn't examine her 'children' in detail. Ja'Nette might be her adopted daughter but Martin would need zoo release papers.

"Then I gotta see your pass, ma'am," the officer said. He had a pleasant half-smile on his broad face, but Ko could see he kept glancing over to Martin who was trying unsuccessfully to hide behind Ja'Nette.

"Oh, I got one of those," Ko said loudly, reaching inside a pocket of her vest. "Somewhere in here," she added, trying to distract him from Martin.

"He with you?" the policeman asked, using his nightstick to point to Martin.

"Sure is," Ko said, aiming the taser dart at the cop's neck. She'd take a chance with the more difficult target rather than risk having the electrified dart bounce off any body armor the cop might be wearing beneath his tunic.

The spring-loaded dart took off with a *thwick* and the cop suddenly gurgled and fell back to the ground. Ko knew he would be trying to get his hands to his throat to pull out the dart — still trailing two wires back to the battery pack in her vest — but the 100,000 volt charge the dart was delivering through its conductive needles was too disruptive to his nervous system for him to succeed. Despite the high charge, however, the darts delivered very low amperage so the shock would not be harmful. For Ko, that made it a perfect weapon. For dealing with humans.

Ko snapped her fingers at Martin and pointed to a spot between two parked cars. She kept her eyes on the open employees' entrance door just off the parking lot. Martin slipped his hands under the cop's armpits and dragged him easily to the cover of the cars. Ko pressed the release button on the wires from the battery pack, reloaded the taser tube, connected the new dart to the battery pack, and hurried off to join Martin and Ja'Nette. No one had come through the door. So far, they were safe.

"Tie and gag," Ko said as she crouched down beside Ja'Nette and an old Grand Am. "Careful about making the loops too tight, Martin."

"Martin know that," the halfling muttered. He pulled two sets of white nylon slip loops from the vest he wore over his sweatshirt.

The cop's twitching hand suddenly punched straight up, smashing Martin's face back with a savage blow to his chin.

Then the cop sat upright and *growled*. A long mane of hair flowed from the cap that tumbled from him. And he had fangs.

Ja'Nette gasped and crossed her arms over her chest.

Ko rocked back out of reach of the shifter's legs and reached to her vest for a can of silver spray. The shifter sprang to his feet, wrenched the dart from his neck and threw it to the ground. He snarled at Ko and ground his heel into the dart, crushing it against the pavement. But before he could attack, his cap flew from the ground, spun through the air, and drove itself onto his face, covering his eyes.

The shifter reacted in confusion, stumbling back against the Grand Am. He howled in pain as Martin's feet slammed into his knees from the side and he crumpled to the ground between the cars. Just as he managed to yank the translocated cap from his face, Ko descended on him, madly spraying the aerosol can.

The creature writhed on the ground, hands covering his face, desperately trying to save his eyes from the stinging spray. Ko could see thick red hives already erupting on the shifter's exposed skin. Then Martin's open hand viciously chopped against the cop's larynx, instantly ending his cries of pain. After the shifter's body had lain still a moment, his hat flipped up through the air once more and landed neatly on his face.

Ko took a breath and turned to Ja'Nette just as the child uncrossed her arms. "Don't waste that."

"Haven't eaten all day," Ja'Nette said proudly. "See? I'm learning."

"Good girl," Ko said, then saw Ja'Nette's mouth open in surprise. Ko wheeled and stared over the car. Three dark, hulking shapes shambled from the employees' entrance, fanning out into the darkness.

"I think we finally attracted some attention," Ja'Nette said.

Dmitri's translucent blue eyes sparkled with small swirling flecks of silver as he held Galen Sword against the wall of the small reception room. His thin, white, fleshless lips pulled back in a monstrous gape over the long, crooked blades of his teeth. He held his other hand in front of Sword's face, clacking his two-inch-long claws together.

"What is he?" Sword croaked out as best he could, trying to free his throat from Dmitri's grasp.

Morgana stood in the center of the room by Roth and made a small pouting expression. "Even we're not sure," she said. "And as you can see, Dmitri's not talking."

Seth laughed.

"But he does have a wondrous blue power," Roth added, walking into Sword's view. "I believe you've seen some of its results? Marcus Askwith?"

"How?" Sword coughed. He looked away from the hideously out-of-place silver crucifix Dmitri wore around his neck. He raised his eyes to Dmitri's face and the horribly swollen skull with tight, dead skin blinked its eyes at him. For a split second after the thick white eyelids opened again, Dmitri's eyes appeared solid black. But then the silver flecks came alive again and the translucent, depthless blue color returned in their light.

"Is it important how he does it, Galen?" Roth asked. "Is it not enough to know that he *can* do it? It's just a simple force of nature, after all. Though not, perhaps, a force of any nature you'd remember."

"He also has the gift of flowers," Morgana said with an affectionate smile at Dmitri. "Yet I'm quite sure he has no wizardry in his line."

"Though the flowers didn't appear to work on you, Galen," Roth said thoughtfully. You didn't remember anything about who was helping you tonight."

Morgana touched Roth's arm. "Or about whom *he* is helping tonight."

Sword recalled the strong scent of flowers he had smelled just after being blindfolded. It had been right after that that he had remembered his meeting with Seth as a child. Perhaps it was a form of interrogation that Dmitri had tried on him. He was glad to know it hadn't worked quite as his captors had wished.

"So, Little Galen," Morgana said, slipping her arm around Roth, "we've tried flowers and reason. Now it's time to try something more ... human, I would say."

Roth nodded. "Torture."

⌒

Ko waved Martin to the front of the car they had ducked behind. She jerked a thumb over her back to tell Ja'Nette where to stay. Ja'Nette crossed her arms and started rocking and humming, building up a charge.

Then Ko jumped to her feet and ran out into the center of the parking lot. It held about fifty cars and the center area was the only clear section. She knew she had to draw their adversaries out, otherwise she and Ja'Nette and Martin would be too vulnerable to ambush.

She heard rapid footfalls to her left. She turned and dropped to one knee. Whatever was coming at her came on all fours, saliva streaming from its jaws, front paws disappearing between hind feet as it sprang forward.

"Three!" Ko shouted. At the last possible second she tucked and rolled to the right. The creature began to compensate perfectly in midair. But suddenly the left side of its face jerked back as if clutched by two child-sized hands.

The creature squealed and fell to the left, stumbling onto its side. Before it could right itself, Ko was beside it, spraying its face with silver halide and driving a thin plastic handgrip, studded with silver needles, into its flank.

The creature twisted backward, wheezing in shock. It threw itself on the ground trying to roll and dislodge the handgrip. Ko leaped back out of range of its wildly waving claws and felt searing pain shoot through her arm as another dark shape swept by her, slashing her on the run.

She was stunned by the force of the blow and her vision flickered. She felt her face press against the small pebbles on the parking lot asphalt. All her senses were operational but limited. Her eyesight flickered again. *Blow to the head,* she thought. *Have to fight it.* Then she felt herself jerked upright, held by the back of her neck. She felt a dozen hot razors rip through her back. She screamed in surprise more than pain.

Then she heard Martin's howl cut the night and whatever held her threw her back to the pavement. She heard mad growls and the heavy impact of bonecrushing blows close beside her. She saw two dark shapes locked in combat. One was Martin.

It only took Ko a few seconds to push up on her knees and elbows. She reached to her vest for another needle grip. Her back blazed with pain. Her arm trembled. But she would not stop.

"Martin!" she shouted, rising to her feet, holding the silver needles above her head, ready to throw herself into the battle before her.

But the bodies had stopped moving.

"Martin?" *Impossible,* she cried within herself. She couldn't have been too late.

And then one body rose from the other and stepped into the light. Martin. He breathed through his mouth. His teeth were stained and his mouth ran with blood not his own.

Ja'Nette ran to her friend and threw her arms around him. She looked up at him and saw the gore in his fangs. The child did not question it.

Martin looked back at the body on the pavement. To Ko, it looked like a puma with an oddly shaped chest. Its throat was torn open. Its blood spurted out in slowly weakening rhythmic pulses.

Martin turned to Ko and looked her in the eye. At last she saw that there was no ignorance there, only wisdom a thousand years older than any Ko could hope to acquire.

"Not want to," Martin said huskily. "Have to. Difference."

Ko watched the body of the puma. It was changing back to its humanform, twisting in on itself as if it were being devoured from within.

"I understand," Ko said. The creature she had sprayed and impaled was also back in humanform. A young woman, pale and naked in the night. "There was a third ... ?" Ko asked. She had lost track in the confusion. Something she had never believed could happen to her.

"That was mine," Ja'Nette said. Her voice sounded older.

Martin hugged her again. "Ja'Nette hunt well. Little sister."

Ja'Nette looked over to the staff entrance door. "But whoever's inside closed the door on us. Probably locked it."

"Probably 'chanted," Martin added. "Blue power not work."

Ko pulled a small plastic-explosive charge from her vest. "That's all right," she said. "I've got a key."

Morgana placed her hand on Dmitri's shoulder and Sword saw it rest on a shape that appeared to be part of no skeleton he could recognize. "Dmitri," she said, "Tomas and I are going to ask Little Galen some questions now. When he doesn't answer, or if he gives the wrong answer, I want you to carve out a little section of his ... let's see, now, shall we keep it simple? His face, I think."

"Leave the eyes to last," Roth agreed.

"Question number one, Galen," Morgana began. "Who is providing you with your back-up and your equipment, such that it was?"

Sword fixed his eyes on Dmitri's flashing claws. "Sword Foundation — it pays the people with me ... pays for everything." He looked at Roth and saw him nod at Morgana.

"Too bad, Dmitri," she said. "Question number two: Who told you to come here tonight?"

"No one told me. They didn't want me to come." He gagged, trying to catch his breath.

"Now we're getting somewhere," Morgana said, pleased. "Who told you not to come?"

Sword made a rasping sound in his throat. He struggled desperately to catch his breath.

"Dmitri," Roth admonished, "please allow Galen to at least touch his feet to the floor."

Dmitri's lips tugged down in a frown and he released his grip enough to let Sword slide to the floor. The grip around Sword's throat stayed loose and Sword sucked in a huge gulp of air. "Thank you," he said weakly, and let his head dip, calculating the period of the swing of Dmitri's cross on its heavy silver chain, now directly in front of his eyes.

"You see, Galen," Roth said silkily, "we can offer you rewards as well as punishments. You should remember that. Now, who told you not to come tonight?"

"Melody Ko," he said in defeat.

Dmitri slackened his grip again and Sword realized his guess had been correct. The creature could somehow sense when Sword lied. Roth and Morgana must be depending on Dmitri to let them know when they were closing in on the truth.

"Very good," Morgana said. "With a name like Melody, is she a troll?"

"No," Sword said. He let his body slump even more against Dmitri's grip. If he could drag out the questioning by not volunteering anything, get Dmitri to relax his hold just a bit more ... The silver cross still swung. Into reach, and out of reach. Back and forth.

Roth let an edge of anger shade his voice. "We're not playing here, Galen. Tell us what kind of adept this Melody Ko is. Which clan is she with?"

"She's a human, not an adept. I don't think she has a clan."

Roth stepped closer. "Then she must *work* for someone who has *contact* with a clan." A dull thump shook the room and Sword heard the glass in the door rattle. Roth glanced over his shoulder for a moment as Seth opened the door and looked out into the corridor. Roth turned back to Sword, staring at him over Dmitri's skeletally thin arm. "So to whom does this Melody Ko answer?"

"I pay her from Sword Foundation but she also answers to Adrian Forsyte." Sword tried to make his body go limp. That thump might have been the explosion of one of Ko's charges. But Dmitri must have sensed a change in his mood. The bony claw tightened around Sword's neck and Dmitri turned to look at Roth.

"Ah," Roth said, "*now* you're trying to hide something."

"Something's going on down there," Seth growled, leaning back into the room. "I'm going to check it out."

"Just stay away from the rotunda," Morgana advised him.

"Yeah, yeah," Seth said, then slipped out the door, claws clattering on the bare floor of the corridor.

But Roth was not distracted. "Dmitri, show Galen what you do when someone tries to hide something from you."

Sword felt Dmitri shift his stance. He looked up at the grinning skull just in time to see a wickedly sharp claw thrust at his face. The edge of it cut Sword just beneath his left eye. He felt it tear through him, felt the red hot heat of it as it sliced through his skin and flesh and even scraped against his bone.

Sword screamed. Dmitri gibbered with pleasure. His chest shook with silent laughter, moving with mad jerks within the soft blue fabric of his loose shirt. He pulled his claw away, no longer white.

Sword felt his blood run down his cheek, across his neck.

"What a pity Orion isn't here," Morgana said, her tongue moistening her own lips as she surveyed Sword's wound.

"Don't even joke about that," Roth snapped at her. He reached out and grabbed Sword's face, pinching him cruelly as he forced Sword to meet his gaze. "Time to face the facts, boy. You've just spent twenty years in a playground compared to what you're going to find here. Welcome to the real world, Galen Sword. The First World."

Ko led them through the smoke of the explosion. The first few lights along the corridor beyond the employees' entrance had blown out in the concussion, but the rest of the broad hallway was well lit and she saw nothing moving. To her right ascended a wide staircase. She guessed that given the slope of the land around the museum, it led to the main floor. The hallway in front of them was a basement corridor.

None of Sword's equipment was putting out a signal. She assumed that meant he had been captured.

"Where would they take Sword, Martin?"

"Depends," Martin said. He sniffed the air, moving his head to the stairway, then to the hall. "Many shifters both ways."

"Would they take him to the Ceremony?" Ja'Nette asked.

"Too early for Ceremony," Martin said.

Ko considered her two options. If the Ceremony were still time away, then most of the shifters might still be upstairs. Would Sword be with most of the shifters, though? Wouldn't his captors want to take him someplace out of the way? Yet why would they risk moving him from a secured area? "Upstairs," she decided. "He's been in here less than an hour. He'll be upstairs with the rest of them."

Martin moved quickly to the stairway, offering no argument. "Many many shifters," he said, then bounded up the stairs on all fours.

Ko paused at the bottom step as Martin stopped to peer around the corner from the first landing. She held out her hand to Ja'Nette beside her. "You did maneuver number three perfectly," she said.

Ja'Nette slapped Ko's open palm. "Fake to the right, translocate to the left."

"Think it's time to call in reinforcements?" Ko suddenly asked.

"Say what?" Ja'Nette said, then followed Ko's gaze to the small red panel on the wall above the first step. "Hey, yeah!"

"Time to attract a *lot* of attention," Ko said. Then she sprinted up the stairs as Martin signalled all clear. Behind her, lagging just for a moment, Ja'Nette nodded her head and three feet away, untouched by human hands, a fire-alarm switch broke through its glass bar and set itself off.

"All riiight!" Ja'Nette shouted over the sudden wail of the siren, and then she ran up the stairs to join her waiting friends.

"They're all *humans!?*" Roth said in disbelief. "*All* of them?"

Sword held his hand to the open wound on his face. His head felt more swollen than Dmitri's, throbbing larger with each beat of his heart. "Except for Martin," he said weakly, and it wasn't all a show now.

"But he's just a halfling!" Morgana protested.

"That's it," Sword said, spitting out the blood that had trickled into his mouth. "Ask Dmitri."

"Twenty years of exile," Roth said, holding his hands on his head, "and this boy without substance came so close to ruining everything in one cursed night."

"But he didn't, Tomas, he didn't," Morgana said, stroking Roth on his shoulder. "It was just an accident of fate."

"Or of Brin," Roth added darkly.

"Where is my brother?" Sword demanded. He knew he wasn't in a position to ask anything, but he didn't care anymore. He could take being shut out of the First World. That had been going on long enough, he knew, and he had been halfway prepared for tonight to have been another in his long list of failures to reestablish contact. And if it hadn't been, then what he had hoped for was an invitation back in, as if his exile had been some type of fairy-tale trial by ordeal which he had passed with honors. But he hadn't expected this: That the First World was just as violent, and as twisted, and as dangerous as his own.

What had he been thinking of all these years? What had driven him into this madness of crystals and werewolves and creatures who looked like the walking dead? Sword touched his hand to his cheek and felt the warmth of his blood upon it, saw it glisten in his fingers. His real blood, his life's blood.

There was no fantasy here. No escape. The time for legends was past. This was no longer a romantic search for his beginnings. This was his life.

He felt Roth staring at him and he met the dark man's eyes. And held them. Roth looked away first. Sword hoped the sudden change of expression he had seen on Roth had been one of fear.

"If I knew where your *brother* was, Galen, then he would be here with Dmitri, and you would still be a happy Second World sheep." Roth glanced back at the door as if expecting Seth's return.

"Enough of this prattle," Morgana said, glancing at her watch again. "What are we going to do with him? And his human friends?"

Roth looked at her questioningly. "I suppose we'll have to — "

A high-pitched fire siren suddenly wailed, cutting off Roth's words.

"Oh, for ... what is it now?" Morgana said with irritation, heading straight for the door to the hallway.

And Sword smiled with relief, because she had finally asked a question he could answer easily.

NINETEEN

Forsyte had reached his limit. Without the van's communications equipment, he was blind and deaf as well as paralyzed. He had only his small transceiver to follow what was going on outside, and now that Ko, Ja'Nette, and Martin had entered the museum, their transmissions were breaking up as badly as Sword's had. But it was the fire alarm that had finally pushed him past the point at which he could no longer follow Ko's careful execution of his plan. Without the van's equipment to monitor her actions, he was useless inside. It was time to move out.

The mechanisms that controlled the van's locking tracks, back doors, and kneeling platform were powered by a separate electrical system and still operational. Forsyte blinked three times and his chair's computer initiated the disembark sequence. The only difference was that this time the van was not parked in the safety of the Loft's garage.

The night breeze, full of the impending storm, felt good on Forsyte's face as his chair rotated to the opening doors. Even with its exhaust and filth, the air of the city smelled like freedom to him. The tracks moved forward on their double worm drive until the chair was transferred to the kneeling platform, and then Forsyte felt himself pushed forward and lowered to the streets of the city.

The chair's computer held a map of the Loft so that getting around in it was usually no more complex than telling the chair where he wanted to end up. The computer then chose the best route and all Forsyte had to do was make sure that it didn't try to roll the chair over 'Bub or any unexpected debris that Sword might have left lying around. But a sidewalk at night, four lanes of traffic to traverse, a museum full of shifters ... Forsyte's mouth quivered into a smile. This was a challenge he could enjoy. This was action and he didn't care what the cost might be. He had had enough of passivity.

He blinked the code that gave him realtime control over his chair, then moved his fingers to the sensitive joystick. He still heard only bursts of static and sporadic partial words from the transceivers of Ko's team so he had no idea what was transpiring. But at least he would be part of it.

He waited for a gap in the traffic, then blinked the chair to its full three-mile-an-hour speed, slowing only when he reached the opposite curb safely. There, the chair's treads easily climbed from the road to the sidewalk, its center-support stalk pivoting to keep Forsyte level at all times.

He turned to the right, and ahead of him by one hundred feet, he could see a group of parking attendants and uniformed drivers swarming about the bulky trailers of the stationary searchlights, watching as a crowd of formally-dressed men and women began to hurriedly exit the museum. The entrance Ko had used was even farther away, around to the building's north side.

Forsyte rotated the chair to see what other possibilities were open to him. In the distance, he could hear the foghorn blasts of fire-truck sirens as they converged on the museum. He knew he had to act fast. His chair had some surprises which he thought might be useful against shifters, but he wouldn't want to use them on firefighters. Unless it was absolutely necessary.

At the far corner, he saw the first spinning red lights of the approaching trucks. He heard the growing babble of confusion among the departing guests. He made his decision and the chair sped off as Forsyte joined the growing battle.

Seth threw open the door before Morgana could open it.

"Hostile force!" the werewolf growled. "Four down at the north entrance."

"Seyshen?" Morgana asked apprehensively. "So soon?"

"They'd never risk the fire alarm," Roth said. He turned to Sword who was still gripped by Dmitri. "It has to be his people. His *humans*."

But Seth shook his head. "Four *dead*, Roth. *Four*. Humans don't kill shifters."

Roth ignored the beast. "Do we know how many of the clan have come down from the rotunda?"

Morgana checked her watch. "By this time, according to the schedule ... maybe a hundred."

"Seth, go direct those who are already down here into the passageway. The others will just have to evacuate with the humans. If the fire department leaves before dawn, they can try to get back in."

"A hundred won't be enough!" Morgana protested. "We need all of them."

But Roth was firm. "We'll just have to attack faster than we had planned. With Pendragon powerless, we can still prevail."

"It's madness, Tomas. Only a hundred. And the Seyshen have Orion, I'm sure of it."

Roth grabbed Morgana by her shoulders as if to shake sense back into her. "Then we shall have Diandra. And we *shall* prevail."

"Diandra?" gasped Morgana. She turned to Sword. "But — "

Then Seth growled at Roth, green eyes staring intently at him, black lips twitching. Roth removed his hands from the werewolf's mother and Seth fell silent.

"What are you waiting for?" Roth spoke sharply to the beast. "Go guide the others."

Seth turned to Morgana for confirmation. "Yes, go," she said. "And be careful. This could be a Seyshen ruse." Seth left the room, the rattle of the glass in the door drowned out by the wailing of the fire siren. Morgana turned back to Roth. "What about Galen?"

Roth thought a moment, then pointed to the blank wall. "The fardoor," he said. "We'll have to take him with us."

Dmitri moaned in disappointment. Sword glanced at the wall. He could see a faint gray hairline describing a rectangle floating just above where he had suspected a secret door might be hidden. The area within the rectangle seemed to flicker. He remembered fardoors. If the working crystal were powerful enough, there was no way of knowing how far away the other side might be. He couldn't risk going through. It was time.

"I know, Dmitri, I know," Roth said. "But we have no time to finish it now."

Dmitri released Sword's throat. This was it. Sword fell to his knees, snatching at Dmitri's crucifix as he dropped down. The heavy chain holding it snapped and Sword dove to one side, scrambling over a club chair with the cross held in his hand.

Dmitri made a sound like a cat on fire. He spun, claws clutching frantically at the empty space around his neck, ignoring Sword. The silver sparks in his eyes winked out and he was left with solid black, featureless orbs. He stumbled blindly.

"Give it back to him!" Roth shouted. "You don't know what you're doing."

Sword shook his head to clear it. Dark spots floated at the edges of his vision. The gash on his face began to bleed more profusely. The wounds on his shoulders from his first encounter with Dmitri throbbed in accompaniment. "But I do know what I'm doing," he said. And at the sound of his voice, Dmitri froze and turned and locked on Sword's position.

"Dmitri!" Sword called out. "Want your cross? Here it is! Here it is!" Sword tapped the cross against the chair he stood behind. Dmitri mewed and stumbled forward, waving his hands before him. "Bad," he wheezed. "Bad, bad."

"Go get it, Dmitri!" Sword yelled. Then he tossed the cross at the blank wall. The rectangular patch on the wall flickered. The cross passed through it, disappearing. "Through the fardoor, Dmitri! Through the fardoor!"

"No, Dmitri!" Roth shouted. "Don't!"

But Dmitri ran to the wall and dived into it and the wall flickered as he passed through. Sword followed swiftly in the creature's wake, stopped by the wall, and swept his hand across it, starting at the outside of the barely-discernible gray line that hovered in position. The rectangular patch collapsed like a soap bubble and the tangled gray line evaporated. From beyond, somewhere within the wall, he heard Dmitri's plaintive wail. Then nothing.

"You animal!" Morgana screamed. "Do you know what you've done to him?"

"I made a one-sided fardoor," Sword said in awe as the term flashed back to him from his childhood.

Blue fire danced in Roth's fingers. "And it will be the last thing you ever do," he said.

Then the door to the hallway burst into a thousand fragments and Sword grinned at the dark shape that hurtled through. His own werewolf had found him.

It was Martin.

⌒

Ko had seen Martin slide to a stop in the corridor, then double back and crash through an office door without stopping to see if it were unlocked. Now she knew why.

A bald man in a tuxedo and a woman in a glittering green gown were pincered between Martin on one side and Sword on the other. Sword's face was smeared with blood and she could see a jagged wound on his left cheek. But he was still standing and his eyes seemed clear. That meant she could concentrate on the bald man. She could see the radiation signature of a blue power emanating from his hands.

"Melody!" Sword shouted to her over the deafening alarms that still filled the air. "If Roth moves his hands, kill him!"

The man froze. Sword's order had been a bluff because Ko didn't have any weapon that could kill instantly, except for additional plastic explosives, so she drew her taser gun and held it on Roth as if it were a different type of weapon. She could see the man's eyes go instantly to the taser, trying to understand what it was. She was relieved he didn't immediately recognize it.

"Shifter?" Ko asked tensely.

"The woman is the one whose signal blew your circuits," Sword said. He moved off to the side, out of Ko's line of fire.

"You have a *machine* that can identify humanform shifters?" Roth asked.

But Sword ignored the question, continuing to slip along the wall to join Ko and Martin as Ja'Nette appeared in the doorway, out of breath.

"Ja'Nette," Sword said, "this man has red crystals in his pockets. Check them and take out everything you can find."

A quick smile played on Roth's face. He looked over to Morgana. "Yes, please, child. Come check my pockets." He obviously had a plan.

"Try again, Roth," Sword said as Ja'Nette crossed her arms and began to rock and hum.

Roth frowned as he felt the pressure of Ja'Nette's translocated hands pat him down. "Marratin bitch," he spit at the child, but said nothing more as Ko raised her weapon.

"Martin, how good to see you again," Morgana suddenly said, turning to the halfling.

Martin stumbled back a foot and Sword was surprised to see him bow his head in reflex to Morgana.

"I see you've enjoyed a hunt, little one" Morgana said smoothly, no trace of fear or anger in her voice.

Martin used both hands to wipe the blood from his mouth but he still wouldn't meet her gaze.

"Human blood?" Morgana asked. "I know how much you enjoy it."

Martin mumbled something to the floor.

"What was that, Martin? Your Victor didn't hear."

He spoke louder. "Martin half-human."

"Is that what they've been telling you?" Morgana raised her eyebrows with arch alarm. "And you believed them? You would give up your father's heritage? The legacy of Astar? Martin. Look at me."

Martin's head shot up and he stared into Morgana's magnetic eyes.

"The blood of the Change flows through you, doesn't it, Martin?" Morgana said seductively and rhythmically. "The blood of the hunt. You smell it, don't you? You taste it, don't you?"

"That's enough," Sword interrupted. Ko didn't like the glassy look that was coming over Martin's eyes.

"*Olan yu ee yanii ee arrtu, Myrch'ntin!*" Morgana hissed. "*Olan yu ee yanii Arkadych!*"

"Nooo!" Martin howled.

"That's enough!" Sword shouted and ran toward Morgana.

Martin crouched down to the floor and patted his hands over his ears, sobbing words in the strange language that Morgana had used.

Sword grabbed Morgana and pulled her back from Martin. But Morgana only laughed at him. Especially when Ko saw Martin's hand close over Sword's arm.

"He'll taste your blood before the sun rises," Morgana taunted Sword.

"Please Galen Sword. Morgana LaVey Victor. Touch not. Touch not."

Sword dropped his hands from Morgana, but without turning from her, said, "When we leave, Martin, will you come with us?"

Martin moaned.

Sword tried again.

"When we leave, Martin, will you come with *me?*"

"Martin, you have to!" Ja'Nette pleaded with him without taking her eyes from Roth or stopping from her task. "You're my brother. You have to!"

Martin backed away from Sword. "Go with Ja'Nette. Not with Galen Sword."

Morgana laughed again. "I see what you're doing, Martin. Children do taste sweeter."

Ko couldn't tell if the Arkady Victor had spoken as she had to hide her disappointment at losing Martin's allegiance, or because she knew Martin better than any human ever would. No matter, at least Martin would not stay behind. She kept her taser aimed straight at Roth. Ja'Nette had almost translocated all the crystals from his pocket. Ko wondered what Sword wanted them for, why they were important.

"What should I do with these, Sword?" Ja'Nette asked as she finished and Sword went to stand with Martin. About ten small crystals floated in a cloud in front of Roth, just out of reach of any sudden movement.

"Give them to me," Sword commanded and held his hands out, cupped.

The crystals floated over to him. "He had a wallet and some other stuff in his pockets," Ja'Nette said. "I put those on the floor."

Sword captured the crystals in his hand. Ko took a quick glance and could see the stones were different sizes, though none was larger than a pea. Some were cut like jewels, others rough-hewn like raw gems, and all were slightly different in color, from pale rose to deep blood-red.

Roth glared at Sword, his rage blinding him to Ko's brief inattention. "Damn you, Galen," he said as the crystals settled into Sword's outstretched hands. "Those were worth a fortune."

Sword slipped them into his pocket. "Then I'll donate them to the Society of St. Linus."

"Ha," Roth said in resigned disgust. "They're worthless now."

Ko didn't understand what he meant but she knew that this wasn't the time for explanations.

"What's the situation in the halls?" Sword asked her.

"It was clear straight along the corridor to a single flight of stairs, then down one flight to the north employees' entrance," Ko said. "We set off the fire alarm so fire fighters should be here any minute, too."

"Good work," Sword said. "There's at least one full-blown werewolf on this level trying to guide humanform shifters downstairs. They said something about a passageway to the place of the Ceremony."

"Other streets," Martin said. "They go other streets."

"Silence!" Morgana thundered and Martin bowed his head again.

"I know what you're thinking, Sword, but we shouldn't go after the shifters," Ko said. The shifters had already come after her and her back still throbbed. She couldn't face them again tonight.

"I don't think we have a choice," Sword said. "Martin, can the Ceremony proceed without the Victor?"

"Yes, it can," Morgana said quickly.

"Not so late," Martin added.

Morgana snarled at Martin and her voice suddenly deepened, becoming something inhuman and rasping. *"You're It, halfling!"*

Martin looked away and made his *ooo*-ing sound.

"You're safe with us, Martin," Ko told him. "We did all right in the parking lot."

"Martin tagged," Martin chanted dismally. "Martin tagged."

"It's all right." Sword moved to look out the open doorway. "She won't be able to tell anyone else. They're coming with us."

"You're mad," Roth said. "You won't get two feet outside the museum."

"I'll eat your heart, Sword," Morgana hissed.

Sword smiled tightly. "It seems we have a difference of opinion. Ja'Nette, put wrist loops on Roth and Morgana."

"Okay," the girl said. She pulled out two nylon restraints from the vest beneath her red jacket. Ko motioned to Roth to hold his hands out together and Ja'Nette translocated the loop over the adept's hands, centered it on his wrists, then tightened it until Ko could see Roth's hands begin to darken. They repeated the procedure with Morgana, though Martin couldn't watch. Sword used tape from Martin's vest to gag Morgana and Roth and then laid out his plan. They were to head back out the north door where Sword and Martin and Ja'Nette would hold the prisoners. Ko would bring the van back to the parking lot with Forsyte and they'd be off.

"What happens if we run into a firefighter?" Ko asked.

"Stun him," Sword said with a nod at her taser.

Oh shit, Ko thought. She didn't even have to look at Roth to know he had caught Sword's inadvertent reference to her weapon and he knew now that it couldn't kill him. His odds had just considerably improved.

"Okay," Sword said, rapidly checking the corridor one last time. "Let's go!"

Martin led the way, sniffing the air without let up. Ja'Nette followed, then Roth and Morgana with Ko covering them from behind. Sword came last, constantly checking over his shoulder.

"Where're the firefighters?" Ko asked. She was surprised that none had come down the corridor yet.

"Probably making sure all the guests are evacuated from the rotunda," Sword guessed. "There has to be a main fire board somewhere that would tell them there's no real fire, that someone just threw an alarm. They won't be doing a sweep."

"So we're going to get out of here?" Ko asked with relief. She hadn't thought it was going to be this easy.

"Appears so," Sword said. "And I've got a lot to tell you once we get these two back to the Loft."

"What are we going to do then?" Ko kept her taser centered on Roth's back.

"I'm not sure," Sword answered, and Ko was struck by the honesty in his voice. "Things are a lot different from what I thought they'd be."

"Good to hear you finally admit that, Sword." She meant it. "Means there's still hope for you."

"There's got to be hope for somebody." She could hear the exhaustion in his voice. Maybe that's where his sudden honesty had come from, she thought. They reached the top of the stairwell and Martin held up his hand for silence. He leaned over the railing, sniffing the air, then silently flipped over and dropped soundlessly onto the landing.

After a few seconds, Ko saw Martin's hand through the narrow green bars of the railing, waving them on. From the landing, she could see that the employee door was untouched on the floor where the explosive had thrown it. Nothing was disturbed.

Then they were out into the night air and cold rain. The storm had broken. She wondered what the falling rain would do to Martin's sense of smell.

"Better give me the gun," Sword said, and she passed the taser to him.

"Keep Ja'Nette back from them," Ko said in a whisper. "She's really being throwing her stuff around tonight. More than she's ever managed before."

"We'll be okay." Sword slipped the taser's battery pack into his pants pocket, then lightly slapped Ko's shoulder. "Be fast."

Ko took a quick glance around. Sword had Morgana and Roth crammed into a corner behind the wall that came out around the stairwell. No light shone into the angle the wall made so they couldn't be seen from a distance. Martin and Ja'Nette stood about ten feet away on the grass beside the parking lot, where they could see the approach from the near corner. Sword stood by a lamp post, hiding the taser with his body from anyone who might look down the long driveway from the street. They were secure and they would only have to hold their positions for about five minutes.

Ko began jogging across the parking lot toward the driveway. The humanform bodies of the shifters they had killed going into the museum were gone, powdery stains mixing with the falling rain. The cold of it took the fire from her wounds, shocking her back into full awareness from the numbing fatigue of combat and the clanging, incessant alarm. She ran easily and smoothly up the driveway. It was going to be good to sit back in the van, to see Forsyte again.

They had done it. They had bloody hell done it. She laughed, opening her mouth to the rain. *Victory,* she thought.

And then the werewolf was on her.

TWENTY

For just a moment, Sword allowed himself to feel the pain that burned within him. His face felt as if Dmitri had scoured half the flesh from it. He could sense spasms building in both shoulders and he had to lean the arm that held the taser against the lampost to keep his hand from shaking. But the pain did not discourage him. It fuelled him. Made him feel alive. Nothing had gone as he had planned or wanted this evening, but he still felt he had won. And with that knowledge, he could stare back into the glaring eyes of his captives. Somehow, within the next few hours he would have the answers that he needed.

Then he heard Ko's sudden shout of surprise, cut off in midword. Both Roth and Morgana started in sudden hope.

"Don't move!" Sword threatened them. He called out to Martin but the halfling had already leapt to the hood of a parked car and stared into the darkness through which the driveway ran. The rain increased in a sudden wave and Martin howled.

Sword saw why.

Ko came back down the driveway carried by Seth as if she were no more than a doll. One monstrous arm wrapped round her waist, the other pulled her head back and down, claws digging into her face, blood mixing with rain. Her vest was gone and Seth held her up so her exposed neck was inches from his fangs. If she were still alive, Sword knew she couldn't dare struggle.

He heard Morgana and Roth moving behind him. He wheeled about to face them and they halted, but their eyes told him they knew who had the upper hand now.

Seth stood no more than ten feet away in the center of the parking lot. Sword gave silent thanks as he saw Ko's eyes move, look at him.

"Release them," the werewolf growled. Saliva dripped upon the taut skin of Ko's neck. "Or the human dies."

Sword straightened his arm, aiming the taser at Morgana's face. "Put her down or your *mother* dies."

Seth leered at him, black lips curling from his enormous teeth. He twisted Ko's head back further and Sword heard her gasp. He blinked through the rain that streamed over his eyes, tensing to see what Seth's next move would be. But Seth didn't make one and Sword knew that the stand-off was even.

"Put the human down," Sword called out, "and we'll back away and you can release your mother yourself."

Seth hesitated. Sword stepped back. "Fair trade, Seth. We all live to fight another day."

He heard the werewolf snarl. He tried to remember anything that he could from his childhood about how a shifter might react in this situation. But there was nothing. Probably because no shifter had ever been in this situation before.

Seth raised his muzzle to the rain and bayed. He snapped his jaws at Sword. "Then you make me the Victor of Clan Arkady! Heir no longer!" He lifted Ko high in the air and his jaws widened.

Sword's scream was without sense, only feeling, only outrage, only horror. He swung his arm around in front in a desperate attempt to fire at Seth, stop him, slow him, anything. But he knew he was too late. In sickening slow motion he saw Seth's mouth gape open. He saw Martin bounding from the car. Saw Ja'Nette running after him. And knew they were all too late. Too late.

The jaws descended.

Seth roared in bloodlust. Then screamed in pain. Screamed in agony as Ko flew away from him and his jaws clamped shut on empty air and he fell to the ground with deadly limbs clawing at the rain-filled air. With two thin wires trailing from his back.

Two thin taser wires stretching twenty feet away to the carrier pods on Forsyte's chair.

Sword didn't stop to think. He ran straight to Ko. She rolled on the pavement, wiping blood from her eyes. She peered over Seth's twitching body. "*Adrian!*" she called out in awe, in love, alive.

Sword gathered the woman into his arms. How much worse could it get? What had he led them all into? What could be worth this?

"Sword!" Ja'Nette shouted. "Behind you!"

Sword turned. Roth held his hands out to Morgana. In them he held the strip of tape that had gagged her. Morgana bit down on the tough nylon loop that bound his hands. She bit *through* it as if her teeth were those of a shark. Roth pulled the tape from his mouth. Blue fire danced on his hands, crackling in the rain.

Sword pulled Ko to her feet. She staggered a step, then shook her head, dazed. "We've got to get to the van," Sword told her. "We've got to get — "

Martin shrieked as Seth arose from the pavement. The werewolf roared hideously as he closed his hands around the wires in his back and pulled Forsyte's taser darts from his flesh. Then he yanked in the opposite direction and Sword saw Forsyte's chair bouncing forward along the driveway.

"The release!" Sword screamed to the scientist. "Hit the release!"

Sword could see Forsyte trying to move his hand along the arm of the chair, but the movement Seth caused was too bumpy. Then Martin hit Seth like a cannonball and the werewolf went down and Forsyte's chair twisted to the right and smashed sideways to the ground. Sword saw the pencil-thin laser beams from Forsyte's glasses spin through the air and tumble along the wet pavement before winking out. But there was no time to go to the fallen scientist. Martin was losing.

Ko and Sword ran at Seth as the werewolf rose over Martin. He brought both massive front paws together and swung them down with murderous force.

"*Nooo!*" Ja'Nette screamed and Seth's lethal blow was diverted by a fraction of an inch, grazing Martin's head instead of crushing it.

Ja'Nette stumbled to the ground, gagging from the force of the translocation she had delivered.

Seth shook his head in confusion, trying to understand what had deflected his blow. Martin's hands clawed at the werewolf's chest and exposed belly. Seth jumped back snarling and snapping. Martin leapt up into a fighting crouch, growling ferociously in return. Seth faced him, crouching, claws extended.

"Need spray!" Ko shouted and ran off to the grass on the right. "Need the vest."

"I've got some!" Ja'Nette called out to her, circling Seth on the other side.

"Over here!" Ko cried and held up her hands.

Ja'Nette pulled a spray can from her red jacket, held it up, then translocated it to Ko without throwing. Seth watched the can shoot smoothly through the air.

"It was *her!*" he roared and turned away from Martin. Martin jumped at him but Seth flipped the halfling from his shoulder. "You won't rob me of my kill again," he snarled. Then he began to move. Fast. Straight for Ja'Nette.

Sword raced to intercept Seth. He heard Ko scream. Saw Martin scrambling back to his feet. Seth's arm shot out and smashed into Sword's chest, sending him flying through the air to land on his back, gasping for breath.

Sword heard Ja'Nette cry out. He rolled on the wet grass. Then saw Seth hold Ja'Nette high over his head, howling in victory.

Ko charged past Sword, spray can held ready. Ja'Nette struggled and kicked. Ko leaped for him. Seth's hind foot lashed out against her chest and Ko crumpled to the ground, spray can knocked from her hand. Then Martin sprang, landing on Seth's shoulders, biting at him, tearing at him. Sword struggled to his feet, searching for the fallen can. Seth whirled, casting Martin off. Seth took Ja'Nette by her ankle and *swung* her at Martin who tumbled backward so the child would not be hurt.

Ja'Nette's scream rose and fell like a siren. *"Melody!"* she called as Seth flipped her back into both his arms. *"Maaarrtiiiin!"* she wailed as Seth brought her to his chest.

"*Maaammmaaaa* — *!*" the child shrieked as Seth's fangs found their mark and sank into her throat and tore and ripped until no sound could ever come from it again.

Sword felt all control pass from his body. His arms and legs wavered, muscles jellied, he fell to his knees in the wet grass.

Ja'Nette's body jerked and went limp. Her arms and legs flopped as Seth noisily sucked at her throat.

Sword heaved whatever was left in his stomach onto the ground. He couldn't speak. He couldn't think.

Ko lay moaning on the grass at Seth's feet. She tried to get up and the werewolf kicked at her again without looking away from his kill. She went down with a sigh.

Then Sword heard a sound he had never heard before, like a thousand nails against a thousand sheets of slate, a sound like all the heavens dying, like demons outraged.

It was Martin.

He had the fighting eyes.

Blazing with the pure fire of a warrior born. Searing from the hidden shadows of his face.

Martin opened his mouth and it was the sound of hell erupting.

Seth threw the drained body of the child to the ground and Martin's attention was diverted for just an instant. Just the time that it took for Seth to spring and land upon him, both arms swinging with fists locked to drive into the halfling's skull and send him smashing to the ground, unconscious.

Seth stood up. Grabbed Martin's leg. Began to drag him back to the museum.

Sword collapsed onto the grass. He was empty. Finished. Utterly defeated.

Two legs appeared beside him. Tomas Roth.

Sword looked up at the adept, tears mixing with blood mixing with rain.

Roth squatted down and grabbed Sword's black hair in his fist, forcing his head back.

"Now you have what you always wanted," Roth said scornfully. "And your punishment is ... you have to live with it."

He threw Sword's head forward, pushing his face into the dirt.
"Goodbye, Little Galen. We shall not meet again."
It was over.

TWENTY-ONE

Ko stared without blinking as she saw the werewolf move away, dragging Martin behind him, disappearing into the museum with Roth and Morgana. She slowly sat up, ignoring the rain, ignoring the blood she coughed from her lungs. There was something missing from her. Something more than the lack of sensation in the dead spot across her ribs. She thought that was probably a shock reaction to something fractured. No, there was something more gone from her. A void she couldn't explain.

Then she looked over to the crumpled red jacket that was balled up around a hard-to-see shape. *Ah, that's it,* she thought. *Ja'Nette.*

Ko got unsteadily to her feet, and walked over to the body. The girl's head was almost completely severed from her torso. Her enormous child's eyes stared unseeing up into the night, not moving as the raindrops broke upon them.

Ko thought she should probably feel something. She thought she should probably feel grief, or sadness, or should maybe even cry. That would be appropriate. But she felt nothing. Somehow, all feeling had vanished when she had seen Seth's fangs sink within the girl's neck.

She turned away from the pitifully small body. She saw Sword lying in the grass about twenty feet away. *Hope he's dead,* she thought, but just kept walking. Forsyte was sprawled in his chair, still held in place by the double shoulder straps he wore. She would have to look after him. That was her job now. Nothing else mattered.

"You saved my life," she said tonelessly to him as she righted the chair. His eyes were wide as he watched her. Ko knew she should probably feel something for him as well. Knew she had, once. But couldn't remember. "Thank you," she said, then leaned over to kiss him. *That would be appropriate,* she thought. Forsyte blinked madly at her. His two operative fingers danced on the arm of his chair. But all the display lights were out. The computer screen was dead. The chair was too damaged. "I'll get your glasses," she told him, then looked around the immediate area. She would have a long talk with him when she took him back to her place. Not to the other place. Not to the Loft. Never there again.

She searched through the grass, looking for the glint of Forsyte's glasses. She ignored the traffic a few hundred feet away. She paid no attention to the man who walked toward her from the dark, moving stiffly, carrying a heavy burden. She didn't want to look up at him. She didn't want to see what he carried. She didn't want to hear his voice. But she did.

Galen Sword stood before her. He carried Ja'Nette in his arms as carefully and as tenderly as if he carried a living baby.

"They have Martin," he said.

"I don't care," Ko answered. She stared at the grass, searching for Forsyte's glasses. Searching for answers. Searching for that which was lost to her.

"Someone has to," Sword said.

She saw only mud and torn-up grass. The debris of battle. "I hate you, Sword." That would be appropriate. She wondered if she would ever feel anything again.

"I know. But that doesn't matter anymore."

"Nothing does."

"You're wrong." He cradled Ja'Nette to him. "Ja'Nette matters. Martin matters. You matter."

"And Adrian?"

"He saved your life. You tell me."

"He matters."

"Ja'Nette saved Martin's life. Do we throw that away?"

Ko felt something then, crawling up from the hidden depths of her. She felt tears somewhere within her, straining to be let free.

"What do you want from me?" she asked him, still staring at the grass, and the dirt, and the darkness.

Sword knelt down and gently laid Ja'Nette's body upon the ground. He pulled the girl's red jacket up around her, the hood supporting the lifeless head. "What do you have to give?"

"For you?" She said it like a curse.

"This isn't about me anymore." He stood again, bowed his head over the child. "This is something more. Something bigger."

"What?" It was a gasp. It was a sob. She held her hands to her face and the liquid she felt there was not rain, was not blood.

"They're evil, Melody."

She hit him. She pounded her fists against him until she had no strength left and he held her arms together, held her to him, as carefully and as tenderly as he had held Ja'Nette.

"Are you telling me that *we're* any different?"

She felt his arms tighten around her and she could feel that there was something different about him. Something changed.

"I don't know what we are anymore. I don't even know what I am. But I do know that we have to try to stop them."

"Why us?" Ko sobbed. "Why?"

And Galen Sword told her the only answer that she could accept. The only answer that could bring back what she had lost.

"We're the only ones who can."

TWENTY-TWO

Forsyte closed his eyes as Sword and Ko rolled him back to the van. He had to. Ja'Nette's body was on his lap, arranged like a sleeping child. He couldn't bear to look down at her and for once was grateful that his paralysis did not enable him to feel any pressure except on his face and his two fingers. Even so, he felt the weight of her death.

The night had been a disaster, of that he had no doubt. The initial thrill he had felt at being outdoors and involved in the excursion, the wild rush when he had fired both taser darts at the werewolf in time to save Ko, those emotions had all left him, gone with the life of this child. Sword's search had ceased to be merely an intellectual pursuit, and though Forsyte sometimes resented the man, he wondered if anyone deserved what Sword must be going through.

But then, Forsyte reminded himself, no one deserved what he himself was going through, and his paralysis was Sword's fault. Perhaps the fates had arranged for events to balance out.

"Fire trucks are gone," he heard Ko say as he felt the chair leave the upward slope of the driveway and reach the level surface of the sidewalk. "No police cars either."

"The clans have to have connections in the Second World," Sword said. "To stay hidden, they'd have to be able to know what was going on within the police, the media — "

"Wouldn't Trank know if something like that were going on in the police? He pulls all those strange cases for you."

Listening to their exchange, Forsyte automatically began pressing his keypad, forgetting that all his onboard systems were dead. Of course the clans had to have agents within all major societal organizations. Police forces, newspapers, even government agencies. To survive at all in modern times, they would *have* to have observers present at every level through which reports of their activities might conceivably pass. Then those reports could be stopped or, more likely, altered before being passed on. It was so obvious. Forsyte could see exactly how such a system could be set in place, becoming simpler to manage each year as the technology for data gathering became more complex, offering more opportunities for intrusion. Without his own computers, though, Forsyte's thoughts could only whirl silently in his head. He sighed, but Ko and Sword didn't notice. They just kept talking as they wheeled Forsyte closer to the parked van.

"Maybe Martin will have heard something about it," Sword said.

"If we get him back."

Forsyte felt his chair slow. "If we don't get him back, then we'll get Seth in his place. And I'll make sure he has a lot to say." There was more than the need to search for his family in Sword's voice now, Forsyte heard. There was the need for vengeance.

An hour later, after setting the hidden charges around the museum's entrance, Sword and Ko stood in the ruined doorway of the museum's north entrance, casting long shadows down the basement hall. The sound of Ko's rifle as she pumped the first cartridge into place echoed in the silence.

"Museum security should have closed this up by now," she said.

Sword scanned the hallway for any sign of movement. Nothing. Forsyte's voder came over his transceiver. "SOMEONE ELSE IS IN CHARGE TONIGHT."

Sword removed his gas pistol from his vest and primed the first charge. Like Ko, he no longer carried darts filled with tranquilizer. The situation had gone beyond that. All the darts now carried full charges of silver-halide solution. Sword wanted to make the shifters feel as if their very blood were on fire, until the silver hit their brains and their inflamed tissues exploded.

"PROCEED," Forsyte's mechanical voice said. While Sword changed into his jeans and vest and replenished his partner's spare vest, Ko had hotwired Forsyte's main communications system into the van's generator motor. As long as the engine of the parked van kept idling, Forsyte would have enough power to reach their larger field radios halfway across the city — wherever the passageway took them.

The passageway to the Ceremony, Morgana had said. *Other streets,* Martin had called them.

"This is how it all started, isn't it?" Ko said quietly. She looked at Sword and he saw the commitment in her eyes. "Hunting for Martin."

"And it's how it all ends."

They began their walk down the basement hall.

Sword had told Forsyte and Ko what he had picked up in his confrontation with Morgana and Roth. The humanform shifters who had arrived at the Society of St. Linus ball were to leave the museum's rotunda according to a staggered schedule. Morgana had thought that about a hundred had made it down to the passageway by the time the fire trucks had arrived. Roth had told Seth that when the firefighters had gone, the shifters who had had to evacuate the museum with the unsuspecting human guests could try to return, back to the passageway.

Forsyte had decided that Sword's and Ko's best chance was to move as deep as they could go beneath the museum's rotunda and wait. Since normal museum security seemed to be absent this night, the displaced shifters would have no problem reentering the building. And once Sword and Ko had found a shifter to follow, Forsyte would enact the plan that would ensure no others could gain entrance.

Only one thing had been left to chance: the timing. From what Morgana had said, Sword guessed that the Ceremony of the Change would take place at dawn, though he could not be sure. The First World seemed to operate by different maps and different times from those of the Second World, and if the passageway deep beneath the museum involved moving through a fardoor, then the Ceremony could be held anywhere in the world, coinciding with any time zone's dawn.

Ko paused in the hallway and held up a laser ranging device, pointing it back the way they had come, then reading the red numbers that appeared in its window. "Two hundred sixty feet," she announced.

"FORTY MORE," Forsyte transmitted. "GUESTS APPROACHING MAIN DOORS."

Ko slipped the ranger back in her vest. The hallway ended at a T-intersection, ten feet in front of them. "Rotunda's thirty feet past that wall, Sword. Right or left?"

Sword checked around the corners. Both extensions of the inter-secting corridor looked identical — gray brick, old yellow linoleum worn through in spots to even older stone. But at the end of the corridor to the left, the lights were out. "That way," Sword said.

Into the darkness.

Forsyte rested easily in his chair in the van. He knew his right arm was badly scraped but he couldn't feel it. There would be time enough for first aid in the morning. But for now, he must do what he did best for Sword — think and plan, and be Sword's eyes on the street, reporting on the innocuous-looking figures congregating around the museum's steps and the now-extinguished searchlights.

He closed his eyes for a moment and pictured Sword's and Ko's position in the museum's basement, mentally superimposing them against an image of the museum's outer structure. It was easier than playing boardless chess with the computer in the Loft. *Why the Museum of Natural History?* Forsyte thought. If the shifters could use fardoors to get to their Ceremony, then they could have arrived individually from all over the world and gathered unobserved in some wilderness area. No, he decided. Fardoors must be limited in some way, or must be too expensive or too energy-demanding to use for so many participants. Forsyte guessed that the Ceremony had to be held in a specific location in the city for a reason. Secrecy, most likely. The shifters had to remain hidden. And where better to hide the Ceremony than wherever they lived in hiding? The Ceremony of the Change must be taking place at the Arkady enclave. Since the museum had been chosen as the nexus for the shifters' arrival, then that meant the enclave must be nearby.

Forsyte visualized a map of the nearby streets of the city. To the east was the park. Perhaps a Ceremony could be held there after dark, but farther north, away from traffic and joggers. To the west was Columbus, then Broadway, apartments over stores and restaurants for the most part, offering no controlled access. But to the north and south along Central Park West ... blocks of gated, high-security condominiums. Private admissions boards to keep out undesirable humans. All deliveries made to security personnel. Perfect enclaves. Forsyte felt the thrill of discovery. Somewhere close by, in one of the nondescript, featureless buildings overlooking Central Park, a den of werewolves thrived in the heart of the city.

How many other buildings were there like it? Filled with what other creatures and adepts who must remain unseen? And in how many other cities? How many small towns had private communities or gated subdivisions? How many farm towns had no place for visitors to stay overnight? *They could be anywhere,* Forsyte thought excitedly. But right now, he knew he must concentrate on the shifters of Arkady.

Seven blocks to the south, the Lincoln Center would be a much better place to disguise the comings and goings of a large number of people. So, he reasoned, the enclave had to be to the north of the museum. And not far. Not far at all.

Anywhere, Forsyte thought as he assembled his conclusions into a sentence his voder could relay to Ko and Sword. *And everywhere.*

The darkness of the corridor glowed green in Sword's Starbrite Viewer. He held it tightly against his face, pushing it into the padding of the bandage he wore over Dmitri's wound, not feeling anything where the anesthetic Ko had injected still deadened his nerves. He heard a door lock click but saw nothing.

"Did you get that?" he whispered.

Beside him, Ko pointed a small sound-collector dish and directional microphone down the hallway and held its earphone to her head. "Right side, twenty to thirty feet."

They moved silently through the dark, their only light now the pale green glow the light-intensifying viewer cast on Sword's grim face.

Twenty-two feet down the hall, on the right, was a closed wooden door. Sword peered through the viewer and read the ghostly letters he saw painted on the door: MOLLUSKS. ARTHROPODS. LONG TERM. He glanced at Ko. She held the microphone to the door.

"Footsteps," she whispered. "Two sets."

Sword slipped a finger under his locator band and pressed the code for 'contact.' Forsyte's voder murmured in his ear. "HIGH PROBABILITY THE CEREMONY IS BEING HELD IN THE ARKADY ENCLAVE. CONDOMINIUM BUILDING NORTH OF MUSEUM ON CENTRAL PARK WEST."

Sword and Ko exchanged a look of surprise but didn't risk speaking. "IF YOU HAVE A CHOICE," the voder continued, "GO NORTH."

Ko collapsed the sound equipment and replaced it on her vest. She slipped on a headband and flipped its eye patch over one eye. Sword did the same, stowing his Starbrite and pulled out a halogen spotlight. He kept one finger on its switch, then reached out to the door's brass handle.

It was unlocked and made the same click they had heard before.

As soon as the click sounded, Sword knew they had lost the element of surprise — if it existed at all. He pushed the door open and instantly flooded the room beyond with the powerful beam of his handheld spotlight.

The first thing he saw was two pairs of eyes glowing twenty feet away as they reflected the brilliant light back to him. One pair was at eye level, the other close to the ground. Then something hissed at him and Ko's gun answered.

A horrifying scream burst out. Sword ran forward and the shadows before him wavered as the spotlight moved in his hand, causing the tall, crammed walls of shelves he ran between to appear to dance back and forth around him, like the waves of a parted sea about to crash overhead.

Then he saw what the eyes belonged to: the two women in saris he had met in the reception line. One crouched, ready to attack, hands at her side with nails like claws. The other sprawled halfway through a trapdoor hidden within an old wooden chest. Her hands were unmoving at her throat. Ko's dart was still in it. The woman's face was swollen and black. Death had been instantaneous.

The second woman sprang at Sword. He swept a specimen case from the shelf beside him and it clattered into her, scattering a collection of small, pastel-colored shells and slowing her for an instant. The instant was all that was needed. Ko's dart hit home. The woman pitched forward, every muscle rigid in agony. There was no time for a final scream, only the soft sigh of her final breath escaping lifeless lungs.

Sword pulled the body of the first woman out of the trapdoor. The door had been disguised to look like a wooden trunk, covered with dust, and was large enough for two humans to enter at a time. Or one shifter to exit.

As Ko went back to close and block the door leading to the hallway, Sword described to Forsyte what they had found.

"PROCEED," Forsyte transmitted.

Sword and Ko descended into the pitch-black passageway. Now it was Forsyte's turn to act again.

Forsyte rotated his chair from the communications console to look out through the passenger window at the museum. A cab pulled up and a man got out. He was still in his tuxedo. So were the three men who waited by one of the long stone benches that flanked the museum's steps. Now that the area had returned to normal, the shifters were returning.

For about ten more seconds, Forsyte thought. He pressed the first code into his keypad and the van's cellular phone made its first call. After four rings, the sleep-filled voice of Kendall Marsh came over Forsyte's earphone. "This better be good," she said groggily.

Forsyte pressed the second code and the voder delivered his preprogrammed message. "THIS IS ADRIAN FORSYTE. I AM AN ASSOCIATE OF GALEN SWORD. HE SUGGESTS YOU BRING A NEWS CREW TO THE FRONT STEPS OF THE AMERICAN MUSEUM OF NATURAL HISTORY IMMEDIATELY."

"This sounds like one of those computer sales pitch come-ons," Marsh complained skeptically. "What's the big deal?"

So much for Sword saying that the woman would come on the strength of his name alone. Forsyte's two operative fingers flew over the keypad and he blinked frantically as he shifted command from his chair to the van and back again.

"I said, what's the big deal?" Marsh repeated, more awake and sounding decidedly irritated now.

"LISTEN," the voder said, then Forsyte switched the transmit circuit over to the van's external mike and pressed the final code.

Eight concussion grenades detonated simultaneously behind the museum's front pillars where Ko had dropped them. They would do no harm to the stonework but the roar of their explosion would resonate for blocks. Then the flare charges went off along the museum's steps and in the trash cans out front, sending out huge billows of glowing white smoke. Combined with the roar of the grenades, it seemed as if the whole front of the museum had been blown away.

Shouts of surprise from the startled shifters followed the first round of explosions. Then the second set of grenades went off and the second set of flares. The sirens erupted only a few moments later.

Over his earphone, Forsyte heard Kendall Marsh chuckle. "Good old Galen's back," she said. "I'll be right down."

Forsyte smiled in satisfaction as the shifters fled.

Ko slipped the false wooden trunk back in position over her head, then jumped down the last five rungs of the old ladder to land on the wooden planks that lined the passageway floor. They squished into soft mud as she moved across them. The passage smelled damp and foul.

"Turn off your spot," Sword told her. She did, flipping her eyepatch up to use the eye that had not been exposed to bright light.

The passageway was lit with a pale red radiance. She recognized it. Crystals were at work here.

To the north and south, the passage looked the same. Bare earth supported every few feet by wooden-beam braces. The construction looked old, built by hand. Something dug in the dark by things unseen. The glow was the same in both directions. She heard nothing and pulled out the directional mike again.

"Forsyte said north," Sword whispered.

Ko used the microphone to check for others moving in the passageway, heard nothing, and stowed the sound equipment again. She brought her rifle back into her hands. Sword drew his pistol. They headed north.

After fifty feet, the tunnel dipped and ran to the east by a few degrees. At the point that its deviation began, a flat red crystal floated close to the low ceiling. It looked almost like an irregular half-square-foot sheet of mica backlit by an incandescent bulb. But Sword stared up at it and said, "That's called a facet. I remember those from ... my home." He reached up to it and his fingers brushed its surface.

The light went out. He brought his hand away. The light slowly came back up. "Remember that if we need darkness," Sword said. Ko said nothing. She suspected that some of the things they might encounter within the passage would have no need for light.

Another fifty feet and the passage branched into four other directions, another facet floating at the intersection.

"How far do you think these things go?" Ko asked.

"Other streets," Sword said and shrugged. He pointed to the most northerly tunnel. "Look at how wet the boards are there. There's been a lot of traffic in the past few hours."

Ko saw the ribbons of mud that had been squeezed up between the passage's floor planks. "I don't think they were people, Sword." They moved on.

They passed two other intersections, still heading north, still following the pattern of fresh mud on the planks, and then the nature of the passage changed. Now the walls were made of white-painted brick, the floor of raw concrete. A metal tube ran along the ceiling, studded with wire-wrapped lightbulbs every ten feet.

Ko sent a signal to Forsyte through her locator band, indicating that they had reached an area where they could no longer risk speaking or receiving a voice transmission through their earphones. She felt three pulses in her band as the scientist acknowledged the message. Everything above was proceeding as planned. She looked at Sword and he nodded.

Almost there, they moved on.

TWENTY-THREE

Martin sniffed the air and knew instantly he had been taken through the layer. He tried to howl his despair but the thick rope that pressed deep into his mouth ensured his silence. He tried to move, to tear at the rope that gagged him and at the cloth that covered his eyes, but other ropes around his arms and legs held him motionless, sitting back against a rough stone surface. He could sense the working crystal in the rope and knew that struggling would be useless. And then he remembered Ja'Nette.

Seth must die.

It was not a coherent thought, nothing which he could explain or describe. His mind did not work that way. It simply became a condition of his being, something known to each cell of him, each thought, each impulse. Ja'Nette had been his sister. Ja'Nette had been his friend. Ja'Nette had been torn open and consumed and taken from him.

In Martin's mind, Seth was already dead.

Then he remembered the Victor Morgana. Martin had been tagged. It was a sentence of death.

He needed information and inhaled mightily through the cloth, learning more about his surroundings by his sense of smell than any human could know by the limitations of sight.

The knowledge he gained was almost overwhelming. There were shifters all around — the Gathering of the Clan Arkady — humanform and shifterform all together. He exhaled, rolling the air through his open mouth, seeking familiar notes. Morgana was present, and Roth. Seth was harder to detect because he had handled the ropes and the cloth that secured Martin, tainting what other evidence of his presence there might be. But Martin struggled with a linear thought, made easier by his recent efforts to talk in humantongue with Ja'Nette and Ko and Sword: Since Seth was heir to the Victor Morgana, Seth must be present for the Change.

Martin inhaled again, searching for other clues to his situation. He caught the soft flower fragrance of a wizard's breath, the sharp electric bite of a glowing Light, other individuals from a dozen different clans, from the lessers and the greaters and the guilds, all observers of the Change, bound by oath and custom.

Only one distinctive scent among the dozen kinds of beings who should be present was missing. Martin inhaled again, exhaled slowly, tasting each molecule, searching and sifting, not finding what he expected, afraid to know what the absence meant.

Then he heard heavy footsteps approach him and the sudden spoor of Seth enveloped him. The cloth was torn from Martin's head. Seth stood before him in the pale rose glow of the nearby facet pillars that ringed the Pit of the Change, deep within the darkness of the layer. The werewolf laughed at him, Ja'Nette's blood still matting his fur.

"I hear you scenting, halfling," Seth gloated. "And I know what scent you miss." He moved his snout through the air, snuffling his nostrils. "No stink of human meat in the Pit this Change." His green eyes bore into Martin. "I wonder why that is, halfling? Surely the Victor knows that there can be no change without a sacrifice of human meat." He shook his head, feigning bewilderment, but his mouth made a cruel sneer. "I wonder where the Victor expects to get our *human* meat? Do you know, *halfling?* Half shifter. Half *meat!*" Seth howled in laughter. He leaned forward until Martin could not escape the scent of Ja'Nette's blood on the werewolf's hot breath. "Just think, halfling. You finally have your wish. You finally will take part in a Ceremony of the Change."

Seth drew back to his full height and spit in Martin's face. Martin snarled past his gag and pulled against the ropes that held him to the rock at his back. But he could not move.

"What good prey you'd make," Seth said. "Too bad you won't even have a chance to run before your heart is plucked." He ran his long pink tongue slowly around his bloodstained muzzle. "No wonder you liked the child," he said, then turned and left as Martin again strained uselessly against his bonds.

Eventually, the pain of his injuries made Martin stop trying to pull free. He would be untied soon enough, he knew, and his efforts would be better spent in pursuit of other strategies.

Martin inhaled again, trying to learn whom among those present he knew. His mind filled with pictures from his storybooks. He saw the Pit of the Change, carved into the dark stone of the layer, ring after ring of stone slabs rising in steps, making seats for all. And in the center, at the bottom, in the final ring, the altar where the sacrifice of human meat would lie beneath the Crystal of the Change Arkady.

Martin saw himself staked out there. He saw how the Victor would change, saw the fangs and the teeth and the scales of her. Saw how the hooks of the Snare of the Silver Death would bite through his flesh and hold open his mouth so she could reach in and reach down and grasp his beating heart. From the inside.

He saw himself spitting in the Victor's face in his final moments of life.

He would not be prey. He would not be tagged. He would be what his little sister had said he could be. He would be human. And he would think.

Sword felt a sudden blast of hot air in the passage, then gagged as an overpowering wave of the stench of rotting meat assailed him. To his right, Ko coughed, covering her mouth, trying to remain silent.

The dreadful odor passed and the air was still again. He risked whispering to Ko. They had moved through the electrically lit brick-walled passages for at least the distance of two surface blocks without seeing or hearing any sign of shifters, and Sword had begun to fear that Forsyte's analysis had not been correct. Until the rotting meat had hit.

"Feeding ground?" he whispered into Ko's ear.

She nodded. "Or sacrificial area."

Sword checked his gas pistol. Martin had told them that a human sacrifice was required for the Ceremony of the Change. They came to another intersection. He felt a breeze pick up in the passage again and tensed. It was the terrible smell again, hot and fetid. Without having to signal their intentions to each other, he and Ko turned into it as one and walked in the direction from which it had come.

The passage opened up, stretching from its consistent eight-foot width to more than thirty. The ceiling arched up from six feet to more than ten. And at the passage's broadest point, the brickwork and concrete flooring suddenly stopped with a clean break. The final electric lights cast the last of their pale illumination, making the point of transition hard to see. Beyond, there was a yawning entrance into impenetrable darkness. The scent of damp mud walls returned between gusts of the fiery, evil-smelling wind.

"What do you think?" Ko spoke softly. "Some sort of cave?"

"Under Central Park West?"

"Maybe we've moved to the east. Maybe we're under the park."

Sword cupped his hand to his transceiver. "Adrian, do you copy? We appear to be at the mouth of a cave of some sort. Melody thinks we might be somewhere under the park. We could also be under the buildings as you thought, but we'd have to be fairly deep. Any suggestions?"

They waited in silence, knowing that Forsyte would first have to think, then program his voder. Finally, the scientist's reply came. "LARGE CAVES NOT POSSIBLE. OLD RAILROAD OR SUBWAY CONSTRUCTION LIKELY. NEWS CREWS ENJOYING EXCITEMENT UP HERE. DON'T WORRY ABOUT VISITORS. PROCEED."

The corners of Sword's mouth tugged upward. He pictured the scene in front of the museum where Ko's diversion charges had gone off. He hoped Kendall Marsh would be astute enough to say she had received an anonymous tip in case anyone asked how she had reached the scene so quickly.

"Looks too big for an old subway tunnel," Ko said, moving to the sharp edge of the brickwork. The light seemed to fall off rapidly beyond her, Sword noticed, almost as if there were a mist ahead.

"Maybe it's an underground train yard," Sword suggested, trying to see what covered the ceiling past the abrupt end of the modern construction materials.

Another gust of foul wind blew at them.

"Whatever it is," Ko said, "they're in there."

"Then that's where we're going."

They passed from the light.

Martin hummed an old Michael Jackson song, very slowly, the way he had heard Ja'Nette do it. It calmed him to think of her. He saw her face, heard her voice. They were the same, she said, and he smiled as he felt pleasure at the memory of that, and all the other things she had said to him. Even when she hadn't realized what she was saying.

"A happy sacrifice?" Morgana questioned as she approached him.

"A simple mind," Roth suggested.

Martin kept his face serene despite the shock of seeing how Roth was clothed. The Victor Morgana, as he expected, was garbed in the ceremonial robe prepared from the scales of the legendary first Victor's moult. Linked together by glowing strands of the finest Lights' gold, the hand-sized scales of the robe glittered green-black, even under the soft light of the facet pillars. But Roth, an elemental, was also clothed in an *Arkadych* robe, though of a lesser moult. Even Martin knew the Roth family line claimed Pendragon as its clan, and the Pendragon ceremonies demanded armor forged from the earth, not the skins of gods.

Roth pulled his heavy robe around him and responded to Martin's expression as a small shifterform werebear removed Martin's gag. "This is the cloak of the future, halfling. When Seth is Victor of Pendragon, the lines will merge."

"Will be war first," Martin said, his voice calm, ignoring the blood that flowed where the rope gag had scraped him.

Morgana moved up to Roth and took his arm in hers. "But first, little one, there will be a Ceremony of the Change Arkady. And the Seyshen will fall before the next Council."

"Not war with Seyshen," Martin said as the werebear used its claws to quickly sever the ropes wrapping Martin's legs. "War with Pendragon."

Roth shook his head. "Pendragon has fallen. The Victor's line has ended. And the — "

"War with Sword." Martin bared his fangs at Morgana.

The Victor of Arkady responded by slapping the halfling, viciously drawing her nails across his cheek, leaving bloody streaks. "How *dare* you?" she hissed at Martin. "Have you forgotten what you are?"

Martin bared his fangs again. "Human meat." But unlike any they had tried to sacrifice before. As they would soon find out.

Roth snapped his fingers and the werebear was joined by two male humanforms, clothed in tanned shifterskins and carrying silver-tipped spears. Martin knew the silver would not be fatal to him as it would be to a full shifter, but the wounds they could make would still be serious.

Roth gloated as Martin rose painfully to his feet, prodded by the spears. "Sword eats the dirt of the Second World, *meat*. His line is ended. His clan is finished. The legends are proven false."

"War," Martin repeated firmly as the humanforms led him forward with their spears. "War with Sword." He knew Roth was wrong. Martin lifted his head. He knew Sword would come.

He could smell it.

Ko felt as if she were breathing sewage, and almost lost her footing on the rough rocky ground, so powerful was the sensation. The temperature in the cavern they had entered from the passageway was easily over ninety, with humidity so thick she was soaked within seconds. The putrid reek of organic decomposition made her eyes sting and her nose burn. She heard Sword begin retching and the sound of it was enough to set her off, too.

"What can it be?" she said weakly.

"Sewage treatment? Maybe this is an old cistern complex."

Ko stared at him, wide-eyed. "Come off it, Sword. Feel the heat, the moisture in the air. This isn't any cave or tunnel under Central Park."

"What is it then?" Sword wiped his face with the sleeve of his black sweater. Ko doubted he'd be wearing it much longer and she was glad for her own sleeveless top.

"Who knows, Sword. I'm only telling you what it can't be." She stared ahead of them. The blackness was perfect and undisturbed.

Behind them, the mouth of the lit section of the passageway appeared like a half moon lying on the ground, sending feeble shafts of light through the hazy air. The light from the passageway seemed to flicker with an almost regular rhythm, as if a giant picture tube were beginning to burn out.

Sword looked back at the passageway Then his mouth opened in surprise. "I've seen that flickering before. We've passed though a fardoor. It's huge."

Ko felt her stomach tighten. Sword had told her about fardoors. Instantaneous teleportation by any other name. Goodbye Albert Einstein, hello Shirley MacLaine.

"Must be an air-pressure difference," she said, remembering what Sword had told her about the flickering effect. "The atmosphere here presses against the fardoor barrier until the pressure is greater than the barrier can resist, then a blast of stinking air bursts through. Like water dripping out of a tap."

"Atmosphere?" Sword asked slowly. "Melody, where do you think we are?"

Ko looked around again. The sky above was pitch black, no stars. The ground was rocky with no sign of vegetation. But they were breathing oxygen, so some place nearby there had to be green plants to produce it. Something nearby certainly smelled dead enough. "No idea, Sword. You said it yourself when you told me about those doors. Could be anywhere." Ko cupped her hand to her transceiver. "Adrian, do you copy?" She pressed the alert signal on her locator band as well.

Sword shook his head, the movement barely perceptible in what little light reached them from the door. "I can hear you coming over mine, but other than that I just get static."

"At least some of the laws of physics are still working here."

"Of course!" Sword grabbed her arm. "The First World, Melody. It *is* an actual place. *This* place."

Ko shook her head. "Martin was clear on that, Sword. The First World isn't a real place. It's like ... the name of a secret society or something. Whatever this place is, it's something else he never told us about."

"It's the First World," Sword said stubbornly.

"Let's go find Martin and ask him again."

"Which way?"

Ko stared directly opposite the glowing opening of the fardoor. "Look straight down there, then move your eyes off to the left by a few degrees."

"There's a red glow. Almost."

"Crystals at work, Sword. I guess even some shifters can't see in the dark."

They headed for it, and the red glow became more pronounced as their eyes became used to the gloom and the white light of the fardoor faded. But after walking down the rough stone slope for a few hundred feet, Ko turned to check on their progress.

"Bloody hell. It's almost gone." The fardoor was now little brighter than the red crystal glow. "There's got to be a heavy mist in here." *Or light no longer behaves like light in this place,* she thought.

"We should leave some sort of marker."

Ko reflected for a moment. Without knowing how long their excursion would take, she didn't want to risk leaving a spotlight behind to exhaust its battery uselessly, and she was determined to keep her explosives and flares until they were absolutely necessary. She thought about signals without light, about caves ... "Give me your transceiver," she finally said.

Sword slipped it from his ear and passed it over. Ko placed it on the ground, slightly elevated on a small outcropping. "For when we come back," she said. "I'll send out a signal through mine and you use the directional mike to locate this."

"Echo-location. Like a bat out of hell."

Ko looked around the almost physical darkness that surrounded them. "The way things look about now, Sword, hell could be a good guess, too."

TWENTY-FOUR

In the Pit of the Change, the Clan Arkady gathered round their three Sacred Hearts. In humanform, the clanmates wore the shifterskins of vanquished foes and fallen kin, fixed in form and tanned by working crystals. In shifterform they wore their true souls and howled within the scarlet glow of the facet pillars. They were bear and wolf and *tagonii*, puma, *orell*, and multi-limbed *lostartes*. Every branch of life except those with gills was mixed in them, from those whose lines had blended with the elder *mammalia*, to the true aristocrats whose lines passed beyond memory to the bloodtide and ancient scales and hearts of firstlife.

The Clan bayed, and screeched, and roared into the darkness as the time of the Change drew near, each family with its own tongue, each line with its own dialect, but all in the common language of the hunter and the prey they shared. Together in the light of their greatest wealth, they were joined as one.

The Greater Clan Arkady.

Their Victor told them it was so.

"*K'llan Arkadych!*" the Victor Morgana called out to her kind in her hidden voice, in the hiddentongue.

All other sound stopped without echo, swallowed by the darkness that surrounded them, as the Victor and her consort, Roth, climbed the low steps of the central altar. The stone beneath them was cut in slabs, black and grooved with the passage of uncountable claws and talons over untold years. This was not the Clan's first Change.

At the center of the stepped stone rings of the Pit that gave space for half a thousand of the *Arkadych*, the altar rose from a raised disk, twenty feet across, which custom called the Greater Heart. Upon it was a second disk of stone, the Lesser Heart, eight feet across and sculpted on its four-foot-thick sides with the twisting coils and veined wings of the Tarl David — first Victor of the Clan. Upon that second disk, in front of which the Victor and her consort now stood, the third and Beating Heart lay stretched out, spread-eagled by chains of the killing silver fit only for prey. The Beating Heart had another name as well.

It was Martin.

He was not frightened and he did not struggle against the chains. He had done what his little sister had told him to do. He had become human. He had thought. And now he had a plan. All he had to do was wait for the proper moment of distraction. A moment would come soon, he knew.

Composed, then, he watched as the Ceremony progressed around him. The Victor Morgana stood by the Lesser Heart, raising her hands over Martin who would become the ritual prey they shared. Beside her, her consort carried the Snare of the Silver Death. The Victor's son remained behind them both, holding the rod on which to gather their robes.

All was silent. All was in readiness.

The Victor shouted the first warning of the Ceremony. "*Tair yu lii'sti!*" Roth held the Snare of the Silver Death to the assembled shifters and clanged its foot-long talon-shaped hooks together. The clanmates did not move. All watched the sacrifice. But Martin knew what the Ceremony meant. With that first warning — the Warning of the Hunt — the Victor had announced the Clan's intention to hunt the prey. Since the ritual prey, tied down, could·not move, the hunters of the Clan were shown to be inescapable, even though their intentions were known. But Martin refused to play his part by struggling, thus spoiling their traditional pleasure in the spectacle, by forcing the witnesses to remain silent.

Next would come the Warning of the Snare, and the ritual prey would be caught and marked by the Crystal of the Change.

"*Varl k'el yu solin!*" the Victor chanted. Martin did not move and again the clanmates could not respond.

Then Martin felt a vibration within the Lesser Heart. He heard the grinding of old stone. He heard the swell of wordless awe that swept through the clanmates in the Pit. Beside the Beating Heart, from the depths of the Greater Heart, through the seal of the Lesser Heart, rose the Crystal of the Change Arkady.

Even Martin trembled as the ageless artifact rose from its hidden chamber. He had seen drawings of it, heard the keepers describe it, even once seen a photograph that had been taken of it. But still the beauty of the actual stone stole his breath, and he sensed the force of its power — both real and symbolic.

The Crystal itself was wealth beyond measure — a working crystal in the shape of an irregular, multi-faceted sphere fully a foot across. It was set in a thin disk of Lights' finest gold, formed to fit each irregularity in the Crystal's undersurface, and the disk was set on a stand made from the shoulders of the kneeling figures of the First Four.

Martin was transfixed by the work's detail. The tiny metal sculptures seemed as if real beings had been coldblasted and reduced to form the figures. Two of them, the humanforms, were made of silver, humanforms — a male and female with perfect physique and pose, caught in a gleaming depiction of life made from the precious metal of the shifters' death. The other two figures were in shifterform, also a male and a female, also perfect, caught in the unearthly brilliance of Lights' gold. The figures knelt, backs to each other, each on one knee, each bent over so the gold disk supporting the Crystal rested on their shoulders.

Martin thought of the legends that the First Four represented. How some adepts had merged their lines with other beings to become a blend of both and how Tarl David had chosen to merge his line without a blending, deciding instead to change from one being to another with the power of the Crystal. A child's story, Martin knew, yet one which found its truth in his own mixed form. And then he realized that incredible crystal must have been used in the stand's creation because he had been entranced by it, forgetting where he was. He shook his head and looked away and heard the gathered clanmates murmur with approval that the Crystal had begun its work so soon.

With a solid *chunk*, the Crystal of the Change reached its final position and the mechanism upon which it was raised locked into place.

Martin looked past the Crystal on its stand and saw the Victor Morgana smile at him, baring her small, almost unnoticeable fangs. "Soon, little one, soon," she hissed at him. Martin bared his own fangs at her and smiled defiantly at the sudden look of rage that came upon her. He would *not* be prey.

Morgana threw her hands into the air and shouted out in a deep inhuman voice the final warning — the Warning of the Change. *"Narta kwo yu tanar!"* Martin did not struggle and the clanmates did not move. As long as Martin made no protest, they had nothing to which to respond.

"You spoil their pleasure," Morgana snarled.

Martin fixed his eyes on her. He had prepared for what he would say next. He had practiced saying it in his mind as his little sister would. "I ... am not ... prey! I am ... *human!*"

For the gathered clanmates, that was as good as a wordless cry of fear and they finally gave the ceremonial response they had been waiting for. They howled in savage release, five hundred of them emptying their lungs in wild cries, mocking the supposed fear of their prey. The Clan ruled supreme.

Morgana smiled regally as she surveyed her subjects and Seth approached behind her to be in position to catch her robe when she would shed it. The green-eyed werewolf snarled at Martin. "If you are human, then you *are* prey!"

Martin simply inhaled, tasting the air. It wouldn't be long now.

The shrieks of a thousand banshees roared in Sword's ears.

"Shifters," he said to Ko beside him. "Gathered in the light there." He pointed to the now almost painfully brilliant red crystal light source about five hundred feet away. It was being generated by a large circle of red crystal pillars.

"Sounds like more than a hundred, Sword. Lots more."

Sword felt a thrill as he made a sudden connection. "That hundred Morgana mentioned ... they'd just be the humanforms who left the rotunda on schedule. But there could be hundreds more, already in shifterform, living in the enclave."

Ko's voice was flat. "And now they're here."

They turned to each other then, imagining what they might face in the next few minutes. Suddenly, Sword doubted that his vest and pistol and all the thousands of dollars of equipment he and Ko wore had any use or meaning at all. But he knew there were no other options for him now.

He studied Ko's intent face in the scarlet glow. He remembered seeing a certain youthful look in her once, a look which had been one of his reasons for distrusting Forsyte's recommendation of her. But there was none of that naïveté present now. There was only the determined set of her mouth, the tight crease above her eyes, the cold stare that came from seeing a friend die. He recognized it as a mirror of his own.

"We can't go back," he said.

"I know."

They heard a deep voice call out in unrecognizable words and it was answered by the multitude of beasts. Sword went through the pockets and loops of his vest, preparing each piece of equipment for immediate action.

"My mother wanted me to be a doctor," Ko said suddenly, and Sword couldn't tell if she were seeking solace in memories from her real life, the way things used to be before she had faced the First World with him.

Sword held out a fist to her. "My mother wanted me to be the Victor."

Ko made a small tight smile, then knocked her fist against his — the sign of equals in the First World. "Guess it's time to show those horror-show rejects a few of the wonders of modern science," she said.

Sword nodded. "It's time to win."

Silently, they moved toward the light.

The Victor Morgana shed her robe and the cloak of the sacred scales fell clattering to the ornate wooden rod Seth held at her back. She uttered the words that told her subjects that though she was naked before them, her true form was yet still hidden. *"Seyta yu tarl g'el. Fah rinnta k'wes see."*

The clanmates rose as one. *"Seyta k'wes see t'Cha!"* they thundered in a single monstrous voice.

Roth and Seth circled the Lesser Heart, fastening the small hooks of the Snare of the Silver Death to the four iron rings around Martin. The halfling moved his arms and legs almost imperceptibly, feeling exactly where the massive silver manacles rested on each wrist and ankle.

"Have you finally decided to struggle?" Morgana asked as she looked down at him.

Martin didn't answer. *No*, he thought, *I am not prey.* He said again within himself the sentence he had practiced: *I am human.*

Seth fastened the last small hook of the Snare and the clanmates roared out approval. Next Martin would be marked by the power of the Crystal. After the Crystal worked the Change and the clanmates shifted, the large hooks of the Snare would be run through Martin's jawbone and his upper teeth and face. The silver chains would be stretched back to the small hooks until the tension was so great in four directions that his head would be immobilized and his jaw would be broken open to its widest extent.

Then, with the Change upon her, the Victor Morgana would reach deep within Martin's open throat, pushing through the soft entrance to the inner spirit of the prey, and with her claws pluck out his beating heart and withdraw it for all to see. And share.

"Arkadych yu!" the Victor roared.

The clanmates rose in an instant wave. Their voices bellowed their response, *"t'Cha! t'Cha!"*

Martin looked past the Crystal to the edge of the layer and his sensitive eyes saw the first softening of the dark. Dawn was coming. The Change would be upon them. The time was now.

The Victor touched the base of the Crystal's stand, holding a finger to the brow of the sculpted kneeling female shifter. *"Arkadych loyan yii!"* Martin saw the sweat pour from her, felt the heat rise in her as her body prepared itself.

"t'Cha!" the clanmates roared again.

Then Martin saw the first ray of the layer's dawn burst through the hole in the sky. The shaft of yellow light, trapped in the layer's heavy mist, burned through the darkness and struck the Crystal. The clanmates' voices rose. The light from the first dawn grew within the Crystal. A matching shaft of brilliant red shot out from the stone like a serpent's tongue and hit Martin square on his chest. He felt a shocking stab of heat where it hit and saw a tiny section of his fur puff in flame and smoke just before the light flared out. But he hid his pain and did not cringe.

And then the shaft of yellow light increased in width and the Crystal glowed and erupted in a spray of brilliant lances of ruby light.

"*t'Cha!*" the clanmates shrieked as they raised their clan rings and amulets to catch the spines of light. "*t'Cha!*"

"*t'Cha! Arkadych!*" the Victor Morgana growled in answer and Martin saw the skin of her belly ripple as the first of her scales began to form.

The Change was upon them.

The Victor *shifted.*

"We're in a bloody cave!" Ko said. "Look at that!"

Sword watched as what was unmistakably sunlight flared through a narrow crevice high above him. At once the area surrounding him and Ko and the horrendous spectacle before them became suffused with a pale illumination. What had once been a featureless black sky became a roof of dripping stalactites two hundred feet above their heads. The circle of red light in which the shifters congregated was now seen to be a natural basin a hundred feet across, finished with black stone slabs cut and arranged in a primitive style that not even Sword's trained eye could recognize.

The mist-filled cave resonated with the inhuman cries of the shifters as they were caught amidst the explosion of blinding scarlet beams refracting from the huge crystal placed to catch the dawn's first light. The red crystal's energy filled them, then spilled from their eyes in double shafts like lasers from Forsyte's glasses. And as the multiplied light grew in brilliance, the shifters began to change.

Those that were already in shifterform stood upright, arms or fore-limbs extended with red fire crackling through their fur, spraying it out on end as if a massive current of electricity ran through them. They lost none of their attributes and Sword realized that they would not shift back to humanform this time so they could be ready to do battle in their war with the mysterious Clan Seyshen.

But those in humanform doubled over, clutching at their naked bodies as hidden shapes within them writhed, displacing skin, deforming bone, and making them cry out with harrowing pain.

"Sword," Ko whispered. "Martin!"

Sword scanned the gruesome arena, until he saw where Ko was pointing — the central raised altar on which the crystal stood in a gold and silver stand. He held his hand to his eyes to block the glare that came from the stone, and in the misty shadow saw a familiar shape stretched out on the altar, bound by silver chains. Martin was to be the Ceremony's human sacrifice. Beside the halfling, Sword saw the naked form of Morgana LaVey twisting in agony as she herself underwent her change. But into what, he could not tell.

Sword stood up from behind their concealing mound of boulders. He and Ko had hidden long enough.

"We can't go down there through them," Ko protested, still hunched down behind the rock shield. "I have to plant the charges first. We have to clear a way with explosives and — "

"Look at them," Sword said. "The way their eyes are glowing. The way they're screaming. They won't see us."

He stepped forward, past the boulders, exposed in plain sight of the shifters gathered below. He looked up at the crevice, now almost filled with the full morning light of this world's sun. *But which sun?* he thought. *Which world?*

"Wait, Sword!" Ko stood up from behind the rocks. "I'm going with you."

"I know."

Together, they entered the Pit of the Change.

As she writhed, Morgana's eyes suddenly opened and looked blindly at Martin. He saw her luminous pupils stretch vertically, becoming reptilian. Scales grew and fluttered across her torso, forming between her breasts, stretching down across her legs. She was unknowing, unseeing, caught up in the torment and the rapture of the Change.

Martin fought the effect of her gaze and closed his eyes to it. He could scent that Sword and Ko were nearby. It was time to act. He strove to bring Ja'Nette back into his mind, the words she had said. *What's the difference between your blue power and what I can do? Both make things move without having to touch them, right?* Big big difference, Martin had told her. But now Martin knew he had been wrong and his little sister had been right.

Blue fire sprang from his hands and feet. He felt the force of it enter the locks of the manacles that held him to the Lesser Heart. He sent his mind out with that force, probing the mechanisms.

He felt the first lock click.

Sword led the way down through the twisting mass of shifters. The creatures slid over and under each other, fur sprouting, fangs growing, the power they absorbed from the crystal blasting from their eyes. None of the shifters of Arkady were aware that Sword and Ko were in their midst. But there were other adepts present, from other clans. Including the elemental, Roth.

Roth screamed Sword's name from the altar. Ten feet away, with the flashing shafts of light from the dawn and the Crystal spraying upon them through the mist, Sword and Ko leveled their weapons at the adept.

"Give us Martin!" Sword shouted over the bestial din.

"You have no right to be here!" Roth cried out in shrill answer.

"You had no right to send me away!"

"Go back now or die with your halfling friend!" Roth raised his left hand.

The answers Roth might have for him no longer mattered to Sword. He pulled the trigger on his pistol and felt the soft rush of the halide dart launching. The silver solution wouldn't kill Roth, he knew, but the dart would slow him down.

But just before Sword fired, Roth rubbed the fingers of his left hand together and a sudden aurora of blue light formed around his body. The dart hit the shield of blue and bounced uselessly to the stone below. Then the aurora faded.

Instantly, Ko fired four darts, one after the other, but the aurora burst back into life for each one.

Roth held up his left hand again and Sword saw a small red stone glowing within it. The adept cupped his hand at Ko and red lightning forked from his fingers to her gun barrel, twisting it in a thunderous explosion.

Ko fell back from the force of it. Her rifle lay on the ground beside her, charred and smoking. Roth cupped his hand at Sword. Sword dropped his empty pistol and prepared himself. But, inexplicably, Roth hesitated. He lowered his arm.

"I have prepared something special for the heir to the Victor of Pendragon," he cried out as he reached within his robe.

Sword tensed, preparing himself for an assault of even deadlier elemental sorcery. But Roth's weapon was not First World. It was Second World. A .45 caliber semi-automatic handgun.

The object was so incongruous in the adept's hand that Sword faltered in his move to dive out of Roth's line of sight. An elemental using a gun? It made no sense.

Roth took aim. Sword looked into the adept's eyes. Roth's finger tightened on the trigger.

Then Martin threw off the chains of the altar in a burst of blue fire and smashed Roth's head in a savage double-handed blow. The gun fired wildly and spun into the air as Roth crumpled at the side of the elevated disk of stone.

Martin raised his fists and went into a fighting stance, roaring out his challenge to the insensate shifters all around him. "NOT PREY!"

Sword pulled Ko to her feet and together they jumped up on the stone disk. The sunlight shining through the crevice had become blinding and a dozen other crevices were now lit up. Through a larger one closer to the floor of the cavern, Sword could see the green of vegetation and the pink of a morning sky.

Sword grabbed Martin's arm. "Come on! Let's get out of here!"

"Not prey!" Martin wailed.

Ko grabbed the halfling's other arm, trying to drag him forward, off the altar. "It's all right, Martin! We have to go *now!*"

"Seth first." Martin pulled away from them easily. He spun around, just as two heavy silver talons swung through the air and dug into the flesh on his chest.

It was Morgana. She pulled on the silver chains, wrenching the twisted talons deeper into Martin, pulling him back into the center of the altar. Martin struggled against her, pulling her out of the shaft of crystal light she stood in. With that, her change stopped halfway, with green reptilian eyes, iridescent scales on her torso, but still with her body in humanform and with honey-colored skin on her arms and legs and face.

A long, pink, and forked tongue slipped from her mouth as she hissed at Martin. *"You are the prey!"*

Martin dug his feet into the cracks of the altar stone. Blood poured from the wounds the talons made. Sword dived for Roth's handgun. He picked it up. He spun and fired at Morgana. The bullet tore open a hole in her chest.

And the hole closed before Sword's eyes, healing itself at a rate too fast to follow.

He fired again and again but each new hit only seemed to give the Arkady Victor more strength. Martin was almost in the center of the altar again. Morgana stepped back into the shaft of changing light. Fangs grew in her mouth. Her change resumed.

"It's the light from the crystal!" Ko shouted. "Shoot the crystal, Sword! The crystal!"

The sudden fear in Morgana's eyes stopped Sword from questioning Ko's strategy. He swung the gun to the Crystal of the Change. He fired and a third of the gigantic gemstone splintered into glassy shards.

Instantly its light died.

Morgana toppled to the floor, losing her grip on the silver chains. Martin fell back from the altar, clutching at the gashes in his chest, wrenching the talons free. And all around, the bellows of the changing shifters stopped as the power of the crystal left them. Instead, Sword heard only a chorus of labored breathing as awareness returned to the clanmates before their Change had been completed.

The Ceremony had been desecrated.

And they knew who was to blame.

TWENTY-FIVE

What surprised Melody Ko most of all was how calm she felt. Her hands still tingled from the shock of whatever type of energy Roth had discharged into her ruined rifle. She was stained with blood from Martin's deep wounds. And she knew that she and Sword had no hope at all of escaping from the mob of staring, panting, half-human creatures that surrounded them. But she felt no fear, and she could see that Sword didn't, either.

She watched as Sword's eyes moved intently over the crowd of beasts that ringed the altar stone. She could see that the creatures were poised to attack the humans who had destroyed their sacred Crystal of the Change. They waited only for a sign from their Victor.

Together, Sword and Ko turned to face Morgana across the altar. The light from outside the cavern was strong now and the sunlit mist bathed everything in a warm, unreal haze.

The Victor of Arkady sobbed. Ko watched with detached fascination as Morgana ran her hands over her unchanged face, trembling as she touched the fangs that overlapped her still-human lips and felt the caress of her serpent's tongue. Her hands moved lower, leaving the smoothness of the skin that was still human and going to the rough, glittering scales that covered her midbody. Ko remembered a word that Martin had used once, long ago it seemed. Morgana LaVey was 'fixed' in midshift. She had become as a halfling, to her kind the lowest of the low.

Roth went to Morgana's side. Blood streamed from his nose and his left ear where Martin had struck him. Together, the two adepts turned as one to stare with outraged hatred at Sword. Morgana's eyes were slit like a snake's. She didn't blink.

Roth raised his glowing hands. Behind him, Seth rose up to his full seven-foot height.

"We shall have three prey at this Ceremony," Roth snarled.

Martin stood, slightly hunched over to favor the bloody wounds in his chest. "Time to die," he said.

Sword jumped up on the altar stone beside Martin. "But not alone."

Ko slipped two concussion grenades from her vest and turned to confront the shifters gathered at Sword's back. *I am seeing things no human has ever seen before*, she told herself. *I am the first scientist to know such things. The first scientist to experience these phenomena.* For her, it was enough. For this gift, she was prepared to accept whatever happened next.

"Your call, Sword." Ko glanced over her shoulder and saw Sword standing tall on the altar, a concussion grenade already in each of his own hands. He raised his head toward the roof of the cavern and shouted out his own challenge. "For Pendragon!" Then he lofted both grenades to either side. Ko threw hers forward into the massed shifters, reaching to her vest for other weapons before the grenades had even hit the ground.

But they never hit the ground.

Red lightning shot through the misty air, enveloped Ko's grenades in pockets of ruby light, then propelled them with Sword's in the direction of the largest cave opening. They exploded uselessly in the air.

Roth's scornful laughter blended into the echoing multiple booms of the grenades' explosions. The Victor Morgana called out the Warning of the Hunt. *"Tair yu lii'sti!"* Through the Pit of the Change, the shifters moved forward, growling low in whatever passed for throats among them.

Sword held his arm out to Ko and she used it to haul herself up beside Martin on the altar stone. The three of them were gathered together, back to back.

"So much for the wonders of modern science," Ko said.

Sword looked over his shoulder at her and suddenly smiled. "Then we attack with whatever's at hand." He reached for the Crystal of the Change.

Morgana squealed. Roth's hand blazed with blue brilliance. "Don't touch that!" he screamed at Sword. "Stay back!"

Ko turned to face Morgana and Roth, caught by their reaction. There was no question that Sword was defeated. What could possibly fill them with such terror? She saw their eyes locked on Sword's hands, a foot away from grabbing the Crystal, as if they were afraid that he might simply brush his fingers against it. Was the Crystal of the Change that sacred to them? Could a human defile it in their eyes just by touching it? Or was there something special about Sword's touch?

Ko grabbed Sword's shoulder as the truth hit her with a force stronger than Roth's lightning. "That's it, Sword! Hold your hands close to the Crystal! They won't touch us if you do."

Sword didn't hesitate. He dropped to his knees in front of the gold and silver stand and the final three-quarters of the Crystal. He held a hand inches away from either side of the stone.

"Get back!" Ko shouted at Roth, and Morgana, and Seth. "Get back or it's worthless to you!"

And they stepped back.

Sword glanced up at Ko, obviously impressed. "Good trick," he said. "Want to tell me how it works?"

"Remember the glowing crystal in Saul Calder's kitchen? You touched it and it flickered, you held it and the glow went out."

Sword's eyes widened. "And the facet in the passageway, when I touched it ... it dimmed." Sword turned to Roth. "And when I touched the crystals that Ja'Nette took from you ... you said that they were worthless!"

"You drain them, Sword," Ko said excitedly. "Whatever power is generated within them, you flatten it out like you're a ... a bloody ground wire or something."

Futile rage seethed in Roth's eyes.

"It's true, isn't it?" Sword asked the adept. He moved his hands closer toward the Crystal and Roth and Morgana gasped in apprehension. "It must be true," Sword said. He laughed in triumph. "And without this Crystal, you can never change back. Never have another Ceremony ... "

"What do you want?" Roth cried out bitterly.

Sword laughed again, triumphant. "Melody, you're brilliant. This is great. This is it!"

Ko leaned over to whisper in his ear. "Uh, Sword, we are still surrounded by about five hundred werethings, here."

"What do you *want?*" Roth repeated desperately.

"Answers," Sword said. "I want answers to all my questions."

Bloody hell, Ko thought, he was doing it again. *Why could he never think more than two seconds into the future?* "Sword, first use the Crystal to get us out of here, then you can ask questions till the ... were-cows come home."

Sword had to think about it for a few seconds, but he nodded. "Yeah, okay. First you let us take this back through the fardoor, back to the city, then we'll negotiate for its return."

Roth shook his head slowly. "How can we trust you not to drain the Crystal after you pass from the layer? At least if you drain it here, we will still be able to kill you." Beside him, Morgana's tongue flicked through the air.

"Because I want those answers, Roth. You know how much I want those answers. And this crystal is what will give them to me. Now, if you don't believe me, let's end it here and now, because *I'm not going back without my goddamned answers!*" He moved his right hand closer and closer to the crystal, until it almost touched its surface, until Roth saw he was not bluffing.

"All right!" the adept called out. "Whatever you want. Yes, whatever questions. Just don't touch the Crystal."

Sword stood up slowly, carefully keeping one hand no more than six inches from the Crystal. He asked Martin to pick up the stone's stand and keep it near his side so, in case an accident occurred, Sword would be sure to fall against it.

Sword and Martin carefully jumped down from the altar. "Shall we agree on a place to meet for tomorrow?" Sword asked Roth.

"No, need," Roth said tightly. "Wherever the Crystal is, we shall find you."

"Just don't forget the Crystal will be by my side." Sword waved his hand over it, to provoke a reaction.

Roth nodded forbiddingly. "Just don't forget that Seth will be by mine."

Martin growled. "Martin not forget. Ever."

Ko patted the halfling's shoulder. "Shh, Martin. Let's just get out of here while we can."

The three of them began to move slowly away from the raised central stone disk, Sword's hands constantly hovering by the Crystal of the Change. "Tell them to move aside!" Sword shouted as they approached the first ring of shifters.

"*Ertu! Ertu la!*" Morgana reluctantly commanded her subjects, and the shifters stepped back, clearing a wide path up from the Pit.

Roth cupped his hands to his mouth. "I hope you find the answers worth it, Little Galen."

Ko looked at Sword and saw he recognized the threat in Roth's words. He spoke softly to Ko. "I hope you're going to have a lot more good ideas tomorrow."

"So do I." Ko knew that Sword and she had not won. They had only gained some time. But at least when they next met with Roth and Morgana, Forsyte would be with her and with Sword.

At last they stood on the final ring of the Pit. Now that daylight penetrated the cavern, Ko could make out the rough path that led up the cavern's sloping floor to the distant fardoor. *No more than ten minutes,* she thought. *Five if we run.* And Roth would never risk attacking them in the narrow confines of the passageway where it would be so easy for Sword to brush against the Crystal.

With the knowledge that they were really going to make it safely away from the shifters, Ko felt a sudden rush of relief pass through her. She found it hard to catch her breath as the tension she had compartmentalized was finally released.

"You going to be okay?" Sword walked sideways, alternatingly looking ahead at the path and behind to the motionless shifters.

"Now I am," Ko answered. "I've just got a bad case of the shakes. In fact, it feels like the whole place is shaking."

"Whole place *is* shaking," Martin said. He came to a sudden halt and Sword stumbled, twisting to avoid touching the Crystal. Martin began to sniff the air excitedly.

Sword wrinkled his own nose. "What can you smell over this stink, Martin?"

"Nothing. Yet." Martin turned his head, and the points of his ears quivered. "But hear something ... hear something ... "

"Look at that!" Ko stared out at the largest opening in the cavern, halfway between the Pit and the fardoor. Beyond was the green of a rich jungle and the blue of an ordinary sky. But through that sky, dark shapes moved. Large and long and swift like enormous insects.

"What now?" Sword groaned. "How big are they?"

Ko watched as the backlit shapes buzzed closer to the cavern opening. They were the source of the sound Martin had heard and now she could hear it as well. She had visions of a prehistoric world filled with giant dragonflies. The shifters turned to stare at the creatures' approach. She heard the murmur of their animal voices. Raised in alarm, she thought, and no wonder. How could any creature that size fly without apparent wings?

The roar of the flying beasts became a rumble, echoing like a roll of thunder in the cavern, rhythmic. And familiar, Ko abruptly realized. Too familiar. Then she saw one settle to the ground outside the cave in a sudden spray of rock and dust and gravel. And as the blowing dust cleared away, she knew she was right in her identification of them.

"Bloody hell, Sword. They're helicopters!"

TWENTY-SIX

Two more came down by the cavern's mouth and Sword saw that Ko was right. Helicopters *were* landing outside the cavern, painted in olive drab. But why? And who was in them?

"They're bloody Sikorskies," Ko said. Sword could hear the stunned surprise in her voice. He could also hear the growing cries of surprise from the shifters and the voices of Roth and Morgana raised and giving orders. Two hundred feet away, the shifters rose from the Pit of the Change and began to form into a line facing the cavern's mouth.

"What the hell's going on here?" Sword asked, but before anyone could say anything more, a string of man-sized silhouettes appeared in the cavern's mouth. The shapes moved forward on two legs, and held long wand-shaped objects before them.

A cry went up from the shifters and the silhouettes turned. And then they opened fire.

Sword pulled his hands away from the Crystal and dropped to the ground. Ko matched his moves exactly. Martin crouched down behind the Crystal and its stand, eyes wide with terror.

"I don't believe it," Ko said. "Those are automatic weapons they're firing. Those are troop helicopters. There's a bloody army after the shifters."

"Not army," Martin said in a broken voice. He took his hands from the Crystal's stand and hunched over in despair, rocking from one foot to another.

Sword watched the cavern's mouth and saw that once the soldiers had moved out of the glare of the cavern mouth, they were clearly human, in green uniforms and helmets. "Those are *soldiers*, Martin. It *is* an army."

"No, no," Martin said. "Not army. Worse than army."

New silhouettes appeared in the cave mouth. Low and sleek, moving over the rocks like molten shadows, slipping though twists and turns faster than anything touching the ground should have been able to move. The shapes flowed like liquid, snaking closer to the shifters, and even when they had left the glare of the cavern's mouth, they remained silhouettes. Inhuman silhouettes.

"What are they?" Sword asked, though he was afraid he already knew the answer like a suddenly-remembered nightmare from his childhood.

Martin made his soft *ooo*-ing sound of anguish. "Seyshen." He grabbed Sword's arm and began to pull him away. "Seyshen Galen Sword! Seyshen!"

"The war ... ?" Sword whispered. Were these the creatures that the Clan Arkady wanted to war with? "*What* are they, Martin?" The swiftly moving shapes were impossible to see clearly in the cave's halflight. They were not human, but neither did they seem to make sense as any type of animal Sword knew.

Martin was approaching hysterics. "Must run! Must hide! Go back fardoor!" He began to scamper off.

"Martin!" Sword called out. "You have to carry the Crystal."

Martin skidded to a stop on the cavern floor. He turned, hesitated, then ran back for the stand and Crystal. "Hurry Galen Sword Melody! Hurry! Hurry!"

A shriek of mortal terror echoed from farther down the cavern, closer to the Pit. More gunshots stuttered through the air. Sword could see a knot of shifters gathering around a seething mass of twisted black shadows. Then he saw a second knot of shifters begin to move away, toward him, and the fardoor.

Ko jumped to her feet. "Let's move it, Sword. They don't look like they're going to worry about who's got the Crystal now."

Sword ran with Ko beside him. Martin loped ahead, carrying the Crystal of the Change. A hundred feet from the flickering halfmoon of the fardoor, Sword looked over his shoulder. A pack of shifters was closing fast. And Seth was in the lead.

Martin squealed, already at the fardoor but not passing through it. The constant roar of automatic gunfire filled the cavern, mixing with the cries of the shifters and an unearthly second sound which Sword instinctively recognized as the screech of the Seyshen.

Sword heard pounding feet behind him, coming closer. He and Ko had fifty feet to cover but the pounding feet behind were faster. Forty. Closer. Thirty. Closer. Twenty. Hot breath all around him. Then Ko broke from the sprint and whirled around, screaming at the top of her lungs.

Sword hit the ground and rolled to a stop five feet from the fardoor barrier. Still carrying the stand and Crystal, Martin rushed to him, made a grab for him, but Sword shook the halfling off and leapt to his feet. "Melody! Have to get Melody!"

Cut off from the approach to the fardoor, Ko was cautiously circling an awkwardly sprawled form: Seth. The werewolf snarled at her, shaking his head, obviously having somersaulted over her, striking his head, when she made her sudden, unexpected stop. Behind her, the band of shifters Seth had been running with were now grouped in one spot, battling with a quick black form that danced among them. Sword saw gouts of blood and heard the screams of dying. A lone Seyshen had ambushed Seth's pack.

Sword held his hands above the Crystal of the Change and shouted to Seth as the quickly recovering werewolf sprang upright on all four feet. "Let her pass or I'll destroy this! Your clan will never shift again!"

Seth rose on his hind legs, glancing back where his clanmates battled the Seyshen. His muzzle twitched with his sharp-fanged smile as he turned back to see Ko dart past him, toward the fardoor. Far off in the cavern, back by the Pit, a full-scale battle was taking place — shifters and soldiers and half-seen shadows. But Seth didn't care.

"You're mine now," the werewolf growled as he began to advance, one step at a time. "All of you." Another step. "Just like the child."

Sword shoved his hand out in front of Martin as the halfling began to move toward Seth. "No! We have no weapons left. Another time, Martin. Another time."

Behind Seth, the small band's fight with a single Seyshen came to an end. The black creature seemed to ripple like water and explode into mist. From the pile of bodies, only two forms rose.

"Go, Melody! Go!" Sword called out. "You too, Martin. Go through the fardoor."

"All mine," said Seth. He lunged forward and Ko scrambled ahead.

Martin lifted the Crystal of the Change and Sword kept his hand above it. Then Melody was by his side. "Keep moving back," Sword said. "Keep moving back." Seth approached almost within reach, trying to find an angle of attack that would separate Sword from the Crystal.

They were steps from the fardoor barrier when Sword recognized the two adepts who had run with Seth's pack and survived the Seyshen's ambush: Roth and Morgana.

"Run you fools!" Roth shouted. "Don't you see what's happening?"

From the Pit, the Arkady shifters had reformed into a single group and were charging up the path, desperately trying to reach the fardoor as the Seyshen and their human soldiers gave chase.

"No closer!" Sword said. "Call Seth off and let us pass through first."

The thunder of the running shifters grew. The gunfire became louder. Sword heard a bullet ricochet from a nearby rock.

"Melody, go through."

"But —"

"Now!"

Sword heard the fardoor crackle slightly. He looked over his shoulder. Ko stood on the other side. She said something to him but her voice did not travel clearly through the barrier.

"Now you, Martin."

"Martin hold Crystal. Martin must go through with Galen Sword."

The retreating shifters were only seconds away.

"Galen!" Roth shouted. "Go through *now!*"

"Call off Seth, first!"

"I'll do it! I'll do it! Just get through and don't touch the Crystal." Roth swept his arms into the air and moved his fingers through an intricate pattern. His blue power blazed forth from his hands as he ran for Seth.

Seth turned to face the elemental. Sword and Martin spun around and sprinted through the fardoor. Seth's arm flashed out and sliced across Roth's face in a spray of blood. The werewolf charged for the fardoor.

Sword and Martin landed on the solid concrete floor of the passageway. Ko shouted a warning. Sword and Martin turned to see Seth prepared to pass through from the cavern. Morgana dragged Roth forward only feet away from the barrier. The retreating shifters were a stampede. Seth flickered through the fardoor, claws extended. Roth and Morgana and the shifters and the Seyshen were moments away.

"*Nooo!*" Martin shrieked as he swung the Crystal at Seth as the werewolf came through on the passageway side. The blow slammed Seth to the concrete floor, halfway through the fardoor. Roth and Morgana began to step through beside him. Blood poured from Roth's face.

"Martin!" Morgana hissed. "Get Sword!"

With a wordless cry Martin threw the Crystal of the Change at Morgana and it hit her and Roth in their midsections, knocking them back. But the force of the throw put Martin off balance. He stumbled. Seth's arm reached out and grabbed the halfling by his throat.

"Your blood will mix with the child's!" the werewolf cried as he dragged Martin down to his waiting fangs.

And too far away to help Martin escape, Galen Sword desperately swept his arm against the flickering floating gray line that defined the fardoor's shape, and pulled his hand through the line so that the fardoor barrier flickered once, then burst and vanished like a soap bubble.

For an instant, Sword saw the astounded look of panic on Roth's and Morgana's faces as the Arkady shifters swarmed up around them. And then there was only a plain white concrete wall with a single door marked EXIT TO THE STREET.

And the hideous, dying scream of a werewolf.

The fardoor had closed.

Most of Seth fell into the passageway. The rest, Sword knew, had fallen onto the floor of the cavern, wherever the other side of the fardoor had been.

This part had Seth's head and his arms and most of his torso, a stump of one leg and most of another. The werewolf dragged himself forward across the floor as blood cascaded from the rippling smooth wound cut by the fardoor's collapse. He growled in animal shock and fury as his leg stumps slid beneath him and he was unable to stand.

Martin rolled away from him, safely forgotten.

Sword watched as Seth lurched on the floor, grunting in rage and pain, until finally he rolled onto his back and lay there, looking up into the electric lights, panting.

"Curse you, Sword," the werewolf gasped. "And curse your child whose blood flows in me." He coughed and blood bubbled out of his black-lipped mouth.

Martin kicked him. Then pounded his fist against Seth's chest. Sword pulled the halfling back.

"It doesn't matter," Seth said, green eyes wavering out of focus. "I know the secret you're trying to hide, halfling *meat*." The werewolf's eyes suddenly worked together and moved to Martin. "The way I had your sweet child ... you wanted her the same way, too. Just the same way." He tried to laugh at Martin's howl of rage but only wet gurgles came forth. The blood did not flow from him as quickly now.

Martin sobbed and Sword held him, comforting him. Had Seth been right? Was Martin really that close to the edge?

"And as for you, Little Galen," the werewolf choked. "As for you ... " He raised a trembling paw, pointing blindly with ragged, bloodstained claws. His mouth drew into a cruel and hateful sneer. "You still ... *stink* like a *human!*"

Then Seth said no more. His paw fell back and, in death, his body began to shift.

Sword stared, numb in mind and body, as what was left of Seth began to shrink in on itself. His silver fur slipped back into his skin. His snout moved back into his skull and the claws shrank back into paws that became hands.

In less than a minute, the bisected body of a young man lay in a thick pool of blood. Somewhere in his face, still twisted in a sneer, Sword thought he saw a ghost of a childhood friend. A boy he used to play with. A boy with whom he had teased the gargoyles. Back in the old school. Back where it had all begun.

Martin pulled away from Sword. He kicked at Seth's body again.

"It's okay, Martin," Sword said, reaching out to the halfling. "It was all he could do. He just said that lie about Ja'Nette to hurt you."

Martin stared up at Sword then, and Sword was shocked to see how much of the shifter still lurked in his dark face. "Not lie," Martin said. "Martin not *want* feel that way 'bout little sister but ... " He began to cry.

Sword let his outstretched hand fall back to his side. *Never forget,* he warned himself. *Half-human. Half-shifter. Never.*

He felt all of the exhaustion of the excursion, of the week, of twenty years, hit him at once. He turned to Ko, seeking solace. Looking for a remnant of normal humanity among the madness of what had just happened.

Melody Ko was on her knees in the middle of the pool of the were-wolf's blood. Carefully, she used the small plastic reflector from her directional mike to scoop up the dark liquid and pour it into the empty plastic casing of her Starbrite viewer.

She worked with total concentration, watching the dark blood drip slowly from the dish to her makeshift container. Her pants were sodden with blood where she knelt in it. Her plastic-gloved hands dripped with it. A smear of it streaked across her face.

All the horror of twenty years suddenly welled up in Sword as he saw what Melody Ko was doing.

"Melody ... why? What are you doing?"

Ko looked up at him and knit her brows. She held up the case that sloshed with the blood of an inhuman creature.

"For Adrian," she said evenly. "He said he wanted some."

And, as if she were still a student doing mundane lab work for her prof, she went back to her task.

Sword shivered. What had his obsessive search become?

He looked down at the floor, feeling the passageway spin around him. He moved his hands out, trying to keep his balance. And then, with a strangled gasp, saw the same dark, inhuman blood on his own hands.

This was what his search was becoming.

And that search was far from over.

TWENTY-SEVEN

It was still raining when they stepped out onto the streets of the city again, a light drizzle. The sky was dark.

"Dawn's still about an hour off," Ko said as she studied the sky.

Sword watched as the door they had come through swung shut behind them. It was unmarked and had no handle, the type of door that let people exit from parking garages and theaters. There were thousands just like it throughout the city. Thousands.

"Condominium building," Ko said, looking from the sky to the unremarkable, gray building beside them. Across the street was Central Park. "Just like Adrian figured." She pursed her lips in silent thought and held the plastic case of Seth's blood closer to her.

Sword took a deep breath and Martin watched him closely. "Martin already check. No shifters near."

Sword tried to smile but found he did not have the strength. "Where were we, Martin?"

The halfling shrugged, then tensed as the motion pulled on the wounds in his chest. "Through the layer."

Sword felt that if he were to sit down on the wet sidewalk, he could fall asleep for a year. "What will happen to them? Roth and Morgana."

Martin bared his teeth — the expression no smile. "Seyshen." It was all he had to say.

Sword wrapped his arms around himself, feeling cold. He wondered how Ko put up with having bare arms, but she seemed unaffected by what had happened, atypically quiet and reserved. She started to walk south, toward the museum.

"Back to the Loft?" Sword asked, falling into step beside her.

She stopped and turned to him. "No. I'm going to get Adrian. Then I'll take him to my place." She looked away, down the street. "We're not going back to the Loft, Sword."

Sword understood. She needed to rest, too. "But later ... ?"

"There is no later, Sword. It's over." She looked at him. "I'm quitting. And Adrian's going to quit with me."

Sword felt he had been hit. "You can't quit. You ... it's ... " He struggled to recall the sense of a new companionship they had just achieved. Back there.

"You got what you wanted, Sword. Your memories are real. You're heir to the Victor of the Clan Pendragon. There are werewolves and monsters and ... Seyshen. And they have their own world. And Adrian and I don't belong in it." She reached out to touch his arm. "And neither do you."

"I *do* belong there."

"The werewolf said it, Sword. You're human. That's why they sent you away. Do what's smart. Stay away."

Sword looked all around in confusion. "But ... you're a scientist, Melody. The things you've seen ... fardoors and glowing crystals. Shapeshifting. How can you walk away from them?"

"A scientist has to understand things, Sword. I've got a blood sample here. We've got Roth's crystals. Tapes of 'Bub and Martin. Pictures of Simone Calder. That's a lot of data to work with. Maybe when we have a theory ... maybe when we start to understand ... maybe then we can try to come back. But not now. Not for a long time."

"Melody ... don't. Please?"

"Good luck, Sword." She started to go.

"Martin go Melody." The halfling began to follow Ko.

But Ko turned and shook her head. "No, Martin. You go back to the Loft. It's a better place for you. Bigger. Maybe safer. You go with Sword."

Martin's face wrinkled, almost as if he were in pain. "But Martin not like Galen Sword. Martin like Melody."

"No. I don't want you to come with me, Martin. I'm sorry." She looked away from the halfling as tears came to his eyes. "I'll get the van back to you in a couple of days, Sword. And there's some stuff I'll want to pick up from the Loft. Take care of yourself." She turned and quickly walked off.

Sword watched her go in silence. Martin sat on the sidewalk beside him and covered his face with his hands, crying silently.

"That's too bad," a voice behind them said.

Sword and Martin both turned in shocked surprise.

It was a young man in a trenchcoat, collar turned up against the rain and the cold. Behind him, the unmarked door swung slowly shut. The man's hair was soft blonde and ... he had his mother's eyes.

Sword felt his skin crawl, heard his heart thunder within him. "Brin?"

The young man smiled fleetingly. He watched Ko walking away. "She seems nice. Competent."

Sword could barely make his mouth function. His thoughts flew in infinite directions. So many questions. "Where have you been? What's going on ... with me? Our ... our parents?"

Brin frowned and held his hands together. "You remember what I told you? In the hospital?"

"That ... I have ... a destiny. I ... must fight."

"*You* must fight." Brin raised his pale eyebrows. "No one else can, now. It's up to you."

"What's up to me?"

Brin's hands twisted together. When they came apart, Sword saw he had removed a heavy gold ring. Brin held it out to him.

Sword took it hesitantly. He had seen it before. He knew he had seen it before. The sword and dragon. The symbol of his clan.

"It's our mother's ring," Brin said quietly. "You should wear it now."

The ring felt hot in Sword's hand. "Where is she? Is she still alive?"

Brin's eyes shadowed. He opened his mouth, about to speak, then glanced quickly over his shoulder. "I can't. I'm ... I'm sorry." He looked down at the sidewalk, as if ashamed. "I ... "

"*What?*" Sword demanded.

Brin turned to the door without a handle. "Wear the ring," he said. Then he held out his hand, cupped his fingers, and blue light flashed around the edges of the door as it swung open before him.

"Brin! Wait!" Sword said. He reached out to grab his brother's shoulder. But Brin turned in the doorway, avoiding Sword's hand. He held up his own hand as if giving a warning. He seemed caught in some inner struggle, on the verge of saying something. But in the end, all he could say was, "Remember. Just ... remember."

"I ... I will," Sword said. And he knew it was an oath.

A small smile flickered over Brin's face. He dipped his head. The door swung shut.

"No! Wait!" Sword shouted. He pounded his hands against the metal door. He shouted at the halfling. "Martin! Open this door! Open this goddamned door now!"

But Martin reached up and took Sword's arm in his hands and gently pulled him back from the door.

"Martin can't open door to passageway," the halfling said. "Brin elemental. Powerful Pendragon elemental."

Sword stared at the featureless door, willing it to open.

It remained closed.

He felt Martin tugging softly on his sleeve. "Come Galen Sword. Come with Martin. Martin want to go home."

Sword looked away from the door. He squeezed his mother's ring in his hand.

"So do I, Martin," he said. "So do I."

JUDITH & GARFIELD REEVES-STEVENS are the acclaimed authors of more than twenty novels, including the Los Angeles *Times* bestselling thriller, *Icefire*, which Stephen King hailed as "the best suspense novel of its kind since *The Hunt for Red October*," and the New York *Times* bestselling thriller, *Quicksilver*, which *Publishers Weekly* called a "warp-speed technothriller with the most engaging underdog protagonists since *Jurassic Park*." They are also the authors of the groundbreaking *Star Trek* novel, *Federation*, and the epic *Deep Space Nine* trilogy, *Millennium*.

This book was designed by Lydia Marano for Babbage Press using a Macintosh G3 and Adobe FrameMaker. It was printed by LPI on 60 pound, offset cream-white acid-free stock. The text font is Minion, a Garalde Oldstyle typeface designed by Robert Slimbach in 1990 for Adobe Systems. Minion was inspired by the elegant and highly readable type designs of master printers Claude Garamond and Aldus Manutius in the late Renaissance. Created primarily for type-setting, Minion lends an aesthetic quality to the modern versatility of digital technology.

THERE IS ANOTHER WORLD

It is the birthplace of all our nightmares. Vampires, werewolves, demons, deadly creatures that have no name or form ... they are all real.

GALEN SWORD WAS BORN WITHIN THAT WORLD

Destined to be an adept warrior, heir to the Victor of the Greater Clan Pendragon. Yet as a child, his birthright and his memories were stolen from him, and he was exiled to a world without substance, without magic, without hope: Our world.

BUT TWENTY YEARS LATER

A mysterious chain of events restores Galen's memory of who he is, and hints at what he might become. Now Galen will stop at nothing to find the truth —and his home. But with no powers of his own, his only tools are those of science.

Now, for the first time, the complete SF/Fantasy crossover series

THE CHRONICLES OF GALEN SWORD

BOOK I: SHIFTER

After three years of failure, Galen Sword discovers an enclave of shapeshifters in New York City. But when he tries to infiltrate their Ceremony of the Change, the beings who exiled him from his own world exact a hideous price.

BOOK II: NIGHTFEEDER

Galen and his team are caught up in the deadly politics of the First World as the Greater Clan Seyshen provokes a war between vampires and shapeshifters that's ready to explode into the streets of New York.

BOOK III: DARK HUNTER

When Clans Tepesh and Arkady unite to destroy Galen, he must forge a dangerous alliance between the vampire, Orion, and a mysterious dark hunter with a startling secret. With them, Galen at last takes his struggle through the layer to learn the truth of his return from exile, and of an ancient monstrous enemy about to conquer both his worlds.

BABBAGE PRESS

... books you can count on

JAMES P. BLAYLOCK
The Digging Leviathan	1-930235-16-X	18.95
Homonculus	1-930235-13-5	17.95

RAMSEY CAMPBELL
The Height of the Scream	1-930235-15-1	18.95

ARTHUR BYRON COVER
Autumn Angels	1-930235-12-7	TBA
The Platypus of Doom	1-930235-22-4	TBA
The Sound of Winter	1-930235-24-0	TBA
An East Wind Coming	1-930235-27-5	TBA

DENNIS ETCHISON
The Dark Country	1-930235-04-6	17.95

CHRISTA FAUST
Control Freak	1-930235-14-3	18.95

JOHN FARRIS
Elvisland	1-930235-21-6	19.95

GEORGE R.R. MARTIN
A Song for Lya	1-930235-11-9	17.95

WILLIAM F. NOLAN
Things Beyond Midnight	1-930235-09-7	17.95

MICHAEL REAVES
The Night People	1-930235-25-9	19.95

JUDITH & GARFIELD REEVES-STEVENS
Shifter	1-930235-18-6	18.95
Nightfeeder	1-930235-19-4	18.95
Dark Hunter	1-930235-20-8	19.95

DAVID J. SCHOW
Crypt Orchids	1-930235-26-7	18.95
Lost Angels	1-930235-06-2	17.95
Seeing Red	1-930235-05-4	18.95
The Shaft	1-930235-29-1	TBA
Wild Hairs	1-930235-08-9	19.95

CONTINUED

JOHN SHIRLEY

Eclipse	1-930235-00-3	17.95
Eclipse Penumbra	1-930235-01-1	17.95
Eclipse Corona	1-930235-02-x	17.95
A Splendid Chaos	1-930235-23-2	TBA

JOHN SKIPP & MARC LEVINTHAL

The Emerald Burrito of Oz	1-930235-17-8	19.95

S.P. SOMTOW

Dragon's Fin Soup	1-930235-03-8	17.95
The Fallen Country	1-930235-07-0	17.95

CHELSEA QUINN YARBRO

False Dawn	1-930235-10-0	17.95

Available from your favorite bookstore or order direct. Discounted to the trade.

Babbage Press • 8740 Penfield Avenue • Northridge, CA 91324
www.babbagepress.com • books@babbagepress.com

Distributed by Ingram Book Co. and Baker & Taylor.